Their Master

S.M. LAVIOLETTE

Chapter 1

A bead of sweat ran down Smith's forehead and into his eye, but his hips, which snapped out a brutal rhythm, didn't stutter or falter.

Beneath him, the whore grunted, her body experiencing the involuntary contractions that heralded an orgasm. Her fourth, by his count.

Smith smirked and fucked her faster, pressing the ball of his thumb against her swollen bud.

She whimpered. "I'm—I'm—*ahhh*—"

Her tight sheath rippled around his shaft, squeezing his cock hard enough to hurt, but he didn't let up. Smith had told her—as he always told the whores he paid, male or female—to alert him when a climax was imminent. She'd not articulated the words, but he'd give her a pass.

This time.

And there *would* be a next time, he decided as he pumped into her slender body so vigorously that every muscle beneath her passion-flushed skin flexed as she struggled to absorb his savage thrusts.

Her eyes were tight with pain at the depth of penetration and Smith could feel his crown bumping against something inside her, a phenomenon he'd experienced with some women in the past.

Indeed, it had occurred the very first time he'd had sexual relations with a woman. He'd been sixteen years old and had chosen an older prostitute named Yvette, well-known for her patience with male virgins. Yvette had screamed like she was being murdered when he'd thrust inside her, weeping and causing an embarrassing scene, accusing him of puncturing her womb.

Even all these years later Smith could recall his mortification.

He'd stayed away from women for years after that, taking only male sexual partners for fear of repeating that disturbing episode. Not until he'd been a more secure man in his twenties had he taken a female lover. Fortunately, his second time had been nothing like the first. Indeed, it had been exactly the opposite. His cock had encountered the same soft barrier as before, but he'd driven the woman to ecstasy rather than tears.

After two such contradictory experiences Smith had sought out a doctor with knowledge of the female reproductive system.

The old doctor had roared with laughter at Smith's naïve question. "You are not entering the womb—that would be impossible, even if you are endowed with a prick well above average. You are nudging something called the cervix. Cervical stimulation can provide pain, pleasure, or even both, depending on the depth and tilt of a woman's pelvis."

"How can a man tell such things? So that he might avoid the wrong women."

"You can't. At least not from a woman's outward appearance. If you engage the services of an experienced working woman, *she* will know her own tolerances."

And so Smith always asked whores before engaging them, even though he knew the question—*are you sure you can you take my longer than average cock?*—made him sound like an arrogant idiot. It was worth sounding like an arse to avoid a wailing woman.

The whore beneath him, Moira, had intrigued him with her response.

"I have occasionally experienced pain," she'd admitted in her cool, dignified way. Smith had been ready to dismiss her, but then she'd said, "And I liked it." She'd smiled at him, the expression turning her rather plain, wholesome features into something wickedly alluring and sensual.

If that hadn't been enough to titillate him, she'd added, "The deeper and harder, the better."

Well.

How could he possibly resist *that*?

And so Smith had been giving it to her deep and hard for at least half an hour.

She would be getting sore—no matter how much pain she claimed to like— and he was gritting his jaws hard enough to crack his teeth. It was time; his ballocks were heavy and aching to spend.

Smith doubled his efforts, digging his fingers into her pale flesh hard enough to leave bruises. For the next week or more, she would remember tonight whenever she looked at her body, and she would think of *him*.

Of this.

Of now.

He smiled fiercely as the last of her orgasm echoed through her body, and then he stopped thinking entirely and surrendered to pure sensation.

***

Moira Dunsmuir watched her client from beneath lowered lashes as he lay face-up on the bed, his eyes closed, his striking features slack. His olive skin was glazed with sweat, the taut V of his abdomen flexing with each breath. His body—free of any hair except the thick, dark thatch on his head—was as hard as iron.

Before coming to Bernina's, Moira had never shaved her body hair. But not only was it common among the whores who serviced Madame Cecile's wealthy clientele, it was a requirement for anyone who wanted to work for *Mr. Smith*.

Moira had known all about Smith's preferences long before she'd met the man—long before she'd come to England, even.

She knew he was forty-five, although you'd never guess it to look at his body. To be honest, it irked Moira that she couldn't stop looking at him—especially his tremendous cock. Before engaging her for the evening he'd had the audacity to warn her about the size of his prick.

"If you have experienced pain in the past, I would ask you to be honest and save us both any unpleasantness." His heavy-lidded eyes had looked politely bored, as if he were discussing the weather.

Moira had struggled not to laugh in his face. She would have believed him arrogant if she hadn't already heard *cock tales* about him from several other whores.

"I've experienced pain in the past," she'd admitted.

He'd nodded and begun to turn away.

"And I liked it."

He'd stopped and then turned back to her, black velvet pupils swallowing chocolate brown irises.

"The deeper and harder, the better," she'd added.

A tiny smile had curved his beautiful lips. "Why, how… delightful."

Despite her intentions, she'd been impressed when he'd undressed and exposed his erect organ. She had wondered, at first, if it was the lack of pubic hair that made him appear so prodigious. But after enduring the exquisite blend of pain and pleasure that came from such deliciously deep penetration Moira knew it was no optical illusion.

It shamed her to admit that she wanted to use her mouth on him—just to see if she could take all of him. Actually, her desire didn't just shame her, it disturbed her.

Maybe what Moira's mother—not that Moira had ever been allowed to call Marie Bardot *mother*—had always said about Moira was true: *You were born to be a whore, Moira, you could not do anything else.* Marie's cold blue eyes had flickered dismissively over Moira's less than impressive person as she'd delivered her verdict. *You might not have inherited the Bardot good looks, but my blood runs strong and true through your veins.*

She'd smirked proudly when she'd said it, as if being the most recent generation in a long line of whores was something to crow about.

Not until this moment, when Moira's mouth was salivating to suck a man's cock—a man who also happened to be the sworn enemy of her family—had she believed Marie's words were true. Indeed, she'd always suspected that her mother's cynical observation was more a reflection of her *own* carnal proclivities than Moira's.

It appeared she'd been wrong.

How could her body want Smith while her mind hated him? What was wrong with her? Was she such a thoroughgoing whore that she welcomed any man to use her if he was attractive enough—even a man like Smith?

Apparently.

Moira tried to take comfort in the fact that she was not the only employee at Bernina's to have fallen for Smith—or at least to have fallen for his magnificent physique and superlative skills in the bedchamber.

It was a universal truth that whores discussed their clients with each other, dissecting their bodies and abilities (or lack thereof) with the cool detachment of accountants reviewing ledgers. The consensus at Bernina's was that Smith was one of the few clients the whores claimed *they* would pay for bed sport.

Moira had been skeptical, but now she knew it was true, and that knowledge infuriated her; Smith had given her more physical pleasure than any man she could remember. His body was like a tool—or a weapon—designed for fucking.

Well, that was fine, because Moira's body was designed for revenge. By the time Smith discovered just what her purpose was, it would be far too late for him to do anything about it.

Smith's eyelids lifted slowly, giving her time to school her features and gaze worshipfully at him, like a woman who'd just climaxed four times in the last hour.

His full lips flexed into a languorous smile. "Thank you."

Moira had been servicing men for years and this was the first time she'd been thanked. How was she supposed to respond?

He chuckled and reached out to stroke her hip. Only her strict training kept her from flinching away from his gentle caress, which was not the sort of touch she generally received—or favored, for that matter.

"What?" he asked. "Has nobody thanked you for the use of your magnificent body before?" His thumb rubbed the thin, sensitive skin stretched over her pelvic bone.

Magnificent? Yet another first.

She shook her head. "No."

"You're a reserved, mysterious little thing, aren't you?"

Like any good whore, Moira had been trained to conceal any emotions other than admiration from the wealthy and powerful clientele she'd served over the years.

But mysterious? No. She was about as mysterious as one of the bland tea biscuits the English seemed to love so much. Or at least she was bland when compared with her parents and her tall, elegant, and darkly handsome siblings.

Moira looked nothing like the rest of her family. She was a throwback to her diminutive, Scottish grandmother—barely five feet tall, pale and freckled, and as curvaceous as a plank—a resemblance that embarrassed her statuesque mother and regal father.

Smith pinched her already hard nipples, drawing a ragged gasp from her. "These are beautiful."

It was a night for firsts; in all her twenty-five years nobody had ever called Moira's insignificant breasts beautiful—not even the men who'd preferred her exactly *because* she was so flat that she could convincingly masquerade as a young boy.

She was stupid to be surprised at his words. After all, her boyish appearance was why her parents had chosen her to come all this way: because Smith preferred his female lovers to be androgynous.

They had considered sending Moira's brother Etienne, first—since Smith enjoyed the full spectrum of male body types, from over-muscled brutes to slight, dainty men—but Moira was the most expendable member of her family.

Etienne wasn't just beautiful; he was also currently under the protection of the Duc de Montaigne and earning their family a great deal of money. Etienne was also clever and managed all the bookkeeping for the family's business, ensuring that the venerated Maison Bardot continued to prosper and maintain its much-vaunted reputation for producing the finest courtesans in France.

There were no wealthy dukes lusting after Moira and she had no head for accounting, so she'd been sent to England to capture and bring home her family's greatest enemy.

Not that she'd done much toward that goal. She'd been in London almost eleven months and tonight was the first time she'd managed to get into the same room as Maximus Proteus Nicolaides, the real name of the man who'd spent the last thirty years of his life known only as Mr. Smith.

Moira had begun to worry that Smith would never notice her. More than once she'd toyed with the notion of pursuing him, but Marie's warnings had been explicit: *"Nicolaides is a man who enjoys the hunt far more than the kill; never show him anything other than reserve. Always be just beyond reach. That is what all men want—a challenge—and Nicolaides with all his wealth and power needs that thrill more than most."*

And so Moira had been forced to exercise patience, and lots of it.

It had taken her three months just to get hired at Bernina's, Smith's preferred—and exclusive—brothel.

If Madame Cecile had known Moira was a Bardot, she would have hired her without a second thought. But Marie had spent thousands of francs and many months to carefully construct Moira's false background and hide any connection to either Maison Bardot or the Bardot family, so she'd needed to impress the madam with her abilities and persistence.

But working at Bernina's didn't necessarily guarantee a person access to Smith.

Week in and week out Moira had watched as the powerful, sexually rapacious, businessman had taken men, women, or both but never her.

Smith wasn't just flexible in the matter of gender; he also enjoyed both ends of a flogger or crop—a unique characteristic in Moira's experience—and she'd heard that he administered whippings as beautifully as he endured them.

His sexual tastes were so varied that she'd begun to believe her mother's assessment was wrong and that Moira held no special appeal for such a man.

As the days had turned into weeks Moira had despaired that he'd ever notice her. Then, earlier that evening—ten months and twenty-six days after she'd stepped off the packet from France—Smith's roving gaze had landed on her.

"What are you thinking about?" Smith asked.

The question startled her. It also reminded her that she was a fool for allowing her mind to wander in his presence.

"Nothing," she lied.

"Nothing at all?" he teased.

"I was thinking how wonderful your hand feels." That was true enough.

"How prettily you lie." His eyes narrowed. "How long have you worked here?" he asked, the question far too close to her recent musing for Moira's comfort.

"Six months."

"How is it that I didn't notice you until tonight?"

"Perhaps I'm not very noticeable."

He laughed, his obvious dismissal of her words flattering. "I think I'm just not very observant."

Moira knew *that* for a lie. Based on all the information her family had gathered over the years there wasn't much that Smith missed. Not only was he an exceedingly wealthy man, but he was a powerful one, as well. Neither of those were characteristics of unobservant men.

"Where were you before Bernina's?" he asked.

"Tosca's. You know it?" Moira asked, playing her part in the conversation.

"Yes, but I have not been there in some time."

Moira knew that, too—and she knew why he no longer went: because his ex-lover—Charles Smith—had recently returned to London and was working at Tosca's. Charles Smith had not been at Tosca's when Moira worked there, but she'd heard stories about the beautiful, mercurial whore.

Smith rolled over and lowered his hot mouth on the nipple he'd been pinching and stroking.

Moira moaned; her nipples were almost as sensitive as her clitoris, but men hardly noticed them because her breasts were so insignificant. They didn't pay much attention to her sex, either—unless it was to shove themselves inside it.

Although she was sore from the vigorous fucking, her inner muscles tightened and her already engorged sex throbbed with anticipation.

"What a deliciously responsive body you have." He nipped the pebbled flesh hard enough to startle a whimper from her, and then switched to her other breast, his hand sliding down her belly toward her slit.

Moira spread for him, and not just because that was what she'd been trained to do. For once, she did it because she wanted to feel those long, sensitive fingers inside her body.

He circled her slick, swollen bud. "Such a beautiful little erection." He penetrated her with one finger and pumped her slowly, the soft squelching sounds obscenely loud in the quiet of the room.

And then he bit her nipple so hard it felt as if he'd drawn blood.

Moira jolted, her back arching as the sharp pain shot straight to her primed sex, shoving her toward another orgasm with ridiculous ease.

"You genuinely crave pain, don't you?" Smith asked once she'd come back down.

Moira had been trained to take a great deal of pain, but it wasn't only her training at work. Smith was right: she *craved it*. For her, sex without pain was as bland as gruel.

"Perhaps I should whip you," he mused, his full, soft lips gentle as they caressed the underside of her breast.

Her cunt clenched at his threat and she felt him smile against her sensitive flesh. "You would like that, I think."

Moira was closer to begging a man than she'd ever been, but would begging work with Smith? She suspected not. He was perverse enough to take as much pleasure in depriving her.

"Ah, too proud to beg," he murmured, easing a second finger into her. "I'll give you what you want… if you just say *please*."

The word *please* pounded on her tightly clamped lips like a prisoner trying to escape its cell. But Marie's words came back to her: *Don't give in too easily; Smith loves the chase more than the capture.*

So, Moira bit her lower lip to lock in her pleas.

Smith chuckled, visibly pleased by her struggle. "That's too bad. I'll just have to try harder." He fucked her with slow, deep thrusts, his thumb avoiding her too-sensitive clitoris while the two fingers buried inside her rubbed that part of a woman's body that could deliver a deeper, more intense climax.

Oh yes, he was skilled, indeed.

"That's right," he encouraged in a low voice. "Ride my hand, darling."

Moira hadn't noticed her hips were moving, but now she gave her body free rein, humping him with abandon.

His mouth caressed over her ribs and he licked and kissed each prominent bone, the gentle action a dramatic juxtaposition to his rough thrusting. "Such a greedy cunt," he praised. "I want you to come for me again."

Smith's crass, wicked command was the nudge Moira needed to send her flying.

Her last thought, as she gave herself up to heaven, was that it was a shame the first man to give her this much pleasure was the same man she'd spent the last year scheming to destroy.

***

Smith returned to Bernina's two days later and engaged Moira along with another whore, a man named Leo, who was one of the most annoying people she had ever met.

You're just jealous because Leo is prettier than you.

Moira couldn't argue with that; Leo was exquisite, petite, and as perfectly sculpted as a classical statue.

The evening had been odd, to say the least.

Instead of whipping her as Smith had suggested the first time they'd been together, he'd tied up Leo and made her watch.

Moira had to admit that Smith knew his way around a flogger. Most clients either got carried away or were too scared to use the necessary force.

Not Smith.

He'd had Moira strip Leo and then tie a leather thong around his cock and balls to prevent ejaculation. It was an attractive look on Leo's disproportionately large cock. For a man who was not much taller than Moira, the small blond was well-endowed, and he made sure everyone knew it.

Moira's job that night had been to service Leo—first while he'd endured his whipping and later while he'd enjoyed his fucking. She was skilled at fellatio, but even she had neared her limit, sucking and swallowing Leo until her throat was bruised and her jaw felt ready to unhinge.

Smith had been hard and leaking almost from the first blow—a sight that had kept Moira slick with arousal, aching jaw notwithstanding. His body really was a masterpiece and he'd been the very image of an angry god punishing a disobedient mortal.

He'd employed a soft flogger, taking a good quarter of an hour to warm up Leo's back, working his pale skin to a sweaty, rosy hue. Smith had become sheened with sweat from exertion but his breathing had remained normal as he'd brought Leo to the brink of orgasm again and again and again—until the younger man had sobbed and begged.

The more he'd pleaded, the more Smith's eyes had burned with unholy glee, his arm swinging faster, the strokes harder.

After what felt like years to Moira and must have felt like decades to Leo, Smith threw aside the whip and mounted Leo's spread, bound body and proceeded to fuck him with the same thoroughness and ferocity as he'd whipped him. He'd ridden Leo to the brink of pleasure over and over, denying him his climax each time.

Really, the man was obsessed with controlling his lovers' orgasms—obsessed with control, full stop.

As annoying as Leo was, he had a lovely prick and was a joy to service—especially with Smith's hot eyes on her all night. And that was no exaggeration; Smith's eyes had flogged Moira as pitilessly as his arm had worked the whip.

Eventually, Smith had climaxed, so had Leo, but Moira had been left swollen and wanting. To add to her confusion, Smith had then sent *her* away and kept Leo with him, even though he'd paid for both their services all night.

Smith's behavior made no sense to her.

Was he tired of her already? Would she be forced to return to Marie and the *Comte* de Blois—Moira's intimidating father—with her tail between her legs? What had changed? Why didn't Smith want her?

To make matters even more annoying, Moira had tossed and turned in her narrow bed after Smith had sent her away. Finally, after hours, she'd given into her body's demands and had frigged herself.

Twice. The image she'd pleasured herself to—both times—had been Smith.

That's not good, Moira, Marie's harsh voice chided.

No, it wasn't good.

But…

Wasn't it to be expected that she was obsessed with the man who was the object of her life?

At least that was the excuse she was clinging to.

Although Smith had come back three nights after the episode with Leo, he'd looked right through Moira and chosen two men.

A few nights after that he'd done the same thing again, and then again.

That would have been bad enough, but the next time he'd returned he'd chosen Moira's hateful roommate—Julia.

Julia must have pleased him because he took her on his subsequent two visits.

Moira told herself she was in agony because her family had put their trust in her and she was failing.

But that was a lie.

The truth was that it hurt to think that such a vibrant, fascinating man had already tired of her.

Chapter 2

Smith stared at the complex legal document on his desk, his eyes glazing over. It was not like him to be distracted, but he'd been out of sorts since his last visit to Bernina's.

Actually, that was a lie. He'd been edgy since the night he'd first taken that young woman, Moira.

He took off his glasses and rubbed the bridge of his nose while his eyes restlessly flickered over his study, coming to rest on the large painting across from his desk.

Smith had hung this particular painting—a portrait of him—in his study because this was the room where he spent most of his time and he adored looking at it.

It was probably wrong to say he adored a portrait of himself—it was certainly a vain thing to say—but Smith didn't care; the portrait was magnificent.

The artist who'd painted it was Nora Fanshawe—the wife of Edward Fanshawe, one of Smith's three business partners—and she'd done the painting without Smith even sitting for it.

This wasn't the only painting of hers that he owned, he'd also commissioned a rather stunning dual portrait for his former lover, Charles.

Charles.

Charles—who coincidentally shared Smith's surname and also Smith's life for almost a year—had been the only live-in lover he'd ever had. It had been an experience that had soured him on ever having another.

Just *thinking* about Charles made him clench his teeth, and he moved his jaw from side to side to loosen it.

While he didn't miss the man himself, Smith couldn't deny that he missed the *idea* of Charles—or at least the idea of having somebody to come home to.

Smith had lost every member of his family—and every person he loved—when he'd been nine years old. Although the experience had traumatized him, it hadn't left him afraid of intimacy or love. He'd hoped for years to have both a wife and children—not that he could replace what he'd lost, but at least he could begin rebuilding.

But the older he'd grown, and the more he'd come to know himself, the more Smith had accepted that he was simply not cut out for monogamy. Perhaps that was the way he'd been made, or maybe it was a result of that nightmarish day all those years ago. It didn't matter what had caused him to be that way. What mattered was that he could never commit himself to only one sexual partner for the rest of his life. Just thinking about doing that made him rebellious and mulish.

He knew many wealthy men kept both a wife *and* a mistress—sometimes several—but he'd seen how bitter those marriages could become. As much as he would like children, the idea of rearing them alongside a woman who hated him for his infidelity was too distasteful to contemplate.

He had been raised by parents who'd loved each other deeply and had been happily faithful until the day they'd been slaughtered. *That* was his idea of marriage—well, without the slaughtering—anything else did not seem worthwhile. And so he'd long ago accepted that a wife and family was not something he could ever have.

His experience with Charles had proven that even living with a lover was not a good idea for somebody like Smith.

While he'd enjoyed the months he'd spent with Charles—at least the first few—the unhappy truth was that he'd begun to get bored with Charles even before their relationship had devolved into nothing but argument and strife.

Smith always became bored with his lovers.

Well, except for Joseph Leather, his valet of a few short months.

But Joseph, or Jojo as he'd called the complex young woman when they'd been in bed together, had already belonged heart and soul to Stephen Chatham, one of Smith's business partners, when she'd come to work for him. The only part of herself she'd ever given Smith was her body.

Those few months with her had been heady. Not only was the master-servant dynamic tailormade for Smith's sexual tastes, but Jojo possessed a gloriously submissive temperament and managed to subsume herself in her master's desires without ever losing sight of who she was.

Smith sighed. Both Charles and Jojo were long gone and he was dwelling on the past when he had more than enough to occupy him in the present.

He gave up the charade of reading the new agreement for his syndicate's recent purchase of a food processing factory, poured himself a glass of Armagnac, and went to stare out the window. But instead of seeing the extensive gardens—complete with a folly and tiny reflection pond—he saw the whore: Moira.

Although the current craze was for hourglass figures, Smith had found Moira's spare—almost masculine—body unbearably arousing. Her skin was pale marble with faint blue veins, dusted with freckles as so many gingers were. Rather than blue or green eyes, her irises were a striking, seductive blend—a mossy cerulean shade that hinted at uncharted oceans and mysterious depths.

She had surprisingly broad shoulders for such a slight woman, her hips boyishly narrow and her belly as flat as Smith's own. The only hint of softness on her spare body was her breasts—slight swells tipped with dark raspberry pink nipples—and her wickedly sensual lower lip, which pouted even when her face was in repose.

Miss Moira Dunsmuir reminded him of a Roman mosaic he'd seen at the British Museum, a scandalous image that had been draped with a black cloth to conceal the most interesting parts. Smith had arranged a private viewing—everything was possible with enough money—and had been enchanted to find two nearly naked females exercising with barbells, their slender, boyish bodies sleekly muscled. The mosaic was estimated to originate around the year 200 A.D. Which just went to show how society's concepts of beauty were constantly changing.

Not only did he like Moira's body type, but her air of reserve had intrigued him. She was like a smooth unrippled pond and he a bratty boy throwing stones to disturb her surface. Not that he'd been successful, no matter that he'd used her harder than he generally used women. That was one of the reasons he usually preferred men: he liked to play rough—sometimes *very* rough—and it had been his experience that most women did not enjoy such brutal treatment.

But Moira had.

Smith didn't understand how he'd managed to overlook her for so long; she was so much his perfect physical type that she might have been specially designed to tempt him.

Too bloody tempting, as it turned out.

He'd wanted to take Moira the next time he'd gone to Bernina's—indeed, he'd gone there specifically with the intention of working her out of his system. But, at the last moment, he'd decided to thwart his burgeoning obsession and take her *and* another whore, whose name he could no longer remember. Although he'd denied her both his touch and an orgasm that night it had been Smith who'd left the brothel feeling irritable and out of sorts.

And here he was, days later, still thinking about her.

He heaved an irritated sigh. His few months with Jojo had left him raw—far more emotionally bruised than he'd been in his adult life—and he had no interest in repeating the experience so soon.

Obsession was… exhausting.

What he needed was a distraction that did not involve Moira.

What he needed was an evening at home, for a change.

His lips curved into a smile.

What he needed was Luke.

He threw back the rest of his drink and left his study and unfinished work behind.

Knox, Smith's current valet, was busy in the dressing room when he entered his chambers but immediately came into the bedroom when he heard Smith enter.

"Good evening, sir. Shall I dress you for dinner?"

Smith pulled off necktie and shook his head. "I won't need you tonight, Knox. Have Luke sent to me and then tell Cook that I'll dine in my room and that he should send enough for two."

"Very good, sir."

Smith unbuttoned his collar and went to his dressing room to deposit his garments on the valet stand Knox kept for that purpose.

The room was huge but spartan, all his garments spaced an exact half-inch apart. Not a stray hair or dust mote sullied the glossy black wood floor.

Smith knew that his servants believed his obsession with cleanliness and order was the mere whimsy of a wealthy man. But he had kept his person and space scrupulously clean long before he was wealthy—ever since he was ten years, one month, and four days old, to be precise.

His mania for cleanliness—and that is what it was, a mania—wasn't whimsy; it was necessary for his sanity and survival.

But he saw no reason to disabuse either his servants or anyone else of their assumptions.

Smith removed only his coat and necktie, leaving the rest for Luke.

He had considered offering Luke the position of valet after Jojo left, but he was tired of replacing valets just when they began to know his habits, so he'd decided that he would not fuck the next valet he engaged. That had ruled out Luke, whom Smith enjoyed fucking very much.

Luke filled a unique position in Smith's house: part-footman and part-whore.

He'd first met the other man at the Birch Palace, a brothel he occasionally visited. Once the employees reached a certain age the madam who owed the Birch Palace—a Prussian woman—helped them find private positions with her clients. Many took domestic positions or amorous arrangements, or anything in between. A few years at the Birch Palace turned out men and women rigorously trained to anticipate and satisfy their employers' every desire.

Smith knew that Luke's personal preference was to serve—indeed, he seemed to *need* it—but he could convincingly provide whatever a master or mistress might want from him: obedient slave, cruel master, or anything in between.

Not only was Luke efficient, intelligent, and possessed of a burning desire to please his employer—in every capacity—but he was glorious to look at, too.

When Luke had first come to work for him, Smith had enjoyed his body almost nightly, unable to get enough of him. But then he had moved Charles into the house.

Charles had taken an immediately dislike to Luke and so—to keep the peace—Smith had dispensed with Luke's sexual services.

After Charles left his house, Smith had found himself traveling a great deal for business.

And then Jojo had briefly come into his life…

Suffice it to say that Smith and Luke had scarcely spent any time together for almost a year.

Smith heard the door open and turned, smiling when he saw the other man.

"Mr. Knox said you wanted me, sir." Luke towered over Smith's five foot nine inches by at least half a foot. Yet he was the very image of docile subservience with his eyes lowered to Smith's feet.

Smith took Luke's chin and lifted his face until he could see the crystalline blue eyes of his beautiful giant.

"I have been neglecting you terribly, haven't I, Luke?"

Twin slashes of color appeared over Luke's elegant cheekbones. "Not at all, sir."

Smith pouted. "Are you saying that you haven't missed me?" he teased, fully aware the poor man could really only give one answer.

"No—er, that is, of course I've missed you, sir." Luke's voice was fervent and his heated gaze was gratifying.

Smith laughed at Luke's flustered demeanor and pretty blush. He knew the other man would be a consummate performer after so many years working as a whore, but Smith enjoyed his act, regardless.

He lightly brushed the back of his knuckles over Luke's chiseled jaw and then lowered his hand. "Undress me."

Luke's huge but deft fingers immediately went to the buttons of his waistcoat and Smith enjoyed his competent ministrations in silence, content to admire the man as he worked.

Once he'd stripped Smith to his skin, Luke reached for the pile of discarded clothing—intending to take it to the hamper in the dressing room—but Smith shook his head. "Leave it for now."

Luke's blue eyes widened. His servants knew that Smith abhorred clutter and usually couldn't bear the sight of even a single scattered garment.

But right now, he needed the other man's mouth more than he needed a tidy room.

He put a hand on Luke's broad shoulder and pressed lightly. "Kneel."

His servant's gaze darkened to near black as he sank to the carpet. A person could fake many things, but pupillary expansion was not one of them, and Smith's already hard cock throbbed at this silent sign of desire.

He wrapped his fist around his shaft and pumped himself until several beads of moisture ran from the slit. "Suck me."

Without hesitating, Luke opened his pretty mouth and swallowed Smith's prick all the way down to the root.

"*Fuck*," Smith groaned, his eyelids fluttering at the sudden burst of pleasure. He'd never had a lover who could take all of him with such ease. Honestly, he wondered if there was anything that could gag the man.

"You feel so good," he said, carding his fingers through Luke's pale, silky hair and holding him full of cock, reveling in both the physical sensation of burying himself in Luke's tight throat as well pure masculine satisfaction at dominating such a large man.

Luke remained motionless, but Smith felt the strain build in his muscles the longer he was deprived of air. He waited until Luke all but vibrated with need and then withdrew just enough to allow him to breathe.

Luke noiselessly filled his lungs rather than gasping or choking; everything about him was graceful, a grace that was all the more amazing given his size.

Smith rolled his hips, fucking Luke's throat with slow, deep strokes, savoring the way the other man's lips and tongue massaged his shaft from root to tip.

Normally Smith would draw out such a pleasurable experience, but not tonight.

Tonight he needed to empty his aching balls so he could concentrate on what he really needed from Luke.

***

Luke was so pitifully grateful to be back in Mr. Smith's room—at his feet—that his eyes filled with tears of joy as the other man plunged into him, the violence of his thrusting giving him an excellent excuse for his soundless weeping.

It had been so long since his master had summoned him that Luke had given up hope of ever being called again.

Several months earlier—devastated and desperate—Luke had finally capitulated to David Markham—one of Mr. Smith's other footmen—who had been pursuing him almost since the day Luke had come to work for Mr. Smith.

Although Luke and David had fallen into an easy, if not especially stimulating, arrangement over the past months, he had continued to pine for his employer.

"Your heart just isn't in this, Luke. You're in love with the master, aren't you?" David had asked Luke one night after he'd performed especially poorly in bed.

Although David's expression had been sympathetic rather than jealous or mocking, Luke had not wanted to admit the truth of the accusation—at least not to another person.

But it was true: he'd fallen deeply, madly, irrevocably in love with Mr. Smith, a man who would never be his. At least not for more than an evening. And, for months now, it had seemed that even a night's pleasure would be denied to him.

He'd resigned himself to suffering in silence but then this evening a miracle had occurred and here he was. Exactly where he wanted to be, on his knees for his master.

"Touch me, Luke," Smith murmured as his fingers tightened in Luke's hair.

Luke seized the rare invitation as joyfully as he seized Mr. Smith's muscular arse, groaning at the delicious feel of his unyielding body beneath his fingers.

Smith never allowed Luke to explore him the way he yearned to do. If it were up to Luke, he'd spent hours exploring every inch of his body with his mouth and hands.

He massaged the hard globes of flesh before caressing around to the front and scraping his blunt nails over the thin skin of Smith's narrow hips and up the hard ridges of his stomach, wishing he had two mouths so he could lick and kiss the fascinating latticing of his abdomen while sucking his cock.

Luke had been a whore at one of London's most exclusive brothels for over a decade and he'd worked alongside some of the most beautiful men and women in England, but he'd never met Mr. Smith's equal for sheer physical perfection.

Although he was not a big man, he was impeccably sculpted and flawlessly proportioned. But even more attractive than his splendid body was the danger that simmered just below the surface of his pleasant smiles and courteous demeanor.

Luke didn't know why he thought Smith was dangerous because the other man had never behaved violently or dangerously in his presence. On the contrary, Mr. Smith was unfailingly kind and soft spoken—with everyone, even servants.

And yet every time Luke engaged in sex with his employer his pulse pounded as if he were about to run into a burning building; he was the most exciting man Luke had ever met, and also the most reserved and unknowable.

All too soon his master's thrusts became ragged and wild and Luke's mouth watered as Smith's shaft thickened, presaging ejaculation.

But instead of emptying himself in Luke's throat, Smith suddenly withdrew.

Luke stared up at him, trapped by his dark, intense gaze as Smith gripped his hair painfully tight with one hand and fisted his cock with the other.

"Open," Smith ordered roughly.

Luke complied instantly and the other man commenced to paint not only Luke's exposed tongue, but the rest of his face, with ribbons of hot spend, milking himself with brutal jerks, until there was nothing left.

Smith growled and then grabbed Luke beneath the arms and pulled him up off his knees, an astonishing feat of strength considering that Luke outweighed him by at least four stone.

He slammed Luke against the wall hard enough to knock a painting to the hardwood floor with a clatter, and then claimed Luke's spunk-covered lips with a savage kiss.

Emboldened by his master's enthusiasm, Luke grabbed Smith's arse with both hands and ground his iron-hard prick against his belly.

Smith's chest rumbled with approval as he licked from Luke's mouth up his cheek, cleaning every drop of his spend from Luke's face. The rasping of his tongue on Luke's temple, nose, and even eyelids, was unbearably erotic.

But as rough as Smith's actions were, Luke felt cherished, almost… loved.

He also felt close to exploding, his balls boiling with the need to ejaculate.

As if he'd spoken aloud, Smith tore open Luke's trousers and grabbed his prick in a painfully tight grasp, pumping him from root to tip.

"You're so hard for me."

Luke whimpered, his hips jerking. "Please."

"No, don't come," Smith ordered, his brutal stroking making that a very difficult order to obey.

And then Mr. Smith leaned forward and spoke words from Luke's darkest, most delicious, fantasies.

"I want you to fuck me, Luke," Smith said. "But first, I want you to whip me."

Chapter 3

Smith adored bondage and physical pain, both dispensing and receiving it.

But the trouble with surrendering to such pleasure was that it left him at his most vulnerable, so he rarely indulged himself, even in his own home.

For years the only people Smith had allowed to tie him up were his close friends Malcolm and Susan Barton, a married couple who shared his proclivities. But Susan had died some years back and since then he and Malcolm had only engaged in annual debauches on the anniversary of her birthday.

Malcolm had recently remarried, so Smith wasn't sure they'd even have those yearly trysts any longer.

He *missed* those sexually liberated times with his two friends; he missed them terribly.

But even though he kept armed guards at the entrances to his house and employed a small army of loyal servants, he was still leery of permitting himself to be bound and gagged in his own home.

Smith's reticence had driven Charles to distraction.

"You don't trust me to tie you up!" Charles had accused him on more than one occasion.

Smith had not been able to refute the accusation; he *hadn't* trusted Charles not to exploit such a position of power. The younger man was simply too mercurial.

Other than Malcolm and Susan, the only person he'd ever relaxed his barriers for was Luke. For reasons beyond Smith's ken—he trusted the big man implicitly. Even so, it wasn't something he indulged in often.

But tonight, Smith desperately needed to give up control and enjoy nothing but sensation for a few hours.

Luke secured Smith's ankles first, buckling soft leather cuffs around each and then attaching straps to the cuffs.

He then flipped up the sections of wood flooring that concealed heavy cast iron rings and fed the straps through the rings and spread Smith's legs wide, until his hips and groin ached from the tension.

Once Smith's legs were secure, he went to an unobtrusive wood panel set in the wall, flipped it open, and turned a dial. Thanks to the miracle of electricity—a subject Smith was interested in—the heavy wrought-iron light fixture descended soundlessly from the ceiling.

Luke attached Smith's wrists to the fixture with more leather straps and then turned the dial in the opposite direction, not stopping until Smith's arms were stretched high over his head and he was almost standing on his toes. The heavy fixture was anchored to an eight-inch beam embedded in the plaster ceiling, which meant that Smith could yank and struggle for the rest of his life and never get free.

Lastly, Luke fastened on the gag, which was fashioned after a bridle, complete with a curb strap, cheek piece, and a thick bit that spread his jaws wide and pinioned his tongue. Leather straps held the device together and fastened with a heavy buckle at the back of his head.

The moment Smith was bound, gagged, and immobilized a transformation came over his gentle, submissive servant, whose face was normally as devoid of emotion as a totemic carving.

Luke's lips curved into a faint, cruel smile, his pale skin flushed, and his blue eyes blazed with arousal.

"So beautiful," Luke murmured, caressing Smith's spread lips with a thick, work-roughened finger.

He'd cinched the gag so tightly that the leather cut into Smith's cheeks and the thick bit forced his jaws wide enough to ache. Not only was Smith deprived of speech and restrained like an animal, but he was also drooling, which was a humiliating side-effect of wearing such a device.

Luke glanced down at Smith's prick, which was back to full hardness even though he'd ejaculated barely half an hour earlier.

"Is this for me?" Luke smirked and then slapped Smith's cock with the flat of his hand.

Smith's scream was effectively choked off by the gag. In a house was filled with servants, only he and Luke could hear the hoarse gurgle of pain.

Tears ran freely down his cheeks, the sight of them drawing a demonic laugh from his captor.

"Like that, did you?"

Despite the tears and scream, Smith's cock was like iron, the copious fluid leaking from the slit a mute testament to his arousal.

Luke slapped him again, even harder, sending ragged bolts of pain from his groin to his belly while his balls tried to retract into his body.

Smith would have doubled over at the agony had he not been bound so tightly.

"You acknowledge a question when I ask you one," Luke snarled.

Smith nodded vigorously, drool streaming from his mouth.

Luke smirked and then slapped Smith hard enough across the face that he tasted blood.

"Good boy," he praised, the demeaning words and painful sting as intoxicating as opium.

Luke left Smith quivering with indignation, rage, and arousal and disappeared into the dressing room, emerging a moment later with two black leather items.

"I'm going to be kind and let you pick which tool I use to punish you. This?" Luke hefted the seven tailed flogger in his right hand. It was a beautiful whip that Smith had ordered from a craftsman in Berlin. The cleverly contoured wooden grip was shaped like a phallus and inset with silver rings that provided a great deal of stimulation when used for penetration.

Luke lifted his other hand. "Or this?"

The second implement was the product of England's oldest and most respected whip-maker, R.Q. Haynes: a plaited riding crop with a wide leather keeper at the tip.

Smith nodded at the flogger. It had been a long time since he'd endured a whipping and he didn't think he was up to the crop.

"Excellent choice," Luke said, once again disappearing, this time behind him rather than into the other room.

Curious—and nervous—Smith twisted his head to see what Luke was doing.

He received a stinging swat with the crop—not the flail—across the back of his thighs for his effort.

"If I wanted you to look in this direction, I would have tied you facing this way. Do it again and you will regret it," Luke said, his breath hot on Smith's neck. "Nod if you understand me," he snapped when Smith did nothing.

Smith nodded vigorously.

Luke was not jesting—he *would* make Smith regret any disobedience. The man was like another person entirely when he got his hands on a whip.

He was bloody delicious. But also rather terrifying.

There were more sounds of movement behind him and then an aggravating silence. Smith's body tensed with dread and expectation. Not that his cock was frightened; indeed, it continued to leak and throb with mindless anticipation.

"We can't have you going off too quickly," Luke muttered as he came around to the front. He had taken off his coat, vest, and shirt and was wearing only black trousers and boots.

Smith groaned at the sight of Luke's naked torso. Not only was he in prime physical condition, but he had continued to shave his chest and armpits even though Smith had neglected him for months.

Something about that silent sign of devotion tugged at Smith's heart, not that he fooled himself that it was desire for Smith that caused Luke to maintain such severe grooming. No, Luke would have continued to prepare himself according to Smith's desires because he was a superlative servant.

Luke dropped to one knee in front of Smith and secured a leather thong around the base of his cock and balls. He fastened the strap snuggly enough to keep Smith from ejaculating too quickly, but not so tightly that it restricted all blood flow.

"How does that feel?" Luke gave Smith's prick another hard slap when he didn't nod quickly enough.

Smith's eyes teared and he squeezed them shut.

"Look at me."

Smith's eyes flew open in time to watch as the palms of Luke's huge hands swatted his engorged shaft one way, and then another.

His howl was no more than a choked whimper and the room tilted, darkness encroaching on his vision as he struggled to hold the other man's gaze.

Luke grunted. "Good lad," he said, but then delivered a final, stinging slap. "Next time you look away or close your eyes I'll whip your cock with that crop."

Behind the brutally tight gag Smith moaned and shook his head vigorously from side to side.

Luke chuckled evilly. "If you make pretty noises like that, I might do that anyway. I bet I could make you come all over yourself with a proper cock whipping."

Smith seriously doubted it. Still, if anyone could make him orgasm by flogging his erect penis, it would be Luke.

Luke commenced the whipping lightly enough, his arm quickly falling into a rhythm.

The soft strips of leather did not hurt—much—on the thin skin of his torso and Smith reveled in his inability to do anything but *feel*.

And maintain eye contact rather than stir Luke's wrath.

Only gradually did he become aware of some discomfort. After a while, each lash felt less like a heated caress and more like a friction burn. And then it began to sting.

One bee, at first, and then dozens, hundreds.

Soon, it felt as if skin was being torn away in strips, leaving only raw, bleeding nerves behind.

Smith shivered and tossed his head; the only movement allowed him. His bound cock and balls throbbed with each beat of his heart and proof of his desire ran down his shaft

And still Luke went on, his biceps bulging with each lash.

"I'll wager you're feeling a bit of discomfort right about now," Luke taunted in a steady voice, his arm falling harder and faster, the knotted leather like nettles digging into his skin.

Slowly, the lash began to drift higher. Luke had mainly been whipping Smith's abdomen, seemingly fixated on the ridged musculature just above his groin.

Only occasionally had the whip hit his nipples, but now he angled his blows so that the knotted leather tips flicked the small, puckered discs of flesh over and over and over.

If Smith hadn't been begging before, he would have been pleading now—which is why he always had Luke gag him—and his throat was soon raw from his muted shouts.

Luke was an expert with a flogger but being whipped on the front of one's body was an entirely different—and tenser—experience than being whipped on one's back and arse.

Especially when one's cock was erect and bobbing.

Luke knew how to keep the flails just close enough to his prick without striking his organ, but everyone made mistakes, no matter how skilled, and the fear that Luke might misjudge one of his strokes was never far from his mind, which only served to heighten the torment.

"You were a right bastard to keep me from coming earlier," Luke said as he slid his free hand down to the wet spot on his black wool trousers. With a few deft flicks he opened the buttons and brought out his erect cock.

Luke was uncircumcised and a dark pink sheath protected the sensitive crown. He began to stroke himself, not pausing his flogging, his actions exposing mouth-watering glimpses of the slick mushroom head.

The other man was big and thick and he knew from experience that Luke's prick would feel like a ship's mast when he buried it in Smith's tight hole.

"I'm so close," Luke warned in a raspy voice, bringing his whip arm down *hard*.

Smith's eyelids fluttered shut, the front of his body on fire.

"Eyes on me!" A single flail struck the head of his cock.

Smith's eyes flew open as he screamed and his knees buckled, his shoulders burning as if his arms were being pulled from their sockets. Even through his tears Smith saw Luke's massive upper body straining and bulging with the effort of his savage flogging. His vision wavered and his head dipped.

Luke laughed at his surrender, threw the whip to the floor, and was behind Smith in a heartbeat. He heard the clink of a glass bottle of oil right before a thick finger pushed at his hole.

"So bloody tight," Luke snarled, sliding an arm around Smith's chest to hold him steady while he fingered him.

Smith forced himself to relax and open himself for Luke's use.

Luke gave a grunt of approval. "You're such a good hole."

He shivered at the vulgar, demeaning praise, shame washing over him when his sphincter puckered with anticipation.

Luke gave a cruel bark of laughter. "You like that, don't you—being my *hole*?"

Smith wouldn't have disagreed with him even if he could.

"You're fortunate that I'm in a kind mood," Luke said. "I've half a mind to fuck you dry."

Smith shuddered at the brutal threat. As big as Luke was, it was going to hurt even well-stretched and oiled.

Luke poured on more oil and fingered him with slow, deep thrusts.

Just when Smith began to lose himself to pleasure, Luke shoved a second thick digit alongside the first.

When Smith whimpered at the sudden stretch Luke slapped his cock with the hand that had been resting on his belly. "Quit sniveling or I'll give you something to whine about," he threatened, scissoring his fingers until tears ran down Smith's cheeks.

After an eternity, Luke gave a grunt of satisfaction and replaced his fingers with the thick crown of his cock. But he didn't enter him immediately, instead only slightly breaching the grudging ring of muscle.

"Bear down and let me in or it will go badly for you."

Smith instantly complied and Luke mounted him with a pile-driving thrust, burying himself balls deep. "Ahh, *fuck yes!*" Luke shouted, his muscular chest clamped tightly to Smith's back as he held his trembling body stuffed full of cock, allowing him a moment to adjust to being stretched and invaded.

"So tight and delicious," he whispered in Smith's ear. "I'd like to shove two pricks in you—you'd like that, wouldn't you?"

Smith groaned behind his gag, his body feeling too small to contain the sensations the vulgar, brutal threats evoked.

"Maybe next time I'll tie you up and then pull three or four big bruisers off the street—huge men with horse pricks who'll go at you all night long. I'd let one fuck your throat while I gave you a good hard ride, stretched you—and then I'd have another man shove in beside me and we'd pound you into next week. When we were done using you, I'd plug all that juice inside you." His laugh was ugly and harsh "But not right now." His voice dropped to a whisper. "Right now I'm going to breed you just like the desperate bitch you are."

Smith's entire body clenched, drawing a tortured moan from the other man.

"Good whore," Luke praised, filling him thoroughly with every thrust, his prick striking that place deep inside Smith that brought almost unbearable bliss.

Just when he thought he couldn't bear much more, Luke's pumping became jerky and wild as he lost control.

"Oh, God. I love being inside you," Luke muttered.

Even through his delirious haze Smith heard the yearning in the other man's voice. Distant alarm bells went off in his mind but were quickly muffled when Luke's fist closed around Smith's swollen shaft, jerking him in counterpoint to the snapping of his powerful hips.

The leather band became an agony as his balls tried to draw up. Mercifully, Luke's free hand fumbled for the thong and untied him. Blood and sensation returned to Smith's abused groin in a rush.

"*Coming*," Luke shouted, hilting himself so deeply it felt like he'd punched through Smith's spine, his thick shaft filling him with jet after jet of scalding semen.

Even in the midst of his orgasm Luke did not forget him, and his fist pumped Smith's prick fast and hard. "Come for me, whore."

The degrading order was like the prod of a whip and Smith's entire body spasmed, the pure shock of pleasure turning him inside out.

He abandoned himself to mindless bliss, the knowledge that he didn't and couldn't do or say a thing setting him free.

Yes, tonight was exactly what he needed; for the first time in weeks, he was at ease, no annoying or distracting thoughts of ex-lovers or intriguing whores.

No sooner had he finished congratulating himself when his willful brain assembled a mental picture of a certain ginger-haired, sea-green eyed woman.

Smith groaned, unwilling to return to the world around him.

But Moira Dunsmuir was back, and Smith was beginning to fear that she might be there to stay.

Chapter 4

"That is checkmate," Luke said. And then added in a more diffident voice, "Sir."

Mr. Smith stared at the board for a long moment and then looked up, his scowl slowly—almost grudgingly—shifting into a smile. "Well done you sneaky bastard. That is three bloody nights in a row you've bested me."

Luke tried not to grin and failed miserably.

Smith laughed. "Go on—have a nice gloat, you've earned it."

Luke grinned. "Thank you, sir."

Smith stood and poured them both more wine before Luke realized what he was doing. When he began to stand, Smith shook his head. "No, I'll wait on you—to the victor goes the spoils."

Luke wanted to tell him that he'd prefer some other *spoils*, but he caught himself in time. As casual and friendly as the past two weeks had been, he was still intensely aware of his place in Smith's household. He was a servant first and foremost and a whore second. They were not lovers or friends, they were master and servant and the moment he forgot that distinction he suspected Smith would send him packing.

"Thank you, sir," he said when Smith handed him his refilled glass.

Smith sat on the settee across from him, his ivory silk dressing gown baring a mouth-watering expanse of bronzed chest. They'd already made love once—before dinner—but Luke could not get enough of the other man. He'd hoped Smith might drag him back to bed, but he could see the other man was in the mood to talk.

"Tell me about your family—you grew up in London, did you not?" he asked.

"Yes, sir. My father is a tailor, although not the sort you'd find on the Row."

"Do you have a large family?"

"Two brothers who work for my father, too. And they've each got three children."

Smith cocked his head. "Do you want a family?"

Luke snorted softly. "I do, but it's not—well, it wouldn't work for me, sir."

Smith merely nodded, well aware of what life was like for men like them.

"What about you, sir?" Luke blurted, suddenly so tired of holding all his curiosity inside himself that he had to let some out or risk exploding.

Smith blinked. "Me?"

"Are you from London?"

"No, but I've lived here a long time, most of my life."

Luke thought that was all he'd say, but then he went on, his dark eyes suddenly distant.

"I come from somewhere so far away from London it might as well be a different world." His gaze sharpened again and focused on Luke. "But I will never go back there. I will live in London until I die." He smiled. "What about you? Where would you live if you could live anywhere?"

Luke gave a startled chuckle. "Lord, sir, that's not anything I've ever thought about. I wouldn't know where to go. I've not been anywhere—except Brighton one summer—so I suppose I'll stay here until I die, as well."

"Why did you go to work at the Birch Palace instead of at your father's?"

Luke shifted in his chair; not sure how honest he should be.

"You needn't censor yourself with me," Smith said, yet again reading his mind. "Nothing you say will anger or offend me."

Luke cleared his throat. And then cleared it again, not really believing he was about to share this part of himself until the words began to tumble out. "I worked for my father for years, and from the age of seventeen to nineteen I was betrothed to a girl from our street," he said, suddenly desperate for this man he loved so very much to know about him. "I cared for her a great deal—I l-loved her, even. But I was always restless." He cut a glance at Mr. Smith.

The other man nodded for him to continue, the knowing glint in his dark eyes telling Luke that he would not be shocked or disgusted.

"I'd had"—he swallowed hard—"a number of, er, encounters with other men—and women—mostly just furtive meetings in dark alleys in the dead of night."

Luke wasn't vain, but neither was he unobservant. He'd seen that women and some men found him desirable and several had made their interest clear to him.

And he had been far too curious to resist.

"None of those encounters were especially rewarding," Luke confessed. "I always felt dirty and ashamed after. And yet…"

"You'd do the same thing again?" Smith guessed.

Luke nodded. "I might have gone on for years working in my father's shop, marrying Katie, and snatching a few hours with strangers once or twice a month." He inhaled deeply. "But then I met a man who taught me… things."

"Things about yourself and how you weren't alone?"

Luke sighed, relieved the other man knew where he was leading. "Yes."

"Tell me about him."

"Even though I met Jake on one of my nighttime forays, in one of the usual places, he was different."

Luke had only ever shared mutual jerks with the men he sought out in dark alleys, but Jake had stunned Luke by sinking to his knees, opening Luke's trousers, and swallowing his prick. It had been the most erotic experience of Luke's young life—far more satisfying than the few sucks he'd had from street whores.

Luke looked up from his old memories to find Smith waiting patiently.

"What stunned me even more than what Jake had done was that he invited me out for a pint afterward. "

Smith smiled. "Your first male lover who was also a friend."

Luke nodded.

That night had opened the door to a whole new world. The pub they'd gone to had been filled with men like them—men who enjoyed both fish and fowl, as Jake had quaintly termed it.

"A bloke like you could earn a great deal of brass, if he had the mind to," Jake had told Luke several months after their first meeting, which they'd repeated with dangerous, careless regularity. "I've got a mate who works in a house behind Piccadilly—in the posh part, too. He's just a footman there, but he's told me plenty about the place. A brothel for toffs who're bent, if you know what I mean." Jake had winked.

As a matter of fact, Luke hadn't had a clue what Jake meant, but he'd been far too embarrassed by his own ignorance to ask. But over the months that had followed he'd learned quite a bit from Jake. And everything he'd learned had made him realize he couldn't go on with the life he'd been living.

"So, what did you do?" Smith asked.

"I'd always known that my… urges would have appalled Katie if she'd found out about them. But I'd believed I could control them. Perhaps if I'd never met Jake I could have gone on with that life. But once I had"—he shrugged. "Well, there was no un-ringing that bell, as the saying goes. So, I did the worst thing a man could do—at least in my family's eyes." He snorted softly. "I became a jilt."

And he couldn't tell anyone *why* he'd ended the betrothal because there hadn't been a reason he could give that wouldn't either earn him more derision or land him in prison.

He met Smith's dark gaze. "My father and mother never forgave me, but my brothers relented over time. If you can believe it, the only person who wasn't angry, was Katie. She said that she didn't want us to marry if I wasn't happy."

"She sounds like a lovely person," Smith said.

"She is. And she married a fine man and has a boy and a girl." Children that might have been Luke's if he'd taken a different fork in the road. But he didn't say that. He'd maundered on long enough.

He saw that his master's glass was almost empty and stood to fetch the bottle.

But when he went to top up his wine, Mr. Smith put a hand over his and took the bottle. He set it aside and took Luke's hand, pulling him down on the settee.

"You are a good man, Luke." Smith pulled the sash on Luke's dressing gown and spread open the flaps, exposing Luke's nude body. He pushed Luke onto his back, his hands and gaze moving to his erect cock.

Luke hissed and arched his back when Smith's strong fingers closed around his shaft.

"You did the right thing, rather than the easy—or selfish—thing. It is painful to give up somebody you love, but sometimes… it is the best thing you can do for them."

Their Master

As Smith lowered his mouth over him, Luke couldn't help
wondering if the other man was speaking from experience or issuing a
subtle warning.

Chapter 5

S mith surveyed the two dozen young men currently at work in the new, well-lighted, and warm furniture making shop and turned to his business partner, Edward Fanshawe.

"This is promising, Edward. *Very* promising."

Edward's harsh features shifted into a rare smile and he patted Smith's shoulder with one huge paw. "Is that a tear I see in your eye, Smith?"

Smith snorted and shrugged off his hand. "This was an excellent idea." He wasn't just talking about the furniture shop, but the entire school, which they'd started a few years earlier to help London's poor and homeless young men.

It had been Edward's idea initially and Smith had just donated money because the other man had asked. But it hadn't taken long before he'd begun to support the charitable endeavor for its own sake.

Smith's three business associates had all spent time in orphanages and workhouses as children and assumed the same had been true for him. He'd never bothered to set them straight because he never told anyone about his past. Ever. Although he'd never spent time in an institution, he'd lived on the streets for years—and had been forced to do questionable, repugnant things to survive—so he knew how hard life was for poor and homeless children.

Over the past few years Smith had come to care for this school a great deal and found that he enjoyed spending time with young men who were eager to better their lives. He liked it so much that he was making plans to convert the rambling ducal estate he'd acquired in Scotland into a similar institution.

He and Edward had started off in just one building and had already expanded to three more. In fact, the reason for their meeting today was to sign papers for a new property, where they would have a pottery, which was something new they were trying.

"Aye, it's a fine thing," Edward agreed, his suspiciously dewy eyes flickering over the twelve young men who were companionably working at various carpentry projects, their instructor moving among them to offer guidance where needed.

Edward, once a carpenter himself, often volunteered his time at the school.

Smith had no marketable skills—well, nothing that wouldn't land the young men in either trouble or jail—so instead of teaching he sometimes took groups of students on field trips to interesting London destinations.

Thus far they had visited the British Museum, the Tower of London, the National Portrait Gallery, and the Royal Botanic Gardens. Although most of the boys came from London, they'd been too busy trying to survive the brutal streets to visit such privileged places.

Thinking of orphans reminded Smith of another matter. "When will you officially become a father?"

Edward's grin threatened to split his face. "Amelia will be with us by the end of the week." The child in question was almost two years of age and recently orphaned.

"So soon! Congratulations, Edward."

Edward blushed, the reaction surprising for a man whose scandalous first marriage and divorce had been front page news for almost a year, and who was generally believed to be one of the most jaded men in England.

"Thank you," he said quietly. "Nora and I are pleased to share what we have."

What they *had*, in addition to an obscene amount of money, was a very loving marriage. Although many in society's upper strata believed the couple to be beyond the pale, Smith knew the girl was extremely fortunate in her new parents, and he was pleased for his friends.

"We'll have you over to dinner once she is settled in—then you can meet her," Edward said.

"I would like that."

After taking his leave of Edward—who would issue the first work orders on the new building—Smith decided to walk home, rather than take his carriage.

"You can go home," he told his coachman, and then glanced at the two guards. Smith was tempted to dismiss them, too, but he had damned good reasons for employing them, so he waved them to follow.

The last time he'd been attacked—a year ago by an enraged worker from one of their textile mills—he had ended up with a black eye and several cracked ribs. Although he'd neutralized that particular threat, there were always more. As the face of—and often enforcer for—his business syndicate, Smith was a magnet for discontent.

Then there were his own, non-syndicate businesses and pursuits, several of which had earned him more than a few enemies.

So, Smith allowed Larry and John to follow behind him—not too close to impinge, but close enough to step in if necessary.

He put his bodyguards out of his mind and thought about Edward's happy news. Smith envied Edward and Nora—both their marriage as well as their impending parenthood.

Families and children were not subjects he thought about often, even though his own family had been both extensive and tightly knit, but he seemed to be thinking about them a great deal lately.

Indeed, ever since Smith's last birthday, when he'd turned forty-five, he'd begun to contemplate his own mortality. Usually, it happened in the early hours of the morning when insomnia imprisoned him in its brutal grasp.

He was well-past the half-point of his life—by a decade at least—although his family had traditionally enjoyed long lives.

Well, until they hadn't.

The screams of his mother and siblings were faint now, as was the smell of blood, gunpowder, and death. In fact, sometimes his memories were so vague it felt as if his past had happened to somebody else.

He supposed, in a way, that was true.

Smith, the man he was now, had no family and no history—not even a first name. All he had was a great deal of money and nobody to share it with or leave it to when he was gone. It surprised him how displeasing that last thought was. After all, what did he care? He would be dead.

But Edward's talk of children had stirred something inside him. And seeing the light in his eyes—not to mention the joy in Nora's the last time they'd met—at the prospect of having a child in their lives had given Smith an odd sense of yearning.

Nora being Nora—which was to say *astute* beyond what was comfortable—she had seen Smith's yearning. "Just because you don't want to marry does not mean you cannot have a child," she had told him the last time he had taken her to tea—something Smith did monthly, just the two of them.

Even though Edward was fiercely possessive of his wife, he had learned not to stifle Nora—something Smith would eternally be grateful for—so he'd never insisted on joining their private monthly teas.

"I wouldn't want to bring a bastard into the world," Smith had said.

Nora had waved away that concern with a flick of her wrist. "Nonsense. It is the dawn of a whole new decade, Smith, and you are one of the wealthiest men in Britain. Any child of yours will have the world at their feet from the moment they take their first step." She had taken his hand and squeezed it between both of hers. "I love you Smith." Her lips had quirked into an impish yet wicked smile. "If not for Edward, I would have set my cap for you."

Although Smith had laughed, he'd been privately pleased by her words, even if it was yet another instance of a woman he esteemed choosing another man over him.

"I want you to be happy," she'd gone on to say. "If you don't want the complications of finding a woman to have your baby, you can always do as Edward and I have done and take in an orphan."

At the time, he'd dismissed her words: he didn't want a child!

But now, after living with the thought for a while, he was beginning to see the appeal. Why *shouldn't* he have a family? Nora was right; he had a great deal to give a child, and not just money. He might have done questionable things in pursuit of business, but he was no ogre to the people he cared about.

A sudden gust of wind picked up and cut between the buttons of his heavy overcoat. Smith glanced at the sky and saw it had turned a flat gray color that heralded snow. He pulled up his collar and marched on rather than flag a hansom even though he was at least a mile from his house. The walk was stimulating his brain, even though it wasn't necessarily making his thoughts any clearer.

He could not do as Edward and Nora were doing and take in an orphan because who would nurture it? A man alone was not enough; a child needed a mother.

Which meant he needed to find a woman who had a child.

Or a woman willing to bear *his* child—and stay in his life to help raise it.

That second thought appealed to him the most.

Yes, it was vain to want to pass part of himself on, but it was certainly no uncommon vanity. People wanted children of their own blood.

Smith sighed and shook the notion away. Finding a suitable woman would be, if not impossible, certainly an arduous task. How did one even go about commencing such a search? She would have to be somebody who could tolerate his… *unusual* appetites and lifestyle. And she'd also need to be somebody whom *he* could tolerate. That was a herculean task even when a person was considering marriage. What sort of woman would contemplate a union with a man like Smith?

Besides, why open his life to uncertainty and disorder now that he'd fallen into such an easy and pleasurable rhythm with Luke?

He smiled just thinking of the other man, whom he'd take to his bed four nights out of seven since resuming relations with him two weeks earlier. They'd enjoyed plenty of lusty sex in addition to entertaining evenings filled with games of piquet and chess, both of which Luke played well.

They had even attended a play one evening, getting more use out of Smith's private box than it had seen in years—and almost none of that use involving the production itself.

They had not indulged in any further rough bondage, even though he knew Luke stood ready, willing, and eager.

Indeed, sometimes Smith thought Luke might be too eager. He hoped the younger man was not forming an attachment beyond the one they'd agreed to in Luke's contract. As much as Smith enjoyed spending time with Luke, he did not wish for another Charles situation. Not only had the end of their affair been ugly, but a goodly chunk of their time together had been unpleasant, too.

But Luke was different. Or at least he hoped he was.

If he'd demonstrated even a hint of jealousy or possessiveness about the nights Smith had ventured out to the Birch Palace—which he'd been using while avoiding Bernina's—then Smith would have ended their enjoyable union.

But thus far all was perfect. So, perhaps Smith was worried for nothing. Perhaps Luke's words that night two weeks ago, *"I love being inside you,"* had meant just that.

Smith hoped so.

Despite his happy arrangement with Luke, Smith still hadn't banished Moira Dunsmuir from his thoughts and he was beginning to believe that avoiding her was foolish. It certainly hadn't worked thus far, and only made her more appealing in his imagination.

Perhaps a better method would be to go to her every night until he tired of her? Wasn't familiarity supposed to breed contempt?

Smith chewed on that notion for several streets, tipping the brim of his hat down when the snow began to fall.

The pleasurable tingling in his groin at the mere *thought* of seeing her again made him extremely uneasy.

But it also filled him with excitement.

Would he really deprive himself of this woman's company just because he was afraid he might become infatuated?

You already are *infatuated,* a cool voice at the back of his mind pointed out.

Smith chuckled to himself. Yes, that he was.

So, what did he have to lose? Why avoid her? Why not *gorge* himself until he tired of her? He would become bored with her—just as he always did.

You didn't get bored with Jojo.

I didn't have enough time *to get bored,* Smith retorted.

Besides, he would do things differently with Moira; he'd not make the same mistake he'd made with Jojo. He'd *take* the time to work her out of his system, and then he would move on.

Smith smiled, a sudden spring in his step.

Even though the heavens had opened and he couldn't see more than a foot in front of him, things suddenly seemed brighter.

He would go to Bernina's and commence gorging that very evening.

Chapter 6

oira stared at the message the footman had just delivered: *Mr. Smith has engaged you for the entire night. Please present yourself for a full grooming, douche, and lavage. The Rose Suite at nine o'clock. C.*

Moira was suddenly uncomfortably hot, even though the small parlor was cool. "What time is it?" she asked her friend Nell, ashamed by the excited tremor in her voice.

Nell glanced at the watch pinned to her black uniform. "It's a quarter past five." She offered Moira the plate holding the scones. "Want the last one?"

"You take it, I'm full."

Mora liked the other girl, who'd been kind to her and was a true friend, but the worshipful look in Nell's eyes made her uncomfortable because she did not reciprocate her feelings.

"You're not leavin' yet, are you?" Nell asked.

"Somebody has paid for the entire night. I must go and prepare." She didn't like the thrill that shot directly to her sex at the thought of the client.

Nell sighed. "I should get back, too."

By *back*, Nell meant to the kitchen. Unlike Moira, Nell wasn't a whore, but a kitchen maid.

Moira took the servant stairs down to the former dining room, which Madam Cecile, the brothel owner, had converted into a bathhouse of sorts.

Amaya, the old lady who handled the trimming, piercing, and general grooming of all the employees was busy, so Moira went to the only available bathtub and turned the handle that would fill it with deliciously hot water, thanks to the rather ugly—but magical—exposed pipes that ran from the large, ugly contraption that heated water.

Her family home in Paris was hundreds of years old and her mother refused to add modern plumbing to the building, so baths were drawn the old way: bucket by bucket.

In Moira's opinion, running, heated water was a luxury worth almost any amount of money.

Her hands shook with anticipation as she considered Smith's impending visit.

She'd not expected to get another chance with him, and she was determined not to waste it. Her monthly meeting with her brother Robert was in two days' time and Moira wanted to have something good to report for a change.

Marie and her longtime lover and the father of her children—the *Comte* de Blois—had always drummed into Moira's head that she and her three siblings owed their mother and father their first allegiance in every situation.

But that wasn't the real reason that Moira had agreed to come to England to capture Smith and drag him back to Paris to face charges for his crimes.

No, it was vengeance for Sandrine that had made Moira not only willing, but eager, to give up a year or more of her life.

She needed to keep Sandrine at the forefront of her mind tonight when Smith attempted to scramble her wits with sexual pleasure and hollow flattery.

Although she knew that was easier said than done.

By the time Moira had finished bathing and washing her hair, Amaya was ready for her.

The old Portuguese woman was an expert at her job and soon Moira was making her way back to her shared room, her entire body hairless and clean—both inside and out.

Bernina's was a small brothel and didn't have enough space to give every employee a room of their own. As the newest worker, Moira had to share a room with a whore named Julia, a woman nobody liked. Because the brothel operated around the clock, the day was divided into two shifts. That was good for people sharing rooms as they rarely had to see one another. But if the person was noisy and inconsiderate—like Julia—it meant you had to be a sound sleeper.

Unfortunately, Moira slept as lightly as a cat, so she'd begun to stuff wads of batting in her ears, but that didn't muffle the slamming of doors or Julia's carrying on with her sometimes-lover, Becky, one of the chambermaids.

Luckily Julia would be gone from their room because she worked day shift so at least Moira wouldn't have to tolerate her presence while she dressed for her appointment Smith.

Moira owned five outfits and rotated them by day. Today's dress was a cream gown that was trimmed with narrow heliotrope ribbon. All she wore beneath it was a single petticoat, plain stockings, and a chemise.

Cecile didn't require her employees to buy a large, expensive wardrobe like Marie did. It had always irked Moira that she'd been forced to spend so much of her hard-earned money on clothing that she could only wear a few times. God forbid some man saw his demimondaine wearing a dress she'd once worn for another.

Madame Cecile also allowed her employees a more casual sort of clothing—not the formal layers upon layers that Parisian society demanded, even of its whores.

The tiny dressing table she shared with Julia was piled high with the other women's pots and vials and powders. All Moira kept on the crowded table was a small tin of lip grease and her tortoiseshell comb and brush set, the only gift she'd ever received from her father. He'd sent it to her on her eighteenth birthday, when she'd joined the family business.

She knew the *Comte* hadn't chosen the gift himself. Likely her mother had assigned the task to some servant.

Moira plaited her vulgar red hair and then pinned it up in an elegant twist, the only style possible with such long, unruly curls.

Once she was ready, she stared at her reflection. The thought of failing her family—failing her beloved sister's memory—wasn't just demoralizing, it was unacceptable.

Tonight, the impossible had happened and Smith had decided to give Moira a second chance.

She could not fail this time; she *had* to ensnare him.

***

Moira was even smaller than Smith recalled, a good eight inches shorter than his own five-foot-nine. Tonight, her slender form was garbed in a simple but tasteful ivory gown with a hint of dark purple on the sleeves and hem.

Her heart-shaped face was as he remembered, as was her copper-colored hair, which was caught up in an elegant knot.

"Good evening, sir." She dropped a curtsey that was breathtaking in its gracefulness, another characteristic he recalled from their prior visit.

"Good evening, Moira. Come, sit with me." He led her to nearby settee, poured her a glass of wine, and sat beside her, close enough that their thighs touched.

"Moira is a lovely name—Scottish, isn't it?"

"Yes, sir."

"Were you raised in Scotland?" If he'd not been staring at her he would have missed the way her sea-green eyes shuttered.

"No, sir. I grew up in London."

She was lying to him—why?

"Is that so? For some reason I thought I detected an accent. In what part of the city did you live?"

"On Cleveland Street." She held his gaze for longer than most dishonest people before dropping her eyes to her hands; hands which lay loosely clasped in her lap.

Smith ran a light finger across the narrow ribbon that banded her puffed sleeve. "I've thought about you often these past weeks." That made her look up, her brilliant blue-green eyes widening.

Smith stroked the sweet curve of her jaw with the back of his fingers; she reminded him of a fairy creature: delicate, mysterious, and intriguing—and ready to flee if startled.

"You gave me a great deal of pleasure the last time I was with you," he continued, enjoying the faint flush his words elicited. He'd been half-hard since she'd entered the room and the slight quickening in her breathing brought him to full mast. It was almost embarrassing to become aroused so quickly—like a boy in his first whorehouse—but Smith didn't care. He wanted her. Now.

His intention had been to become better acquainted, but that would have to happen after he'd taken the sharp edge off his hunger.

He smiled, amused by his own eagerness. "Open my trousers, Moira."

She obeyed, her slender fingers working the buttons quickly and efficiently. Smith lifted his hips to allow her to push down both trousers and drawers. Without being asked, she slid a cool hand around his hot shaft and he hissed in a breath.

"Stretch out on the settee, lie on your stomach with your bottom up here. I want to play with you while you suck me."

She startled at his command and Smith thought how sad it was that so few men seemed to care about their partner's satisfaction, especially when they were paying for sex. To Smith it was a badge of honor to make his lover climax, no matter who they were. After all, if he wanted to fuck something mute, dumb, and without thoughts, he'd use his fist.

Moira stretched out, holding herself up on one elbow and using her other hand to work his cock. It wasn't the most comfortable of positions, but he'd not keep her this way long.

Smith watched her work his cock, her hands small but strong and deft. Whoever had trained her in the erotic arts had done a superlative job and she stroked the silky skin with just the right amount of pressure, the slick, soft pad of her thumb grazing the sensitive area below his crown.

He laid a hand on the back of her head, only needing to apply slight pressure, and she lowered her mouth to his erection.

She didn't take him inside her mouth immediately, but bathed the sensitive head with hot breath, her hand still working his shaft.

Smith inched up her skirt, exposing muscular legs with lovely, shapely calves sheathed in prim white cotton stockings and nothing but a chemise covering her bottom.

His mouth watered at the sight of such perfection and he cupped one firm buttock, his hand a large dark brown star on her milky-white arse.

She chose that moment to tongue his slit.

"*Fuck!*" His hips jerked and she rewarded him with another lick, the tip of her tongue pointed and probing, but still she did not take him into her mouth.

Moira was a tease—a delicious, taunting, tormenting tease—who gave him only a hint of sweet, wet heat and made him suffer and squirm.

Smith grinned and slid his hand lower, his finger dipping into her cleft but not stopping at her back hole—not yet. He needed to contort himself slightly to reach what he wanted, but it was worth the effort. Her outer lips were freshly shaved and swollen, her inner folds wet and hot, and her pearl engorged and slick.

She wanted him. Or at least she wanted to come.

Tonight he would give her that and more.

***

It annoyed Moira to admit that Smith's thick, heavy cock was a thing of beauty. Not only that, but he smelled and tasted remarkably clean, with only a hint of masculine musk.

Even more important than his beautiful cock and well-groomed person was his courtesy.

Every other man she could remember had fucked her mouth as if she were an inanimate object. Never had a man touched *her* body while she pleasured him. And good *Lord* did Smith know how to use his fingers.

"Spread your thighs wider, darling," he murmured, his hand rhythmically caressing from her entrance to her clitoris, using her body's copious moisture to slick her.

Indeed, Moira was mortified by how wet she'd become for him.

Remember who he is and be grateful your body is responding as it does. He will believe you are his creature.

Moira's body tightened at Marie's unwanted advice and the hand stroking her toward ecstasy stilled.

"Did I hurt you?" he asked.

Mouth stuffed with cock, Moira gave a miniscule shake of her head. To distract him, she relaxed her throat and took him deeper, but still not all the way.

He groaned. "Christ, you're good at that."

Even a slight amount of praise was like nectar to her, making her yearn to please him more. It was a pathetic reaction, but she had long ago come to terms with her desperate desire for acceptance. Even from the man who'd killed her sister.

A sudden, stunning, bolt of rage shot through her body at the thought and it took enormous discipline to keep from inflicting any damage.

A moment of pain—no matter how dire—would not be worth ruining all her months of scheming.

Rather than clamping down, she opened even wider, which allowed him to slide deeper than anyone she'd ever taken in the past.

"You are amazing, Moira."

The sounds of pleasure he made helped check her anger and she deliberately swallowed around him, earning a guttural growl of approval.

"Such a delicious, fuckable mouth." His hips pulsed gently while his fingers continued their magic between her legs.

Moira was close to climaxing when he tapped her bottom with the hand that had just been driving her to madness.

"Up," he said. "I want you to finish undressing me."

He smirked at her obvious unwillingness, helping her to sit up.

"I'm going to fuck your arse. And later, when I am ready again, I will take your cunt." His smirk grew. "I'm going to own all three of your holes before the night is through."

Moira had been a whore for almost eight years and never had anyone spoken so crudely to her. The effect on her was electric and her fingers flew over the buttons on his waistcoat and shirt while he removed his necktie.

She dropped to her knees to remove his shoes and stockings while he shrugged out of both coats and shirt, together.

Moira paused at the awe-inspiring sight of his muscles moving like steel cords beneath his olive skin, a chiseled work of art.

He was a handsome man—perhaps too angular for classical male beauty—but masculine and striking. His lips were full and sensual but not feminine. The only soft thing about him was his eyelashes, which were so lush his eyes looked as if they'd been darkened with kohl.

Moira scrambled less than gracefully to her feet and then reached for her garter while he kicked aside his trousers and drawers

"No, leave it on. I want you to straddle me." His hands closed around her waist and he steadied her while she placed a knee on either side of his hips. "Hold up your skirt," he ordered once she was kneeling. "Yes, higher—let me see you." His probing gaze settled on her bare slit and he made a noise of appreciation. "Rest your hands on my knees and lean back."

Moira obeyed, which opened her wider.

His lips curved into a smug, possessive smile. "So pretty," he said, stroking her lower lips with a finger. "They're pouting," he murmured, amusement in his voice. "Why is that, I wonder?" His eyes lifting to hers. "Do you think I'm going to deny you an orgasm again tonight?"

Moira flushed, uneasy that he'd guessed the direction of her thoughts.

He grinned at whatever he saw on her face and leaned back, draping his arms along the back of the settee. "Use your cunt to get me wet."

Again she jolted at his crudity, both aroused and repelled, but her body was trained to obey and she lifted her hips, notching his cock between her swollen lips and moving up and down, slicking him with her embarrassingly wet sex.

"Did you go back to your room and pleasure yourself that night, Moira?"

He laughed before she could even formulate an answer.

Moira dropped her irritated gaze to his prick rather than the knowing, amused glint in his dark gaze.

Smith flexed his hips rhythmically, his shaft grazing her bud with each pump.

Once again he worked her to the brink of climax and then stopped.

Moira had to bite her tongue to keep from begging.

His arms slid from the back of the settee and he reached behind her, spreading her cheeks and prodding at her back hole.

His eyebrows lifted appreciatively when he discovered that she was slick with oil.

"Very nice," he murmured, pushing his thumb into her. "But next time I want to be the one to stretch and prepare you."

Next time.

Moira was so excited by the words that she forgot to answer.

"Understood?" he asked, his eyes hot but his expression stern.

"Yes, Smith."

He nodded and positioned himself at her entrance before pulling her down slowly.

Moira burned inside even with all Amaya's preparation, and his cock was like a molten rod inside her tight passage but she pressed down harder, until he filled her to the root, the pain of penetration making her so wet it was as if she'd already come.

He gave a breathless laugh as he shifted his angle slightly and flexed his hips, skewering her deeper and keeping her filled.

Moira shivered, finding it difficult to breathe she was so full. It hurt—*he* hurt—but she couldn't get enough of him, the pleasure and pain so intwined she didn't know where one left off and the other began.

But as full as she was, her cunt felt empty… so empty.

She opened her mouth to beg for his fingers but bit her lip before she could give in to her body's demands.

Instead of pleading for more, she ground her bottom down, taking him deeper and then tightened her inner muscles.

He hissed in a breath. "Such a good girl," he praised, fucking up into her with sharp thrusts that darkened her vision. "I wish I had more to give you."

If he gave her any *more*, she probably would have lost consciousness.

"Ride me," he ordered, sitting back to watch.

Moira was woozy and shaky as she raised herself up until his crown stretched the tight ring of muscle, and then sank down again.

"Yes… just like that—slow and deep."

She began to post him, taking every inch of him.

His burning gaze dropping to her sex and he lazily thumbed her clitoris.

Moira shivered at the addition of yet more sensation.

"Please, Smith," she whispered, her inner muscles fluttering and contracting on nothing, begging to be filled.

Smith smirked. "Such a greedy little pussy," he chided, but he lowered his second hand and pushed two fingers into her cunt, pumping while his thumb worked her overstimulated bundle of nerves and his big cock filled her to the root.

It was just *too*… much.

"Come for me, Moira," he ordered as her body shook with the effort of containing so much sensation.

Her hips jerked and her fingers dug into the hard, striated muscles of his shoulders as the most intense orgasm of her life rolled through her body.

For the first time ever, Moira gave herself up to her own pleasure without any thought of the man who was paying her.

***

"More wine?" Smith asked, raising the half-empty bottle.

"No thank you," Moira said.

That was the last thing she needed to do: drink too much and let her control slip even worse than it already had when she'd screamed out her orgasm and then fallen into a brief but deep sleep.

She'd never done that with a client—it wasn't her job to climax until she lost consciousness. It was her job to ensure her partner did so.

Instead, she'd woken to find Smith watching her.

"Tell me about yourself, Moira," he said now.

"About me?" she repeated, stalling.

"And no more lies about growing up in London."

Moira was momentarily unnerved that he'd uncovered her first lie so quickly. The story about being raised in England had been for prospective employers rather than Smith, and Marie had said it didn't matter if he saw through. "*A man like Smith will enjoy snooping and catching you in a lie or two, being such a liar, himself,*" she'd assured Moira.

She could only hope the other falsehoods her mother had concocted wouldn't be so easy to detect.

"I'm sorry I lied," she said after a long pause. "It was necessary for my safety."

"Oh?"

"My name isn't Moira Dunsmuir. It's Catherine Duvalle."

"I thought I detected a slight accent."

She nodded. "Yes, I'm from France, but what I told you about my grandmother coming from Scotland is true. My mother spoke English to me when I was growing up, so that is why I am fluent. Moira is my middle name and Dunsmuir was my grandmother's maiden name, but I grew up in Marseilles."

"And you left your life behind to move to London. Do you have friends here? Family?"

Moira shook her head. "No, I am alone here."

"How intrepid you are," he said, a slight smile on his lips.

"Not really. I had to move. You see, I got into trouble there."

"What sort of trouble?"

"I borrowed money I couldn't repay. Fleeing to Paris wasn't far enough; I needed to leave the country. I knew the men looking for me would not think I'd leave France because they don't speak English and wouldn't consider it themselves."

"So, you are a wanted criminal, are you?" His eyes glinted with amusement rather than condemnation.

"Well, maybe not a criminal, although I suppose most people consider evading one's debts criminal behavior."

"I suppose they might."

"You are mocking me."

"A little," he admitted. "Should I call you Catherine, instead of Moira?"

"I would prefer you continued to call me Moira. Madam Cecile doesn't know there are men after me or she never would have consented to hire me." Moira gave him a worried look that wasn't entirely feigned. "You won't tell her, will you?"

"No, I won't tell her that you are using a fake name," he said with an odd smile.

Moira could only assume he was thinking of his own assumed name and how few people knew his real one.

Rather than pursue the matter, as she'd feared, he asked, "How are you finding London?"

At least this was a question she could answer honestly. "Cold, rainy, and gray."

"That does not sound like the endorsement of a person who will stay here long."

If only he knew how short her duration would hopefully be, and how it would coincide with his departure.

"What about you? How long have you lived here?" she asked him.

"Most of my life."

"Where did you move here from?" Moira was genuinely interested because Smith's history wasn't something the *Comte* or Marie had ever shared.

But Smith wasn't sharing, either.

"Somewhere else." His gentle but firm smile made it clear the subject was closed. "It is a hard life you have chosen."

Moira shrugged. "Most work for women is hard."

"I cannot argue with that," he said, his response surprising her. "Did you choose your career or was it forced on you?"

It wasn't a question Moira expected. Men in Paris knew exactly who Moira Bardot was and who her family was, so nobody had ever asked why she did what she did.

Until leaving home a year ago Moira herself had never considered it odd that her mother expected her children—male and female—to enter the family business.

But the longer she lived away from Marie and Maison Bardot, the more she realized her upbringing had been unusual, to say the least.

Had she chosen to become a demimondaine?

Moira hadn't made a conscious decision, or any decision at all. She'd just done what her siblings before her had done.

But if she had a child—not that she had any plans in that direction—she would want something better for him or her. Whoring was lucrative work, but it was not the sort of future she'd want for somebody she loved.

She looked up from her thoughts to find Smith watching her intently, making her aware that she'd allowed her mind to drift. Again.

"I wasn't forced into it if that is what you are asking. Besides, it has—"

Moira realized that she'd been on the verge of admitting that the lifestyle paid enough for her to eventually retire when she recalled that she was supposed to be hiding from gambling debts.

He lifted an eyebrow. "It has—"

"It has been a good enough life," she finished lamely. "A woman doesn't have many choices other than marriage or domestic service." She gave him a mocking smile, "But wait—those are really the same thing, aren't they?"

He chuckled. "So, not a devotee of either marriage or scrubbing chamber pots. Well, I can't say that I blame you."

"You are not married?" she asked, even though she knew the answer.

"Would I be here if I were?"

Moira laughed.

"So cynical for one so young," he chided, setting aside his glass, and reaching for her. "Let's see if I can't do something that will make you more… optimistic."

Chapter 7

John Sheffle—the man Smith had engaged to investigate Moira Dunsmuir or Catherine Duvalle or whoever she was—was an annoying bastard, but he was an astounding ferret when it came to acquiring difficult-to-come-by information.

Smith had hired the man after he'd gone to Moira seven nights in a row. That was the same day he'd finally admitted that he was, without a doubt, smitten. He was nowhere close to sated even after a week of gorging. If anything, he'd become more interested in her with each day that had passed.

Despite his resolution not to engage another live in lover, he'd decided it was time to look into Moira's background as he suspected that he would soon be making her an offer.

Right after hiring Sheffle, he had needed to go to Glasgow on business and had been kept longer than expected. A week away from Moira had given him a bit of perspective on his current obsession, but it hadn't dampened his enthusiasm for her in the least: he wanted her— exclusively. At least on her part.

Provided Sheffle had discovered nothing disagreeable, he'd be offering her a carte blanche sooner rather than later.

But Smith had much more in mind than a simple sexual arrangement.

That morning meeting with Edward all those weeks ago—when they'd discussed Edward's adopted child—had planted a seed. The seed had sprouted and grown during the days he'd been away from home with plenty of time to think. The eventual fruit of that seed had surprised even Smith.

Today he would learn what Sheffle had found out—and whether Smith could have what he wanted: Moira.

"What do you have for me?" Smith asked after he'd curtailed Sheffle's monologue about a carriage accident he'd encountered that morning.

Sheffle slid a grimy leather portfolio across Smith's desk.

Smith stared at the filthy item for a moment before gritting his teeth and flipping it open with the tip of his fingernail.

"What you'll see is—"

Smith held up a hand, cutting off the verbal flow. "Let me read it and I will ask questions."

Sheffle made an irritable burbling sound in his throat but sat back and shut his mouth.

Catherine Duvalle, also known as Moira Dunsmuir.

Age: twenty-five, arrived in London, unattended, eleven months ago on The Petrel *from Marseilles.*

Smith looked up. "How did you find out what ship she arrived on?"

"I was followin' her work history when I hit a dead end after goin' back eleven months." He gave Smith a sly look. "Since you said money wasn't an object, the first thing I did was go around to some of the better whorehouses."

Smith snorted at Sheffle's notion of *research*.

"Go on," he said.

"I found she'd looked for work at the Birch Palace but hadn't been hired. I went through a few others before I got to Tosca's, which looks to be the only place she worked before she got hired at Bernina's. I found the girl she shared a room with and gave her a few bob to loosen her lips."

When Smith didn't praise him for his cleverness, he went on. "She didn't know much," Sheffle admitted. "But she *did* know that Dunsmuir had mentioned where she'd lived before moving into her room at the brothel. A right narsty pit of a place called Pigeon Court. I went there and found the landlady. She said Dunsmuir never caused trouble, never had guests, and paid on time before she buggered off." Sheffle grinned, and it was a gruesome sight. "I thought I'd found nothin'. But then, just as I was about to go, the old lass let it fall that Dunsmuir came to her from a fellow down at the docks. The old crone has an arrangement where—"

"The man refers potential renters to the landlady and receives some sort of finder's fee," Smith finished for him.

Sheffle nodded. "Aye. Anyhow, I went and found the bloke. With enough persuasion, he remembered the girl and looked her up in his book. There she was: not Moira Dunsmuir but Catherine Duvalle, traveling without a berth from Marseilles."

That meant steerage, which meant Moira had had a grim journey, as Smith knew all too well.

"The whore at Tosca's said she saw Duvalle writing a letter in a foreign language and asked her what it was. Duvalle got flustered and hid whatever she was writin'. Told her that she'd grown up in Marseilles but begged her not to tell anyone she was part French. She said Englishmen didn't like foreign whores, especially not French ones. Said the reason she could talk such good English was because her Ma had been Scottish."

Smith looked down at the single piece of paper and turned it over; it was blank on the back. He looked up. "And?"

Sheffle shrugged. "And what? That was it. That's where the trail led." He hesitated and then added, "Er, unless you want me to go over to France?"

"Do you speak French?"

"Not a word." Sheffle sounded very proud of his ignorance.

"Then I don't need you to go to Marseilles," Smith said. But that didn't mean that he wouldn't send somebody who *did* speak French.

"Probably ain't nothin' to find over there, anyhow," Sheffle said.

Maybe. Maybe not. But Smith was nothing if not thorough.

In the meantime, however, Sheffle's investigation would suffice.

Now Smith just had to pay a visit to Moira and make his offer.

***

Smith stared at Madam Cecile. "Gone?"

"Yes, she left a week ago."

"Why?"

"She became ill and couldn't work. And before you look at me that way, *no*, I didn't give her the boot."

Smith smiled. "I didn't think you had, Cecile." Indeed, the madam was kinder to her employees than anyone else he'd met in the business.

"I told her she could stay—we just had a kitchen helper get married, so she could have earned her keep, which is what she was concerned about. But she wanted to go."

"Where?"

"I have no idea."

"Do you know what made her ill?"

"She said it was a return of some sickness she'd had before."

"Could she be pregnant?" Now wouldn't that be ironic?

"It did not look like morning sickness to me." Cecile shook her head. "I'll be honest, she looked like hell, Smith. She was waxy, gray, and sweaty, walking in a hunched over sort of fashion. I wish she'd stayed, but the girl is stubborn and secretive to a fault."

"I want to talk to the woman she shared quarters with," Smith said.

"I'll send for her, although I doubt that she'll have much to tell you." Cecile pulled the velvet servant cord. "Julia and Moira were not friends." She hesitated and added, "Julia is—to be honest—a pain in my arse. She sets the whole house on edge, but—as I'm sure you'll agree, having taken Julia several times yourself—she's a lovely piece of tail." She snorted. "Provided you gag her."

Smith had to smile at the madam's apt description. He *had* gagged the wench and she indeed had a lovely tail. She was a voluptuous brunette—whereas he typically favored skinny and fair—but he'd enjoyed himself quite thoroughly, although he'd mainly taken her because he'd known she shared quarters with Moira. Yes, he was a bastard that way.

"Fetch Julia," Cecile told the footman who opened her study door.

The young man hesitated. "She's still sleeping, ma'am."

"Wake her," Cecile said in a chilly voice.

"Yes, ma'am."

When the door shut, Cecile turned to Smith. "Are you sure I can't pour you a glass?" She lifted her own one-third filled crystal tumbler.

"No thank you." His weekly partner meeting was later that night and he never drank before talking business.

"Do you want me to stay when Julia comes?"

"I think she'll be more forthcoming without you here."

"Then if you'll excuse me, I'll go and see to some business." She gave him a peck on the cheek and left him in her private study.

He liked Cecile—enough that he'd loaned her money to purchase this building and start anew after she'd been arrested and bled dry by solicitors and barristers to defend herself against a multitude of indecency charges. It had been a difficult time for her and Cecile had been forced to assume the identity of the person on her birth certificate, which was Henry James Brinks.

They'd been partners for almost eight years and she'd always dealt honestly with him, never giving Smith any reason to regret his decision. She took care of her employees and was fair.

His thoughts turned from Cecile, back to Moira. What the hell had happened? Why wouldn't she have remained at Bernina's and taken Cecile's offer?

Smith had worked himself into a grim mood by the time the door opened a quarter of an hour later and Julia sauntered into the room, her pretty face sporting a very sulky expression. He could see by the state of her plaited hair and dressing gown that she must have been dragged from her bed.

As ever, Smith stood when a woman entered the room, a courteous gesture that eased the hostile glint in her eyes.

"Good evening, Julia." He gestured to a chair and she lowered herself like a queen.

"You've been scarce," she said, smoothing her skirt with a coy look through her lashes.

Smith ignored her impertinent prying and said, "I have a few questions for you."

"Oh?"

"Do you know where Moira went?"

She scowled. "Why is everyone asking about her? She's a scrawny tart who—"

"Who else is asking?"

She pursed her lips and Smith leaned toward her, whatever she saw on his face caused her to sit up straighter. "Why are you looking at me like that?"

"I know you want to be helpful," he lied. "So, I'm going to assist you in that endeavor." He reached into the inner pocket of his coat and extracted £10 from his notecase.

Avarice sparked in her lovely brown eyes when he held it up.

"Answer my questions—honestly—and this is yours. Do you understand?"

She nodded; her gaze riveted to the money.

"I want to hear you say it, please."

"I'll answer all your questions honestly and you'll give me the money."

"Good. Now, do you know where Moira went?"

"No."

Smith stared.

"What? You asked for the truth—that's the truth."

He continued to stare.

"You can give me beastly looks all you want, but I still don't know," she said, exhibiting commendable—if ill-advised—backbone. "However, I *do* know what was ailing her and it wasn't an influenza."

"What was it?"

Her lips curved slightly. "She had a bad client."

"Bad how?"

"He beat her."

Smith's jaws clenched. "She told you this?"

"No, her nightgown slipped off one shoulder and she had welts, bad ones. Some had split and the blood was on her nightgown. I told her that she'd never get those stains out, that it was ruined."

Smith's head buzzed, the sensation not one he experienced often, but one that almost always presaged violence. It took him twenty or thirty seconds to re-establish control over his boiling emotions.

"Did she say anything?"

"She said it was an old nightdress and—"

"Not about the nightdress." He had to shove the words through his teeth. "About whoever gave her the welts."

"Oh. Well, you've met her, so you know it's not as if she talks very much. I told her she should go to Madam and tell her who did it, but she didn't want to."

"Did she tell you who did it?"

Julia hesitated, but then shook her head. "She didn't, but I knew." A shadow of something like guilt flitted over her face. "He was handsome—*really* handsome—and all of us were panting for him when he came in. And then he astounded everyone and selected Moira."

"His name?"

"He said his name was Mr. Brown."

"Mr. Brown," Smith repeated in a flat tone.

"I'm not lying, *Mr. Smith*." She cut him a pert, pointed look.

"What did he look like?"

"He was lovely and his clothes were expensive." Her eyes flickered over Smith. "They were like yours, but not all black." Her dismissive look told him what she thought about such an affectation.

"What about his face, hair, how tall was he?"

"He was about your height. His hair was such a pale blond it was almost silver and he had the most unusual, brilliant blue eyes. He looked like an angel." She made a prim face. "But beauty is as beauty does, as my ma used to say."

"Had you seen him before?"

"No—and I would have remembered. None of the other girls knew him, either."

"How much did Moira pay you to keep the information about her injuries to yourself?"

Her jaw sagged, but she quickly recovered herself and puffed up, no doubt preparing to defend her honor.

Smith held up the banknote as a reminder.

All the air she'd sucked into her lungs came out in a dispirited sigh. "Fine. She gave me a crown if I kept her secret."

For the first time, Smith felt genuine dislike for the girl. People who couldn't keep their word were useless; one's word was the only thing a person truly owned in this world.

"I think she must have been sick in the head," Julia said as she examined her cuticles, utterly oblivious to Smith's annoyance.

"Oh?"

"Cecile wouldn't have chucked Moira out, she liked her for some reason, and yet she insisted on leaving. It was stupid; she was almost bent in half with pain but she packed her things and left. Not that packing took much effort since she never spent any money on clothes."

"Anything else you remember?"

"No—wait, yes, there is. When she was packed, she lifted up her mattress and then turned on me like some kind of wild animal, shouting, '*Where is it? What have you done with it?*'"

"What did she think you'd taken?"

"I don't know—she never said, she just ranted."

Smith stared.

"I swear I'm telling the truth!" she insisted, and then scowled. "She wrinkled my silk dressing gown so badly I'm not sure the laundress will be able to press it flat."

"You have no idea where she went?"

"No. We didn't talk about personal things. We hardly saw each other; that's the way it is here, we work different shifts. Not that we would have talked if we *had* spent time together. She wasn't the sort I wanted as a friend."

Smith imagined that went both ways. "Anything else you can remember?"

Julia paused, her brow furrowing, and then she shook her head. "No, that was the last she said, although she rolled around curled up on the bed for half an hour before she left, so she must have hurt herself when she manhandled me. Which only serves her right."

Smith experienced some very unpleasant feelings looking at her smug, self-righteous face. Although he hated to reward such a venal person, she'd held up her part of the bargain.

"Thank you." He handed her the banknote, which she quickly snatched.

Smith stood to open the door for her.

Rather than leave, she turned to him. "Did you talk to Nell?"

"Nell?"

"She's a maid here and she's been pining for Moira, for all the good it did her. She might know where Moira went."

Smith nodded his thanks and closed the door behind Julia. He pulled the servant cord and a footman answered his summons so quickly that Smith knew Cecile would be aware of the depth of his displeasure and wanted to do what she could to alleviate it.

Quite frankly, he was more annoyed with himself than anyone else. Why was he chasing after a whore he'd fucked a handful of times?

Why was he about to disrupt a perfectly enjoyable agreement with Luke in anticipation of something that might very well—indeed most likely—would prove to be a mistake?

But Smith knew why he was there, and it infuriated him. He had to be the most predictable man in London—hell, in all of England. Dangle an emotionally distant man or woman in front of him and he was hooked, like a hound on the trail of a fox, unable to rest until he'd brought his quarry to ground.

The door opened and a young woman entered. She was tall—a good deal taller than Smith—and solidly built.

"I'm Nell, sir." She dropped an awkward curtsey. "Madame Cecile says you want to talk about Moira."

"Thank you for coming, Nell. Please have a seat."

"Er, beggin' your pardon sir, but I'd rather stand."

"Whatever makes you most comfortable." He smiled, hoping to put her at ease. "Madame is right; I'm concerned about Moira."

"Aye, so'm I. She left without sayin' *anything*." Her face crumpled and a tear rolled down her cheek and she brushed it aside with a loud sniff. Smith noticed there were dark smudges beneath her large hazel eyes, as if she'd been missing sleep.

He offered her his handkerchief and she stared at it like he was offering her a live cobra.

"Go ahead," he urged gently.

She took the pristine white square with thick fingered, work-scarred hands that were bigger than Smith's.

"Do you know what was ailing her?"

Nell shook her head. "I could see that she hurt bad. I knocked on her door when she didn't come for supper. She didn't answer until after I'd knocked and knocked and knocked. She was *gray*, sir. I haven't never seen anyone go that color."

"Does she have friends? Family?" he asked, already knowing the answer, but hoping he might be wrong.

"No, she were alone. She came all the way from," she paused, her brow furrowing. "Well, I don't rightly know where. But she said her family was all dead. I met her the first day she came." She smiled at the memory, but quickly came back to the present and fear flashed in her eyes. "I'm afraid for her, sir. She won't take help—even if I knew where to find her—that just isn't her way." She met his gaze squarely for the first time. "Can you find her and help her, sir?"

"I'll find her," Smith promised.

Whether he could help her would be up to Moira.

Chapter 8

Moira still hurt—both inside and out—but at least she could eat and dress and use the chamber pot without calling for Mrs. Dauntry, her landlady.

"Cracked ribs is wot you got," the older woman said—at least a dozen times every single day.

As much as Moira hated asking anyone for help, she'd had to ask this time—there'd simply been no choice. She'd been in so much pain—and so scared that she'd suffered internal damage—that listening to Mrs. Dauntry's incessant babbling was a small price to pay. Well, in addition to the shillings she'd paid her, of course.

Even when Moira was no longer in constant pain, she was still terrified.

After leaving Bernina's the first thing she'd done upon reaching the relative safety of the dingy room at Pigeon Court was send a message to her brother Robert.

When no answer had come, she'd sent a second message—this one to his landlord, a French émigré who had given Robert a place to stay as a favor to Marie.

It had been two days before she'd received an answer from the landlord: Robert hadn't been seen in over ten days.

Ten days.

That meant that what Mr. Brown had told her that night was most likely true: Robert was dead.

Robert had been almost twenty years older than her, so she'd never known him well, but he'd been her favorite among her two brothers.

It wasn't that she didn't love Etienne—of course she did; he was family—but she could never bring herself to *like* him. He was the sort of person who would pour salt on an open wound if you asked him for a sticking plaster.

Robert had always been kind, if distant, toward her and Moira had looked forward to spending some time with him while she was in England. But as matters had turned out, they'd met only once a month, and then only if there was news to exchange.

And now he was probably dead and she'd never get to know him.

Yet another death to lay at *Smith's* door.

The vicious thought gave Moira pause. As good as it felt to have a target for her hatred, she knew it wasn't Smith who'd killed her brother. She knew that from the killer's own mouth.

But if Smith hadn't taken her sister to begin with, then Moira and Robert would never have come to this wretched city.

After receiving word about Robert, Moira had sent a letter to the address in Marseilles that Marie had made her memorize.

"Only use it in case of dire emergency. And never use any name except for Lauren de Beaufort."

Moira had always believed her mother's insistence on such secrecy had been overly dramatic—was Smith really such a fearsome enemy? But now she realized that her family was facing more than one threat, at least if the mysterious and violent Mr. Brown was to be believed.

In any event, it would likely take time—days, maybe even weeks—before her mother responded to her message. In the interim Moira had barely any money. As battered and scarred as she was, thanks to Mr. Brown, she wasn't sure when she'd be able to seek work again.

Even if she went back to working in a brothel, she'd never again work at a place like Bernina's. Or Maison Bardot, for that matter. Wealthy, powerful men didn't want scarred whores, they wanted fresh and youthful. At almost twenty-six she was a long way from dewy, and now she was physically damaged.

Smith spent a fortune on expensive, beautiful whores and was unlikely to want Moira the way she was now, no matter how much interest he'd been showing before Mr. Brown had destroyed her plans.

As much as she'd wanted to stay at Bernina's—at least to recuperate before returning home to France—Mr. Brown had given her three days to leave London, warning her that she'd meet the same fate as her brother if she lingered.

Thanks to whoever had stolen the small stash of money beneath her mattress, Moira couldn't even afford steerage passage back to

France. She still suspected Julia of taking it even though she'd acted confused when she'd accused her.

In any case, she barely had enough money to pay for another week at Pigeon Court.

Moira looked down at the still-vivid bruises on her wrists as she fastened her sleeve; she was such a mess. How had she not seen Brown for what he was?

She told herself that it wasn't her fault, that nobody could have guessed such a gorgeous, pleasant, well-spoken man was really an evil spirit masquerading in human form.

After all, look at Smith and how he managed to fool everyone, even Moira—who knew the truth about him—into believing he wasn't a murderer.

As much as Moira enjoyed physical pain, she'd not liked the sort that Brown had dispensed.

Worse than the pain had been the look in his eyes as he'd methodically broken her—nothing but a blank, blue stare as he'd asked her '*Why are you here?*' over and over again.

At first, she'd wondered if Smith had sent him.

Moira had told him everything, not withholding any of the truth—about Smith and her sister and her parents—but Brown hadn't seemed interested. Indeed, he'd looked almost dismissive, as if she didn't have the information he wanted.

He'd finally stared down with his dead gaze and said, "Go home Mademoiselle Bardot and tell the *Comte* and your mother to enjoy their golden years and give up their plans or they'll be getting a visit from a man who makes me look like an angel of mercy. You have three days to leave or you will end up just like your older brother. There is nothing left for you in London but an unmarked grave."

Moira had gone over his words again and again but had found no answer for why their plans for revenge against Smith had attracted the attention of a man like Brown.

More and more she suspected there was some *other* plan he was referring to. But what? And why would her mother and father send her here without telling her about Brown or the obviously dangerous people he represented?

Moira simply could not believe this was all about avenging her sister, which meant her parents had lied to her.

That thought was her constant, nagging companion during the days she'd laid in her dingy, cramped room. Was it possible that she'd given up a year of her life for nothing but lies?

If she'd not been in such incredible pain, she might have dragged herself from Bernina's to the Thames and flung herself in.

Instead, she'd come back to Pigeon Court—the ridiculous name some wag had given the falling down collection of shacks—and immediately reported to Marie, just as she'd always done. She was pathetic, like a trained animal that couldn't think for itself.

Pigeon Court was cheap, familiar, and had seemed like as good a place to die as any other. Now, ten days later, it appeared she would remain among the living. It also appeared that her mother was taking her time to respond and Moira was almost out of money. She needed to look for work or she would soon be homeless, freezing, and starving like so many others she'd seen in London.

She'd considered going to Robert's lodgings and seeing if there was anything of his she might sell to raise money, but she was terrified of going anywhere Brown might see her.

She could always write herself references from fictitious employers back in Paris, if need be, and take a job cleaning fireplaces or scrubbing toilets. It would be hard work, but it would be honest.

Moira snorted as she brushed out her greasy, tangled hair. What did it say about her that she believed sucking cock and spreading her legs for men she disliked was easier work than being a scullery maid?

You don't have to go back. In Paris you will be an aging, scarred whore. How much will you be worth? Wouldn't it be better to stay here and find work? You are as well educated as any lady—you could easily forge letters of recommendation and become a governess. You could—

What sort of traitor do you take me for? Moira demanded, putting a stop to the far-too-appealing thoughts. *The sort who would leave behind the only family I have left?*

The voice scoffed. *Family? You mean your mother, the Comte, and Etienne? If you don't bring Smith back to Paris with you, none of them will want you to return.*

Moira had no quick retort for that claim because it was true.

And all those other thoughts—traitorous or not—were almost painfully appealing.

In Paris she would always be the daughter of Marie Bardot. In England, she was Moira Dunsmuir, a nobody.

She *had* received the education of a lady and spoke fluent English, French, Italian, and Spanish. She could play the piano and harp well enough to acquit herself without embarrassment. She could paint watercolors and was a fair hand at embroidery. Why couldn't she use all that knowledge to teach children instead of entertaining wealthy men who—

"*No.*"

Moira startled herself with the low word.

Her parents might have lied to her but she had given them her word—something that had value for her—and she was no deserter. While she might not be able to get into Smith's house via his bed there had to be another way to get to him when his guard was down.

And Moira would find it.

But she couldn't think about all that right now. Just surviving the next few weeks would take all her attention.

Moira lifted a chunk of her hair and sniffed it, wincing away from the stench. She'd sweated for days without a wash. That was one of the perks of whoring in a fine house: frequent bathing. If a person wanted to bathe at Pigeon Court, then she needed to haul water up the rickety steps and heat it herself.

Since Moira could barely lift her own feet and had only a miniscule hearth in her room, she would have to go without.

She sighed and quickly plaited her greasy hair and then glanced into the basin of filthy water that Mrs. Dauntry had brought up to her—for a price, of course—which was her only mirror.

The image reflected at her was even worse than she'd imagined. She looked gaunt-eyed, ill, and twice her age. With greasy hair.

The surface of the water rippled and Moira felt the footsteps through her bare feet before she heard them.

The tread wasn't heavy and labored like Mrs. Dauntry's, it belonged to somebody who moved quickly and easily up the rickety, makeshift stairs that led to her room.

Brown! He'd found her!

The thought galvanized her and every muscle in her body tightened, as if poised for flight. Her eyes flickered around her small room even though she knew there was only one way out; she was on the third floor and the only window was no bigger than a loaf of bread.

There was a tin plate beside the basin of water and Mora grabbed it. It wasn't much of a weapon, but it would have to do.

The feet stopped outside the door and there was a light knock. "Moira?"

Moira's jaw sagged. No. She must have imagined the voice. *I couldn't be—*

"Moira?" Smith called out, louder this time and undeniably Smith. Another knock. "I know you're in there." There was a pause, and then, "The spies told me so."

By *spies* he meant all the children who floated around the filthy courtyard below like bits of paper on the breeze while their mothers and fathers were off at work—or engaging in criminal activities.

There were dozens of them and they would have seen Smith's expensive clothing and equipage and come running like wild dogs to fresh meat.

Moira glanced again at her reflection in the filthy water; she didn't want him to see her this way, but she'd be a bloody fool to send him away.

"Open the door, Moira."

Moira sighed and tossed the tin plate onto the table with a dull *clang.* She removed the bar from the door and opened it.

There he was, dazzlingly clean and mesmerizing handsome, like a perfectly polished jewel dropped onto the dung heap that was Moira's life.

"Well," he said, brown eyes gleaming with triumph and a faint twist of a smile on his full, wicked lips. "Here you are."

She'd only ever seen Smith indoors, under gaslight. In the cruel light of day—albeit a polluted, brownish-tinged light—she saw the lines around his mouth and eyes were deep. His skin, however, was even lovelier, more burnished. His eyes, which had always looked almost black, were actually the rich brown of strong French coffee.

As always, his exquisite body was clad in black and he emanated such power, wealth, and confidence that the hairs on her body stood on end, as if he exerted some sort of electrical pull.

He held a cane in one hand and a large wicker basket over his other arm.

"Are you going to invite me in, Moira?"

As if in a daze, she stepped back and he entered; Moira closed the door but didn't bar it. When she turned, he held out the basket. "I thought you might be hungry." When she didn't reach for it, his smile just grew larger. "You *do* remember me, don't you?"

She shook herself from her fugue and took the basket. "Yes, of course. Thank you. Why are you here?"

He laughed at her abrupt question and her face heated.

"Not that I'm not glad to see you," she added, and then grimaced at how unconvincing that sounded.

But he just smiled and shrugged, his powerful shoulders shifting the fine fabric of his coat as if it were another layer of skin. "I'm here because you intrigued me and then you were gone."

It wasn't what she'd expected him to say. Not at all.

"If I intrigued you so much then why did you suddenly disappear?" Moira clamped her jaws shut; furious that she'd let such telling words slip.

His heavy lids lowered and he stepped toward her and it took all the courage she could muster not to step back.

"I was called away on business for longer than I anticipated. Did you miss me?" He reached out a black leather sheathed hand and stroked her jaw, the touch warm and smooth and bizarrely comforting.

Quite suddenly—and irrationally—Moira wanted to push her face into his palm and sob out all her fears and worries.

Instead, she jerked back from his touch. "Why are you here?"

"I thought you might need a friend."

"We're friends?" Moira felt as if she were reading a novel and had suddenly skipped several pages.

"If you like."

She held his gaze, almost sweating with the effort; he was not an easy man to stare down.

Why are you repelling him? Now is your chance to lure him in. It was Marie's voice, again. When would Moira stop hearing her mother in her head?

Except this time the voice was right.

Moira was behaving like a fool but couldn't seem to stop herself. Something about him seeing her amid such squalor, and looking like death, damaged her bruised, broken pride.

He smiled at her, leaned back, and propped one foot on the wall behind him while lazily spinning his cane.

She broke first. "I'm not the same person I was the last time you saw me. I'm… damaged."

"I understand you were beaten."

Moira snorted and rolled her eyes. "Julia?"

"Yes. I'm afraid you wasted your money."

Money that Moira could have put to far better use.

"Did you know the man?" he asked.

"No." At least that was the truth.

"I assume he was sent to collect from you?"

"Collect?" The question was out of her mouth before she remembered. "No," she said hastily, even as something that looked like suspicion flickered across his face. "He wasn't sent by the people I owe in France."

He hesitated for a long moment before asking, "What was his name?"

Moira didn't want to tell him *anything* but she suspected that *Brown* had been a false name, so why not? "He said his was Mr. Brown."

"You sound skeptical."

She shrugged.

"What did he look like?"

"Why are you asking me about this man?"

"Humor me."

Well, what did it matter? If Smith had hired him, then he already knew. And if he hadn't hired him? Well, it was doubtful the two would ever cross paths in a city of a million people.

"He was about your height, very pale ash blond hair, brilliant blue eyes, and the face of an angel."

He lifted one eyebrow but didn't push any further on the matter. "Why did you leave Bernina's? You know Cecile would take care of you."

"Her customers would not pay for somebody like me. She would keep me on out of a sense of duty, pity, or guilt; I'll not be her burden." Something suddenly occurred to her. "How in the world did you find me here?"

He smiled, reached into his coat, and extracted a banknote from his notecase. "I've found that if you pass enough of this around, you can find almost anyone or anything."

"But why would you *want* to find me?"

"I want to see what he did to you."

Moira gaped, and then shook her head, unable to make sense of this man. "Why would you want to see that?"

"Do you care what my reasons are?" His words were dismissive but his expression was mild—gentle, almost. He held up the banknote, which was big enough to pay her way home to Paris in style. "I'll trade you; you show me what he did and you can have this."

Moira swallowed, her eyes on the money. What did it matter if he saw her? She had no shame when it came to being naked; how could she? Besides, the longer she could keep him interested, the better her chances were of getting close to him. If he wanted to be *friends*, she'd accommodate him.

She set the basket he'd given her on the table and reached for the buttons she'd done up only a short time earlier. The dress wasn't one of the gowns she wore to visit customers, but a faded old muslin that had seen better days.

His dark eyes followed her fingers as they worked their way from her chin to her navel, his nostrils flaring when he saw that she wore nothing but a single petticoat and chemise beneath the ragged gown. Given the condition of her ribs Moira couldn't have laced up a corset for any amount of money.

Once the last button was open, she carefully pulled off the sleeves, biting back a wince.

"You needn't remove it entirely." His eyes flickered over the bruises on her arms, shoulders, and one particularly ugly mark at the base of her throat. "Turn around."

She obeyed, keeping her spine straight and her posture proud. Why shouldn't she stand tall? Receiving a beating—and surviving such violence—was nothing to be ashamed of, no matter how much it diminished her value. The only person who should feel shame was the vicious villain who'd wielded the whip.

The thin floorboards creaked as Smith came closer and goosebumps formed on her skin as she felt the heat of his body behind hers.

"A crop," he said.

"Yes," she replied, even though it was not a question.

Warm breath bathed her neck and shoulders and her body tensed in anticipation of his touch.

"The wounds look clean—uninfected. But you are right; the scars will always be visible."

Moira's throat was suddenly too thick to speak, his proximity making her skin feel unbearably tight and fragile, as if it would crack when he touched her.

But he didn't touch her.

Instead, the heat disappeared and she heard his light step recede.

"You may dress yourself."

Her hands shook on the buttons. How was that for irony? She could strip for a man without any qualms, but putting her dress back on left her flooded with shame? There was something wrong with her.

When she'd fastened the last button, she turned.

He was leaning in the same position, as if he'd never moved. "What are your plans?"

"Plans?" She shrugged. "I don't have any."

"I'm willing to offer you a position."

Moira's eyebrows lifted. "You want me even after this? Even… scarred?"

"Yes," he said without hesitation.

She lowered her eyes, unable to meet his steady gaze and unable to believe he wanted her.

And also unwilling to admit how much that thought warmed her.

Here was the chance she'd been waiting for. She should jump on it.

Perhaps he wants you to scrub his floors, not warm his bed?

Moira swallowed down the unhappy thought and looked up. "What sort of position?"

His lips curled up at the corners and the lines around his eyes deepened, which only made him look more attractive. "I want you to be my lover—to live in my house—and I also want you to bear my child."

Moira's mouth opened and Smith laughed at her expression— doubtless one of shock.

"Are you mad?" she demanded.

"Possibly. But I want a child and your time in this business is likely over—as you yourself stated—so it seems an excellent opportunity for both of us."

"You think I'm so damaged and desperate that I'll agree to be your broodmare?"

Something flickered in his eyes at her rude tone but his smile didn't falter. "If you do not want to be my lover and bear my child then I can help you secure more traditional employment."

The word *lover* hung in the air between them, the images it created causing a predictable pulsing between her thighs and a not so predictable ache in her womb.

"How do you know I'm even capable of having a child? I've never been pregnant. Maybe I am barren."

He shrugged. "At best, you will become pregnant, at worst we will enjoy a year of each other's company." He smiled. "Not exactly a hardship for me."

Or her, either. Moira didn't like the way her body heated and softened in response to his words and smile. It irked her how badly she wanted to accept, and not only—or even mostly—because it would further her family's goal.

She wanted more time—another chance—with him because of *him*.

For a moment Moira wished that Marie was there to slap some sense into her.

Before she could come up with a response, he extracted an envelope from inside his coat.

"Here are the details of my offer. There is also the name and address of the employment agency I use." He tossed the heavy envelope down beside the banknote and then closed the distance between them, not stopping until they were toe-to-toe and Moira had to crane her neck uncomfortably to meet his gaze.

His eyes roamed her face. "Take a week to carefully consider my offer—read the contract and then read it again. And again." One side of his mouth pulled up. "If you decide to sign it, I will hold you to the terms—all of them—don't doubt that for a second. If you don't decide to sign it, I wish you all the best in life. I've instructed my employment agency to assist you in finding whatever work you seek." He traced one of her eyebrows with his gloved finger, caressing down her cheek, and then lightly over her lower lip.

Moira filled her lungs with the intoxicating scent of expensive leather and opened her lips, flicking his finger with the tip of her tongue.

He hissed softly and his pupils swelled until his eyes looked black.

They stood motionless for a long, tense moment; their gazes locked.

And then he dropped his hand, turned, and walked out of her hovel without another word.

***

Children swirled around Smith like a school of ragged little fish as he crossed the rubbish-strewn courtyard toward his carriage. More than a few of the light-fingered urchins took nibbles at his watch chain as if it were a brightly colored lure.

Smith gently fended away the questing fingers and handed out coins, as well as several introduction cards to the older boys. The school he and Edward operated accepted anyone over the age of twelve who showed a willingness to learn a trade. They never turned anyone away empty-handed, often placing younger boys in domestic positions or other types of work if carpentry wasn't a good fit.

He couldn't help smiling at his coachman and two guards, all of whom were looking rather harried at having spent a quarter of an hour fending off so many raucous children.

Pigeon Court was not the sort of place that most Londoners would want to go if they didn't have to. It was filthy, cramped, disease-ridden, and infested with criminals. Smith was perfectly at home there, but then he'd spent his first years in London in an area that wasn't any better.

Smith stared out the window as the carriage rolled away from the claustrophobic alleyway. But instead of cramped streets filled with huddled buildings he saw Moira—the brutal welts on her pale freckled skin and the haunted look in her sea green eyes.

He'd been angry hearing about the beating she'd endured; actually seeing it had filled him with a rage that had briefly blinded him.

It hadn't been difficult to identify *Mr. Brown* using Julia's description of the man—but Moira's description had confirmed it. Her assailant was really a man named Owen Onions—no wonder he'd adopted a less clownish alias—and he was a bully boy for whomever had enough money to pay him.

Onions seemed to have dropped off the map shortly after he'd assaulted Moira, so Smith did not yet know who the man had been working for that night.

Whether Moira's French creditors had sent him or she was in trouble for something else, he didn't know and Moira had not seemed inclined to tell him. But he'd find out. He'd find out everything.

Smith had hired somebody whose specialty was investigating criminals—another man with an amusing name, Joe Bacon.

If anyone could find Onions, it was Joe.

And when Joe finally found and apprehended him?

Smith smiled and flexed his gloved hands.

Well, then he and Mr. Onions would spend some time together and the other man would learn what it felt like being on the receiving end of a whip.

Chapter 9

Luke desperately wished for more and brighter light as he gorged on Mr. Smith's sleeping face and relaxed body.

His mouth watered to nibble the other man's exposed nipples, but even if he possessed the courage to do something so audacious, he didn't want to wake his master from a rare moment of sleep and deprive him of rest.

Indeed, Luke almost never saw Mr. Smith asleep; the other man seemed to survive on brief cat naps here and there and a few hours every few nights.

Like everyone else, Smith looked younger while he slumbered, his chiseled features relaxed. His lips looked even fuller and were slightly parted, his muscular chest rising and falling gently, tiny specks of black sprouting on his chin and cheeks.

Luke could watch him for hours.

He knew such behavior crossed the line from adoring to disturbing but he simply did not care. These past few weeks had been blissful. He'd joined his master in his bed almost every night since he'd returned from Glasgow, his days spent on a cloud of joy, anticipating the next time they would be together.

But beneath that joy there lurked something darker.

How much longer could something so good continue? How much longer until—

"I can *feel* you thinking."

Luke startled. "I'm sorry, sir. Did I wake you?"

Smith opened his eyes, his lips curving into a smile that shot straight to Luke's balls.

"No, you were as quiet as a mouse." He reached out a warm hand and caressed Luke's face. "But your body is tense." He glanced at the clock. "I've already slept too late; it is past time I got up." He stretched and yawned, his movements causing his muscles to ripple and flex in a way that left Luke breathless.

He swallowed down his lust and realized he was staring—again—and reached for the sheet, preparing to get out of bed.

Smith's hand shot out and closed around his wrist. "Stay a moment, I wish to speak to you."

Luke's belly tensed at the other man's expression—gentle yet… reserved. "Yes, sir?"

"I wanted to let you know that I am in the process of engaging a live-in lover."

The stabbing in Luke's chest was so painful that he glanced down to see if Mr. Smith had actually plunged a dagger into him.

But there was no blood. The wounds were invisible, no matter how much it felt like his heart had been hacked out of his chest.

Luke swallowed several times to force down the bile and vomit that threatened to choke him before looking up to meet Smith's gaze. "Are you terminating my employment, sir?"

"Lord no!" Smith squeezed Luke's shoulder. "I'm sorry; I did not express myself very well. I'd like you to stay on, but in a slightly different capacity, if you are amenable."

Luke wanted to sob with joy and relief, but he merely nodded and said, "Of course I will stay, no matter the capacity."

Smith's dark eyes softened at his calm response and he knew that he'd pleased his master by not indulging in histrionics, which Smith loathed.

Luke had worked for Mr. Smith while his last lover, Charles, had occupied the big suite of rooms adjacent to Smith's. Charles was a stunning young whore who'd met Mr. Smith at Tosca's, a brothel that was almost as exclusive as the Birch Palace.

Unfortunately, Charles's temperament had been as ugly as his appearance was beautiful.

He'd hated any attractive men who worked for Mr. Smith—which was most of the all-male household—and had made their lives hell, trying to force them to quit.

He'd saved the worst of his temper for Luke and Smith's valet at the time, an older man who'd worked for Smith for years and had warmed his bed on occasion.

Charles had caused scene after scene, seemingly unaware of how such behavior had revolted Smith and driven him away.

Revulsion was the last emotion Luke wanted to see in his master's eyes.

"I want you to know that my hiring a new lover is no reflection on you, Luke," Smith said. "You please me greatly."

But not enough that you don't need somebody else, too, Luke wanted to say, but did not.

Instead, he said, "Thank you, sir." He cleared his throat. "Might I ask what my new position will entail?"

"I'd like you to be the body servant for my new lover, Miss Moira Dunsmuir."

Luke's eyes bulged. Smith's new lover was a *woman*? He knew the other man engaged female whores, but for some reason this surprised him. "Er, of course, sir."

"Does the fact that she is a woman change your mind?"

"No, sir, not at all. I'll be pleased to offer my services to the lady in question, provided she finds me suitable."

"How could she not find you suitable—as well as desirable?"

Luke flushed at the warmth in the other man's eyes. "Thank you, sir."

Smith leaned forward and kissed him—a long, lingering kiss that caused him to harden and scattered his already frazzled wits.

When Smith pulled away Luke had to clear his throat several times before asking, "Will this be a full-service position, sir?"

"It will include whatever she wants," Smith said, and then cocked his head. "I know you served female clients at the Birch Palace, but I don't know if that was your preference?"

Luke's current preference was to serve only the man across from him, but he knew what Smith was asking.

"I enjoy women as much as men, sir." Normally that was true, but nothing about his current situation was normal. He'd made the worst mistake of his life and had fallen in love with his employer. It would rip him in half to watch another person—male or female—supplant Luke in his master's bed.

Perversely, just thinking about such a humiliating event was enough to make his already hard cock leak even more. Luke had given up wondering why he reveled in pain and degradation, but that didn't mean he had to like the effect on his body.

He saw that Smith was watching him intently and wondered—not for the first time—if the other man had realized just how much such humiliation aroused him.

But no, why would he? He employed Luke to service his needs, not the other way around. Besides, he didn't know how Luke felt about him; falling in love had not been part of the contract Luke had signed and he should never forget that. Indeed, Smith had made it quite clear when he'd hired Luke that the arrangement would never become anything other than master and servant. If Mr. Smith ever discovered the way he felt, Luke suspected he'd be sent packing so fast it would make his head spin.

"I will be glad to take the new position, sir." Luke hesitated and then added, "It is an honor to serve you in any way I can."

Smith looked pleased by his declaration, and if he'd noticed the raw emotion throbbing below the surface of Luke's words, he gave no sign of it.

"There is one other thing," Mr. Smith said.

"Yes, sir?"

"Miss Dunsmuir has agreed to bear me a child."

Luke's jaw dropped. "But—but that is wonderful, sir!"

Smith looked nonplussed at his obvious joy, the uncertain expression sitting strangely on his normally confident features. "Er, thank you, Luke. You like children, do you?"

"I adore them." Indeed, it broke his heart that he'd never have any, but he kept that to himself. Instead, he said, "I might have mentioned that my brothers have children?"

"Yes—two brothers, was it?"

"Yes, sir. Six children between them, five boys and one charming girl and I often visit them on my free day." Luke smiled fondly. "My brothers and sisters-in-law have threatened me with life and limb if I don't stop spoiling them."

Smith chuckled. "You sound like the perfect uncle."

"I hope so, sir." Luke had to bite his tongue to keep from asking whether or not Mr. Smith would be marrying the woman. Or was she going to give up the child? How would such an arrangement work? There had to be money involved.

"You have questions?" Smith asked.

"Will you be marrying Miss Dunsmuir, sir?"

"No, Luke."

Luke couldn't tell if it was sadness that flashed across the other man's face. But at least he wasn't angry at Luke for prying.

A child! There would be a child in the house!

He couldn't help grinning. A child was, in Luke's opinion, exactly what the master needed. Nobody should live without family and he'd not seen a single relative in the time he'd lived under Mr. Smith's roof. He needed family.

"You look very pleased," Smith said.

"Oh yes, sir. I'm thrilled. I adore children. They give life… meaning."

He wasn't nearly so delighted by the prospect of another lover moving into the house, but he already shared Smith, so that was nothing new.

He was also relieved that Mr. Smith wasn't replacing him because he was deficient in any way. He had a perfectly acceptable reason for setting Luke aside: children. If Luke were a wealthy, powerful man he might do the same thing.

"Any other questions?" Smith asked.

Luke had dozens, but they weren't the sort that his master was likely to tolerate.

So, instead, he said, "No, sir."

"Good. Now, let me show you a small token of my appreciation."

"Appreciation?"

"For being so amenable."

Luke had no response for that—why wouldn't he be amenable? He was a servant.

But it seemed Mr. Smith didn't need any response because he rolled onto his hands and knees and then backed down the bed. "Spread your legs for me.

The muscles in Luke's thighs twitched and jumped as he hastened to obey, but his mind became snagged on an unpleasant thought: would this be the last time he'd be the recipient of such a gift? What if this woman was as possessive as Charles had been? Would Smith put him aside as he had done before—to avoid causing conflict?

Smith's strong fist tightened around Luke's cock, putting a stop to the questions and concerns swirling in his head. "You really do have a lovely prick, Luke. Let's see if I can take all of you today."

Luke bit back a gasp of pleasure as the man he loved attempted to take him to the root.

One last worry gnawed at the edge of his bliss, like a rat taking a bite from a chunk of cheese.

Should Luke have said *no* to his master's request to act as servant to his new lover? After all, as much as he reveled in humiliation, would it be too painful to sit by while the man he loved took another? Had he made a terrible mistake? Should he—

Mr. Smith swallowed and his throat squeezed Luke's thick shaft like a hot silk sheath.

Luke cried out and lifted his hips, fucking into him even deeper, all his worries dissipating like fog on a hot, sunny day.

Chapter 10

The seven days between Smith's visit and Moira's journey to his house passed even more slowly than the nightmarish days she'd spent half-delirious with pain after Mr. Brown's beating.

All her life, Moira had worked—even when she'd gone away to school it had not been for pleasure, it had been to study and learn the skills, manners, and graces necessary for a successful demimondaine.

She'd left school at seventeen and spent a grueling year under Marie's tutelage learning the practical skills necessary. And then, immediately upon turning eighteen—just like her siblings, her mother, her grandmother, and great-grandmother before her—she'd accepted her first protector, Oliver Linville.

Oliver was the heir to an ancient title and significant fortune. He'd been seventeen, a year younger than Moira, when they'd begun their association. Like so many of his class, Oliver's father had provided his son with a professional lover, hoping to avoid the rapacious women who often lay in wait for wealthy, immature young men.

Although they'd been close in age, they'd been leagues apart in experience. While privileged, arrogant Oliver had gained his meager sexual experience from servants—likely unwilling ones—on his father's vast country estate, Moira had learned her trade at the knee of a master of the seductive arts—or a mistress, she supposed was more accurate: her own mother.

Maison Bardot did not broker virgins; it provided attractive, well-spoken companions who'd been rigorously trained to provide sexual satisfaction to even the most jaded palate. Not that Oliver had been jaded at that point.

No, that hadn't happened until almost two years had passed.

At the beginning of their liaison, Oliver had come to her every night and often during the day. His father had provided a love nest for them, where Moira lived and was always available for Oliver's needs.

Over the years he had visited her less and less. By the time she was twenty, he'd stopped taking her out in public. Moira knew that he'd formed a rather unfortunate liaison with an actress who had become pregnant with his child.

She'd discovered her arrangement was over when Oliver had shown up at the pied-à-terre, fucked her one last time, and then told her she had a day to vacate the house because he was installing his new mistress.

Fortunately, Marie had anticipated the situation and had selected her new protector, so Moira had moved from Oliver's apartment directly into her new home, a far larger and more luxurious establishment that had been paid for by Bernard Chastain.

Chastain—the ludicrously wealthy owner of more slaughterhouses than any other man in France—was the type of client Marie despised, but she'd not been able to turn down the money he'd offered.

"His sort would not even have been fit to kiss your hem a hundred years ago," Marie had groused when she'd told Moira about her next lover.

But times had changed in France and it was hard to ignore a man sitting on millions of francs, even if they'd been made in abattoirs.

Bernard had been fifty, paunchy, and missing most of his hair, but Moira had liked him a great deal more than the younger and more beautiful Oliver.

He'd been married for over thirty years to a woman who'd given him ten strapping sons and daughters and no longer wanted his cock anywhere near her person. It had been Madame Chastain who had sent her husband away to find a mistress.

Bernard had been so sweetly grateful to Moira for the use of her body it had seemed like a miracle after Oliver's crude, brutal behavior. He'd been deliriously happy upon discovering that she was willing to accommodate his every desire with a smile on her face.

Moira had liked him—he'd been kind and generous and had showered her with expensive gifts right from the beginning. She suspected she would still be with Bernard had he not died in an unfortunate and gruesome accident while demonstrating a new method of killing a cow.

By that time, she was twenty-two and her bloom had already faded. Unable to secure a new protector, she'd entered the establishment simply known as *La Maison*, the most expensive brothel in Paris—although it gave Marie fits to hear it called thus.

But Moira had never fooled herself. No matter what a person chose to call it, La Maison was a whorehouse and Moira was a whore. While she'd not hated her job, she'd been grateful for the chance to come to London. Even now—scarred and broken—she was in no hurry to go back.

After Smith's visit to Pigeon Court that day, Moira had written a second letter to Marie—even though she'd not received an answer to the first—telling her about the new development. Well, she'd told her about everything except agreeing to have Smith's child. There was no reason to share such information, not when it would never happen.

Moira had used some of Smith's money to pay her landlady to deliver food and water—and launder her clothing—and had spent the intervening days eating, sleeping, and resting.

By the morning of the eighth day the bruises had mostly disappeared, even the worst of the welts had scabbed over, and her ribs ached rather than screamed. The scars would be there for the rest of her life, but the pain had faded. At least the physical pain.

Although Moira didn't think of the attack during the day, she'd had nightmares about Mr. Brown. His beautiful, angelic features had branded themselves on her brain, especially the deadness in his eyes while he'd whipped her bloody, asking her the same question over and over again: *"Why are you here?"*

Moira's mind shied away from the last hour of that night—before she'd lost consciousness—and she buried the memory in a dark, deep hole at the back of her mind, rolled a boulder over it, and resolved never to expose it to the light of day.

"Mr. Smith will see you now, Miss Dunsmuir."

Moira's head jerked up and she found the same attractive, black-suited servant—Michael, he'd said his name was—who'd admitted her waiting for her.

She followed him through a house that was solely decorated in shades of gray, black, and ivory. Truly, she had never seen the like. The only splashes of color evident were the many paintings on the walls and the objets d'art in glass cabinets.

The servant stopped in front of a glossy black door and knocked.

"Come in," a familiar voice called out.

Smith stood when Moira entered the room and his face broke into a smile. "What a pleasure to see you, Moira. Please, have a seat." He motioned to a big leather wingchair across from his desk. "Would you please have tea sent up, Michael?" he asked his servant, not taking his eyes from Moira.

The only person who'd ever looked so thrilled to see her had been her sister Sandrine.

Feeling slightly off balance by his reception Moira dropped a deep, formal curtsey.

"Very nice." Smith's eyes sparkled with appreciation.

She handed him the envelope that held his contract. "I've signed it."

"Thank you." He placed the envelope on his desk, which held only an open ledger and pen.

"How are you feeling?" he asked, resuming his seat behind the desk after she sat.

"I am ready to work."

"That's not what I asked, Moira," he asked, his tone and smile gently chiding.

"I feel much better, thank you."

"Good. But I have summoned my physician to examine you later, just to make sure."

"Oh. That's not necessary."

This time, he didn't smile. Instead, he cocked his head. "You didn't read the contract as I asked, did you?" He spoke as softly as ever, but something in his gaze made her want to sink into the luxurious chair.

She considered lying but decided against it—not when he had already guessed as much.

"No, I didn't read it."

He leaned back in his chair and laced his hands over his flat midriff. "I'm not going to tell you how unwise it is to sign your name to something you've not read," he said, his voice cooler than she'd ever heard it. "That is your own affair. However, when I ask you to do something, I would like you either to comply or tell me why you would rather not." He gestured to the document on his desk and his mouth curved into a smile that made her shiver. "You would know that if you'd read the contract."

Now look what you've done! Marie shouted in her head. *Your impulsive, stubborn behavior will end with you ruining everything!*

"I've not yet signed my name and now I'm not inclined to do so," he continued.

"You're right," Moira blurted, scrambling. "It was foolish to put my name to a contract I haven't read."

"It won't offend me if you don't want this arrangement. Moira."

"No, no—I do want it." Even to her own ears the words sounded forced.

She wanted to scream; what was *wrong* with her? This was exactly what she'd been working and scheming towards for months and months. Why was she trying to sabotage herself?

Perhaps you've still got a shred of conscience? Another voice, not Marie's, whispered.

Perhaps you have unanswered questions and suspect your parents might be using you for something you don't agree with?

Perhaps you like *Smith more than you like any of your remaining family.*

The last thought was like a slap.

Could that really be true?

Moira saw that Smith was waiting—patiently—and shoved the chaos in her head aside. "I do want this," she said, more quietly this time.

"I want you to be sure, Moira. If you have a child with me, we will be in each other's lives for a very long time."

"Why did you pick me?" she demanded, not caring if she was jeopardizing everything with the question. She simply *had* to know. "There are thousands of women in London who would be grateful for such an offer. Why do you want to have a child with me?" Her voice broke on the last word and her eyes suddenly stung.

Smith stared at her a long moment before answering, his eyes darker, more intense than they'd been only seconds before.

"Because I can't stop thinking about you. Because you make me feel alive. Because I'm… drawn to you."

Moira inhaled through both her mouth and nose and still she couldn't seem to fill her lungs with enough air.

She heard Smith exhale slowly, as if he, too, was having difficulty breathing.

"I don't know you well—yet" he admitted. "But I respect and admire what I do know. You are beautiful and appealing, but it is your intelligence and resilience that I find most attractive. Those are the same characteristics I'd want in my child."

Moira's body tightened at his words and she had to blink harder than ever to keep from crying.

When had anyone ever said such things to her? How could such lovely sentiments be so painful?

Because you are going to betray him.

Thankfully Smith didn't seem to need an answer because she probably would have started sobbing.

"My terms are *rigorous*—some might even say *arduous*." He gave her a humorless smile. "It would be unfair to you—perhaps even catastrophic—to accept your signature on this contract at this point."

He was right and Moira felt like an idiot. She'd been entering into contracts since she was eighteen. It was critical to know what the other person expected.

Not only that—and it pained her to admit this—but Smith had been generous and kind to her and had asked nothing in return. He'd offered to help her find work whether or not she accepted his offer. Nobody else had sought her out and brought her food, given her money, and cared what became of her.

His kindness left her sick with guilt, and that infuriated and confused her.

Think of Sandrine.

Moira forced herself to summon an image of her loving, beautiful sister the last time she'd seen her and then took a deep breath and met his patient gaze.

"Will you give me a second chance? I—I don't want to wait a week again; I just need an hour to thoroughly read through the contract. Please, Mr. Smith," she added when his expression remained closed. "I'm not an innocent maiden—I know why I'm here. Just give me enough time to read it through—as I should have done. I will tell you if there is anything I cannot accept."

Not that there would be.

The door opened before he could answer, and a servant—yet another man dressed all in black—entered with a tea tray.

"Thank you, Thomas." Smith gestured to a low table that was in front of the glowing fire. "Go ahead and put it there."

Once the servant had deposited the tray and left Smith turned to her. "Why don't you make yourself comfortable? You can enjoy a cup of tea and something to eat while you read."

***

Moira flipped to the last page an hour and a quarter later. It was the second time she'd read the contract through.

Her body had begun to sweat—and not only from proximity to his crackling fire—as she'd read.

She'd been mad—*mad*—to sign such a thing without reading it.

It wasn't that any of his expectations were monstrous, but the degree of autonomy she sacrificed by signing was similar to an actual marriage.

The monetary compensation for becoming his live-in mistress was unheard of in her experience. And if she bore him a child she would receive a generous income until her death, a life estate in a town house, a full staff, including but not limited to a butler, housekeeper, footmen, groom, cook, maids, nannies, nurses, governesses, tutors, et cetera.

A town carriage and a traveling coach, access to a private railcar and villas across Europe, a second house in the country, and on and on.

Surprisingly, Smith didn't want a slave in return for such largesse; far from it. Indeed, some of the clauses *required* her to speak her mind in certain situations and one paragraph listed activities that required her initials to approve.

And even approval didn't signify complete acceptance, as there was *another* paragraph that stated it was her responsibility to inform him of any change in attitude or acceptance.

There were only a few non-negotiable items.

First, he expected her to give up any outside sexual attachments for the period of one year.

He, on the other hand, would continue to do whatever he wanted and see whomever he pleased.

The obvious double standard amused, rather than angered her. She'd never been jealous about sex or sexual partners. After all, she'd only ever known sex in a transactional context and she certainly couldn't imagine being jealous of Smith's amorous adventures.

In her opinion, a genuine friendship was far more intimate and precious than sex.

As for romantic intimacy? Well, that was as foreign to her as the surface of the moon. Men were not romantic with their mistresses or whores. At least not in her experience.

The most interesting sections in the contract were those detailing hygiene.

She must consent to cutting her hair, shaving her body, bathing twice each day, and using only the grooming products provided. He disliked perfume, cosmetics, and a list of other toiletries.

The contract was mind-boggling in its complexity.

But there were two paragraphs that stood out from all the rest.

First, there would be no leaving before the year was over. Even if she repudiated their arrangement and forbade him to touch her again—yes, he'd reserved that right for her—she would have to remain under his roof until the year was over.

Second, any child conceived during their time together would live with him—always.

Of course, women and their offspring were the property of their husbands, so that was not especially shocking. But he would *not* be her husband, so how could such a thing be legal?

Moira suspected that when a man was as wealthy and powerful Mr. Smith that legality became fluid.

Even though she knew their union would not last long enough for any of this to be an issue—and she would see to it that there was *no* child—it still left her on edge to sign away such significant rights.

But she had no other choice.

She glanced up from the document.

Smith hadn't left the room while she read but was seated at his desk, working on the ledger

He was looking at his work, rather than her, and she took the rare opportunity to study him unobserved.

Surprisingly, Smith wore spectacles to read. Rather than make him look weak—as her father had always claimed, refusing to wear his glasses, even though it meant he could hardly read—he looked intimidating with a frown of concentration on his face.

Seeing him this way made Moira realize that he was rarely without a smile curving his lips. A teasing smile, a sensual smile, a dangerous smile, and a half dozen others flickered through her mind.

Along with those smiles came other memories: his naked body sweaty and flexing above or beneath her; the almost satanic expression on his face when he stimulated her to orgasm—or deprived her of one—and his dark, fiercely possessive gaze when he spent inside her.

The resulting heat from that erotic montage wasn't surprising; after all, the man had given as much pleasure as he'd taken, unprecedented behavior in her experience.

By signing the contract, Moira had guaranteed that he would continue to provide her with sexual pleasure—not to mention a luxurious home, wardrobe, money, and a future that was free from want and fear.

And a child.

Moira shook her head, her heart speeding. *No. No child.*

You could accept his offer and forget about Marie and the Comte's plans and—

But that was the sticking point: Moira could *never* forget that Smith had killed her sister.

So, no. She couldn't simply sign the contract and live happily ever after.

You could always ask him what happened.

Moira scoffed at the insidious voice. *And end up as dead as my sister?*

Smith must have felt the weight of her gaze because he looked up, his intense concentration dissolving and his pleasant mask shifting subtly back into place, a querying smile curving his lips. "Finished?"

"I have one question."

He replaced the pen in its holder, removed his glasses, and closed the ledger. "Yes?"

"It's about paragraph twelve."

"I remember the paragraph. Go on."

"You say you would want the child to live with you. For what purpose?"

"To raise in an environment of safety and affection."

Moira blinked, momentarily speechless.

He raised his eyebrows. "You look so surprised, Moira. Do you think I keep a big caldron in my kitchen for children?"

His whimsical answer startled a laugh out of her. "Would I be permitted to visit the child?"

"It is my hope that you would want to continue living here—whether we were lovers or not. After all, that would be better for the child than visits."

Moira couldn't think of a response.

"What have I done to make you think that I would deprive a mother the right to see her own child? Or that I would make my own child suffer the loss of its mother?"

Her face heated at his question. He was right—*she* was the lying snake. Thus far he'd not lied to her—at least not that she knew.

"Why would you want to keep me around?" she asked.

"I am a firm believer in the necessity of a mother's love."

She almost laughed; he would change his mind in a hurry if he ever met Moira's mother. But she understood what he meant, in principle.

"Do you have a loving mother?" she asked. Why not? He'd told her to ask questions.

It was his turn to blink, and the series of emotions that flickered across his face were so myriad and rapid, she couldn't identify them all—but she recognized one: a pain so deep, raw, and wrenching it was like a punch to her chest.

"Yes, I did," he said, his eyes lowering to his closed ledger for a moment. When he looked up again, his gaze was pleasant, his smile bland. "Anything else?"

Moira shook her head, not trusting her voice; what had happened to this man? Who had hurt him?

"It is a year of your life, Moira. Are you sure?"

"Yes," Moira said, not that she'd be with him even a fraction as long. "What should I call you?"

"Smith is fine."

"Just *Smith*?"

He smiled. "Just Smith."

Chapter 11

Smith rang the servant bell and less than a minute later the door opened.

Her new employer smiled warmly at the man who entered and then turned to Moira. "This is Luke Cooper and he will be your body servant."

Luke bowed. "It is a pleasure to meet you, Miss Dunsmuir," he said in a low, pleasing voice.

Moira nodded at the towering man, a flutter of excitement in her belly as she took in the vision of masculine perfection: well over six feet tall, heavily muscled, with the chiseled features, striking blue eyes, and cornsilk blond hair of a Viking.

And he was going to be her personal servant?

Moira had no issue being waited on by men; indeed, it would have been odd had she still possessed reservations about her body by this point in her life. Having a body servant—Moira smirked at the old-fashioned term Smith had used, which sounded almost biblical—as beautiful as Luke would doubtless be an enjoyable and titillating experience.

"Luke will help you freshen up, give you a tour of the house, and then bring Doctor Felson up when he arrives."

Luke opened the door for her.

They walked in silence through the hushed house and Moira couldn't help staring at the art on the walls, a great deal of which appeared to be erotic in nature.

Smith only had the one painting in his study—the portrait of him. It had been mesmerizing and she'd had a difficult time not staring. It was an excellent likeness, but the expression in his eyes had been haunting and wild—not a look she'd ever seen on his face.

Luke opened a door at the end of the hallway, banishing Moira's thoughts with the room beyond.

"My goodness!" Her eyes skittered around the room—jumping from the goldleaf and purple velvet furniture to the six towering armoires, finally settling on a huge bathtub shaped like a clamshell.

"It's quite spectacular, is it not?" Luke said.

"I've never seen anything like it."

"I believe Mr. Smith had it specially made."

"And does he use it often?"

Luke gave a startled laugh. "Never. At least not that I know of."

"I suppose he had it made for Charles," she couldn't help fishing. From what she'd heard about Smith's former lover this sort of room would have appealed to him.

"Er, yes, that is true." Luke looked nonplussed that she knew about Charles.

Moira had hoped the question might make him open up on the subject, but it appeared that Luke was not a gossip.

"I thought we might start with a bath before I show you your rooms and the rest of the house."

"That sounds wonderful."

Luke turned a bronze handle and water came gushing from the swan shaped tap.

He turned to her and gestured to the large room around them. "This room separates your chambers from the master's. Mr. Smith suggested you treat it as your dressing room, although there is a smaller one of those on the other side of your bedchamber, if you wish."

The room reminded Moira of the boudoirs that were still popular among the wealthy in France. Although she'd never seen a seashell bathtub.

"May I undress you?" Luke asked.

"Of course."

He commenced to remove layer after layer of clothing like a man who'd had ample practice, quickly getting her down to her corset, which she'd worn for the first time since her beating, albeit much looser than usual.

Moira was accustomed to female servants babbling while they waited on her but Luke was cut from different, quieter, cloth. If he thought anything about her scars and bruises, he kept it to himself.

"Have you worked for Mr. Smith long?" she asked once she was down to her chemise.

"Almost two years," he said, dropping to his knees to remove her shoes and stockings.

That meant he'd been living there through Smith's last lovers—Charles and Joseph Leather. He probably had all sorts of interesting tales to tell, if she could only winkle them out of him.

"How many servants live here?" she asked.

"I think perhaps twenty—although that doesn't include the men who come each day. They don't live here."

"Men?" she asked, even though she knew Smith employed bodyguards around the clock.

Luke stood and then began to pluck the pins from her hair. "Guards accompany Mr. Smith whenever he leaves the house and there are always four here—two at each entrance—whether he is here, or not."

"Goodness, that sounds... excessive."

"There have been attacks on his person."

"Ah. His work must be dangerous."

Luke merely nodded at that comment, refusing to be drawn.

Although she'd known about the guards before coming to Smith's house today, she'd learned about his security firsthand when she'd needed to give her personal information before getting close to the front door. Apparently only people whose names were on Smith's pre-approved list were allowed to enter.

Luke tested the water. "How do you like it?"

"Hot."

"Then this is perfect. Let me just help you with your chemise and we'll get you in here."

He lifted the garment over her head and carried it to the hamper. He was very tidy. In fact, the entire house was the neatest, cleanest place she'd ever seen.

He offered her his huge hand. "It's easy to slip on the sides of this tub," he explained at her quizzical look.

Moira took his hand and stepped into the big shell, lowering herself into the almost too-hot water with a sigh. "This is divine."

"Would you like to relax for a while, or shall I wash your hair?"

"Oh, hair, please." She'd been washing her hair in cold water and could never really seem to get it clean enough.

"This is a most unusual bathing chamber," she said, as Luke pulled the rolling cart of vials, bottles, and jars closer.

"Bathing was one of Master Charles's passions."

"I can see it might become one of mine."

He smiled. "If you don't care to use the bath for any reason, there is a shower bath on the other side of your dressing room." He poured a generous dollop of shampoo from a glass decanter and rubbed his large hands together.

Her eyes drifted shut as he massaged the shampoo into her scalp. Luke wasn't just gorgeous; he was also incredibly skilled with his fingers. Moira became so relaxed that she'd almost drifted off to sleep when he stopped.

She lifted her heavy eyelids and watched as he reached for the tap, flipped a lever, and suddenly water came out of a device that was attached to a hose.

"How ingenious," she murmured as he used the attachment to rinse the soap from her hair.

"It's a marvelous convenience and Mr. Smith has even installed them in the servant quarters."

That must have been quite an expense. Moira couldn't see her mother doing the same thing for her employees, who were required to haul their water and share dungeon-like bathing chambers in the bowels of the ancient Paris building.

Luke turned off the water and poured something onto her head that smelled so good it made her salivate. "What is that delicious smell?"

"It is bergamot." His fingers were firm yet gentle on her scalp, which was always sore from carrying around such a heavy pile of hair. She had once suggested cutting her hair shorter but Marie had vigorously protested. *It's the only attractive thing about you*!

So, that had put an end to *that*.

Luke's hands moved to her neck and shoulders. Moira knew how to give sensual massages, but Luke was a master. She felt his touch in her very bones.

"Where did you learn such a skill?"

"I used to work at the Birch Palace."

"Ah… I see." Although she didn't—not really.

"I was a whore, if that's what you're wondering."

Luckily the hot tub could account for her horribly flushed face. "And now you are a personal servant. That is quite a change of occupation."

"It's not so different," he said. "Service is service, after all. I enjoyed my work at the Birch Palace, but it was becoming increasingly difficult to find anyone interested in a thirty-five-year-old *boy*."

Yes, Moira was familiar with that. At barely five feet and not quite seven stone she was small and girlish looking—if you didn't examine her face too closely—but she was obviously a grown woman past the first flush of youth.

Luke helped her from the tub and then commenced to dry her.

"You will spoil me, Luke."

"It is my job and my pleasure to spoil you, Miss Moira."

"Just Moira, is fine."

"Mr. Smith would not appreciate such liberties."

"Is he such a strict master, then?"

"He's strict but fair. And exceedingly generous."

This time Moira heard something that sounded near worshipful. So, the gorgeous servant was infatuated with his employer, was he? She could see how that would happen easily with Smith.

Luke led her over to one of the *three* fireplaces that were crackling away in the enormous room. "Just hop up on here," he patted a strange-looking leather covered table, which had multiple drawers in its polished wood base. Beside it was a cloth covered cart that contained a basin, a stack of cloths, and a variety of scissors, razors, and other grooming materials.

Moira used the two steps to mount the table.

He met her gaze, a slight stain spreading over his cheeks. "I've been instructed to shave you. It can be, er, intimate."

"I'm accustomed to such grooming and will not run screaming," she assured him.

Based on the explicit detail in Smith's contract—and his own immaculate hygiene—Moira knew he'd expect his instructions to be followed to the letter.

She hadn't shaved since leaving Bernina's and had been itching as the hair all grew in, so she was looking forward to being smooth.

"These are for your feet." He gestured to two metal devices at one end of the table. "I'm going to put a heel in each." He lifted her left foot and guided it to the metal cup.

"I've never seen such a table."

"Mr. Smith owns a company that makes them," he said as she put her right heel in the cool metal. "Apparently they are a new invention for use in doctors' offices." He did something with a brass crank that raised the back of the bench. "Go ahead and slide down a bit and then lie back and relax."

Once Moira did so, he lifted the lid on a huge silver tureen, the sort that hot soup might come in, and took out several steaming towels.

"This will make removing the hair easier," he said, unwrapping the towel around her body and laying a steaming cloth over her mound. "I'm going to adjust the stirrups now."

He moved first one and then the other foot outward, not stopping until her thighs were spread wide, the suggestive pose enough to make her exposed sex pulse with interest, her mind racing with the uses that could be made of such a table.

Once he'd positioned her the way he wanted, he tucked a second warm cloth over her spread cleft.

"Lift your arms, please."

When she had a hot towel in each armpit, he covered her exposed torso with a thick towel. Moira was deliciously cozy—perhaps the warmest she'd been in weeks.

"Tell me if you get cold," he said, and then set about stropping a razor.

"I came here from Bernina's," Moira said, suddenly wanting him to know at least that much about her, since he'd confessed part of his own past.

"Yes, I know. One of the other servants said he saw you there." Luke finished one blade and moved on to another.

Moira's mind boggled at the thought of a servant who could afford to go to the expensive brothel.

"His sweetheart works there," Luke said, as if he could guess what she was thinking.

"Who is it?"

"Leo Tinsley."

Moira snorted. "I didn't imagine Leo as the sort to have a steady lover."

"Yes, he is quite a handful," Luke said, looking amused.

This was just getting more and more curious. Ex-whores as *body* servants, other servants seeing current whores, the master of the house hiring a live-in-whore… Moira almost felt at home.

"Why so many?" she asked when Luke moved on to yet a third razor.

"They tend to dull quickly, so this will keep the skin from getting chafed."

Old Amaya had used only one razor and had wielded it like a butcher scraping the bristles from a pig. Not that she'd been clumsy or had ever cut Moira, but she'd certainly never gone to so much effort.

Once Luke was satisfied with his razors, he quickly soaped and shaved each underarm.

When it came time to work on her sex, he moved the rolling stool to the end of the bench, pushed the stirrups one notch wider to accommodate his massive shoulders and removed the towels.

Moira knew she'd be swollen and slick—how could she not be with such a gorgeous man waiting on her hand and foot—and Luke couldn't help but notice the obvious signs of her arousal. Part of her wanted him to say something. Another part—the part he was currently exposing—wanted him to *do* something.

She really was a harlot.

But if Luke noticed anything, he didn't show it. "Now, relax and I'll have you smooth the way the master likes in just a few minutes." He went to work, the razor flickering with almost worrying speed as he stretched skin and shaved areas that she didn't recall getting attention in the past, leaving no part of her untouched in his quest to eradicate every last hair.

Once he was satisfied, he used yet another steaming cloth to clean away the soap, returned the stirrups to their original position, helped Moira to her feet, and then wrapped her in a thick, soft robe that must have been warmed by the fire.

He led her to a dressing table and sat her in front of the mirror, his gaze on her hair. "It is so glorious that it seems a shame to cut it," he said, picking up a strand and pulling the corkscrew curl to its full length. He met her gaze in the glass. "But I'm afraid Mr. Smith wants it trimmed."

Moira nodded.

"How short shall I go?" he asked.

Moira gave him a reassuring smile. "Short."

"Are you sure?"

"It's just hair; it will grow back."

***

Moira felt as if she'd shed a stone by the time Luke was finished. When she glanced down at the floor it looked like Luke was standing in a sea of copper.

"Well?" he asked, an anxious notch between his eyebrows. "What do you think?"

"Have you ever heard of *coiffure à la victime?*" she asked, running her fingers through the short, tousled curls and loving the feel and look of the new cut.

Luke shook his head.

"It was a haircut that some women wore during the French Revolution to protest brutality. It looked very much like this." She smiled at him. "I like it." she said, taking a last look at her reflection before standing. She *loved* it, maybe especially because she knew Marie would hate it. "Thank you, Luke."

He looked genuinely pleased. "It's my pleasure. Well, let's get you into a dressing gown and slippers. I'll have just enough time to show you around before the doctor arrives." Luke opened one of the armoires and took out a dressing gown of pale pink silk. "How about this?"

"It's gorgeous." She had always dressed in nice clothing, but never anything so feminine.

The dressing gown fit perfectly, as did the matching satin slippers, and Moira couldn't help staring at her transformed appearance. She had always worn clothing that was plain to the point of severity. Pink was the one color her mother had specifically told her to avoid, but it made her pale skin appear rosy and vibrant rather than sallow. Moira smiled at her reflection; she had never looked better.

"Where did this gown and slippers come from?"

Luke opened the other armoires and she saw dozens of garments hanging inside each. "Mr. Smith had a selection delivered earlier in the week. If there is anything you don't like I will send it back."

Moira couldn't help smiling at Smith's arrogance; not for a minute had he doubted that she would accept his offer. Had there ever been a time when he'd *not* got what he wanted?

He got Sandrine, didn't he? If you are beginning to like him too much— admire him or feel gratitude toward him, then remember your sister.

Moira's smile slid away.

"Is aught amiss?" Luke asked.

She shook her head and forced another smile. "No. Everything is fine."

Luke led her through a connecting door into a room that was just as large as the one they'd just left.

Rather than white and gray marble, the floors were wood stained ebony and buffed to a shine. Expensive looking rugs with intricate patterns woven with dozens of shades of gray, black, and white were scattered around the room.

A fire roared in the massive fireplace, whose marble surround was taller than Moira, and the bed was a monstrous four-poster, the thick posts easily nine or ten inches in diameter, its canopy and curtains made of a creamy gauze.

Moira couldn't help feeling a bit overwhelmed, not only from the luxury around her, but at how impeccably neat and clean everything was.

"Everything is very, er—"

"Perfect?"

Moira nodded.

He hesitated, then said, "Mr. Smith is a pleasure to serve, but he is particular about some things."

Moira thought back to the extensive contract she'd signed. Yes, *particular* was a good word to describe him.

"His chambers and yours will be thoroughly cleaned every day—from top to bottom, including fresh bedding. He bathes in the morning, evening, and always after he uses his private gymnasium." He cleared his throat. "You will be expected to bathe in the morning and evening as well. You might say he is obsessed with cleanliness."

It sounded more like a mania, but Luke's meaning was clear: Moira had better develop a similar mania.

What had happened to Smith to make him this way? Or perhaps it was just a byproduct of being so wealthy that he could afford to indulge his every whim.

Whatever his reasons, having multiple baths a day, changing clothes frequently, and sleeping in fresh sheets every night wasn't exactly a hardship.

"He despises clutter or mess," Luke continued. "How the servants keep our quarters is our own affair, but he is particular about the way we present ourselves in public. He provides us all with multiple sets of outer garments and underclothes—unheard of generosity when it comes to clothing one's servants—and he also expects us to take baths at least weekly. He has a most, er, acute sense of smell."

"Yes, he mentioned that." He didn't care for perfumes—unless he'd selected them—nor strong-smelling lotions or powders.

Luke gestured to the unopened door on the east wall of the big room. "His chambers are through there."

Moira was a bit startled; always in the past her protectors had maintained a certain reserve with her—mainly to enforce the differences in their statuses, she'd always suspected. Never had any of them lived in an adjacent room.

Luke opened the door for her.

Moira hesitated. "I'd hate to intrude."

"The master instructed me to show you all of the house." His tone made it clear that he had no intention of doing anything other than exactly what Smith had instructed.

She stepped through the doorway into a room that was almost a mirror image of hers when it came to color and furnishings. There was one detail that was different: the enormous painting above the bed.

Moira's lips parted as she stared at it, not quite sure what to say.

It was Smith, reclining on a chaise, one arm draped around a gorgeous naked young man. An *erect* man, with a big silver ring in the crown of his prick.

Never had she seen such a blatantly sexual painting of two men together. If the portrait was ever made public, Smith could go to jail for violating indecency laws. Or perhaps he was so rich that he didn't need to worry.

It was clear, from Smith's bare arm, shoulder, and a bit of his knee, that he was also naked. He wore an expression that was more relaxed than she'd ever seen, his fascinating, mobile mouth pulled up on one side in a barely-there smile, his fingers brushing against the other man's erect nipple.

"It is striking," she said when it became apparent Luke was waiting for a response.

"Yes."

"Charles, I presume?"

"Yes."

He was certainly prettier than Moira.

The feeling in her belly wasn't jealousy, but something even stranger and equally useless: competitiveness.

Why did she want to compete with one of his lovers?

She forced her thoughts away from that question and her gaze away from the mesmerizing painting and looked around the rest of the room, which was, unsurprisingly, immaculate.

But it was his dressing room that was most eerie; all the clothes—black, of course—were hung with precise equidistance.

"It almost looks as if—"

"A ruler has been used?" Luke asked, pulling a short wooden ruler from the breast pocket of his coat.

Moira goggled. "Good God."

His eyes crinkled with amusement. "All the items in the house are placed where he wants them." He shrugged. "It might seem draconian, but it's just as easy to put things back where he likes them as it is to put them elsewhere."

"Should I get a ruler? Will he expect my room to be this way?" Or her person?

Luke chuckled. "No. Your room is your personal space." His pale blond eyebrows descended. "Unless Mr. Smith made a provision that says otherwise in your contract?"

"No."

"Then you needn't worry. One thing he is very good about is making sure that what he wants is clear and then not changing his mind."

Moira suspected that was true, but it didn't do anything to make the situation any less overwhelming.

Indeed, it only made her dread—even more—what a man like Smith would do if he ever learned that one of his employees was lying to him.

Or scheming against him.

Chapter 12

Moira was curled up in a comfortable chair with a book when Smith entered her room later that night.

He came to a halt in front of her chair before she could stand, his dark, unnerving gaze roaming her person. "You look lovely," he pronounced. "And your hair is delightful."

Moira was both pleased and startled by the warmth in his gaze. "Thank you. I—I like it. Please"—she gestured to the chair across from her— "won't you join me?" she asked, intensely aware of her position in his household, which was essentially that of mistress.

"Thank you."

"Would you care for a drink?"

"Yes, please. Whatever you are having."

"It's wine—from dinner. It's excellent. Thank you for having such a lovely meal sent to me." She filled the extra glass that had been delivered along with the bottle. At the time, she'd assumed it must have been a mistake because Smith had left a message that he'd be gone for dinner. She should have known that nothing was a mistake in Mr. Smith's house.

"Thank you," he said, when she handed him the wine.

Moira hesitated before returning to her chair, uncharacteristically unsure of herself.

You're a Bardot, for God's sake. Pleasing a man is bred into your bones.

"Would you like to feel my hair?" she asked on impulse. "It is like a sheep's."

He laughed. "How could I resist such an intriguing offer?"

Moira sank to her knees beside his chair.

His pleasant expression shifted into something hungry and predatory, and his flaring pupils told her it had been the right thing to do.

He slid his hand into her tousled locks. "Soft," he murmured. "Not at all like a sheep."

"Have you ever felt a sheep?" Moira asked pertly, earning a chuckle and smile from him.

She was relieved that she was finally easing into her role of attentive, admiring lover, a role that had always been as natural as breathing in the past, and yet seemed so difficult with this man.

Perhaps that is because you were not planning to betray all your other lovers?

Moira banished the thought and met Smith's far too probing gaze.

"No, I don't recall ever touching a sheep. You've caught me out in a lie, already. I see I shall have to be more careful."

That makes two of us.

His fingers trailed over her cheek and settled on her throat.

Moira pressed against his palm, strangely comforted by his touch.

"What were you reading?" he asked, his hand tightening around the sensitive skin and then stroking, the caress enough to make her purr.

"Great Expectations."

"Is it good?" he asked, his expression almost dreamy as he sipped his wine and explored her with his fingers.

"It is good so far, but… ominous. I took it from your library. Haven't you read it?"

"I suspect that either Mason, my secretary, purchased it or perhaps my friend Nora Fanshawe left it."

"The painter?"

"You know her?" he looked surprised.

"No, but I've seen her work." Moira leaned closer, so that he wouldn't have to stretch to continue his divine stroking. "I saw one of her paintings, the one that won a prize—I'm afraid I don't recall the name of it."

Smith smiled. "That's because it was simply titled *Male Nude, #14*. The wretched woman refuses to come up with titles that are descriptive. She also painted the portrait in my study as well as the nude above my bed. I take it Luke gave you the tour?"

"Yes, he did. The one in your bedroom is… most striking."

He stroked her jaw. "It is the ultimate in vanity for me to have consented to the painting and doubly vain to hang it above my own bed, is it not?"

"Consented? You mean it wasn't your choice?"

"I lost a bet with the young gentleman in the painting. As the winner of the wager, he demanded that portrait."

"It is magnificent."

"*You* are magnificent," he said softly. "That pale blush color suits you; you have glorious skin and hair." He stood and helped her to her feet, his hands going to the ties on her dressing gown. "I spoke to the doctor after he was finished with your exam and he said you were in good health—even your back."

Moira had liked Doctor Felton, a young man who'd not seemed shocked by her shaved body, her scars, or her presence in Smith's house. While he'd examined her most thoroughly, he'd been respectful and had explained what he was doing every step of the way. All in all, it was the most illuminating doctor visit she'd ever had—and she had endured plenty, both at home and at Bernina's; brothels that employed diseased whores would not be in business long.

Smith slid her dressing gown from her shoulders and then strode the few feet to drape it across the bench at the foot of the bed.

When he returned, his dark eyes flickered over the nightgown she wore, which was the same pale silk as the dressing gown but there was much less of it.

He cupped her breasts and Moira hissed in a breath as he thumbed her hard nipples. "I adore your body, Moira. The more I think of putting a child inside you, the more it arouses me."

Moira sucked in a breath at both his words and the hot, possessive look on his face. There was no denying that being desired by a man like Smith was a powerful aphrodisiac. He could have anyone he wanted—male or female—and yet he had chosen Moira, a woman who'd always been the least of her family.

"The doctor told me you were twelve days from your last courses."

His words snapped her from the sensual daze he'd induced with his caressing.

Smith grinned at whatever he saw on her face and then pinched her nipples hard enough to send twin shocks of pain and desire straight to her pulsing core. "Is it indelicate of me to speak of your courses?"

Moira had certainly never discussed such a thing with any man—not even a physician, until today.

"You needn't answer; I know it is." He pinched and pulled her aching nipples. "But as I plan to breed you it seems wise to deal with the matter head on, don't you think?"

Moira's face flamed at his words and she lifted her hands to her cheeks, stunned that she could still blush.

Smith chuckled. "How lovely you look with roses on your cheeks." He released one of her nipples and slid a hand down her belly to her sex, his finger pushing the thin fabric between her swollen lips. "Mmm, you are wet and so hot," he muttered, gently flicking her sensitive bud. "I think you like my crude, direct manner of speaking."

Moira couldn't demur; she'd never had a man say such things to her.

She spread her legs to give him better access and he fingered her, doubtless ruining the lovely nightgown in the process.

"Doctor Felton told me there are days of the month when you are more fertile. Are you, in general, regular in your cycle?"

Even the doctor had not inquired so closely.

Smith seemed to read her thoughts, "I am quite nosy. You see, I want to know everything about you, Moira—no matter how private or insignificant."

Unease slithered down her spine at his declaration. She shrugged it off; what he meant was that he wanted to know everything about her physically, to aid conception. Not that he wanted to know how she was scheming to capture him.

She met his open, curious gaze and said, "Yes, I am very regular."

"Good. According to Felton, the next four or five days are your most fertile days." He removed his distracting finger from her slit and brushed an errant curl away from her eye, his lids lowering slightly as he caressed her cheek. "For the next week I will fuck you every day—multiple times." He smiled. "After all, practice makes perfect, doesn't it?"

How was this man so good at tying her tongue—and brain—in knots?

All she could manage was a nod.

"Undress me, Moira," he said, his eyes twinkling with humor at her no doubt stunned expression.

Moira was grateful to have a task to focus her badly scattered wits and she set about undressing him, something she could do in her sleep.

She draped his coat and waistcoat over the valet stand that had been placed not far from her bed—doubtless for that very purpose—and then removed his shirt.

Moira paused before she carried the linen to the hamper, her breathing quickening as she took in his exquisite torso.

"You shall make me a vain monster if you stare at me that way, Moira."

She lifted her gaze from his body to his smiling eyes. "You should be vain," she said, for a change not lying through her teeth.

He stepped closer and unfastened the few buttons on her gown before lifting her gown over her head.

He made an approving noise in his throat as his eyes swept her up and down several times. "You are perfection, Moira."

She'd stood naked before hundreds of men in her life. Not since she'd been a young woman with her first lover had she felt so very *conscious* of her body. And never had a man's words warmed her so utterly.

What was happening to her?

Smith lowered himself in the chair.

Moira shook herself and draped both his shirt and her nightgown over the valet stand before sinking down on her knees before him.

He looked completely at ease with a person at his feet, his hands resting on the arms of the chair like a pasha as he gazed down at her.

Once she'd removed his shoes and stockings, she pushed his knees apart and unbuttoned his flatteringly tented placket.

He didn't speak, his heavy-lidded eyes tracking her every move as he lifted his hips and she pulled off both his drawers and trousers, carefully folding them and setting them on top of his shoes.

His ridiculously big cock was hard and slick and he groaned when she lowered her mouth and took him as deeply as the angle allowed.

"Mmm, you have a delicious mouth."

His words sent ripples of pleasure through her body. As usual, he smelled and tasted clean, with only the faintest hint of musk.

"Take me deeper, darling," he murmured, shifting his hips to accommodate her better, his fingers stroking through her short hair.

Moira took him into her throat, but still could not swallow his entire length. It must have been enough, because he gave a murmur of pleasure and his hips began to gently thrust.

Sucking him was a challenge, but the noises he made and the way his breathing hitched and stuttered was beyond erotic. She wanted to make him come apart, to hear him cry out and lose control.

Instead, he laid a hand on her jaw, stopping her before carefully withdrawing himself.

"Come up here." He helped her to her feet and then held her hand while she placed a knee on either side of his hips.

The flaring of his pupils and the sound he made when she straddled his thighs was enough to make *her* vain.

"So very pretty," he murmured, his gaze flickering from her sex to her breasts. "Kneel high," he instructed, and then placed the fat head of his cock at her slippery, swollen entrance and eased himself inside. "God, you feel wonderful." His hands closed around her waist and he pulled her down slowly while lifting his hips off the chair.

She whimpered at the depth of penetration, her eyelids fluttering as waves of pain-soaked pleasure swamped her.

"Eyes on me."

Moira opened her eyes and discovered their faces were only inches apart, his pupils blazing into hers.

He flexed his hips.

Moira gasped.

"Does that hurt?" he asked, his smile wicked.

"Yes."

"Good." His fingers dug into her hips and he worked her with slight, but potent thrusts, barely moving. "I adore fucking you," he murmured. "You must always tell me if I haven't satisfied you, or if there is a way to give you more pleasure."

Moira honestly couldn't image that happening, but said, "Yes, Smith."

"Now," he said, cupping her bottom with both hands and standing, his cock still buried inside her. "I need to taste that freshly shaved pussy of yours." He carried her to the bed and laid her across the mattress "Spread your feet and let your knees fall open."

Once she was spread like a butterfly, he lowered himself between her thighs and sucked her swollen nub into his mouth.

She'd not exaggerated his prowess in her memories. He was every bit as attentive to her needs as he'd been before, and it wasn't long before she was crying out and climaxing in his hot, eager mouth.

While she convulsed and shuddered, he positioned himself at her entrance, and thrust into her so hard that he drove her up the bed.

"I can't get in you deeply enough," he rasped, lifting her legs over his shoulders and bending her in half. "I've thought of nothing all evening but *this*," he forced the words through clenched teeth, stroking into her harder and faster, his thrusts becoming less controlled, his grunts louder and wilder until Moira felt his shaft begin to swell.

"Coming," he muttered, sheathing himself to the hilt and flooding her with pulse after pulse of hot seed.

An unfamiliar feeling of calm washed over her as she lay beneath his hard, hot body. She wasn't just physically satiated. In that moment, she was also… content.

If you don't sneak away and cleanse yourself, you might have a child with this man. You could stay with him. You could have a family—one who might actually love and appreciate you…

Moira squeezed her eyes shut as if that would cut off the traitorous thoughts.

Smith killed Sandrine; he is the enemy, not the answer to my prayers, she reminded herself.

Why was that becoming harder and harder to remember?

***

True to his word, Smith bred Moira several times a day that first week.

Sometimes he appeared in her room, sometimes he summoned her to his, and on one memorable occasion he mounted her on the big black desk in his study, sunlight blazing through the uncovered windows.

He was vigorous and voracious and didn't care who happened to be around when he decided that he wanted her.

More than once he'd come to her while Luke was busy doing something in her dressing room.

Those were the only assignations that she'd not quite enjoyed. Although Luke had never shown it by a look or a word, Moira was beginning to suspect he was more than just infatuated with their employer.

It took her until the end of the third week—after Smith had all but mounted her in front of the man—before she worked up enough nerve to broach the subject.

"Luke in love with me?" Smith repeated, and then laughed. "Ridiculous."

"He is certainly infatuated with you," she'd retorted, nettled by his easy dismissal.

He'd not refuted that quite so quickly. "Perhaps."

"You were lovers?"

He'd lifted an eyebrow at her question.

"I'm sorry, that was an inappropriate question."

"Perhaps," he said again, and then gave her one of his disarming grins. "But I enjoy questions of any sort from you, Moira. Yes, Luke and I are lovers."

Are, not *were*.

The mental image of the two men together had sent a bolt of arousal directly to her core.

But she'd also been confused. When, exactly, did Smith get the time to fuck the other man?

The answer was that he hadn't—at least not lately. No matter how virile he was, there simply weren't enough hours in the day and Smith had stayed with her most nights.

"Is Luke not bothered by my presence here?"

Smith's smile had slid from his face. "Has he given you any indication that he resents you?"

"No, no," she hastened to assure him, alarmed by the way his warm brown gaze had frosted over so quickly. "Quite the contrary. He has been most welcoming."

"Good. As to your other comment—regarding infatuation—I think you are wrong in that, as well. He and one of the footmen—David—are together."

Moira knew which one he meant—yet another exceedingly handsome man. They would make a handsome pair. She hadn't pointed out that just because Luke was with one man, didn't mean he couldn't want another.

"Whatever gave you that idea that he is infatuated with me?" Smith had asked.

"Nothing really," she'd lied, not wanting to expose the way the other man's eyes followed Smith whenever they were in the same room. "I—I, er, just wondered at the nature of your relationship."

"Relationship? He is my servant and I am his employer; we both signed a contract to that effect." His clipped tone had indicating that was the end of the matter.

Joseph Leather—Smith's prior valet—had also been a servant and her brother Robert had been certain that Smith had been in love with Leather.

Of course, that was not information she could admit to having.

And so, Moira had let the matter be.

Chapter 13

Luke was in the kitchen with several other servants—which is where he'd been spending his evenings since Miss Moira had moved into the house—when one of the service bells went off.

Michael craned his neck to see the bells. "That's you, Luke—it's Miss Moira's room."

"They must have worked up an appetite," Frank, one of the grooms said, making all the others chortle.

"I'm glad the master's stayin' around more now," Cook piped up. "Gives me a chance to earn my keep. Sometimes it's a wonder he pays me at all considering the paltry amount of food he takes at his own board."

"Aye, well, I reckon he'll stay close now that he's got a reason to," Clark, one of the inside servants commented, setting off a series of speculations about the master's newest lover.

Luke left the men to their chatter, ignoring the twinge of pain that had blossomed in his chest at their words. He'd bled inside and continued to do so with every pleasant greeting and nod he exchanged with Mr. Smith, who'd not called him to his bed even once since Miss Moira's arrival.

Even as miserable as he'd been, Luke had provided excellent service. He'd been trained by the very best at the Birch Palace, and it was a badge of honor to obey his master's orders both quickly and respectfully, without giving any sign of how much Smith's neglect was crushing him.

As he mounted the stairs to answer the bell, it occurred to him that if his desire to please overwhelmed even his own anguish at losing his lover to another, then maybe it wasn't love at all that he felt.

He was wrestling with that thought when he entered his mistress's bedchamber.

The sight that met his eyes drove everything from his mind.

It was Mr. Smith, naked and sprawled on top of the bedding. Beside him, slit-eyed and sweaty, was Miss Moira, her bare torso rising and falling rapidly, as if she'd been sprinting—or fucking Smith, which was guaranteed to leave a person just as breathless.

Mr. Smith was absently stroking one of her breasts, the image of a man whose every sensual need had been satisfied.

"Ah, Luke," his master said, "there you are. I would like my slippers and a robe—tell Knox I want the velvet one, it is quite chilly. Miss Moira would like some of Cook's shortbread. I've promised her that it is the best in Britain. Is that not true, Luke?"

He cleared his throat and managed to croak, "That is the general consensus, sir."

"There, you see?" Mr. Smith said to Miss Moira, tweaking a nipple hard enough to make her squeak. "Luke *never* lies." He pulled her body on top of his and the two lost themselves in kissing, forgetting that Luke even existed.

Luke silently left through the connecting door and then sagged against the wall, struggling to catch his breath.

The emotions that battered him were so confusing he felt as though he was losing his mind. Bitter rejection and rampant arousal struggled inside him like drunken street brawlers. His sadistic mind's eye kept replaying the scene he'd just left: the two lovers entangled in each other arms, their bodies naked and sweaty.

For all that his eyes prickled with unshed tears of frustration, his cock throbbed so hard it was a wonder they couldn't hear it in the next room.

Luke laid a hand over his bulge, not to stroke, just to hold himself—desperate to find some comfort in touch… even if it was his own.

But all he felt was a soul-rending desire for a man who'd cast him aside without a care.

He never lied to you. There has never been any love—at least not on Mr. Smith's side. To him you're merely a servant he hired to fulfill particular duties. And now those duties have changed.

Luke couldn't argue with the chiding voice. This was all his fault; he'd allowed his feelings for the other man to career out of control. And now watching Mr. Smith behave with somebody else the way he'd only recently behaved with *him* was the punishment.

The pain he was feeling made sense.

It was the arousal that was throbbing inside him that left him confused and maddened; how could such agonizing humiliation make him so bloody hard?

Because you're a self-destructive fool, that was why.

Luke smiled grimly at the thought. He *was* a fool.

If he'd truly wanted happiness then he never would have rejected what David had offered him daily—until he had finally stopped.

But clearly Luke had no interest in somebody who wanted and loved him.

He was sick in the head and had only himself to blame.

Yet he couldn't make himself leave. Just thinking about never seeing his master again made him feel ill. He loved his job, even when it caused him gut-wrenching pain.

Luke dropped his hand from his groin, sighed, and went to look for Knox in the master's chambers.

The valet was nowhere to be seen, but Luke easily found the dark grey velvet robe and slippers his master had asked for. He briefly considered bringing them to Smith himself, but he knew that when he gave instructions, he expected them to be carried out to the letter.

So, he rang the bell for Knox and waited, taking the opportunity to explore Mr. Smith's pristine dressing room, smelling the various items of clothing and hoping for the scent of the man he'd come to worship, adore, and yes, love.

But Knox's dutiful obedience to their employer's wishes meant there was not a whiff of Smith's person or even a stray hair anywhere.

Luke stroked the sleeve of one of his master's many black coats and wondered what had happened to the other man to leave him with such obsession for cleanliness.

On one rare, glorious occasion Smith had summoned Luke to his bed directly after leaving his gymnasium, not bothering with his usual wash.

The feel of his hard, sweaty body and the scent of his clean sweat and musk had almost made Luke delirious.

Many of the men he'd been forced to service over the course of his career as a whore had been less than well-groomed. If somebody had told him a few years ago that he'd *want* a sweaty lover he would have laughed.

But sometimes he worried that Mr. Smith was *too* sanitized. It was as if he'd washed away some part of himself in the process, leaving only a clean, perfect vessel.

"Luke?"

He looked up from the coat sleeve he'd been holding to find Knox giving him a quizzical look. "You alright, mate?"

Luke smiled, so conditioned that it came without a thought, but not without effort. "I'm fine. His lordship wants the velvet robe and slippers and wishes you to collect his clothing."

Knox laughed. "He must have been mighty randy if he was able to overlook such clutter."

"Yes, he must have been," Luke agreed, trying to forget the times when his master had been in a rush for him.

***

Smith smirked when the door closed behind Luke. Sending the man on such a demeaning errand—and reveling in his stoic, delicious suffering—had left Smith as hard as iron.

While Smith didn't agree with Moira's assessment that Luke loved him, he had begun to suspect the other man had developed a certain… possessiveness toward him.

Smith would either smash that inclination or Luke would have to find himself another job, because he would be damned if he'd tolerate another Charles in his house.

He grimaced at the thought of his former lover and turned to Moira. She was curled up on her side like a small cat, her face slack from the three orgasms he'd given her.

He didn't know what it was about her, but he was insatiable for her. She'd been with him for weeks, now, and his lust for her showed no signs of diminishing. Quite the reverse, in fact.

Even though she was no longer in the fertile period of her cycle he had continued to come to her every night and take her at least twice, usually more.

And now Smith wanted her again, so he slapped her exposed buttock. "Hands and knees," he ordered, smirking when she cut him a sleepy, sulky look but quickly obeyed his command and presented her sweet little bottom for his enjoyment.

Smith knelt behind her, positioned his cock at the opening to her tight, swollen pussy, and entered her with a firm thrust, chuckling at her earthy groan and the way she pushed back, trying to take him even deeper.

There was something about fucking a lover in such an animalistic position that always felt filthy and forbidden.

It also allowed for deep penetration, which meant more of the pain his Moira craved.

Smith kept his back to the door so the first thing Luke would see when he entered with his tray of shortbread would be Smith's arse.

Luke, being the good servant he was, would stand and wait until Smith told him otherwise.

He grinned at the thought. He was a sick bastard to find Luke's reaction so bloody arousing.

Still, he wasn't a *complete* bastard; he wouldn't be tormenting the other man if Luke didn't have such a raging desire to be humiliated.

Almost as raging as Smith's desire to humiliate him.

He'd wager a thousand pounds that Luke's cock had been stiff and leaking when he'd entered the room to find them in a state of erotic dishabille.

Smith knew he'd been neglecting Luke—and he would make amends to the other man soon—but the prospect of impregnating Moira entranced him and he'd rapidly become obsessed with putting a child in her belly.

Moira, he knew, was equally obsessed *not* to bear his child, and kept a cleansing kit hidden in the corner of one of her armoires to ensure she didn't fall pregnant.

Rather than anger him, her rebellion intrigued and amused him.

He'd responded to the threat of having his seed washed away by keeping her close after breeding her, not leaving her alone until the following morning most days.

Smith had taken Luke into his confidence on the matter and the other man—after expressing his shock and disapproval that Moira would try to evade her contractual responsibility in such an underhanded manner—had helped to ensure that she had no time to cleanse herself, using the pretext of drawing a bath or grooming her or fussing about in her dressing area to make her covert activities more difficult.

"You can rely on me to be both subtle and diligent, sir," Luke had assured him.

Smith had come to understand that the other man really *did* look forward to having a child in the house. He was so enthusiastic that he'd even asked Smith if he might begin preparing the old nursery for use.

Smith was charmed by Luke's interest and suspected he would make a superlative nanny when the time came.

As for Moira and why she was so determined to cheat him?

Smith didn't really know what her motivation was. It might be something as simple as not wanting to give birth at all. Or maybe she didn't think he deserved to have a child. Many people would agree with her if that was the case. Smith's household was unconventional in the extreme and he had no intention of ever getting married; to some people it would be a sin to give a child to a man like him.

Not to mention his sexual tastes, which most people would view as not only debauched, but worthy of prosecution.

Well, whatever her reasons, Smith couldn't help admiring her for trying to violate the contract. After all, that was part and parcel of any business agreement: the constant one-upmanship, the urge to dominate and succeed at the expense of one's opponent.

Moira would never gain the upper hand with Smith, but that didn't mean that he didn't enjoy her efforts.

***

After leaving Knox to deliver the robe and slippers Luke descended to the kitchen, which was surprisingly empty. Mr. Smith allowed a keg for his employees and most evenings the men simply stayed in, rather than going to a pub where the ale would cost money and be inferior.

But they'd all disappeared and only Cook remained, idly flipping through the newspaper, which Mr. Smith always shared with his employees once he'd finished reading them.

Cook perked up at Luke's entrance. "Yes?"

"He'd like some shortbread, if you have it."

"Aye! I've a batch from this afternoon." Cook leapt up and hurried to assemble a tray.

Luke opened his mouth to tell him just the shortbread, but then decided the tea might be welcome. Indeed, he would take up a bottle of sherry from the new case the master had just received. He knew Mr. Smith did not care for it, but perhaps Miss Moira would enjoy a glass with her shortbread.

"I'm going to the cellar," he told Cook.

"This will be ready in five minutes."

Luke thought about what he was doing—making a special trip for a bottle of wine for the woman who'd supplanted him—and snorted softly. Most people would think him a pathetic fool for taking pains to please his replacement. He knew that he should be jealous and angry at her—she'd taken the man he loved—but he couldn't bring himself to dislike, or even resent, her.

If Smith didn't have Miss Moira upstairs, there was no guarantee that he'd be with Luke. He'd always spent more evenings in the arms and beds of other lovers than he ever had with Luke, or even Charles.

His lips twitched into a smile; the man did not have it in him to be monogamous. Smith's wandering ways had never bothered Luke; it only bothered him when he'd failed to wander back in Luke's direction.

He genuinely liked Miss Moira, who was quiet, polite, and easy to please—unlike Charles. He grimaced at the memory of the beautiful young man. He wouldn't have tolerated Charles's tantrums and spoiled behavior for a day. Mr. Smith had not only tolerated him, but he'd also indulged him outrageously.

Until the day he hadn't.

If Luke was the sort to be jealous, he'd have been jealous of Charles because he had *never* been worthy of Smith.

Luke loved Smith. He was sure of it. After all, he was old enough to know the difference between love and lust, love's less noble relation. He wanted Smith to be happy, even if Luke wasn't part of that happiness. Weren't you supposed to want the person you loved to be happy?

He shook his head, irritated by his own dithering, and quickly located the sherry.

Once back in the kitchen Luke arranged the bottle and two glasses—just in case—on the tray Cook had prepared, deciding not to open the bottle until he was sure it was wanted.

When he got to Miss Moira's room, Luke balanced the tray, opened the door, and stopped in his tracks.

His master's backside faced the door, giving him a glorious view of his tight bottom, muscular thighs, and pendulous sac, which jolted with each violent thrust.

Luke's lungs seized and he stared, frozen in place like a startled hare.

Should he set down the tray? Or just leave.

Or should he—

As if sensing him, Mr. Smith slowed his thrusting and looked over his shoulder as he reached beneath his lover's body. Whatever he did to Miss Moira drew an immediate groan of pleasure.

"Yes… *please*, Smith."

He held Luke's gaze as he masturbated the woman, his lids heavy and his face slack with lust. Luke felt skewered by his dark gaze, his feet rooted to the floor.

As if satisfied by whatever he saw, Smith gave a slight nod, turned away, and resumed his rutting even as Miss Moira cried out that she was coming.

Luke didn't know whether to crow or weep that the other man had not dismissed him.

He did neither.

Instead, he stood by the door, the tray in his hand, and waited quietly like the excellent servant he was.

***

The hair on the back of Smith's neck prickled and he turned at the primitive warning; Luke had returned from his demeaning errand with the tea tray, complete with some wine.

Smith squinted at the bottle and saw that it was sherry, which he only kept for his guests, not caring for it, himself. Which meant that Luke had brought it for Moira.

That small evidence of the other man's desire to please his new mistress relieved him.

Moira had been wrong about Luke; he didn't love Smith and wasn't jealously infatuated like Charles had been, or he certainly wouldn't be so considerate of her.

Smith's lust mingled with relief. Luke wasn't about to descend into histrionics like Charles had, which meant that Smith could happily keep both his lovers,

The selfish thought made his cock throb so hard he almost came.

But instead of giving into to his need, he reached beneath Moira's body and stroked another orgasm from her responsive bundle of nerves, reveling in Luke's gaze.

He cut the other man's tented trousers a triumphant smirk and mentally collected the thousand pounds he'd wagered with himself, and then turned away, plowing Moira's tight cunt with renewed vigor.

Life, he thought as he hilted himself balls deep and emptied his load in Moira's hot, eager body, could not get much better than this. Smith would remember that thought later.

Chapter 14

S mith came back from the weekly meeting with his three syndicate partners earlier than usual.

Although he generally stayed afterward and played cards with his partners, tonight he was eager to get home.

He hadn't seen Moira for over a week thanks to a sudden—and unavoidable—journey to Liverpool. Although he had expected to stay away only three days, the trip had extended to seven.

He'd spent almost every minute immersed in a series of labor discussions with the employees at the ship works the syndicate had purchased eighteen months earlier. As of right now there were no problems at the facility and Smith wanted to keep it that way by listening to worker grievances.

Amazingly, Smith was the only one in his four-man syndicate who possessed the social skills necessary to interact with their employees and not make matters worse.

Gideon Banks was so teeth-grindingly arrogant that he had touched off an armed conflict with workers the only time he'd gone to a negotiation.

Edward Fanshawe was so rigid that he had once sacked every employee at a glassworks when they'd refused one of the terms on a contract.

As for Stephen Chatham? Well, he rarely managed to utter more than three words in a row, but his unsettling gray stare had a habit of causing workers to become so flustered that the number of clumsy accidents always soared when he stepped onto a property.

All that was to say that Smith was the one who had to trot around Britain putting out fires.

He'd spent day after day in the manager's office, meeting with various workers. Although the manager kept the premises clean and tidy—no doubt somebody had warned the man about Smith's cleanliness issues—Smith had still felt as if he had grit in every pore by the time he left.

He'd gone directly from the ship works to his private railcar, so bloody exhausted that he'd only had time for a rushed bath before he'd fallen into his comfortable, but lonely, bed on the train. He'd slept for an unprecedented six hours, waking too late to have another bath before the train reached London.

As a result, he'd felt like clawing off his own skin by the time he got to the weekly syndicate meeting.

As a result of his rushed schedule, he was both exhausted *and* wound up tighter than a watch spring; he needed to expend some energy or he'd not be able to sleep tonight.

"I'm going to take an hour of exercise before bed, Knox," he said as his valet stripped him. "I'll bathe afterward. Have Cook send up a tray for me—something light."

"Very good, sir."

In Liverpool his only exercise had been calisthenics in his hotel room, so he was grateful to be in his own gymnasium, where he had bags for boxing, barbells, and various weight strengthening equipment, like the sand-filled canvas bags sized to fit either ankles or wrists.

Floor-to-ceiling mirrors were positioned along the walls to allow him to observe himself from all angles while he exercised. Was that an act of shameless vanity? Undoubtedly, but that did not bother him. He liked to see whatever part of his body he was currently working.

Gideon Banks—the Earl of Taunton and one of Smith's three business partners—had barged his way into Smith's private area a few months ago and his eyes had gone wide as they'd taken in the room.

When he'd learned that Smith exercised naked in front of the mirrors, he had immediately said, "I'm going to set up a room *exactly* like this—Alys will adore watching me: her very own naked and sweaty object of masculine perfection."

Smith had laughed: that was Gideon in a nutshell. The man managed to make towering conceit not only attractive, but strangely adorable.

Still, as arrogant as the statement had been, Smith knew Gideon was correct: his new wife adored her husband as much as he adored himself. To be fair, Gideon was also madly in love with Alys. After a somewhat rocky start the couple were deliriously happy now and greatly enjoying their first child.

Smith shrugged aside thoughts of Gideon and his happy family and warmed up his body with a series of stretches.

He had discovered that exercising was as addictive as fucking, drinking, or gambling—maybe even more so. After all, he had never gone a day without exercise, but he'd gone weeks without the other activities, even sex.

Smith hefted two barbells and began to work his arms, curling the weights slowly to keep his form correct, his gaze fixed on his shoulders and biceps in the mirror.

His exercise regimen was brutal, yet—perhaps because of the pain—the exertion invariably left him aroused. He supposed that wasn't surprising since he loved pain and got hard both giving and receiving it.

Tonight, was no exception, and by the time he'd been at it half an hour his shaft was rigid and pulsing. Smith ignored his nagging erection—he never pleasured himself during exercise—and allowed his mind to dwell on Moira, something he'd had little time to do in the past week.

He wondered what she had been doing to fill her days. He had brought up the subject of all the free time she'd have the evening before he'd left, when they'd been lounging in bed.

It wasn't only curiosity that had made him ask. Charles had become bored with too much time on his hands, and a bored Charles had been an unhappy Charles, which had meant a miserable Smith. Boredom was a good part of why their relationship had deteriorated so quickly.

Well, he admitted, boredom *and* Smith's inability to commit to only one sexual partner.

In any case, Smith did not wish to lose Moira to boredom.

"I have always wanted to learn to draw and play the piano," she'd admitted when he asked.

"At the same time?" Smith had teased, surprising a rare laugh out of her.

"I thought I'd try them singly, at first. Would you mind if I engaged music and drawing tutors?"

"I would be delighted if you did so."

"I know you do not have a piano, but I understand people often go to the houses of their tutors."

Smith hadn't said anything at the time but had left word for his steward to procure a piano and have it delivered. The house had a music room, after all, but nobody had ever used it.

His boyhood home had been filled with music—his sisters and mother had all played the piano—and he would dearly love to have music in his house. Although he supposed it might be longer than a year before a student learned anything.

In any event, she now had her piano. He was interested to see if she'd made progress on finding tutors. If not, he'd ask Nora Fanshawe about painting masters, no doubt she'd be able to recommend somebody.

Smith didn't want Moira to find living in his house lonely or tedious, as Charles had done. If Moira maintained interests and hobbies of her own, perhaps she would be content when the attraction between them began to cool, which it would. His amours always cooled, and then he moved on.

Maybe a day would come when he no longer followed his urges, but until then, he would take lovers if and when he wanted.

"You're like a dog that is constantly in rut, Smith!"

Constantly seemed a bit of an exaggeration, but Charles had had a point.

When Charles had signed the contract, he'd insisted he was delighted with Smith's rules and Smith had stupidly believed the other man. Or perhaps Smith had *wishfully* believed him.

But Charles had become more agitated each time Smith had exercised his contractual rights. It was a vicious circle: the more Charles complained, the more Smith wanted to get away from him.

As furious as he'd been at Charles, he'd been even angrier at himself; he was old enough to know better.

The situation had deteriorated, until they'd not shared a bed for days and days. Their final weeks together had been unbearable.

"Why am I not enough for you? What do you want?" Charles had screamed before he'd given Smith an ultimatum that could only end one way.

"Prince Vladimir Zhukov has asked me to accompany him to Russia. If you can't make the changes I need, I'm going to accept his offer—regardless of your damned contract."

Smith had released him from their agreement on the spot.

Rather than be grateful, Charles had gone mad, throwing things, breaking things, asking over and over, "What will it take to make you contented—*happy*?"

It had been pointless to explain to Charles—yet again—that Smith had, before the incessant fighting, been happy living with him.

Yes, he'd shared his body with others, but his heart—for lack of a better word—he'd reserved for Charles, the only person who Smith had been *intimate* with. Without intimacy, sex meant nothing to him. The distinction was a critical one to him, but Charles had just dismissed it as self-serving.

Perhaps it was, but that made it no less true.

When Charles had snatched up a letter opener and attacked the portrait Nora had painted of the two of them, Smith had known that Charles had to leave.

The last he'd seen of the younger man was his forlorn, tear-streaked face when Smith had left him in a suite he'd paid for at the Clarendon, the same hotel where Prince Vladimir and his entourage had been staying.

Smith scowled at the unpleasant image and added a pair of five-pound weights to his ankles before he began the last of his sets, which was fifty lifts. He dried his hands on a towel and then jumped to catch the metal bar that hung several feet above his head.

A lift, in his opinion, was an almost perfect exercise. Muscles from his neck to hips bunched and flexed, the blood engorging and defining every part of his body, not just his prick.

He stared at his reflection, making sure to maintain perfect form with each lift, and counted silently in his head.

One, two.

It bothered him that thinking about Moira always seemed to lead to thoughts of Charles—as if he were doomed to unhappiness when it came to his lovers.

Three.

It wasn't that Moira or Charles were anything alike, quite the reverse, in fact.

Four, five.

Besides, he and Moira had entered into this agreement for entirely different reasons than the one he'd had with Charles. This was a union for a specific purpose: a baby. Hopefully she would become pregnant and have a child they could share, love, and raise like rational adults. Like a family.

Smith smiled at the image. His body, which had been flagging, enjoyed a surge of energy.

Six, seven.

He thought about tomorrow and Moira and the things he would do to her.

Eight, nine, ten, eleven, twelve, thirteen, fourteen.

A pearly stream dripped from his prick as he imagined Moira naked before him on her knees, lips stretched around his cock.

"*Christ*," he grunted, as the vision struck him with the force of a locomotive.

Fifteen, sixteen, seventeen.

Smith's arms strained, his body shaking with effort.

Eighteen, nineteen, twenty.

He grunted loudly and hoarsely, his biceps and abdomen on fire. A week away from his gymnasium had affected him more than he'd believed.

A soft knock startled him and he looked away from his reflection toward the door. Not the one from his chambers, but the one that led to the corridor. Only one person would knock on that door.

Smith's gaze returned to his reflection, his eyes briefly flickering over the weeping slit of his cock before he did his next lift.

Twenty-one.

So, Moira had come to him, had she? How… intriguing.

And revitalizing. Smith counted off three more lifts in rapid succession.

Twenty-two, twenty-three, twenty-four.

He smiled, lowered himself slowly, and then called out, "Come in."

***

Moira didn't want to knock on Smith's gymnasium door at one o'clock in the morning, but neither did she want to engage in yet another argument with her faux *music tutor*, Mr. Victor Turnbull tomorrow.

Especially not when she'd been bickering with him for what felt like years.

Turnbull knew nothing about the piano and she doubted his name was either Victor or Turnbull.

What she *did* know about the man was that Marie had sent him.

"She wanted me to tell you that you have less than six weeks," Turnbull had informed her the first time he'd visited.

"Why? What happens in six weeks?" she'd retorted.

"I don't ask questions; I just relay the messages."

Moira hadn't been able to blame him for that; it was Marie who should have sent instructions by letter rather than passing such information along to a stranger—not to mention such a stupid, arrogant one.

"It will be easy enough to change the day or time of your lessons when the time comes, but *you* need to conceive of a way to get your brother and whoever he's bringing with him into the house," Turnbull had ordered, as if Moira were some sort of servant—and a dumb one, at that.

It had amused—but not surprised—her that Turnbull didn't know who Etienne's accomplice would be. Marie had kept the *Comte*'s identity a secret to protect him, and only him. If this stupid kidnapping scheme were to fall apart, her father would not be among those who were arrested.

"Do you think I haven't already been trying to work that out?" Moira had snapped at Turnbull, playing scales on the piano while they spoke. Fortunately, one of them knew something about music. Although Marie had spent money to procure a false identity for Turnbull, the man didn't know a piano from a porpoise.

"So, what have you come up with, girlie?" Turnbull had persisted.

"Nothing yet. You know the guards never leave a door unattended—what am I to do? Shoot them?"

Not only were there always four men on guard—two at the front and two at the back—but they were armed and prepared to maim, or even kill, to protect their employer.

"Just do whatever it takes, girlie," Turnbull had shot back. "We need to fix a date and time if I'm to get everything else in order."

Girlie.

"Smith has been in Liverpool for almost a week. How am I to set a date if he isn't even here?"

"Isn't it your *job* to keep him here? Open those thighs—or that mouth—and give him a good reason to stay."

Moira had wanted to punch him in the face so badly she'd had to bite her tongue until it bled to stifle her rage.

Instead of smashing a poker over his head, as he deserved, she had taken every opportunity to introduce him to the other servants—and the guards—hoping that making him familiar would help to make him appear harmless.

He was certainly *useless*, as far as Moira was concerned, but she doubted that would help convince Smith's guards to dismiss him as a threat.

Even when Smith was away, the guards were on the doors. They'd taken Victor's name and address, as they did with every visitor, and she *knew* that somebody had investigated the false background Marie had paid for.

All she could hope was that her mother had fashioned a fake identity for Victor that was better than the one she'd devised for Moira.

Gambling debts driving her from Marseilles! Moira didn't even play cards—although she was quickly teaching herself since Smith had said that he wanted to take her to his bloody gambling club when he returned from Liverpool.

And now he was back, but he'd not come to her first. No, he'd apparently missed his gymnasium more than her.

Which meant Moira needed to go to him.

Victor's last words to her today had been, "*Keep* him in town or I'll be telling the boss who is to blame for any delays."

And so here she was, knocking on what was widely considered to be Smith's private sanctum.

Ugh. Moira felt like an idiot for questioning her actions, but she didn't know Smith or his habits well enough to guess if what she was about to do was a good idea.

She hadn't even known he was coming home today. It had been Luke who'd delivered the message before dinner.

Indeed, Smith had not contacted her at all this past week.

Left alone with nobody but Victor and her new drawing master—Victor's idiot nephew, Dennis, who knew nothing at all about art—Moira had found herself increasingly drawn to her handsome, pleasant, and unerringly helpful personal servant.

Luke was also as difficult for her to read as a book written in Chinese.

As accustomed to sexual activity and multiple partners as she was, Moira had still been disconcerted the night she'd realized that Luke had patiently waited with a tea tray while Smith had fucked her.

Marie had always cautioned her children to behave with decorum around servants. *Finding a decent servant is much more difficult than finding a wealthy protector*, she'd said more than once.

Clearly things were different in Smith's household because he'd appeared unsurprised by Luke's presence, merely wiping the sweat from his face before directing the placement of the tray.

"Sherry? What an excellent idea, Luke," Smith had praised, smiling up at his servant and seemingly not caring that he was sweaty, naked, and liberally smeared with both their juices.

"Thank you, sir." Luke had been unperturbed, serving them without so much as a flicker of an eyelid.

Once Luke had gone, Smith had turned to her, his smile sly and his eyes hooded. "I hope you did not mind that Luke observed us." He fed her a bite of shortbread, and then held the wine to her lips. "Good?"

Moira had swallowed obediently and said, "Delicious. And no, I don't mind."

His smile had grown. "Excellent."

She *had* wondered what Luke thought of her.

You're dithering, Moira. Knock on the door and get it over with.

She sucked in a deep breath and knocked.

"Come in," Smith called out after a pause.

She opened the door and then froze.

Smith was naked, hanging from a bar, his body taut and sheened from exertion.

He was also erect.

Moira's face scalded, as if she'd lifted the lid off a furiously boiling pot.

"Hello, Moira. I'm almost finished here," he said in a strained voice.

She swallowed. Good Lord, he was… Well, she didn't quite have a word to describe him. She'd seen him naked many times, of course, but never quite so… completely.

"Close the door and have a seat." He lifted himself slowly and deliberately, the action causing a fascinating cascade effect on the muscles of his arms, chest, and abdomen.

Moira gracelessly dropped into one of the two chairs that were on either side of the door, unable to look away. She'd been correct about people paying to watch him; he was mesmerizing.

Her mouth was producing more saliva than she needed for a week and her thighs were slick. She'd not had an orgasm since the last time she'd been with him. Indeed, those had been his last words to her.

"No playing with your pretty pussy while I'm gone," he'd ordered, his words playful, but his eyes hard. "This is my cunt—mine alone."

There was no way he would have known if her fingers had slid between her swollen lips after Luke had shaved her—how could he? — but she had obeyed his order just in case.

Moira saw he wasn't looking at her but staring straight ahead at his reflection. Their eyes met in the glass and his lips curved, his body moving smoothly and regularly, just like a well-oiled machine.

"I like your eyes on me," he said.

Moira knew he did; he was exceedingly vain.

It bothered her how attractive she found him, not only his body, but his personality, which was unique in her experience. Moira had been around wealthy, powerful men all her life and they had, almost without fail, been arrogant and rude. Not just to her, but to anyone subordinate to them. Yet Smith was one of the most courteous and polite people she'd ever met.

Thus far she had seen no sign of the cruel, brutal, and inhuman man her parents had described.

Although she had no proof—except her parents' warnings—she sensed that something dark and dangerous lurked beneath his polite façade. Something that acted like a siren's call on her.

Who was Maximus Nicolaides, really, and what was he to her mother and the *Comte*?

But now was hardly the time for such distracting questions, so she pushed them to the back of her mind and stared at the man she'd come to seduce, manipulate, and betray.

The last few lifts were agony and she could see his body attempt to rebel and slip his control. But he triumphed over his fatigue and held the last lift longer than the others before dropping lightly to the floor.

He took a clean cloth from a pile and wiped his brow, face, and hands before tossing it into a nearby basket and turning to her, hands fisted on his hips, eyebrows raised.

Moira acted without thinking, sliding from the chair to her knees and hands and crawling toward him, closing the short distance between them.

She sat back on her heels, slowly running her gaze up the hard, slick length of his body until she met his eyes. His lips had thinned, giving him an uncharacteristically stern look, and he stared down at her from beneath heavily lidded eyes like a conqueror surveying a defeated foe.

Or a god eyeing a supplicant.

Moira closed her hand around his thick cock and lowered her mouth.

He sighed as his fingers combed through her short hair. "I've missed you, Moira."

She swallowed convulsively at the praise and his hips gave an involuntary buck. Her eyes watered at the depth of penetration and every muscle in her body strained to pull away, panic fluttering in her chest.

"So good." His fingers drifted over her temple, her cheeks, and settled on her lips as she slowly pulled off, inhaling through her nose and filling her lungs to near bursting.

He pushed a finger in beside his cock, stretching her lips painfully thin.

"Mmm." It was a low, animal hum, and he pulsed in and out of her a few times before removing his wet finger and using it to trace her stretched lips. "Touch me," he ordered softly.

Moira ran her hands up his thighs, not stopping until she reached the sharp bones of his pelvis and the thin skin that separated his hip from the V of his lower abdomen.

When she dug her fingers into the ridges—or tried—he gave a low chuckle and tilted his hips, pushing himself deeper and sliding his hands around the back of her head, gently pulling her down onto his cock

"Make it last." The words were a low growl that sank deep in her belly.

Moira opened herself to him, tonguing the pulsing vein along the underside of his shaft, worshiping every inch, reveling in the noises he made as she worked him.

She brought him to the brink slowly, and then again, and again, until his callused fingers fisted her hair and he fucked her with punishing thrusts.

"Take it," he growled, his eyes burning into hers as he flooded her throat with jet after jet of hot seed.

Moira milked him gently until he shivered and pulled away.

He gave a groan of contentment. "Good girl." He stroked her hair and she rested her head on his hip, preening at his touch and praise, her body empty and aching to have him inside her.

All too soon, he roused himself and helped her to her feet.

He looked down at her with drowsy eyes and kissed her, tonguing deeply before pulling away with a smirk. "I love the taste of myself in your mouth."

Moira pushed her hips against him.

He chuckled at her shameless begging. "Strip for me."

Moira's fingers trembled as she tugged at the sash that held her rose-colored dressing gown closed.

Once she'd deposited the dressing gown and nightgown over the chair he said, "Turn, spread your feet, and bend over; rest your arms on the back of the chair."

Moira's skin prickled with awareness as she presented herself to him.

His hands, warm and rough, spread her cheeks and hot breath bathed her cleft. "So wet," he muttered, his thumb sliding between her slick, swollen lips while another finger flicked her sensitive bud. He played with her, spreading her, kneading her, teasing her, until she felt like crawling out of her own skin.

"Quit squirming," he ordered, but she heard his amusement.

And then his hot wet tongue probed her entrance and he fucked into her with lazy strokes, thumbing her clitoris while his other hand used her body's moisture to slick and probe her arse. Suddenly it felt like there were hands and tongues everywhere, stroking her bud, caressing her slick folds, and penetrating both holes.

Moira came fast and hard, her loud cry echoing in the cavernous room.

Her orgasm had barely faded when Smith's deeply satisfied *mmmm* brought her back to reality. He slid his hands around her, cupped her breasts, and gently raised her upright.

"Better?" he asked, trailing kisses over her shoulder, his lips soft on the scars.

Moira could only nod and press back against him.

He released one of her breasts and traced the mostly healed wounds on her back. "Do you have any pain?"

"They've not hurt for a while. Every evening Luke rubs a salve on them." Which left her just as frustrated with arousal as his shaving.

Moira paused and then asked, even though she didn't want to, "How do they look?"

"Like you've been in a war and survived."

"They are ugly." It wasn't a question.

"They are part of you, so that makes them beautiful." The feel of his lips tracing a scar made her throat prickle and she had to swallow to hold down a sudden sob.

But she mustn't have been entirely successful hiding her emotions.

"Shhh," he whispered, kissing the sensitive shell of her ear, the gentle touches undoing her more than Brown's brutal beating had.

Nobody had ever touched her with such tenderness. Certainly neither of her parents, although her sister Sandrine had done what she could—what their mother had allowed.

But Moira didn't want his kindness; the only thing she wanted from him was Sandrine, and that was something he could never, ever give her.

That's a lie, Moira, and you know it—you want far more from Smith.

You want everything.

Moira squeezed her eyes shut at the traitorous thought and pushed back against him, the comforting shelter of his hot, muscular chest against her back only making her feel more miserable and guilty.

"I need to be whipped," she whispered. "Please."

His body tightened at her words, but he merely held her.

"I want it, Smith." A bubble of hysteria rose inside her. "Please, I need to be—"

Moira bit her lip just in time to catch the last part of that sentence: *punished for what I'm going to do to you.*

He squeezed her gently. "I'll give you what you need."

Moira almost wept with relief. "Thank you."

"But not tonight."

Moira blinked. "Er, I'm sorry?"

Smith chuckled, kissed her again, and then turned her around and grinned down at her, lust flaming in his dark eyes. He took her nipples between his thumbs and forefingers, pinching them hard enough to make her eyes water. "I'm afraid I couldn't do you justice in the state I'm in tonight, darling."

"But... *when?*" she whined.

"Soon," he promised. "Soon I'll whip these pretty tits until you come."

Moira moaned. His words alone were almost enough to make her climax, and she pressed into his palms, her breasts tight and aching. "Please."

Instead of easing her need, he released her and kissed her lightly on the nose. "Good night, my Moira."

And then he strode toward the door to his bedchamber and disappeared into his room, leaving her alone.

Moira stared in slack-jawed shock; for the first time in her life, a client had left *her* wanting more.

Chapter 15

Moira scarcely had a moment alone with Smith until three nights later, when they met in his study before dinner.

It was the first time that he would be taking Moira out, and they would be joining his friends at a restaurant. He'd ordered a new gown for the occasion even though Moira already had dozens that she'd never worn.

Like all the other clothing he'd chosen for her, it was romantic and feminine and there were no crinolines, cages, or bustles; just a corset, chemise, and petticoat of silk beneath a flowing velvet gown that was reminiscent of a style depicted in medieval paintings.

Her armoires were full of such garments, which had come out of the dress reform movement and were designed to promote not only more comfortable clothing, but also to prevent the countless fires caused each year by huge cages and bustles knocking into candles and lamps.

"I'm thrilled my house won't burn to the ground, but I must admit that I like it because it affords easier access to your body," Smith had admitted as he'd made her model the ice blue velvet ensemble—complete with a full-length, fur-lined cloak—right before they'd left the house.

"Indeed, you look too delicious not to fuck." He'd then proceeded to bend her over his spotless desk and work two orgasms out of Moira before emptying himself inside her.

"I think not," he'd said when she had asked for a moment to clean herself before they left the house. "I want to imagine you with my spend running down your thighs all night while we sit in public, surrounded by people."

And that is exactly what was happening right now.

Moira shifted in her seat, her thighs sliding against one another, as she sat at the table with Smith and his friends.

It surprised her that such a man—too untrusting to share even his real name—would have friends, but Smith appeared more relaxed than she'd ever seen him.

There were two couples at the table, a huge, bear-like man and his tiny wife—Edward and Nora Fanshawe—and a towering gentleman named Stephen Chatham and his tall, thin companion, whom he'd introduced as Josephine Leather.

Moira knew this was the same Leather who'd been Smith's former valet—and, if her brother was right—also his love.

A third couple, the Earl and Countess of Taunton, had not yet arrived.

"Gideon and Alys will be along shortly," Nora Fanshawe said, and then grimaced. "I'm afraid I made them late."

"How did you make them late?" Smith asked.

"They brought over their son to meet Amelia and Nora wanted me to steal him," Edward explained dryly, sipping the wine the sommelier had brought and nodding to the hovering man.

"Amelia is our daughter," Nora said to Moira. "Edward would not participate in the abduction, so young Gideon escaped our clutches."

Moira was charmed by the other woman's playfulness.

Smith clucked his tongue. "What? No kidnapping, Edward? Since when did you become so law-abiding?"

Edward snorted.

Nora ignored their teasing. "The good news is that Alys promised we could borrow young Gideon for an entire evening this coming Friday."

"Ah, yes," Smith said. "That is the evening they are going to dine with the Queen, is it not?"

"Gideon is so nervous it is adorable," Nora said.

Edward rolled his eyes.

"Women think that everything about Gideon is adorable," Smith explained to Moira. "I daresay you will fall under the same spell when you meet him."

Moira was intrigued. The Earl of Taunton had frequented Bernina's before he'd married and she'd heard plenty of stories about his voracious sexual appetite and outrageous behavior.

"What sort of an arse names his child the same name as himself?" Edward demanded.

"Gideon's sort," Stephen Chatham said in a soft voice, which bore a slight Yorkshire burr. "I fully expect him to name any future sons the same thing."

"And likely his daughters, too," Smith added.

Everyone chuckled.

"You three are terrible," Nora scolded. "Gideon is a lovely name and it suits the boy."

"It's a perfectly fine name," Edward said with some exasperation, "but it leads to confusion when there are two Gideons in the room."

"Especially when both of them act like infants," Smith said.

The others chortled, even Nora, although she gave Smith a chiding look. "You shouldn't be so awful to poor Gideon."

"You see how she defends him?" Edward demanded. "Truly, Gideon can no wrong in the eyes of any woman, even an intelligent one like my wife."

"How are you enjoying fatherhood thus far, Edward?" Smith asked, wisely changing the subject.

Edward exchanged a quick look with his wife, so much love passing between them that it gave Moira a sharp pang of envy.

"Amelia is a handful," he admitted. "The nurse we engaged said two years is often called the terrible twos."

"Which can then become the terrible threes," Nora added.

They all laughed.

"She is a bundle of energy and into everything," Edward said proudly.

"I'm just relieved that she doesn't cry or have nightmares. She lost her parents five months ago," Nora explained, looking from Moira to Josephine. "They both died in a carriage accident. Fortunately, Amelia wasn't with them."

"Where has she been living since that time?" Josephine asked.

Moira felt Smith's body jolt slightly at the sound of the other woman's voice.

When she turned to him, she was astonished to see that his cheeks bore evidence of a slight blush.

He met her curious look with a bland smile, but Moira was not fooled. For a man who showed almost nothing of what he was feeling, a slight tensing and faint blush were the equivalent of shouting out emotions from anyone else.

Moira suspected he still bore deep feelings for his former valet.

She studied Josephine from beneath her lashes, fascinated by this woman who had attracted the attention—and love, apparently—of two wealthy and powerful men.

She was slender to the point of gauntness and possessed features that were, at best, average. The most arresting thing about her was her thick spectacles, which grossly magnified her slate gray eyes.

Moira knew the simple but elegant brown chignon must be a wig since Leather still served as Chatham's valet.

Her brother Robert—who'd been a reserved and difficult man to know, himself—had been intrigued by the enigmatic woman.

"I tell you, Moira, when Leather is dressed in her black suit you would never guess that she is a woman," he'd marveled. "She valets Chatham during the day and then warms his bed at night, just as she did for Smith during those few months that she lived with him."

A light touch on Moira's shoulder made her look up.

"Where did you go?" Smith asked softly. "You looked miles away."

"I'm just enjoying being out," she said, realizing after she'd said it that she meant it.

His hand slid up her thigh and Moira glanced around at the others.

"None of them can see what I'm doing," he said, cupping her mound. He stroked a finger between her lips, the fine fabric of her chemise snagging on the bristly hairs of her sex, making her squirm.

Moira shifted in her seat, wishing that Smith had allowed her regular shaving that day.

"Hmmm, that must be uncomfortable," he whispered, petting her mound harder and intensifying the discomfort.

"Why do I feel like that was the point?" she murmured tartly, earning a grin from him.

"As much as I enjoy your suffering, that was not the reason for the delay."

"What was?"

"I'd hoped to have time to shave you myself—but business matters conspired against me these past few days."

"You want to shave me?"

"Why should Luke get all the pleasure?" he retorted.

Moira wondered if Luke had been telling their employer how aroused she became when he groomed her.

"Would you like that, Moira? If I were your servant?" he asked.

Although he was barely speaking above a whisper Moira felt that everyone around them must know the shocking things he was saying—and guess the way her body responded: like a well-trained pet—but a quick look around showed nobody was paying them any mind.

"Yes," she whispered. "I would like that." In fact, it annoyed her how much it stimulated her to imagine Smith tending her as closely as Luke did.

"Then you shall have it." He leaned even closer. "I don't think I told you how charming you look this evening."

That made her smile. "You did. Several times."

"Ah, have I been gushing?"

Moira smiled. "Hardly that, but you have been most… generous."

"I want to be generous with you." His expression was suddenly solemn. "I want to give you everything you desire."

Moira swallowed, uncomfortable beneath his probing gaze.

"Nora has a showing at a gallery in ten days—would you care to go?" he asked when she remained tongue-tied.

"I'd love to."

"Then I will tell Nora to add our names to the guest list."

They turned back to the conversation to find Nora saying something to Josephine while their men stared at them in silent adoration.

"Quite nauseating, isn't it?" Smith teased, following her gaze. "Wait until you meet Gideon and Alys, he is just as smitten."

"You find that nauseating?"

"No. I'm merely envious."

Before Moira could respond, not that she knew what to say, the Earl and Countess of Taunton arrived at the restaurant, turning heads as the maître d' escorted them to the table.

Everything she'd heard about Gideon Banks was true; he was quite the loveliest man she'd ever seen, a golden haired, blue eyed god.

His wife, although very pretty, could not hold a candle to her magnificent husband and the pair put Moira in mind of those species of bird—like peafowl—where the male eclipsed his humbler mate.

As Smith and the other four greeted the newcomers Moira couldn't help envying how much they seemed to like one another—how comfortable and happy they all appeared, even though they were each, in their own way, social outcasts.

"Moira," Smith said. "Allow me to introduce the Earl and Countess of Taunton. Gideon, Alys, this is Miss Moira Dunsmuir."

The countess gave her a welcoming smile that turned her merely pretty face into a beautiful one. "Please, call me Alys."

The earl visually stripped off Moira's clothing with his angelic blue eyes and she would have known without being told that he was a devil who only resembled an angel.

"Charmed, Miss Dunsmuir. You may call me Gideon, although I far prefer *my lord*."

Moira laughed.

"Unfortunately, he's not jesting, Moira," Edward said.

The dinner was noisy, amusing, and over far too quickly.

As Moira watched the others, she knew a moment of intense yearning. What would it be like if she could truly be a part of this intimate, fascinating group?

She enjoyed the fantasy for a long, pleasurable moment.

But then she turned to the man who made such a future impossible.

Smith, who'd been arguing with Nora about something painting-related, caught her glance and raised his eyebrows inquiringly.

Moira stared at him a second too long, grappling with the painful memory of what this man had done to her sister.

He killed Sandrine.

The improbable fantasy future she'd just created dissolved in the blink of an eye.

She had only one future, and it didn't include Smith.

At least not for much longer.

Chapter 16

The footman hadn't even shut the carriage door before Smith pulled Moira onto his lap. "Did you enjoy your evening?"

"Very much," she said honestly.

"I was hard all night from looking at you."

"Were you?" she asked with an arch, teasing look. She'd made it her business to stroke his groin when he was least expecting it, keeping him hard in case he should flag. Which he hadn't. She'd told herself it was just part of her duty as his mistress, but the truth was she enjoyed being able to touch such a man—such a body—whenever she chose.

"You were a cruel tease and you know it." He bit her neck hard enough to make her whimper. "And you deserve to be fucked. Hard." He claimed her mouth violently, consuming her with his raw need.

When he released her, he flipped up her skirts and petticoat and then used his thighs to force her knees apart. His cool fingers pushed between her swollen lips and he sucked in a breath. "You're drenched for me." He thrust a finger inside her, fucking her slowly. "I am saddened you are not enceinte."

Moira's courses had come while he'd been away on his business trip. "So am I," she said, not sure if she was lying, or not.

Smith had taken her so often—and then kept her with him afterward—that she'd rarely been able to take measures to prevent conception so she'd been alternately surprised, devastated, and relieved when she'd woken to blood on her sheets.

Moira hadn't mentioned the matter to him so Luke must have reported to him, something she'd assumed he was doing given Smith's mania for control.

"While it is a shame it just means we shall have to try twice as hard this month," he said.

"Twice as hard might kill me."

"Hmmm. What is the saying? *That which doesn't kill you, only makes you stronger?*"

She laughed. "I shall be extremely strong soon."

He lowered his mouth over her throat and sucked so hard she knew there would be a mark.

When he released her, his amusement had fled and his face was hard with lust. "I'm going to pump you full of my seed day and night, Moira."

Her body clenched at his heated look and crude words.

He smiled when she tightened around his fingers. "Do you find the image of yourself full and rounded with my child arousing?" he asked, easing in a third finger. "I've discovered it's enough to get me hard no matter where I am, or who I'm with."

Moira grunted when he splayed his fingers, stretching her, and then smirked. "Anywhere?" she teased. "And with anyone? I imagine that could be quite… embarrassing."

He barked a laugh. "You little witch, you're damned right it can be embarrassing."

She couldn't help grinning as she imagined him meeting with other titans of industry, his trousers grotesquely tented.

"I have never understood the predilection to hide away a pregnant woman. I cannot wait to take you out and show you off as the physical manifestation of my virility." He laughed at the obnoxious words and Moira couldn't help joining him.

"That is so masculine and arrogant, is it not?"

"Very," she agreed, privately liking the image more than she ought.

He leaned back and unbuttoned his trousers. "No time like the present to begin." He positioned his wetly gleaming crown against her entrance and thrust hard, taking her deeply enough to make her wince.

"Does that give you a bit of an ache?" he mocked, his thumb working her throbbing bud while he fucked her hard enough to make her dizzy. "Tell me what it feels like."

"It is the most intense combination of pleasure and pain—and it hurts—" the last word was a raw gasp as he hilted himself and then kept her full. Moira struggled to take enough air into her lungs, bright spangles obscuring her vision. "I need—"

"I know what you need," he rasped, his hips commencing to drum. "When we get home, I'm going to whip your tits."

His words pushed her over the edge and Smith gave a triumphant shout and buried himself to the hilt, his thick shaft jerking and spasming inside her.

***

Smith sprawled out on his carriage seat, watching Moira straighten her clothing. "Luke is quite a whip hand. I hired him from the Briar Palace."

"Yes, that is what he said."

"I'm going to have him prepare you for tonight. Would you like that?"

Her hands trembled slightly as she smoothed down her gown. "Yes. I would like that," she finally said, meeting his gaze, her expression unreadable. "A great deal."

Smith grinned. His Moira: what went on inside her head? Whatever it was, she wasn't sharing. At least not with him.

"Oh? What else would like him to do to you?" he asked.

"Anything you wish," she said without hesitation.

Well, well, well. What a lovely evening awaited them.

Smith summoned Luke immediately when they arrived at the house.

"Undress your mistress and then accompany her to my chambers."

Luke's brow furrowed only slightly, but he nodded and the two left.

Up in his room Smith had Knox undress him, pour him a drink, and then he dismissed him for the evening. He settled in a chair before the fire, and reflected on the pleasant evening.

Moira had genuinely enjoyed herself—he'd seen that much in her eyes—and his business partners and their spouses had liked her. It had been an excellent evening. He'd suffered a brief pang seeing Jojo with Chatham, but it had passed. She was happy and that pleased him. Smith wouldn't have wanted to keep her if she'd wanted to be with somebody else.

The door to his chambers opened and Moira entered, wearing an emerald-green dressing gown, Luke on her heels.

One look at Luke's blank face told Smith the man hadn't guessed yet at his role this evening.

"I want you to strip and bind Moira for me, Luke—in the usual way."

142

A jolt of some emotion—surprise? Anticipation?—ran through his big body, but he simply nodded. "Yes, sir."

Smith stretched out in his chair and stroked himself as he enjoyed the mouthwatering spectacle of his servant preparing his mistress for his use.

They made an attractive pair—Luke towering and bulging with muscle and Moira so slight and fairylike. The juxtaposition of Moira naked and Luke fully clothed in his blacks was likewise a sensual contrast.

Smith savored the way Luke's massive but gentle hands cuffed, strapped, and restrained Moira, until all she could move was her head.

He was a very lucky man—he knew that. He might have searched London for years and never found two treasures like the gorgeous pair before him.

When Luke held up the gag, Smith shook his head. "Not tonight. Nor the blindfold," he said, smirking at the relief on Moira's face and filing her reaction away for future use.

"Raise her arms a bit more," he instructed Luke. "Yes, that's good," he said, once the straps were pulled tautly enough to stretch her just to the point of discomfort.

Smith put down his drink and stood to better inspect her. She was slender, but her muscle tone was sleek and hard. The scars on her shoulders and back sent a bolt of fury through him each and every time he saw them.

He had counted them—the ones he could see—and Onions would receive triple that number when Smith finally got his hands on the man. Ninety-nine strokes would be a great deal for a body to bear. It might kill him.

He turned away from that satisfying thought and looked up at Luke, "Fetch the lighter of the German floggers and a leather thong." He went closer to Moira while Luke left the room, running a light hand over her prominent, delicate ribs.

She was breathing raggedly, her lips slack and parted, the expression in her eyes one he recognized intimately: she was slipping away from herself—from her cares—already.

Lucky, lucky Moira.

Smith ran a finger through her wet, swollen folds and groaned at the feel of their mingled juices. He lifted the finger to her lips and she sucked him into her mouth, her eyes hazed, lids drooping.

Smith felt Luke approach and removed his finger with reluctance, tugging the sash on his robe and shrugging out of it before taking the flogger from Luke.

He spread his feet and stared at Moira while Luke dropped to his knees and wrapped the leather thong around his cock and balls.

Her sea green irises had receded like an outgoing tide, leaving only twin black pools of desire. She moistened her lower lip with the tip of her pink tongue, the gesture making his cock jerk in Luke's firm grip.

Her slack, lazy expression shifted into a smug smile—a smile that told him she was perfectly aware of the power she had over him, and that she merely needed to flex to make him pant and beg like a dog.

Smith chuckled. Fuck, but she was delicious.

He tore his gaze away from Moira and looked down, wondering why Luke was still on his knees.

The huge man stared up at him, his eyes burning with raw yearning and some other emotion—

Good Lord!

Smith gaped in stupefaction at the familiar face—a face now wearing a very unfamiliar expression. Was that… *love?*

Luke's bland mask slid into place and he stood.

But it was too late: Smith had seen the truth and Moira had been right.

Bloody hell.

Playful sexual humiliation was one thing, but taunting somebody who'd allowed their emotions to become involved? That was torture.

"You may go," Smith said coolly, more displeased with himself for his misjudgment than with Luke for his disastrous lapse.

Smith looked up to find Moira watching, always watching.

Unlike the man he'd just dismissed, *her* mask never slipped. Maybe that was because it wasn't one. Maybe she really felt no more for Smith than what she showed him: occasional amusement and desire.

Rather than bother him, that possibility only made him want to disturb her placid surface more than ever.

The perverseness of his reactions did not elude him. He had just dismissed a man who might very well love him while keeping a woman who might not even *like* him.

Smith snorted and hefted the whip. "Ready, darling?"

***

Moira had been flogged many times, both by skilled and unskilled hands, but Smith—not surprisingly—was different than anyone who'd come before.

She had wondered if she'd ever enjoy the experience again after what Mr. Brown had done to her. She needn't have worried.

What Brown had done was brutal abuse.

What Smith did to her was… well, it was sublime.

In the past, the whippings had been for her clients' pleasure. Smith being Smith—which was to say singular—the experience was all for her.

First, he took the time to bring her along almost agonizingly slowly, his strokes like caresses… until they weren't, until her nipples and the thin skin of her breasts were on fire.

Until she was floating above her body, watching the scene with a sort of dreamy detachment.

Then he tossed aside the flogger and dropped to his haunches in front of her spread sex, using his tongue as deliberately as he'd just used the whip, licking and sucking and teasing until she came back to herself with a vengeance, occupying every inch of her body with an awareness that was almost painful.

And still he teased.

"Please," she gasped, when he'd brought her to the brink yet again and then left her there.

His dark eyes crinkled at the corners and his lips closed around her bud and tugged, stretching her almost painfully before releasing her.

"Mmmm, I do like it when you beg."

"*Smith.*"

He chuckled, lowered his skillful lips and tongue, and proceeded to give her what she'd begged for—three times in rapid, euphoric succession.

She was still reeling from her third climax—too sensitive for anything more—when Smith sat back on his heels, unfastened the thong that bound him, and closed his eyes as he gently stroked his freed cock.

He was, quite honestly, the most erotic sight Moira had ever seen: his face covered with her juices, his lips swollen, and that ridiculously big prick in his slim, elegant hand.

"I love watching you," she said hoarsely, the words escaping before she knew what she'd said.

His heavy lids lifted and a lazy smile curved his lips. "You please me, Moira," he said, the simple praise strangely intoxicating.

She almost retorted: *not as often as you please me* but was—thankfully—coming out of her sex-induced stupor.

Smith stood and then disappeared behind her. A moment later she felt oil drizzle onto her lower back. He used his hands to coat her cheeks, kneading the muscle with brutal fingers, until only her bonds held her upright.

He used one, two, and finally three fingers to stretch her, opening her gradually and gently while his other hand reached around her to the front of her body, his thumb pressing against her pulsing core.

"Come once more for me, darling," he whispered, his magical hands working her front and back, driving her toward bliss yet again.

She was still floating when he positioned his cock at her well stretched hole and entered her slowly, deeply, until she felt sure he must be encountering some vital organ.

He licked and bit and sucked her neck hard enough to mark her, his body shaking with the effort of entering her so carefully.

"So good, Moira." His words were slurred, as if he'd been drinking for the prior hour rather than servicing her every need.

He'd taken great care preparing her, but it still hurt, and tears squeezed from beneath her eyelids as he held her full, his chest pressed against her back, the pounding of his heart thudding through her body. Never had she felt so … enveloped, so possessed, so *owned*.

And then he began to move, giving her every inch with each stroke, faster, deeper, harder with each thrust, until the slap of skin on skin and grunting filled the room.

"Going to fuck you *hard*," he warned right before he clamped onto her neck with his teeth, biting hard enough to break the skin as his hips beat against her, driving his cock painfully deep with each thrust, like an axe splitting her in two.

"Mine," he whispered in her ear with a ragged breath, and then filled her with lash after lash of scalding heat, their bodies pulsing as one. "I own you."

Moira was beginning to fear that he was right.

Chapter 17

Every day Luke expected the summons from his master, word that his services were no longer needed. He both dreaded it and yearned for it; at least if Mr. Smith dismissed him, he could stop dreading the inevitable.

The night he'd foolishly exposed his love for Smith had been one of the lowest points in his life. The look on Smith's face: disdain, disgust, and disappointment, had gutted him. All he'd wanted to do was crawl into a hole and lick his wounds.

But that had not been an option.

Instead, he'd needed to be ready to serve Miss Moira once she left Smith's room—whenever that happened to be. Just because Luke was bleeding inside did not mean he could ignore his work.

Indeed, the only thing that had offered any solace in the days after that awful night was work.

Unfortunately, his mistress was tidy and clean and made almost no mess for him to tend to. He knew she was only trying to be considerate; doubtless she could not imagine a person so pathetic that they needed to serve in order to feel useful.

Luke was the only servant who took care of Miss Moira's room, just like nobody but Knox was allowed to clean Smith's chambers. Most valets or ladies' maids would revolt at such demeaning work, but Luke preferred doing the cleaning himself rather than tolerating the presence of other servants in his domain.

On the same evening that Luke had exposed his feelings to Smith, he'd stripped off his coats, donned his heavy apron and gloves, and had cleaned Miss Moira's already clean rooms rather than sit and stare at a blank wall or try to socialize in the kitchen.

He knew why he chose to clean her boudoir that night. It was because it was nearest his master's room and he'd been able to hear every yell and grunt as he'd crawled around the already gleaming marble floor, scrubbing the cracks and corners with a small brush.

Luke's behavior shamed him, but he simply could not stop himself.

Later that night—morose and miserable—he'd gone to David's room for the first time in weeks.

"I can't, Luke," David had said, his hazel eyes heavy with sleep, the dark hair on his chest visible in the V of his nightshirt.

When Luke had only stared—no doubt with a similar mute misery that had so disgusted Mr. Smith—David had sighed, smiled tiredly, opened the door, and drawn Luke into bed with him.

But when Luke had reached for David's cock, the other man had stopped him.

"No. Not anymore. It is too painful for me." He'd folded Luke's much larger body against his chest. "I want you too much to share you, Luke, with him or anyone else. The comfort of my embrace is all I can offer you."

The simple words had been like a knife in his chest.

What was wrong with Luke that he couldn't want David, who was kind, handsome, and thoughtful.

And monogamous.

Why couldn't Luke be happy and stop yearning for the moon? Why did he want Mr. Smith more with each act of rejection?

Worst of all had been the throb of lust he'd experienced under his master's cold and disgusted gaze: even his contempt had aroused Luke.

He deserved to be thrown into Bedlam and displayed to gawkers: *Pay a penny to look at this poor specimen of manhood!*

In the weeks since Smith had dismissed him, Luke had fisted himself to the same scene over and over: Mr. Smith, naked and hard, sneering down at Luke's cringing form.

The dreams took off in dozens of different directions after that, each one wilder than the last.

Luke sucking Smith while Miss Moira watched.

Luke and Smith using her together.

Luke being stripped and brutally mounted in front of her, and then kicked into the street, naked and wanting.

And on and on.

He squeezed his eyes shut, as if that could stop the visions from unfurling in his mind.

It had to stop.

He had to make it stop.

But instead of stopping, he lay there in the darkness, eyes closed, and once again reached for his erect cock.

***

Smith was reviewing a proposal to purchase a canning operation when there was a soft knock on his study door.

"Yes?"

The door opened slowly and Moira entered. As usual, the sight of her fiery hair and pale, freckled skin made him smile. He removed his glasses and stood. "How lovely to see you." He gestured to a chair across from him. "Please sit."

"Thank you." She glanced at his desk. "I hope I didn't—"

"You must never feel that you are interrupting me, Moira. I am always at your disposal." Her cheeks flushed charmingly at his words. "What can I do for you?"

Her big sea-colored eyes flickered nervously around his office. "I just wondered—well, there was a dress delivered a while ago."

"I'm glad to hear it. I worried it might not be ready in time."

She swallowed. "There was also a jewelry case."

He smiled. "Yes."

"I—well, are those real diamonds?"

Smith laughed and sat back in his chair.

Her pale skin flushed scarlet. "I didn't mean that the way it sounded. It's just that it must be very expensive if it is real. The stones are… well, it's beautiful. I would be afraid of losing it."

"It is yours to lose." Smith saw her horrified expression and amended his words. "It is insured, Moira. You can wear it without worrying."

She swallowed and nodded. "And you want me to wear the gown tonight—to Nora's gallery showing?"

"I would like that."

Again she nodded, and then blurted, "You didn't come to me last night." The attractive flush deepened. "It has been a week since, well, you know."

Smith *did* know. The past week had been beyond trying as he'd fought with both mill management and workers about the installation of several of Gideon's new inventions.

149

Although he'd not had to leave town—the mill in question was only about an hour outside London—he'd left before first light and returned home near midnight every day.

It had been a grueling week and when he'd arrived home last night—after one in the morning—he'd fallen into bed and slept deeper than he had in years.

"I'm sorry," she said, twisting her hands. "I don't mean to—"

"Come here," Smith said, pushing his chair away from his desk. When she came closer, he pulled her onto his lap. "I've missed you, too. I spoke to my partners earlier in the week and explained that this cannot go on." All three men had agreed—guiltily—that Smith had been stretched to breaking while they'd been enjoying their domestic bliss.

Smith laid a hand on her flat belly. "What we need is some time away; I've decided we will go to my house in Scotland after the holiday."

The holiday in question was Guy Fawkes Day. Normally Smith would have left before the chaotic festivities, but he simply had too much to do this year.

"Would you like to visit the land of your ancestors?" he asked her.

"Yes, I've never been."

"I shall take you." Smith leaned close and kissed her breast. She wore a pale pink velvet gown without pads, bustles, or cages. The romantic, relaxed design suited her slender build and diminutive size.

Smith sucked her nipple until it was peaked and hard and then sat back and smiled. "I'm afraid I've marked your gown," he said, thumbing the damp spot.

She reached down and stroked his erection.

He groaned. "God, that feels good, Moira."

"So… we will be in the city for Guy Fawkes?" she asked, squeezing his crown in a way that cleared his mind of any other thoughts.

"Mmm, yes. Do you enjoy going out into the crowds?" he asked, closing his eyes, dreamy and relaxed under her firm, skilled hand.

"Last year was my first year in England but I had to work so I did not get to go out and join in the festivities."

"Shall we make our own Guy and march him toward Parliament?"

Smith hissed in a breath and opened his eyes when she deftly unbuttoned his placket and slid her cool hand around his hot shaft.

"You are very naughty, my dear." He stared into the complex blues and greens that made up her irises. "How is your sketching progressing? Do you need a model to sit for you?" He showed her his profile and struck a pose.

She gave a delighted gurgle of laughter. "You are *so* vain."

"Yes, I am," he admitted. He fluttered his eyelashes playfully, "But I am an excellent sitter." He bit her nipple and she shuddered, her hand closing around his shaft.

There was a scratch on the door and Moira's hand froze.

Smith sighed "I'm sorry," he said, "But I'm expecting several important messages today."

Moira nodded and released him.

"Come in," he said, not taking his eyes from her flushed, pretty face.

The door opened and Michael entered. "A message has arrived, sir—from France," he clarified, holding out a salver with a single envelope on it.

Smith stared blankly at his servant. This wasn't the message he'd been expecting; this was the one he'd been dreading.

His reaction to the fat envelope was visceral; he didn't want to read whatever it contained.

Did he need to read it?

Undeniably.

Smith shook himself and smiled at his patient servant. "Thank you, Michael—set it on my desk." When the door closed behind the other man Smith turned to Moira. "Thank you for coming to me. It pleases me that you are eager to spend time with me." He claimed her mouth with a deep, searching kiss, briefly considering bending her over the chair and taking her right there.

But the envelope on his desk nagged at him.

When he pulled away, he caressed her cheek. "I'm afraid I need to take care of this," he said. "But I look forward to spending the evening with you."

She nodded and stood, wearing an odd, shy smile. "I'm looking forward to this evening, too."

Smith watched her leave and then turned to the envelope. It looked innocent, but he suspected that it would disappoint, if not enrage, him. Should he read it? Or toss it into the fire?

He took a letter opener from the desk drawer and slit the back flap.

***

Moira shut the door to Smith's study and slumped against it, letting out a shaky sigh. She wanted to run—not stop to gather anything, not even the bit of money she kept stitched into her old coat—just run.

But where could she go?

She pushed herself off the door and walked with heavy steps toward the stairs. She'd been feeling sick for three days, ever since receiving Turnbull's message:

Miss Dunsmuir:

Remember, remember the Fifth of November! This is just a brief note to remind you I shan't be able to come during the usual time. Would seven o'clock on the 5th be too inconvenient?

J. Turnbull

It wasn't exactly creative, but the meaning was clear: Victor and his minions would come for Smith on the evening of Guy Fawkes Day.

While November Fifth was far too soon for her taste, it would be a good evening for Marie's plan because it was a day when normal routine was suspended and most of the servants had the evening off.

Smith's armed sentries would still be on duty, of course, but Moira had been working on the problem for weeks now.

While none of the eight men who took turns at the door were stupid enough to let their guard down for *anyone,* she had managed to make a certain amount of headway with at least five of them. She'd seized every opportunity to talk to them when coming or going. Whenever she'd gone out of the house she had stopped at a bakery or pastry shop and brought back treats.

Was it nakedly manipulative? Yes, it was, but food—she knew from experience—was often better bribery than money, which the guards certainly would have balked at taking.

While three of the men had thanked her but demurred, the others had—at one time or another—accepted the treats with obvious pleasure. All she needed was for at least one of those men to be on the servant door on the evening of the Fifth.

The men took half-hour breaks four times during their shifts, meaning there were four brief windows of time with only one man on either door. Moira had acquired a harmless, but effective, emetic that

152

would ensure there would be trouble keeping even one man to his usual vigil. Her solution relied a great deal on luck, but there was no other choice.

Victor, who'd been coming and going twice a week for almost eight weeks would come later than usual that day. Instead of departing after the lesson, Moira would hide Victor in an unused cupboard in the music room.

"This is a stupid plan," she'd told Victor when he'd described how things would work.

His piggy eyes had narrowed. "If you don't like it, you can complain to those in charge."

Marie, in other words.

"The guards will check when you don't leave the house," she'd told him.

"Not if they're shitting themselves blind, they won't."

Moira had winced at both his crudity and her guilt. She liked Smith's guards—they were always respectful and kind to her. Indeed, she liked them a great deal more than she liked Turnbull.

"What if one of them *does* decide to come looking for you?" she'd persisted.

"Well, then you'd better hide me good, hadn't you, girlie?"

Moira had stared at the loathsome man, closer than she'd ever been to putting a stop to the mad plan and confessing everything to Smith.

Naturally, she had done no such thing.

It's not too late. You could run away—far and fast—and not be here on the Fifth, her inner voice urged her now as she made her way from Smith's study to her room.

Moira snorted softly as she opened the door to her bedchamber, relieved that Luke wasn't inside. It wasn't that she didn't like him—not at all. In fact, she'd come to rely on his unfailing good humor and kindness—but she needed some solitude to collect her wits.

She needed to root out the doubts that seemed to plague her more each day. She would have given everything she possessed for just five minutes with Marie and the *Comte* and the chance to make them explain *everything.*

You should have done that before tossing your life aside and coming to England.

Yes, she should have. But she'd been so gutted about Sandrine—and so vengeful—that she'd been an empty vessel they'd filled with whatever they'd wanted. Now, with time and distance, more and more questions wormed into her mind.

Moira wanted to do what was right, but she no longer was sure what that was.

Chapter 18

Smith read the information from France three times.

And then he had a glass of his favorite Armagnac, the maelstrom of emotions inside him worse than anything he'd felt in over thirty years, not since he'd watched everyone in his family tortured, raped, and slaughtered before his nine-year-old eyes.

His emotional reaction surprised him; he'd not believed that he had the ability to feel such pain anymore. Such betrayal.

After finishing his drink, he went up to his gymnasium and proceeded to engage in two hours of brutal exercise. He worked his body until he hurt—beyond what was wise—but he couldn't stop.

The pain didn't lead to an aching erection this time. Indeed, he was the farthest thing from aroused. As emotionally defective as Smith was in so many ways, at least he did not find blazing fury sexually stimulating; it left him feeling hollow and dead inside.

By the time two hours had passed his rage had diminished from an inferno to a white-hot glow. His body was sweat-slicked, his blood coursing through every muscle and sinew. He could have continued lifting dumb bells and doing sit-ups, lifts, and push-ups for the next ten hours.

Fortunately, his mind, which had been like a rabid animal trapped in a too-small cage—had calmed. It was time to stop before he injured himself. He was no longer a young man. If he damaged his body, it would take a long time to heal. And even healing was no longer guaranteed at his age.

Besides, he had no more time for foolish indulgence; he had a great deal to do and very little time to do it.

The first thing he had to do was cancel the evening with Moira. He needed to leave at once—he should have already done so—but he'd wanted to see her.

No, he *needed* to see her. And he knew exactly where she would be at this time of the day.

Smith dried himself off, slipped into his robe, and went to the room she called her *boudoir*.

Luke glanced up from the exam table, where Moira lay nude but for the steaming cloth draped over her pelvis, her heels resting in the metal stirrups.

Her eyes widened and she blushed—as if being caught in such an exposed position embarrassed her.

Luke paused in the act of stropping the razor.

"I'll take over, Luke. Leave us," Smith said, striding toward the table. Something occurred to him as he looked at her lounging, naked form. "Before you go, bring in the jewelry case that was delivered today."

Luke bowed his head. "Of course, sir."

Moira watched her servant leave as if he were the last lifeboat on a sinking ship.

Smith pulled his sash and shrugged out of his robe, letting it fall to the floor, unable to pull his eyes from her naked breasts. They were so small they scarcely filled his palms. They were the perfect handfuls, the tiny nipples a dark pinkish brown against her almost translucent skin. Lately he had envisioned them full and swollen with milk for their child. But right now, he remembered how they'd looked welted from the whipping he'd administered a few weeks before.

He wanted to do that again right now. But it was never wise to wield a whip when one was angry. It probably wasn't wise to wield a razor, either, but Smith reached for the blade Luke had been stropping.

Moira flinched slightly.

"Shhhh, you needn't look so nervous," he lied. "I have plenty of experience with shaving." That, at least, was the truth. "I groomed myself for years before I could afford servants." He tested the edge with his thumb, leaving a small line of ruby drops. "You may have noticed I have something of a mania for hygiene."

It wasn't a question but she gave an uncertain nod. "Yes."

"Oh, don't worry about offending me," he said, sucking the blood from his thumb and then taking the foaming brush from the cup of shaving soap that he had specially made. It contained a high degree of fat in the blend, which made shaving sensitive areas far more comfortable.

The door opened and Luke entered. "Please put them on Miss Moira," Smith smiled at Luke so warmly that the other man fumbled with the large velvet box.

Moira pushed up onto her elbows, even more confused than Luke. "What—"

"I'm afraid I must leave tonight. I have unavoidable business for the next few days." His mouth flexed into a genuine moue of regret. "I must cancel our plans for this evening but I wanted to see you in the diamonds—and nothing else."

If anything, she looked even more confused. "But—when will you return?"

"Don't worry. I'll be back before the fifth. I haven't forgotten that we are going to spend the holiday together. I give you my word that I will be entirely at your disposal after that."

Moira's eyes flickering from Smith to Luke and back as the other man fastened the magnificent diamond necklace around her throat.

"Make sure it is snug," he told Luke, his eyes on Moira. "It is meant to fit tightly—a choker is the word the jeweler used. There is even a tiny lock. But I won't have Luke put that on you tonight," he assured her, amused by her startled expression.

It was the single most expensive gift he'd ever purchased for anyone. Smith had to admit it looked well on her—five rows of diamonds that blazed like white fire. The earrings were double tear drops and suited her heart-shaped face and short hair.

Luke stepped back once he'd screwed in the second earbob.

"You may go, Luke."

The door shut behind his servant and Smith ran a finger over her diamond collar. "You look magnificent, Moira. These stones are almost beautiful enough to adorn you."

She swallowed, the necklace cutting into her skin when her throat flexed. "Thank you, Smith."

The pulse at the base of her throat was pounding like a tiny drum. He leaned over and kissed it, lingering over the delicate spot before straightening.

"You are welcome, Moira."

Smith took the towel from beneath her arm and soaped her armpit, where tiny glints of reddish-gold hair were breaking through her pale skin.

"I appreciate that you agreed to such rigorous grooming. I know it seems… excessive, but I cannot stop wanting it. Needing it. For years I tried to combat my obsession for both order and extreme cleanliness, but I finally decided there were other battles more worthy of my time."

Her lips parted, but she said nothing.

"You want to know what made me this way?" He smiled at her hesitant nod. "I've never told anyone else." He replaced the brush and then picked up the razor. "But hopefully you will be the mother of my child, so you should know."

Her pale skin flushed. Was she feeling guilty about cleansing herself? Or something else?

Well, no matter.

Smith stretched the skin and then stripped the area of hair in only three swipes of the blade. He glanced up and caught her staring, her eyes so wide the whites were vivid.

"You see how quick and painless that was?"

"Yes," she whispered.

Smith wiped away the soap with the still-hot towel and then tossed it into the nearby hamper.

"Using separate blades is the key to a painless, close shave," he said conversationally as he picked up the second razor, tested the edge, and then moved to her other side and commenced the same process.

When he was done, he went to the foot of the table and raised the level of the stool until it put him at the correct angle. He then slid a hand around each of her ankles and exerted gentle pressure. The mechanisms that locked the stirrups into place clicked as he opened them wider.

"This table is quite ingenious, isn't it?" he asked, continuing to push.

"Yes."

"I have to admit it gave me …*ideas* from the very first moment I saw it." He raised an eyebrow. "Did it give you any ideas, Moira?"

"Yes, Smith. It did." The tension around her eyes told him that she was beginning to feel discomfort at being opened so wide.

Smith halted his pushing and examined her spread thighs. The tendons that joined her thighs to her pelvis were prominent beneath the smooth, white skin. He caressed them with light touches that made her shiver.

"When I was young—not quite ten—I was freezing to death in a snowstorm. I had nowhere to stay, no money to buy my way into even the meanest of flophouses. So, I broke the lock on a cellar door and hid in a huge bin of apples."

Smith looked up from the snow-white cloth that covered her sex and met her rapt gaze.

He clucked his tongue. "Here I've been chattering and this towel has become cold." He took another heated towel from the silver warmer and replaced the one covering her. "Better?"

She nodded.

"Servants discovered me in the cellar, of course." Smith held her worried gaze and chuckled at the memory—at least that part. "Not only had I eaten my body weight in apples, but so much food on a starved, shrunken stomach had made me ill. I must have made a disgusting, pitiful picture—smeared in shit, vomit, and apples, bony, and sickly."

Smith rested his hand over her mound, squeezing it lightly as he skated dangerously close to the edge of the ancient, unpleasant memory.

"Naturally the servants were furious. Not because of the broken lock and stolen food, but because they had to clean up after me. So, they took their revenge in a most ironic fashion. Can you guess what they did?"

Dread had replaced discomfort on her face and she shook her head.

Smith's jaw tightened, even after decades. "They took me to the outhouse and pushed me down the hole."

Her jaw sagged.

Smith nodded at her expression of revulsion. "It was… well, even after all these years I don't have the words to describe the experience. I don't know how long I was in there—more than an hour, less than a day—before the stablemaster pulled me out. The house belonged to a very wealthy man, somebody so rich and powerful that he likely never even knew that a filthy urchin had eaten his apples and defecated in his root cellar."

He watched as a single tear slid down her cheek, sparkling almost as much as the stones around her neck.

"I couldn't seem to get clean enough afterward, no matter that the stablemaster had thrown bucket after bucket of freezing water over me. He gave me a brush that was no longer good enough for the master's horses and I used that to clean myself, scrubbing until I was bloody."

Her mouth opened, but nothing came out.

Smith almost felt bad for her. "Let's move you down just a little," he said, taking her narrow hips in both hands and bringing her toward him, the action opening her even wider.

He didn't stop until she winced, using pain to cruelly pull her thoughts away from a skinny boy trapped in a shithouse.

"Does that hurt, Moira?"

She cleared her throat. "Yes, it hurts a little."

"Just a little?" he teased.

"Perhaps a little more than a little," she conceded.

"Do you like it?"

She wiped away her tears with the back of her hand and nodded. "Y-yes, I like it."

"Would you like more?" He slid a hand up her thigh.

Her pupils flared to life at his touch. "Yes, Smith. I want more." And then she slid down the table without any prodding, the pained lines around her eyes deepening.

"Good girl," Smith praised, removing the towel that concealed her sex. He groaned at the sight that met his eyes. "You are so beautiful—so perfect," he said, aware of the roughness in his voice and the throb in his now rock-hard cock. He'd not believed he could get an erection after what he'd read earlier, but her pink, wide-spread cunt had cured him.

"And you're aroused," he said wonderingly, rubbing her slick, swollen clitoris and reveling in the grunt of pleasure the caress elicited.

"Yes, Smith."

"Do you always become aroused when Luke grooms you?"

She inhaled and then paused.

Smith chuckled. "I won't be angry if you say yes. Luke is masculine perfection; it would be difficult not to notice him—especially when his hands touch such intimate places. I find it titillating to think of you becoming aroused for him."

There was a soft sigh, and then, "Yes."

He glanced down to where his fingers had not ceased their idle stroking. She was so slick and lovely.

"Perhaps when I've seen to this current crisis, we can do this again, Moira? But have Luke join us."

An emotion flickered over her face too quickly for him to read it. Excitement? Arousal? Something else entirely?

"I would like that," she said.

"So would I," he said, not lying. He lowered his eyes to her spread sex, torn by regret and arousal. "I have to leave soon, but I need to taste you before I go."

One last taste.

***

Moira was finding it extremely difficult to relax under Smith's touch. For the first time ever, she wasn't even sure she could climax.

His lips and tongue were as magical as ever and yet… yet she couldn't help feeling uneasy at his odd mood.

In the span of half-an-hour he'd taken her from arousal to horror back to arousal again.

She'd been startled when Smith had shown up, naked and slick from exertion, eyeing her with a strangely intense gaze, his body *glowing* with health and vigor.

Moira knew he'd gone into his gymnasium not long after she had left his study earlier. According to a conversation between Luke and Knox, he'd been in there twice as long as usual.

Moira never would have heard the conversation if somebody hadn't left the communicating door ajar.

"This much exercise cannot be good for him. Why does he punish himself like this?" Knox had fretted, concern for his employer evident in his voice.

"Something is probably wrong with one of the syndicate's businesses," Luke said. "That's what he always does when there are problems: goes into his gymnasium. He told me it helps him think." Luke's tone was almost proprietary, as if he were Smith's confidant.

Well, she'd known they were lovers, just not how close they were.

"That's not the *only* way he manages his problems," Knox said with a low chuckle. "Why don't you go offer your services, Luke. It's been a while, hasn't it?"

"Unfortunately, that is no longer my place." Although Luke's voice had been as well-modulated as ever, Moira had heard the tension beneath the words.

"Knocked you back, did he?"

Luke made a dismissive sound. Even through the door it sounded forced. "It's his way—he was the same with Mr. Charles, although that was because Charles had a tantrum if the master so much as *looked* at another man or woman." He paused, and then said, "With Jo Leather he was different."

"Ah, yes. The incomparable Mr. Leather."

This time it was Luke who laughed. "Is that jealousy I detect?"

"Who wouldn't like to warm the master's bed," Knox said, apparently so sure of the answer he didn't even wait to hear it. "Tell me, how was Smith different with Leather?"

"Well, he was *happier* for one thing. Leather had no pretensions to anything more than serving him and didn't mind if the master had outside interests."

"The man *does* have an impressive sexual appetite," Knox marveled. "Gives me hope that my pecker won't just up and die when I reach forty—" his voice had begun to get fainter as the men moved away and Moira didn't hear Luke's response.

Luke had arrived in her chambers soon afterward to begin the business of getting her ready for the evening.

And then Smith himself had appeared.

Although he'd said their evening was cancelled, he'd then taken the time to share a story he'd never told anyone else. A story that had been as sad as it had been awful.

Moira had seen him so clearly in her mind's eye: a skinny boy, freezing and wandering the streets, eyes hollow with hunger and exhaustion.

The flat, emotionless way he'd delivered the tale had been belied by the anger in his eyes.

Or perhaps he was angry for some other reason?

He certainly hadn't seemed angry afterward, nor was he showing any sign of anger at present.

Indeed, he was behaving with such animal enthusiasm that the room echoed with the loud, earthy sucking and primitive grunts and growls, all of which were as erotic as the masterful way he worked her cunt.

Suddenly his head whipped up and his gaze locked with hers, his hand not pausing it's thrusting. "Your mind is wandering. You must tell me what you need if I'm failing you."

Moira opened her mouth to lie—but then he shifted his angle and struck something inside her that caused every muscle in her body to tighten at once.

She cried out and gripped the sides of the bench.

"That's better," he said, hitting the same spot again and again and again, until she gave in, drowning in wave upon wave of pure sensation.

Moira's eyelids felt heavy and it took effort to lift them. The first thing she saw was Smith, staring at her. She squinted, disoriented. "Was I—did I fall asleep?" she asked, noticing that the stirrups were no longer spread wide and her body had been covered with a towel.

"Only for a few minutes."

"I'm sorry. I never usually—"

"Shhh. You don't need to apologize. Giving you pleasure makes me very happy, Moira."

His words sent a warm rush of … something coursing through her body.

But then Moira noticed that Smith didn't look happy at all. If anything, he looked unspeakably weary.

"Are you—is anything amiss?" she asked haltingly.

"No." He smiled, his gaze so alert and warm that Moira thought she must have imagined any exhaustion.

He *tsked*. "I came here intending to shave you and got carried away." He ran a finger lightly over the towel that covered the prickly skin on her mound.

"Oh," Moira said. "I completely forgot."

He laughed. "I enjoyed making you forget. But now, unfortunately, I had better be on my way." He paused and then said something… odd. "Unless you wanted something else from me?"

She gawked at him; a jumble of thoughts fighting to get out of her mouth:

Please don't leave!

You're in danger, and it's all my fault.

I'm so sorry.

I've fallen in love with you.

Moira's jaws ached with the effort of keeping them closed.

His dark eyes bored into her, his lips parted slightly. "Yes?" Smith urged, sounding almost breathless.

"I—" She bit her lip, and then forced a smile. "I wish you safe travels."

Chapter 19

November 5th

Moira's palms wouldn't quit sweating.

From the moment she'd woken up that morning—far too early, but unable to sleep—until twelve hours later, her hands had been cool and clammy. She'd never experienced such anxiety in her life.

That's because you've never before betrayed a man whose child you are carrying—a child you've been hiding from him.

It was true.

Moira must have become pregnant not long after her last courses. She'd briefly deliberated letting Smith know—perhaps he would trust her more and it would be easier to get Etienne, Turnbull, and his idiots into the house—but had, ultimately, decided the information belonged only to her.

God help her if Marie or the *Comte* ever learned the truth.

It had been easy to conceal, all she'd needed to do was get a small amount of blood from a butcher shop.

She should have taken steps to rid herself of the child during the five or six days when she was supposed to be having her courses, but she had dithered and dithered until it wasn't possible to do what was necessary and still recover in time for Smith's return.

You want this baby.

Moira paused her anxious pacing and glared at her wide-eyed reflection in the looking glass; that was a lie. She didn't want a child—she was a whore, for pity's sake. She'd never thought to have children.

And why is that, pray?

Moira rubbed her damp palms on her dressing gown and then grimaced, glancing at the fabric. Thankfully she'd not ruined it yet with all her sweating and fussing.

It was new, delivered just that morning. A message in Smith's bold handwriting had accompanied it:

Moira,

Wear only this and your diamonds.

S.

This was a dressing gown of flowing red silk that looked like blood poured over her naked body.

It was the most seductive garment she'd ever worn—pure sin—the striking color not one she'd have believed she could wear.

And the diamonds? Well, those were fit for a queen.

Never had Moira possessed such beautiful clothing or lived such a luxurious existence. If she'd not been here under false pretenses, she would have adored the opportunity to find real tutors and learn real skills.

Instead, she spent her time associating with fakes: fake drawing masters, fake music tutors—

Fake parents.

Moira froze in mid-pace.

Why would she think such a disloyal thought? Marie and the *Comte* had housed and clothed her from birth, sent her to school—

Sold you into a life of prostitution.

Moira stood in the middle of her room, frozen, her heart pounding as long-ago words drifted back to her—Sandrine's words.

"We should have been given a choice."

Moira must have buried the memory in the back of her mind, but now it had crawled into the light.

Why now?

You know why. Because you are pregnant. Is this the life you want for your child?

The question smashed a dam Moira hadn't even known existed and memories flooded out.

Suddenly she recalled the time she'd overheard Marie shouting and Sandrine weeping—crouched in the window seat in the library. It was their favorite room in the house where they'd all been born; a house that lived in the shadow of the most exclusive brothel in Paris.

Moira, only twelve at the time, had been surprised to find her sister at home. Sandrine had her own house by then, paid for by her powerful, wealthy, and influential patron, the Marquis de Bouvier.

"Why didn't you tell me sooner?" Marie had shouted.

"Because I knew you'd demand that I get rid of it!" Sandrine's face had been wet with tears; her lovely blue eyes red-rimmed.

"Of course, you will get rid of it!"

"Why couldn't I have the baby and pay somebody to care for it?"

"Are you mad? Do you think the marquis would want a bastard? You *know* this is not what these men expect. You can have children later—as I did—when you no longer command the price you do now."

Sandrine had resisted a little more, but in the end, she had complied with Marie's wishes.

Her sister had never really been the same after that. Oh, she'd been just as lovely, but a light had gone out of her.

The same thing will happen to you.

"Shut. Up," Moira hissed into the quiet room, pinching the bridge of her nose hard, praying the pain would drive away the incessant voice.

Her parents would be furious if they found out she was to have Smith's child. They would make her get rid of it.

Go to Smith and tell him the truth. Don't go through with this mad plan. Stay with him, raise the child in the luxurious house he has promised you.

Moira growled. *How could I possibly stay with the man who killed my sister?*

The savage thought quieted the voice.

But she knew it would return.

***

"You look magnificent this evening, my dear," Smith said, his hot eyes roaming over her body.

She lifted a hand to her throat as his gaze lingered on the diamond collar. "Thank you."

He looked magnificent himself wearing his ivory robe, the deep V exposing a goodly amount of his torso.

Moira's gaze moved on to the huge array of food spread over two tables, which the servants must have erected especially for the occasion. "Goodness."

Smith laughed. "Quite outrageous, isn't it? Cook was worried we might starve as he has the evening off, so he took precautions. Don't worry, you won't have to eat it all."

"It looks delicious," she said, her stomach churning so badly that she felt ill just looking at it.

"The wine should be decanted," he said. "Will you bring me a glass? I'm feeling quite lazy tonight."

"Of course." Moira went to where the bottle and glasses sat.

"I hope you don't mind that we won't be making our own Guy and joining the bonfire," Smith said.

She carefully angled her body so that it was between the wine and her employer. "I'm relieved not to go out as it seems rather a madhouse."

"It will get worse before the night is through."

Moira knew that Turnbull—who was currently hiding in a cupboard in the music room—was counting on that chaos to aid their cause.

"Are you sorry that you aren't participating in the celebrations?" she asked as she flipped up the stone on the gaudy ring she'd purchased a week before, exposing the white powder she'd acquired from the chemist.

"I'd much rather be here with you," Smith said.

Moira swallowed down the stab of shame she felt at his words as she tipped the powder into to the glass with shaky hands and then sloshed the wine around until it was dissolved. She took a deep breath, fixed a smile on her face, and turned.

"Thank you," he said, taking a big swallow before setting the glass on the end table.

"You look a bit tired," she said, settling beside him on the settee.

"I'm never too tired for you, Moira. I thought we might do something special tonight as I've neglected you so badly recently." He pulled her into his arms and claimed her mouth with one of the deep, mind-destroying kisses at which he excelled.

"Special?" she said, when he released her, silently praying tonight wasn't one of the nights he wanted to restrain and whip her. As much as she enjoyed it, she shuddered to think of Victor seeing her that way.

He traced a finger down her temple and jaw. "I'm in the mood to be bound and punished—how do you feel about that, Moira?"

Her jaw sagged.

He laughed softly. "You look shocked. Do you not enjoy wielding a whip?"

"Yes—of course I do," she lied quickly. While she'd been trained to dispense punishment, it was not something she enjoyed.

He smiled. "Excellent."

It's perfect, you fool. Marie's voice was so clear in her head she almost looked around the room for her mother.

It *was* perfect. But it was also something Smith had never indicated he wanted from her. Why tonight of all nights did he want such a thing?

Smith kissed down the line he'd just traced with his finger. "I've been thinking about it for a while," he said, yet again reading her mind. He sat back, his eyes a bottomless black. "You mean a great deal to me and I want to share everything with you, Moira. I am very happy with our arrangement. But sometimes I wonder if you are?"

Her initial reaction was shock; how could he not see how happy she'd been with him these past few months?

The only thing that had made her *unhappy* was Turnbull and the need to scheme and plan.

"Is that such a difficult question?" he asked, making her realize she'd been staring at him rather than answering him.

"No, of course not. It's just…" she bit her lip and Smith raised an eyebrow.

Just tell him the truth, for once. What will it matter after tonight?

"It's just?" he asked.

"It's just that I'm surprised that you couldn't see how happy I've been." She swallowed and then added before she lost her courage. "I'm happier than I've ever been in my life."

And I'm about to destroy it.

***

Smith enjoyed watching her fit the leather cuffs and straps to his body, her movements both graceful and economical.

"This is something you've done often," he said.

She nodded, even though it hadn't been a question.

"Which do you enjoy more, Moira—giving or receiving?"

She blinked at his question, as if her mind had been elsewhere. Indeed, all evening—through the meal she'd barely touched and the conversations she'd scarcely taken part in—she'd seemed distracted.

"I—er, well, I like both."

It wasn't the first time she'd lied to him—not even the first time this evening—but it was clumsy at best.

Smith almost felt sorry for her.

Once he was bound hand and foot, she glanced at the bridle gag and swallowed. "Are you sure you want—"

"I want it."

"And—" she gestured to the crop with the fat keeper.

"Yes, I'm sure of that, too. It will feel exquisite on my chest and stomach."

"Oh. You don't want your back—"

"No. I want to look at you while you whip me."

She smiled—or tried to—but it was more of a rictus.

Smith cocked his head. "If you don't wish to do this, you don't have—"

"No! No, I *do* wish to do this," she said, giving him a smile that was almost convincing. "I will enjoy it." She swallowed and then raised her hands with the gag.

"Might I have a last swallow of wine?" he said. "I'm feeling parched."

She turned abruptly and brought him the glass.

When she held it up to his lips, he drained it in one long swallow and sighed. "Thank you. I am ready."

Smith had allowed her to remain clothed, even though he normally preferred to have his lovers naked. She looked lovely in blood red, a color he'd not been sure of with her hair, but it looked magnificent.

And he adored seeing his collar around her elegant neck.

Ever since their first evening together at Bernina's, Moira had exhibited complete confidence in their sexual interactions. It was true she sometimes blushed or looked confused about other matters—like personal questions or when he became vulgar—but when it came to sexual pleasure, she had the poise and grace of a much older woman.

But tonight, she was so very, very anxious.

Smith yawned around the gag in his mouth, or at least he tried to, swamped by a sudden wave of lassitude.

While his mind was hazy and sluggish his cock was rock hard and weeping in anticipation of his whipping.

The crop was a dangerous implement in the wrong hands. It required finesse to give pain without damage.

Moira's first few blows were uncharacteristically timid, but somewhere around the fifth or sixth strike she fell into a rhythm that employed just the right pressure.

The bodice of her dressing gown was low, exposing her chest and the gentle swells of her small, raspberry tipped breasts.

Smith sighed at her perfection, watching with increasingly heavy eyes as her skin became slick and mottled.

She worked him with the skill of a virtuosa, until each strike with the unforgiving tool was exquisite agony.

Smith didn't notice that tears were running down her face until she tossed aside the whip and wrapped her arms around him and pressed her body to his burning torso. She hugged him hard enough to make his ribs creak.

"I love you," she whispered against his temple.

Or that is what Smith thought she said, but there was an odd buzzing sound in his head, so he might have imagined the words.

Indeed, he must have.

When she pulled away, he wanted to look at her, but his head had become strangely heavy on his neck and kept falling back.

She slid a hand around the back of his skull and held him upright.

"Mo—Mmm—" Smith lost track of what he'd been trying to say.

"I'm so sorry," she said, choking on the words, tears streaming. Almost as if *she* were being punished.

Something moved in the corner of his blurry vision.

"Step away from the bastard, girlie," a flat male voice ordered.

Her warmth disappeared and a hand gripped Smith's hair and jerked his head up. The sneering face of John Turnbull, Moira's music teacher, rippled and shifted before him.

"Well, look at you. All trussed up like a holiday goose." He laughed harshly and then punched Smith in the gut.

"No!" Moira yelled. "What are you doing? You don't have to—"

The next blow struck Smith in the jaw and his head exploded with pain and bright white spangles.

"Stop it!" Moira screamed

"Shut up, girlie!"

"No!" Moira shouted. "This isn't—"

The fist struck him again and Smith's head once again exploded with white stars. He was distantly aware of the sounds of scuffling, a woman screaming, and then darkness claimed him.

Chapter 20

A re you sure you don't want to go?" David asked Luke for the fifth time.

"I'd only sour the mood," Luke said, yet again. "You go ahead—enjoy yourself."

"Really?"

"Yes, really."

David sighed and shook his head. "You need to forget about him, Luke."

"Just *go*."

"Fine." David snatched up his woolly scarf and headed out the door.

Luke waited until the door slammed to sink down onto his bed. He'd been arguing with the other man for half-an-hour, after David had drawn the shift tonight and Luke had offered to cover him.

Mr. Smith had said only one servant was necessary—along with the four men on the doors—so Luke would be on duty alone tonight.

It was just as well since the last thing he felt like doing was joining the revels.

He doubted he'd be summoned tonight as Mr. Smith and Miss Moira had dined in the master's chamber and Luke and a few others had already cleared away the heaps of remaining food.

Earlier that evening, as Luke had groomed and prepared Miss Moira for her night with Smith, she'd looked so downcast that he'd broken one of his own rules and asked her a personal question. "Are you not feeling well, Miss Moira?"

She'd smiled, but he could see it had taken effort. "No, just gathering wool. Are you going out to join the revels?"

At that point Luke had not yet convinced David to switch shifts with him, so he'd said, "Yes, miss, with several of the others."

"I hope you enjoy yourself."

After he'd finished dressing her, she had taken Luke's hand and said the strangest thing, "Thank you for being so kind to me."

It was just as well that she'd hurried from the room as he'd been too confused to reply.

He was still pondering her odd behavior hours later. Rather than look elated at the prospect of spending the evening with the master—who'd been away most of the past week—his mistress had looked almost… terrified.

Luke's stomach rumbled, interrupting his pointless fretting. He sighed. If he wanted food, then he'd need to get his arse off the bed and get down to the kitchen. He could fret just as easily while shoving food into his mouth.

The house was strangely quiet as he made his way down the stairs. He reached the third floor and was about to descend when movement at the far end of the corridor caught his attention.

There was a man walking—no tiptoeing—toward Miss Moira's room.

Luke squinted; it was the music teacher—Victor Turnbull was his name—who'd left the house hours ago. Or so he'd believed.

He opened his mouth to demand what he was doing, but something about the way the man was skulking urged caution.

As Luke watched, Turnbull opened the door, peered in through the narrow gap, and then slipped inside.

What the bloody hell?

Luke strode toward Miss Moira's room.

Hold up there, Luke. How do you know this isn't one of the master's amusements?

He skidded to a halt in the middle of the hallway, his brain darting in ten different directions at the thought.

But none of the directions led to his master wanting anything to do with the ill groomed, crude, repulsive music tutor.

A loud female scream broke the silence and Luke jolted into action.

"Stop it! What are you doing? You're—"

It was Miss Moira's voice and it was coming from Mr. Smith's room. Luke turned and ran back the other way. But when he yanked on the handle to Smith's room it didn't move.

It was locked.

Miss Moira screamed again and Luke ran to the door Victor had just disappeared through. Rather than flinging it open, he had the presence of mind to peer inside first, as the other man had done.

The voices were louder, meaning the connecting door must be open.

Miss Moira started screaming again and Luke threw caution to the wind.

Luke slid to a halt when he passed through the open doorway into the other room. "Good God!" he shouted, his gaze snagged by Mr. Smith's bloody, obviously unconscious form.

He took a step toward him and then stopped when he noticed his mistress struggling with the music teacher, the two rolling around on the floor. "What in—"

Luke heard the footstep behind him right as his head exploded.

His last thought as he careened into a table and sent something smashing to the floor was that his master would be very angry about the mess.

***

"If you *touch* him again I'll—"

"You'll what?" Etienne's voice came from behind Moira.

She jerked away from Turnbull and saw her brother standing in the doorway between the two rooms, a body crumpled at his feet.

"Luke!" Moira pushed up off the floor and stumbled toward them, dropping to her knees beside Luke and lowering her head to his.

She closed her eyes when she felt a puff of air against her cheek. Thank God! He was alive. Bruised and unconscious, but alive.

Moira struggled to her feet and glared at her brother. "What is going on?" She flung an arm at Smith's unconscious, bleeding body. "These maniacs are—"

"Doing exactly what I told them to do," Etienne said coolly, wearing an expression of distaste as he looked at her. "Calm yourself, Honorine. You are behaving like a hysterical fool and you look like a cheap slut."

Moira flinched at his words. Although he'd spoken in French, the loathing in his tone meant the two Englishmen could be in no doubt what her brother was saying.

He strode over to where Smith still hung, his body sagging against his bonds, and grabbed him by the hair.

"Etienne! What are you—"

"The pig is caught in his own snare, eh?" He spat in Smith's face and then flung his head back. "Cut this piece of excrement loose and then tie him up good and tight. You can roll him up in one of these rugs to carry him out. You must hurry! The two guards on the front of the house are still unaware that the servant entrance is unguarded, but they won't be for long."

Moira grabbed Etienne's shoulder and he whipped around fiercely enough to send her staggering back a step.

He sneered at her, his eyes pulsing with dislike as they slid up and down her person. "Go put on decent clothing." His lips twisted. "Or are you so happy being his *putain* that you don't want to leave?"

"Why are you treating him this way?" she demanded, ignoring his slur—which was ironic as *he* was every bit as much a *putain* as Moira. "We are just supposed to take him back to Paris, not—"

Etienne gave an ugly laugh, which seemed obscene coming from such an angelic looking man. "You really are stupid, Honorine. We aren't taking him *back*, you fool."

"What do you mean?"

"You will see." He smirked and turned away.

"Wait." Moira reached out to grab his shoulder.

Etienne spun around and his arm moved like a blur, the force of his blow knocking her to the floor.

Moira's vision swum as she slowly pushed herself up, wiping the blood from her lip and staring at this man who was supposed to be family—who was supposed to love and care for her.

Etienne glared down at her as if she were filth.

"What did I ever do to make you hate me so much?" she asked.

"You were born," he shot back without hesitation. He pointed to Luke's unmoving body. "Who is this?"

Moira crawled toward the fallen man, propelled by fear. "He is just a servant here," she answered, even though he'd been asking Victor and Morris, who were unbuckling Smith's ankles.

"He is no danger to you," she added when Etienne ignored her.

"He saw our faces," Victor said. "We need to kill him."

"No!" she shrieked. "You can't—"

"Shut up before you alert those louts at the front door!" Etienne snarled, and then turned to Turnbull. "Whatever you are going to do; do it quickly. I am going to make sure that nobody *else* sneaks up on us."

He gestured to Moira. "If you are coming with us, you'd better cover yourself."

"You can't let them kill him. I won't let you."

Etienne reached into his overcoat and his hand came out with a revolver. "You really are stupid—it's a good thing Marie and the *Comte* knew better than to feed you anything but lies. Now get away from him unless you want brains all over you." He snorted. "Which would be the only brains you'd ever have." He pointed the gun at Luke's head.

Moira threw herself between the pistol and Luke.

Etienne smiled and pulled back the hammer. "Two birds, one bullet, as it were."

"You're mad," she gasped. "What do you think the *Comte* and Marie will say when they find out what you've done."

There was a noise behind her and Etienne's head whipped up.

"What is going on here, we should be gone by now," a familiar voice demanded in French.

Moira turned clumsily on her hands and knees. "Father!" she cried, remembering only when she saw his wince of disgust that *father* was not a name she was allowed to call him. "Etienne is threatening to kill this man—he's just a servant."

"He saw the two imbeciles," Etienne explained, with a jerk of his chin toward Turnbull and his nephew.

Thibaut, the ninth *Comte de Blois*, ignored his only surviving son as if he were an insect. His cold, slate-blue gaze slid away and settled on Smith, whom they were rolling into a carpet.

And then he did something Moira had never seen before: he smiled.

"Bring him," he ordered in heavily accented English, snapping his fingers at the two men.

"And him?" Etienne gestured to Luke with the gun.

"You would kill somebody to protect a pair of criminals?" Thibaut scoffed, once again speaking French.

Etienne opened his mouth, but nothing came out. Turnbull and his nephews stared from her father to her brother, their furrowed brows telling Moira they didn't understand French.

When Etienne hesitated, the *Comte* shook his head and snapped his fingers at the two men. "Go!"

They picked up Smith's body and hurried from the room and the *Comte* followed them, leaving his children without a second glance.

Fury distorted Etienne's handsome face as he glared at Moira. "See what you've done?" He lowered the hammer and shoved the gun back in his coat. "Stay here with your *servant* if you want. I won't ask father to wait for you."

And then he, too was gone.

"Luke?" Moira shook the huge man's shoulder. Luke's eyelids flickered, but he didn't move.

Moira brushed back a tear. "I'm sorry, Luke." She kissed his temple. "I'm so sorry."

She pushed to her feet and stumbled to her dressing room, snatching up the beautiful fur-lined cloak Smith had bought for her and wrapping it around herself.

And then she went to join her family.

Chapter 21

W ake up, you pig!"

The icy water did more to wake Smith up than the slap in the face.

When he opened his eyes, it was to see three people staring at him. One face was new to him, one face he'd not seen in thirty-six years, two months, and six or seven days—depending on what day it was now—and the last was a face he'd believed he might one day come to love.

Smith dredged up a smile for the *Comte*. "It has been a long time, my lord."

Thibaut, the *Comte de Blois*, glared at him with a hatred so raw that it verged on madness.

"You must be Etienne," Smith said to the angry young man who bore more than a passing resemblance to both his sister and Blois

Etienne Bardot scowled.

Smith turned to the third person.

Moira's face was blank—more unreadable, even, than usual. "Hello, Honorine."

Her blue-green eyes bulged and she looked from Smith to her father, as if hoping for something from him—reassurance, perhaps.

Smith wasn't surprised when Blois ignored her; he knew the *Comte* gave more care to the thoroughbreds he raised than he did to his illegitimate offspring.

Blois strode toward Smith and struck him with the flat of his hand, hitting him hard enough to almost knock over the chair Smith was tied to.

Moira gave a startled yelp. "Please, don't—"

The *Comte* ignored her and struck him again.

"Where is the body?" Blois demanded.

Smith shook his head and blinked up at several *Comte*s. He smirked. "I'm not going to tell you, so you might as well kill me now." His smirk grew into a grin. "And then you will *never* know."

Blois roared and jumped on him, knocking over the chair, and coming along with it. "You bastard! You demon!" His hands tightened around Smith's throat and he squeezed, slamming his head on the ground over and over.

Smith grinned up at the man's demented expression, wishing his vision wasn't darkening quite so quickly. Wishing he could get a better look at all the pain and suffering he'd caused the other man.

Because *this*—this insane agony in the *Comte*'s maddened eyes—was worth dying for. He'd waited three-quarters of his life for this moment, and it was... delicious.

Smith laughed—or at least tried to—but no sound came out of his mouth.

He heard Moira yell, the sound distant and tinny. "Stop it, you'll kill him!"

"Get back!" Etienne Bardot shouted.

There was more shouting—and scuffling—but he could no longer see clearly.

"Give that back, Honorine! *Arrrgh*—"

A pistol went off, the noise deafening even in Smith's head, which had been ringing ever since Blois's first slap.

"Get off him, my lord," Moira said in a loud, but calm, voice.

"What do you think you are doing, Honorine?" the *Comte* thundered.

"Get off him, *now*!"

The *Comte*'s hands loosened and then he pushed to his knees using Smith's battered ribs as a springboard.

Smith wasted no time filling his burning lungs with cool air, his vision slowly clearing.

"You were going to kill him," Moira/Catherine/Honorine Dunsmuir-Duvalle-Bardot accused. She held the gun in both hands, but the barrel still jumped and shook.

"Put that gun down," Blois ordered, struggling to his feet, his son rushing over to help him.

"You said we were taking him back to France to stand trial for Sandrine's murder," Moira said.

Smith laughed, although it sounded more like a death rattle. Poor Moira—she would always be Moira in his mind—she was so very, very young.

"Give me the gun, Honorine," Blois said, fury pulsing in his voice.

Moira's hands shook even worse, the gun pointing in a direction that was far too close to Smith's cock and balls for him to be entirely easy.

"Stay back—I won't give the gun to you. Not until I know what this"—she waved the pistol around the room, scattering the two standing men like roaches exposed to light— "is all about."

"How dare you question *me*, you—"

"No more lies!" Moira's voice broke on the last word. "I want the truth, *now*."

"He killed my only son!" Blois shouted back at her, his voice shaking with rage.

Moira and Etienne exchanged a long look in the awkward silence that followed their father's declaration.

For his part, the *Comte*'s pale face flushed at his words, but he didn't try to take them back.

Moira turned to Smith. "Is that true?"

"No."

"You *liar!*" Blois lunged for him yet again.

"Get back, my lord." Moira's voice was like steel.

"She wouldn't really shoot us, my lord," Etienne said taking a step toward his sister.

Moira pointed the revolver in the direction of her brother's feet, closed her eyes, and squeezed the trigger.

Etienne's blood curdling shriek told Smith she'd got remarkably lucky with her shot.

"You fucking bitch!" he sobbed, rolling around on the floor, clutching his foot. "I should have killed you when I had the chance."

Moira ignored him and pointed the gun at the *Comte*, who'd begun to creep toward her.

He stopped and flung up his hands.

"I want the truth."

"I've already told you the truth," Blois snapped.

She gestured to Smith. "Lift up his chair."

Blois crossed his arms. "I will *not*."

"I've already shot my brother. No doubt it will be easier to shoot a man I am not even allowed to call *father*. Now, lift the chair."

Smith laughed and then winced at the pain in his head and chest.

Scowling, Blois lifted the chair and let it fall with a bone-jarring thump.

Moira stared at Smith. "You knew my real name. You knew who I was all along."

"Not *all* along."

"Why didn't you say something to me? Why didn't you stop all this from happening?"

"Because he is an evil, sadistic bastard who likes to toy with his victims." Blois spat.

Moira looked at Smith. "Is that true?"

"It is partly true."

She gave a half-amused, half-disbelieving snort. "Which part?"

"I am no bastard," Smith said, staring at one of the two men still alive who knew exactly who he was. He turned back to Moira—a far more attractive view. "But I confess to occasionally being evil, sadistic, and toying with my victims. Of which the *Comte* most certainly is one."

"But you didn't kill his son?"

"I am not a child killer. Or a child rapist." He turned to Blois. "Unlike some."

"What does that mean?" she asked her father.

"I have no idea," the *Comte* shot back.

Smith heard the lie in his voice and could see that Moira had, too.

She swallowed, as if making some decision, and wrenched her gaze back to Smith. "What about my sister?" Moira asked, her voice higher than normal. "Or is that a lie, too—that you killed her?"

"That is a lie, too." Smith turned to Etienne, who was leaning against the wall wrapping his necktie around his bleeding foot. "Go and open the door."

"Go to the devil! I don't take orders from you!"

Moira looked from Smith to her brother. "Open it, Etienne, or I'll give you a matching pair." She pointed the gun in the direction of his uninjured foot.

"Honorine—"

"*Now.*"

He flung up a staying hand. "All right, all right, calm yourself," he muttered, crawling toward the door with a pitiful whimper.

Smith kept his gaze on Moira, rather than the door, and was not disappointed.

Her beautiful eyes threatened to pop out of her head. "Sandrine!" She shrieked and ran for the door, apparently forgetting the gun in her hand, which hit the stone floor and skittered across the room.

The *Comte* ran toward it but his shoe struck it before he could grab it and it went twirling across the floor.

"*Tut-tut.* I don't think so, my lord."

Smith looked up at the sound of Malcolm Barton's voice and sagged with relief to see the huge bastard filling the doorway, holding the biggest gun Smith had ever seen and pointing it at Blois.

The *Comte* quickly raised his hands.

"Bloody hell, Mal. Is that a punt gun?" Smith asked.

Smith's oldest friend chuckled and ran a big paw down the barrel. "I call her Vickie—after the Queen. Because she's always the most dangerous piece in any room."

Smith laughed, even though it made his head throb.

Moira—who'd finally let go of her sister long enough to breathe—hurried toward him, but then stopped a few feet away, her expression fearful and anxious, as if she worried he wouldn't want her to touch him.

"Come untie me, darling."

A choked sob tore out of her and she dropped to her knees and started to release an ankle.

Sandrine hurried over to join her sister, working on Smith's hands.

"I hope you brought me some clothes," Smith said to Edward, who'd just eased past Malcolm and his gun, the two hulking men making the small room feel even smaller.

"Be patient—somebody is bringing them." Edward smirked. "The last thing we all want to look at is your saggy bollocks."

Smith snorted.

"These are too tight," Sandrine muttered behind Smith's chair.

Edward produced a knife and handed it hilt-first to Sandrine, who speedily sawed through the ropes.

"Where are we?" Smith asked, flexing his freed hands, and wincing when the blood began to flow.

"An abandoned dairy a few miles off the North Road," Malcolm said.

Luke appeared in the doorway and pushed past both Malcolm and Edward.

"Thank God you are alright, sir," Luke cried out, the relief in his voice flattering.

Smith grinned. "I'm relieved that you are up and about, Luke. That looked like a nasty knock on the head you took."

"You saw that?" Moira asked, looking up from the knot she'd just untied. "I thought you were unconscious by then." She rubbed his freed ankle.

"I might not have been as far gone as I appeared," he admitted, standing and helping her to her feet before turning to Luke, who had an armload of clothing.

Smith set a hand on Luke's shoulder and stepped into the trousers the other man held open for him, wincing when he tried to bend too quickly.

"Did you get those other two packages for me?" he asked Edward, allowing Luke to button him up since his hands were still numb.

Edward rolled his eyes. "Aye, we've got your *packages*. And a proper pain in the arse one of them is, too. As for the other one? Well, he's cried and pissed all over the floor of my carriage—you owe me for that. We've got both outside."

Moira looked up at him at his face. "You need a doctor. That cut on your—"

"Shhh, don't worry." Smith cupped her face and gave her a reassuring smile. "I shall be fine."

"But—"

"I'll see to myself soon," he said more firmly. "But first I need to finish here."

Her face seemed to crumple and she clutched at his hand, squeezing it hard enough to shift the bones. "I'm so sorry," she choked out. "I never expected any of this. We were supposed to take you back to France. Because of Sandrine."

He gently pulled his hand free. "Go and stand with your sister, Moira."

She hesitated, swallowed hard, and then obeyed.

Smith slipped on his shirt, waistcoat, and coat and waited while Luke buttoned the garments.

There was a commotion behind Malcolm and Edward—who were guarding the door like two massive gargoyles—and Gideon's handsome face shoved between their shoulders. "Smith! Holy hell, you look like you went ten rounds and lost."

Smith looked from Gideon's grinning face to Edward and Malcolm and said one word. "Really?"

Malcolm shrugged. "Sorry. We needed four hands and Edward and I only had three between us," he held up his gloved hands, one of which only had three fingers—as if Smith didn't know what his hands looked like. "Besides," said, the unmasked side of his mouth pulling into a grin. "He seemed keen enough."

"What?" Gideon asked, his head whipping from man to man. "Why are the three of you smirking at me like—"

"Thibault!" a female voice screamed as a body shoved past Gideon and burst into the increasingly crowded room.

Moira stepped toward her. "Marie!"

But Marie Bardot had eyes for only one person and she hurried across the room—not sparing a glance for Moira, her bleeding son, or even her supposedly dead daughter.

"Thibaut! My God, I was so worried for you." She flung herself at him.

Blois didn't seem to notice he had a sobbing female attached to his body; he never took his hate-filled gaze off Smith.

"Well done keeping her restrained, Gideon," Edward said dryly.

"She *bit* me, Edward!" Gideon retorted, shaking his hand. "Do you have any idea how filthy the human mouth is? It's a good thing I'm wearing gloves."

"Go and get the other one," Edward said. "Not that he's in any shape to either bite *or* run," he added dryly.

Gideon huffed, but turned on his heel and left.

When Smith turned to Moira, he knew what he'd see. But that didn't make it any less gut-wrenching. Both her and her brother were staring at their parents—if you could call them that—with yearning and disbelief. Only Sandrine regarded Blois and Bardot with cold contempt.

Everyone turned when Gideon dragged a filthy, barely moving bundle into the room.

"Where do you want him, Smith?" Gideon gagged. "He smells. *Bad.*"

"That's far enough," Smith said. "Lift up his head so Moira can see him."

Gideon grabbed a handful of filthy pale blond hair and pulled it back from the man's face.

Is that Mr. Brown?" he asked, already knowing the answer.

Moira recoiled. "That's him. That's Brown."

"This is actually Mr. Owen Onions." Smith turned to Marie Bardot. "Do you recognize Mr. Onions, Madame?"

Bardot whipped around and spat in Smith's face.

"Marie!" Moira gasped, staring at her mother with horror.

Smith took out the clean handkerchief Luke had just brought him and wiped the spittle from his chin. "I'll take that as a *yes*."

He turned back to her daughter. "If it seems a bit of a tangle, Moira, that's because it is. You see, your mother had one purpose to send your brother Robert to London and Blois had quite another to send *you*. I'm afraid Robert was the victim of Mr. Onions, who killed Robert at the behest of one of his employers, the especially nasty owner of a smuggling organization that makes a hefty profit kidnapping unwary British girls and selling them on the Continent." He turned an unpleasant look on Marie Bardot. "People are far more tractable when they find themselves stranded in a foreign country and cannot speak the language."

As Smith knew from personal experience.

He turned back to Moira. "Your mother has been using them as suppliers for brothels she owns in Dijon, Marseille, and Lyon."

Moira's stunned expression told him volumes.

Smith had to admit at least one of the weights on his chest had been lifted; he would have hated to believe that Moira had known about those houses of misery but had done nothing to stop it.

"Your mother sent Robert over here with instructions to set up a new network—one that would cut out Mr. Onions' employers. They took umbrage at her plan and your brother was their victim. As were you."

Smith tilted his head to get a better look at the man who'd inflicted such a vicious whipping on Moira.

Onions recoiled from his stare and raised his tied hands. "*Please*, no more," he begged in a voice made ragged by screaming.

Smith smiled. "Hush, now, Mr. Onions. What did I tell you about talking out of turn?"

Onions threw himself face down, blubbering and sobbing, and commenced to crawl toward Smith, likely to kiss his feet.

Thankfully Gideon stopped him.

The other man had been remarkably easy to break, not much of a challenge at all. When Smith was done with Onions—which he would be, soon—the other man would serve as an object lesson for what happened to a person who touched what belonged to him.

Smith turned back to the French madam and her lover, both of whom were staring at him with loathing and a pleasing amount of fear.

"Now, where was I?" he asked. "Oh, yes, Marie's incursion into *run goods*," he said, using the street cant for selling virgins. "Blois would never dirty his hands with trade, although he has certainly enjoyed the fruits of your mother's business for decades. No, what he really wanted was to get to me, but he is too much of a coward to do it himself. You aren't the first person he used to do so, neither is Sandrine." He smiled at Moira's lovely, gentle sister. "He prefers to have others do his dirty work. Don't you, my lord?"

Blois stared stonily, his gaze on something at Smith's feet.

Smith bent down to pick up the revolver. He opened the chamber; four bullets, three more than necessary. He snapped it shut and turned back to Blois, who was now watching him with more than a touch of apprehension.

"I can only assume you're here because you are desperate, my lord. I daresay the pounding your financial interests have been taking over the last two or three years might be behind your actions."

Smith raised his eyebrows and grinned as horrible comprehension dawned in the other man's eyes.

"*You*?" Blois gasped. "But… *how*?"

"You would be amazed by how much a desire for revenge can motivate a man to be inventive. Would you like to sit?" Smith offered, pushing the room's only chair toward him. "No?" Smith said when the other man continued to stare. He shrugged. "Please yourself."

"You are the devil," Blois said in a voice that was a mere husk of his commanding baritone.

Smith closed the distance between them, until their faces were only inches apart. Blois tried to back away but was stopped by the wall behind him.

"I *am* the devil," Smith agreed. "And you are the man who made me what I am today."

He realized his breathing had begun to quicken and he was squeezing the pistol grip until it cut into his hand.

It was unlike him to allow his emotions to seize control.

But then this was an event that was decades in the making.

"Madame Bardot," he said, not taking his eyes away from Blois. "You will take your son and go back to France. The next time I see either of you—or anyone you might think to send after me—I will come to Paris myself and kill you both." Marie Bardot gasped, but Smith ignored her. "Gideon, take them to the docks and put them on the first ship to France.

Marie Bardot hesitated, stepping closer to the man who'd bred multiple children on her and didn't give a tinker's curse about any of them—or her, either probably.

"But what about Thibaut?" Marie said. "Can he not go back with us?"

Smith turned to her without veiling his thoughts, allowing her to see the person he kept locked inside.

She recoiled and backed away, her lips parted, eyes wide with fear.

Smith nodded at Malcolm and Edward. "Take the others outside and wait for me."

"Smith?" Moira said, taking a step toward him, her hand out, her voice shaking. "Please. I know he was behaving brutally, but he wouldn't have killed you. Can you not—"

It was Blois who laughed, a surprising show of spirit. "You think to plead with the devil?"

Edward laid a hand on Moira's shoulder.

"Go with him, Moira." Smith dimly regretted that Moira had to be here for this, but he had lost the ability to think of anything or anyone except the man across from him

And Blois only had eyes for *him*.

They were, he realized, more intimate than lovers in some ways, their hatred binding them so tightly it was difficult to think of anything else with Blois so near.

He felt a light touch on his shoulder. "Please… Maximus."

Smith startled at the sound of the name, which he'd not heard in decades, and whipped around. "*Go*," he hissed.

Whatever Moira saw—not the Smith she knew—made her jerk her hand away.

This time when Edward led her away, she went without protesting.

The door closed behind them and Smith turned to Blois and smiled. "Alone at last."

Chapter 22

Moira felt as if she were trapped with people who couldn't understand the language she was speaking.

She clutched Edward Fanshawe's arm when he closed the door. "Don't let him do this—that is my father in there. He might not be much of a father, but he is the only one I have."

Edward gave her a stony look and led her away from the door without speaking.

Moira turned to her sister—kind, loving, sweet Sandrine—and flinched at her cold expression.

"Sandrine—surely you—"

"What?" Sandrine demanded when she saw Moira's stunned look. "He deserves whatever Smith does to him—he deserves far, far worse. And our *mother* got better than she deserved. She should be in there with him, taking her own bullet. Not to mention Etienne, the heartless sycophant."

Moira's jaw sagged.

Sandrine grabbed Moira's upper arms and shook her hard enough to rattle her teeth. "Don't spare Blois even one more thought, Honorine. You have already given him—both of them—far too much of yourself and your life."

"But Sandrine—"

"Don't you understand what they have done to you—to all of us? They made us *whores*, Honorine. What kind of parent does that? And what about Robert? Marie turned him into the sort of man who bought and sold little girls! Just think of all the lives they have ruined."

Moira felt as if she were in a dream. Could they really be standing there arguing while one man cold bloodedly killed another only a few feet away?

As if to answer her question, the crack of a pistol came from inside the small stone building.

Moira jolted and looked at the faces of those around her.

Sandrine's chin was high and she wore an expression of fierce vindication.

Edward Fanshawe looked vaguely uncomfortable, as if somebody had just committed a mild solecism.

Luke looked as blank as he always did—unless he was gazing at Smith.

The other man—the one with half his face covered behind an ominous black leather mask, Malcolm, Smith had called him—kept his single eye on the quivering lump that was Onions, who was huddled at his feet.

Nobody cared about the shot they'd heard.

You don't either. You just want your betrayal to have meant *something.*

The words were like a kick, knocking the breath from her lungs.

Could that possibly be true?

The door opened and Moira rushed toward it.

Smith caught her in his arms and held her. "No."

She struggled, but it was like fighting against an immovable object. "I want to see him."

"No, you don't." He towed her gently but inexorably toward the two carriages that seemed to have appeared from nowhere.

"Let me go, Smith!" She pounded on his arm, shoulder, chest—any part she could reach—but it was like striking a tree.

Sandrine's arm slipped around her. "Stop, Honorine. Stop it. You will make yourself sick. *Honorine!*"

Sandrine struck Moira across the face hard enough to snap her head back.

Moira's jaw dropped and she stared at her sister.

"I'm sorry," Sandrine said coolly, taking Moira's unresisting arm and leading her to the carriage.

Thomas, one of Smith's footmen, held open the door and handed them inside, not making eye contact.

"I will ride on the box with Thomas," Luke said, giving Moira a pristine handkerchief before darting away.

Smith's battered, bruised face was unreadable. "Sandrine will take you home—she will stay with you."

He shut the door before Moira could respond and she stared out the window at him as the carriage rolled away.

Sandrine took her hand and pulled her closer. "Come and talk with me. How many years has it been? "

"Almost six," Moira said softly.

Sandrine gave an odd laugh. "Has it really been that long?"

"Marie and the *Comte* said you were dead. They said they didn't know what had happened to you until two years ago when they found out that it had been Smith who'd killed you."

Sandrine sighed and shook her head. "The one thing they didn't lie to you about was my death—we made sure they believed that."

"But… *why?* One minute you were living under Minister Bujold's protection and the next you told me you'd met a man and that he was going to take you away."

Sandrine scowled. "Bujold! That swine. You know he beat me? It was the only way he could achieve sexual satisfaction."

Moira had seen her sister's bruises and remembered how frightening Bujold had been when he'd confronted Marie after Sandrine's disappearance.

"I don't understand," Moira said. "Was Smith the man you met?"

"In a way." Sandrine sighed. "It was all a ploy, Honorine. They—the *Comte* and Marie—*forced* me to lie to you. They also forced me to come to London, using lies just as they did with you, but a different set of lies." She snorted. "Back then they were more direct than they were now, with you."

Sandrine paused and inhaled deeply, visibly upset.

"I was to approach Smith directly and throw myself on his mercy, beg him to help me. I was to tell him that I could give him damaging information about our father, whom Smith has hated for years. I don't know the story between them, but it goes back a long, long way. Although Smith never told me how it started, I'm sure Blois did something terrible to deserve his animus." She gave Moira a firm look to go with her declaration. "I was supposed to worm my way into his trust and then kill him."

"They wanted *you* to do it?" Moira could not believe what she was hearing.

"Yes. They gave me poison to use."

Moira stared, speechless.

"I knew I wouldn't do it even before leaving France." Her beautiful blue eyes flickered around the inside of the coach, as if she were trying to collect her thoughts. "The *Comte* told me that I was to kill Smith because he had killed his son. I remember thinking to myself: *Why should I murder to avenge somebody I was never even good enough to meet?*"

"That is more than the *Comte* ever told me," Moira admitted, sickened by how stupid she had been. How gullible.

Sandrine looked up from her clasped hands. "I didn't want to leave you, but I *needed* to get away, Honorine. I—I thought Bujold might kill me with his beatings. Marie told me the only way to get out of my contract with him was to run away." Sandrine scowled. "Of course, Marie wouldn't give me my money when I left—you know how she always held the contents of that damned vault over our heads!"

Yes, Moira knew.

Sandrine sighed and went on in a calmer voice. "So, I took the chance they offered and I made it my way out. Once I was here, I told Smith the truth. Instead of killing me, he saved me."

Moira felt like she couldn't get enough air: Sandrine had done what she couldn't do—and she had freed herself.

While Moira had handed Smith over to people who would have killed him.

"Honorine?" Sandrine leaned closer. "What is wrong?"

"Moira." It was a struggle to get even that word out.

Sandrine's forehead furrowed. "I'm sorry?"

"Call me Moira—not Honorine. Honorine Bardot is dead."

It remained to be seen what happened to Moira Dunsmuir.

***

"I want at least *part* of the story—I've earned it," Gideon proclaimed. "Don't you agree?" he asked Malcolm and Edward, both of whom hesitated.

Smith snorted and looked from the glass of American whisky—called bourbon—to his three friends.

"Do we need to do this *now?*" he asked. "Because I'd really like to climb into my bathtub and soak for three days, eat a good meal, and sleep for a week." He yawned and then winced at the pain in his face and ribs.

Malcolm wore a resigned, but stubborn look. "Think of it as a tax, Smith, the price of friendship."

Gideon and Edward nodded.

Smith had to laugh at that.

And then winced again.

"Besides," Mal added. "You know every damned detail of my life." He glanced at Edward and Gideon, who immediately nodded. "So, it only seems fair we learn a little about yours."

They were sitting in Malcolm's study. Although Edward and Gideon had only met Malcolm Barton at his wedding the year before the three men were already on the way to becoming friends.

Indeed, Smith thought sourly, when he'd told Malcolm what he was doing, the man had gone behind his back to rope in Edward—and apparently Gideon, whom he'd not learned about until today.

"It is for your own good," Malcolm had had the nerve to say when Smith had confronted him about bringing in Edward.

In retrospect, Smith was very, very grateful to have had the assistance of all three men. Things had become ugly today and he and Malcolm would have had their hands full without the other two.

It was late. The day had been taken up with matters like returning Onions to the hole where Smith was keeping him and then picking up Blois's two henchmen—Victor Turnbull and his son—and seeing that they were given to the captain of one of the syndicate's ships, a rather fanatical man known for taking ex-convicts as crew and motivating them to lead God fearing, crime-free lives.

Lastly, they'd had to dispose of the *Comte*'s body.

Smith raised the glass to his mouth, took a sip, and then winced when the liquor burned the split in his lip.

"Hurts?" Gideon said.

"Only when I smile," Smith quipped.

"You wouldn't have to deal with any of that if you had just let us pick them up before they came for you," Malcolm pointed out unhelpfully.

"Or even if you'd let us take them *after* they broke into your house," Edward added.

Smith knew that was true. As soon as he'd received word from Joe Bacon about the November Fifth plan, he could have picked up Turnbull and his nephew—or waited to take all four when they came to Smith's house.

Had he done so, he doubted that Moira would have ever believed him when he told her what her family had planned for him.

But that wasn't the real reason he'd done things the way he had.

"If I'd taken them then, Blois would have never sent the message he did," he explained.

"A message to whom?" Gideon demanded. "Christ, Smith! Just what the hell is this all about? Who was Blois to you? What is going on? Why does everything about you have to be so…*tangled?*"

"You're whining, Gideon," Edward said before turning to Smith. "But you *did* promise us some answers. Starting with who the hell you really are."

Malcolm nodded. "I think we've earned a bit of trust."

Smith sighed. Yes, they had.

"At least we should know your real name," Gideon added.

Gideon had started a game of sorts, years ago, where he would try to guess Smith's Christian name. Smith had promised to tell him if he guessed right, knowing that he never would.

He'd only told his real name to one person in London, Nora Fanshawe, after she'd essentially blackmailed him. But Nora had never mentioned it again.

Gideon, on the other hand, would probably be relentless.

"I haven't been called by my real name for so long that Smith is now more *real* to me. My birthname is Maximus Proteus Nicolaides."

"What kind of name is *that?*" Gideon asked.

Malcolm's forehead, at least the half not covered by the black mask, wrinkled. "Er, Greek?"

"Yes."

"So… who are you? And why are you hiding?" Gideon asked.

"Who am I?" He snorted softly. "I'm the last direct descendant of John VI Kantakouzenos, the longest-lived ruler of the Byzantine Empire."

All three men stared.

Predictably, it was Gideon who recovered first. "Wait a moment— if you are a descendent of"—he looked at Edward and frowned. "Who is in charge of the Byzantine Empire? A king? Queen?"

"As it was an *empire* it would have been an *emperor,*" Edward said dryly.

Gideon ignored the dig, his forehead wrinkled. "Emperor? Does that mean—"

Edward rolled his eyes. "Yes, Gideon, that means Smith probably outranks you."

Smith and Malcolm laughed, and Gideon sputtered, "That's not what I meant."

Smith suspected that was *exactly* what he meant. Ever since Gideon had learned he was an earl he'd been obsessed with status.

"I wasn't the best student at the orphanage," Edward said, "but the Byzantine Empire fell long ago, didn't it?"

"Yes, very long ago—the middle of the fifteenth century. John the VI was eventually forced to step down, living out his last years as a monk in The Peloponnese, in the Despotate of Morea."

"And where is that, exactly?" Malcolm asked.

"It's the area now within the Kingdom of Greece, where his son was Despot Manuel Kantakouzen who—"

Gideon moaned as if he were in physical pain. "Please, *stop*. Is there going to be much more of this? Because I *hated* history in school. All those dead people with unpronounceable names and places I've never heard of."

Smith laughed. "While my ancestor was no longer an emperor, my family managed to prosper, until they were the wealthiest and most influential force in Mystras—which had once been the capital of the Morea."

"That's a walled city, is it not?" Edward asked.

"I'm surprised you've heard of it."

"Nora's got me reading mythology lately," Edward admitted, his cheeks darkening slightly at his admission.

"Yes, it is a walled city," Smith said. "Or at least it was. Now it's a walled ruin. In the 1830s the city suffered a dreadful fire and was afterward abandoned."

"A natural fire, or arson?" Malcolm asked, the unburned side of his face grim.

"Oh, it was very much intentional." Even now, Smith could sometimes hear the screams of his sisters, his youngest brother, and his mother. "Every member of the Nicolaides family died in that fire. Except me, and I should have died that day, too."

And he would have, had he not disobeyed his mother.

"So, how is this connected to Moira's father?" Gideon asked.

"It was Blois who was there that day—he and seven other men, all armed. It was a joint military action—France and Great Britain. He'd been sent by French officials to ensure there would be no rebellion in the countryside. It didn't take many soldiers to terrorize a village filled with women, children, and elders."

He poured himself another drink and then held up the bottle, but the others shook their head.

Smith continued. "The independence movement had been raging across the area for over a decade, but the allied powers had managed to broker a fragile peace. They wanted to ensure there were no other rebels to threaten the new Kingdom of Greece that was to be established—complete with a foreign king chosen at the Convention of London. The Nicolaides name was well respected and people had approached my father several times to take sides, but he had remained neutral. His neutrality didn't matter to Blois and his group, who looked upon their mission as an opportunity to enrich their own coffers."

Smith took a drink and hissed at the pleasurable burn.

"You needn't tell us about this if you don't want," Malcolm said in a quiet voice.

"Wait—I want to know," Gideon blurted. "What?" he demanded when the other two men glared at him.

Smith smiled. Judging by his small audience's reactions, it was a feral smile. Well, he was feeling feral. He was also ready to speak the truth for the first time in over thirty-five years.

"I am still alive because I was obsessed with collecting bird eggs. I'd heard of a rare bird nest and was desperate to be the first capture a prize for myself. Unbeknownst to my parents, I sneaked out of the schoolroom, where my tutor had me studying. The journey to the nest was a bit precarious and quite far away.

"I was distracted by many things along the way—just as nine-year-old boys tend to be. It wasn't until I saw smoke—a great deal of it, coming from the direction of Mystras that I began to run like I'd never run before."

Smith moistened his lips, which were suddenly dry. "The townspeople were milling outside the walls, but there was nobody from my family. People tried to stop me from entering, but I easily broke through. Once I was inside, I saw that the fire burned strongest in the area where my family lived—in the biggest house. There were screams coming from the large courtyard where our family spent so much time. I climbed up on a stump and looked over the wall…"

Smith closed his eyes for a moment, knowing what he would see when he looked into that courtyard.

There were men—eight of them, although he did not know their exact number until later—and what they were doing at that moment was branded on his mind's eye.

Two had large sacks that were so heavy they were dragging them—pausing to push silver and plate from the large family table that was set for a meal that would never happen.

Two others were dragging the bodies of his older brother Gaius and his father, their limp arms and legs and the broad smears of blood on the stone courtyard telling a silent tale.

But it was the last three men he remembered most clearly.

They had caught one of his sisters, his mother, and his father's youngest sister, his quiet, shy Aunt Alexa, and were doing… things to them.

His nine-year-old brain didn't know about rape. At least not until that day.

Later, he would recall the men as they'd been in that moment: laughing and pillaging and raping while smoke swirled around them. It was like some of the religious paintings of Hell that Smith would later see—a cautionary tale: behave, or you will end up *here*.

A small pile of bodies—he couldn't see their faces, but he recognized his sisters' dresses—lay off to one side of the courtyard, close to the fire.

As he watched, a man dressed in a soldier's uniform climbed off his thirteen-year-old sister Phile and bent to pull up his trousers.

Phile crawled away, her dress torn off her slight body, smears of blood all over her. She managed to get to her feet just as the man buttoned up his trousers. He caught her easily, grabbing her long, wavy hair—Phile's pride and joy. He then raised his arm and Smith saw the blood splash, even though Phile was hidden by the man's body.

Something broke inside his nine-year-old brain and he charged screaming, flinging himself onto the man who was writhing and thrusting on top of his aunt. He was screaming and pounding his fists, blinded by tears and rage.

A hand gripped his hair—still long because it was spring, before the summer shearing he and his brothers had so disliked—and yanked him to his feet.

He was surrounded by laughter and the babble of voices in a language he did not know. He kicked and fought and bit, until another hand struck his face and knocked him to the ground.

His head rang and he was aware of his mother and aunt, weeping and screaming.

"Run, Maximus! Run!"

But he couldn't run. He couldn't even move, because the man towering over him—an impossibly tall, dark-haired man with a cruel sneer—planted his booted foot on Smith's chest. He said something in his language to the others, both of whom had finished their raping, and the men laughed.

One of them said something back to him, and the words *Monsieur la Comte* stuck in his mind.

A voice came from the small olive grove—where the youngest children played most of the day.

Smith's captor and his henchmen laughed harder and nodded, pointing to Smith.

Smith heard his two young sisters before he saw them. Five-year-old Xenia and seven-year-old Mya, his favorite among all his siblings.

As he watched in speechless horror, one of the other men approached the group. He said something, his hands going to his trousers. A gesture that would have been meaningless only minutes earlier made Smith scream like an enraged animal.

He somehow managed to break free of his captor, only to be seized by what felt like a hundred hands. Another man ripped off Mya's cotton shift and then pinned back her arms—

"Smith!"

Smith punched and kicked, vaguely aware of shattering glass and a pained grunt.

"Bloody hell! *Smith!*"

A body fell on top of him and arms twisted around his neck, choking off his air. Another hand grabbed his arm and squeezed.

"Smith! Stop! It is Malcolm, Edward, and Gideon. *Stop.*"

Smith blinked and the haze of smoke cleared, the screams disappearing.

Malcolm and Edward loomed over him; their expressions horrified.

"It is just us—your friends," Malcolm said, breathing heavily.

"And you're bloody crushing me," Gideon grunted, his voice vibrating through Smith's back and making him realize that he was lying on top of the other man. "Can I let you go now?" Gideon asked, his arms still tight around Smith's neck. "Or will you try to kill us with a damned glass of whisky?"

Smith's hand, he saw, was damp and bleeding, his fingers clutching a bloody shard of glass.

"He's fine, now." Malcolm held out a huge hand.

When Smith took it, the bigger man pulled him to his feet with ease. Smith glanced around the room, appalled by the destruction he'd caused. "I'm sorry, I—Good God, did I cut you?"

Malcolm glanced down at the sleeve of his coat, which was indeed cut. "Just a scratch. Here, sit. I'll get you a fresh glass."

"Isn't anyone going to help *me* up?" Gideon asked from his position flat on the floor.

Smith went to the supine man and extended his arm.

Gideon stared at his hand and then at Smith. "Are you sure you won't try and kill me with a pen nib or some other seemingly harmless item?"

Smith snorted. "I promise."

Once everyone was resettled, chairs were back upright, and a servant had been summoned to clean up the broken glass and spill, they all sat in silence, clearly waiting for the rest of the story.

Smith took a deep breath before continuing. "When I returned to the area years later, I learned that the same thing that happened to my family happened in at least a dozen other places. Not all were looted or burnt to the ground, and not everyone was murdered, raped, or sold into slavery, like what happened in Mystras, but nobody escaped the roving bands of soldiers unscathed."

"That's what happened to you? Blois sold you?" Gideon's face was no longer confused and disgruntled; it was now a mask of cold fury. Smith knew about the year and a half the other man had spent in an orphanage, where he'd been sold and sexually exploited.

"Yes, one of the men—an English soldier—sold me along with several others," he said shortly. That was a story he would not tell—to anyone.

"You have no family left—at *all*?" Malcolm asked.

"None that I could find. Blois and his men were very… thorough."

"And the men who were there that day—you said it was just eight of them?" Gideon asked.

Smith nodded. "Yes. It has taken me years, but I found each of them." He didn't explain what he did when he found the men, but he could see by their faces they could guess. "There is only left alive one, now."

"That's why you wanted to wait until after Blois captured you. He sent a letter to the last man?" Malcolm guessed.

Smith nodded, thinking about the name it had taken him thirty-five years to get. "I wasn't sure he would do it—for years he'd been careful not to communicate with the man who'd been his English counterpart—but it was worth the risk."

"So, who is the last man?" Gideon asked.

Malcolm gave a snort of disbelief while Edward turned to Gideon and said repressively, "That is none of our affair, *my lord.*"

Naturally Gideon was unrepressed. "I think I earned the right to know today. Especially after Smith almost killed me." He crossed his arms and stared. "Well?"

Smith couldn't help chuckling. "Sir Clayton Tyler."

Gideon's brow furrowed. "That name sounds familiar."

Edward slapped a hand on his forehead and muttered something beneath his breath.

"What?" Gideon demanded.

Malcolm explained. "Clayton was high up in the Home Office—I don't recall his actual title, but he was driven out and it was a big scandal. Something about missing money." Malcolm's gaze was speculative and worried as it rested on Smith. "He had accumulated a great deal of power over the years, so it took some doing to oust him."

"That is the story," Smith said.

Gideon whistled. "Lord! An ex-minister?"

"Not a minister," Malcolm muttered, his gaze still on Smith. "But still a powerful man."

"You aren't going to go after *him*?" Gideon asked.

Edward took one look at Smith and then sighed. "Oh, yes he is."

Gideon leaned forward in his chair and rubbed his hands together. "What is the plan, then?"

"The less you know about this, the better," Smith said. Gideon opened his mouth, doubtless to argue, but Smith said, "On this I stand firm."

Gideon shrugged. "Fine." He smirked like a man who knew he would eventually convince Smith otherwise. "What about Blois's son?" Gideon asked. "Did you kill him?"

"*Gideon,*" Edward said, briefly turning to stare at the ceiling, as if seeking divine assistance.

"What?" Gideon demanded. "We all know what Smith has done in furtherance of the syndicate's interests" He sneered at Edward. "Or do you believe the number of deaths that occur whenever somebody displeases Smith is a *coincidence*? The man is like a bloody human plague."

Humor glinted in Malcolm's eye when he glanced at Smith and he could see his laconic friend was amused and charmed by Gideon's open, outrageous manner.

Smith looked at the younger man. "I'm not a child-killer, Gideon," he said. "Although I suppose being a child abductor is hardly any better. In my defense, Blois was a cold, manipulating bastard who made his other children's lives—both illegitimate, and his three legitimate daughters—a misery. And his wife was a lover of Morpheus long before I took her infant son twenty-one years ago. The couple I gave the boy to couldn't have children." He gave Edward a significant look. "They are neither rich nor poor, but good, salt of the earth farmers. Yves—as the new *Comte* de Blois is now called—is happily married with a child of his own on the way. Fortune has smiled upon Yves and he is a wealthy man in his small village." Smith had seen to that. "If he had remained with Blois he would have been warped and twisted and probably like his father. And also poor after I finished with the *Comte*." Smith shrugged. "So you could claim he is better off, all around."

"Still, you took him from his parents," Gideon said. As a new father himself, Smith could see the notion was a nightmare to him. "Blois never knew whether his son was alive or dead?"

"No, he didn't."

"Did you at least tell him the truth before you shot him?"

Smith smiled. "No."

"Christ, Smith." He shook his head. "That is so cruel there should be some new word to describe it. The poor man must have gone insane."

"That *poor* man killed my entire family," Smith said coolly. "I will neither attempt to justify nor apologize for my actions."

"We're not asking you to," Edward said hastily. "Are we, Gideon?"

Gideon's jaw clenched, but he finally dropped his gaze and shook his head. "No."

"So," Malcolm said after yet another uncomfortable silence. "Only one name left."

"Only one."

"We are here for you if you need any assistance giving Clayton what he deserves," Edward said.

Gideon nodded. "Too right we are."

Malcolm nodded.

Smith merely said, "Thank you."

"Clayton is rumored to be a dangerous, slippery bastard," Malcolm said. "One part of his responsibilities was allegedly handling some of Britain's most lethal, er, covert operatives."

Smith knew he meant the government agents who sometimes carried out Her Majesty's commands in a quieter, far less legal manner. Killers, in other words.

Smith took another sip of whisky, savored it, and then smiled at his oldest friend. "It is fortunate for me that I enjoy a challenge."

Chapter 23

Moira and Sandrine talked until dawn, and still Smith had not returned.

She learned Sandrine was married to a solicitor and had two children. And that she lived in a village only a short distance outside London.

Moira knew she would be happy for her sister's good fortune once the numbness wore off. But, for now, there were simply too many shocks still reverberating through her stunned mind.

Not the least of which was the knowledge that her sister had once been Smith's lover.

Moira had never felt jealousy before, but she'd heard enough about the emotion to recognize it. She could see it in the way Sandrine spoke that she still cared deeply for Smith.

"He saved me, Moira. He made the life I have today possible. I didn't mean to, but I fell in love with him." She gave a sad laugh. "He did not return my feelings, but he was kind and caring and did more for me than either of our parents ever did. I am still ashamed that I believed the worst of him for so long—" she stopped and bit her lip, her creamy skin flushing in a way that had always sent men into rut. "I didn't mean it like that. I know you thought he was responsible for my death. I understand why you were so adamant that he needed to be brought to justice and—"

"I was a fool to ever believe the *Comte* or Marie were interested in anything legal."

A pathetic fool.

"You mustn't blame yourself—"

"Shhh, don't worry." Moira took her sweet, gentle sister's hand and squeezed. She couldn't bear to hear Sandrine try to explain away what she had almost done to a man who'd shown her nothing but kindness.

A man she loved.

The father of her child.

"How long have you known about me being here?" she asked her sister.

"He came to me about a week ago," Sandrine admitted. "I wanted to come to you then—I begged him to tell you that I was alive and well, but he wanted to wait."

Because Smith had wanted Moira to trust him.

To *choose* him.

The reality of what she'd done—handed him over without even giving him a chance to defend himself—made her feel ill.

Sandrine laid a hand on her shoulder. "Moira? You suddenly became so pale."

"I'm fine. How long will you stay?" she asked, unable to talk anymore about what she'd done.

"At least until Smith returns. He put me up in a hotel and I've been waiting for… well, *this* to happen for several days. I cannot stay too much longer. I have an able nurse for the children, but… I miss them."

"Of course you do." That is what normal parents did: loved and missed their children.

Sandrine hesitated and then said, "I'm sorry I never wrote to you— never told you what happened. But Smith said it would be best to break all contact with that life. He worried they would send somebody for me if they knew I was alive."

Smith had been right. Now that she knew what Smith had done to the *Comte*—taking his heir—she understood her blood-father's obsession all these years.

"Are you sad?" Sandrine asked.

Moira didn't need to ask what she meant. "I'm not mourning the *Comte* himself," she admitted. "But I'm mourning the loss of what family I had."

"Now you have me," Sandrine said. "And Molly and Sarah and my husband, Albert."

Moira embraced her sister, suddenly weary to her very bones. "Thank you, Sandrine. You must be tired—it is late."

"It has been a long day," Sandrine agreed.

"Get some rest. I will see you in the morning."

Moira found Luke waiting for her in her chambers.

"I told you to go to sleep," she said, shaking her head at his perfectly coifed, dressed, and groomed person.

"I did, Miss Moira. I napped for an hour."

She snorted. "I'm too tired to argue."

Luke's lips twitched into the slightest of smiles as he began to undress her.

"Has Mr. Smith returned?" she asked as Luke knelt to strip off her stockings.

"No, miss."

"Do you know when he will?"

There was a slight hesitation and then, "I'm sorry but I don't know. Would you like me to ask Knox?"

"No, that's fine."

Smith would come back when he felt like it.

Or not.

***

Smith spent that night and a good part of the next day at the suite the syndicate maintained at their gambling club. It had been years since he'd used the rooms, not since he and Gideon had occasionally gone on the prowl together, often bringing back lovers to share.

He knew he shouldn't avoid seeing Moira—that he should go home and allow her to confront him—but he needed to gather information about Clayton before the man disappeared for good. And for that, he needed a clear head. The drama that awaited him at home would need to wait a bit longer.

Once he'd bathed and slept for an hour he'd sent for Doctor Felton, who'd shaken his head and *tsked* at Smith's various cuts and bruises, declared that three of his ribs were bruised—perhaps even cracked—and prescribed two weeks of rest.

Smith thanked him, ignored his advice, and spent the afternoon chasing down Clayton's whereabouts, calling in every favor that he'd accumulated over the years from his various criminal connections.

Information was thin on the ground, but by the end of the day, he'd found somebody with something to sell.

It was almost midnight when Smith left his carriage and bodyguards in front of the Victoriana Hotel—a dingy, rundown establishment that Her Majesty likely wouldn't appreciate using her name.

His skin prickled as he passed through the grimy lobby, and down a narrow, gloomy corridor. He kept his eyes straight ahead to avoid looking too closely at the filthy kitchen as he slipped out the back door.

Parking at the hotel and sneaking out seemed like too much precaution to take, but it made his two guards less agitated about him walking the few foggy blocks to the meeting place alone.

Barry and Howard had been on duty when Smith had been abducted. He'd told the men beforehand about the plan and had instructed them to accept whatever food Moira gave them, and to pretend as though they'd become ill. He'd also insisted that they let Blois take him from the house.

The guards had been extremely unhappy with his decision, arguing until he'd finally allowed them to follow Blois's carriage when it left Smith's house.

Smith knew that his friends had believed he was mad to go along with the kidnapping, but he'd never really been in much danger between the guards and his three friends.

Tonight, he'd left his guards behind because he didn't want anyone else hearing the information that he'd paid for. Not because he didn't trust them, but because conspiring to murder a public official—even a former, disgraced one—was a serious crime. Neither Howard nor Barry needed to expose themselves to such risk.

Smith didn't need the exposure, either, but bloody Clayton had gone to ground like a fox immediately after Blois had sent him that damned message and he simply couldn't think of any other way to get information about the man.

Ahead of him the battered sign for the Crab & Badger Pub emerged from the gloom, the two lamps beside the door barely managed to cut the combined darkness and filthy fog.

The fug inside the ancient pub was scarcely any better than outside.

The man he was to meet, Red Jasper, sat in the far corner, a bar wench balanced on his knee. When he saw Smith, he gave the girl an ungentle shove.

Smith handed the disgruntled lass a larger denomination coin—but not so large as to draw unwanted attention—and said, "Two pints."

Once she was gone, he took the seat beside Red Jasper, rather than across from him, which would have put his back to the entrance. Although he'd been using the other man's services for decades, that didn't mean he trusted him.

Red Jasper grinned, exposing an astoundingly white pair of teeth—none of which had been gifted to him by Nature. "S'been donkey's ears, Smiff."

Not long enough, in Smith's opinion, but he had nothing to gain by being insulting, so he offered the other man a brief smile and said, "Indeed it has. What do you have for me, Red?"

Red leaned closer, the smell that came with him enough to make Smith's eyes water. "This'll cost more'n the usual."

He *always* charged more than the usual, which—Smith thought with a smirk—rather made that the usual, didn't it?

"Fine. What do you have," he repeated.

"The man in question 'asn't got no family to speak of. 'Ee 'asn't got no bolt 'ole in the country, neither."

Smith knew all that. It hadn't surprised him that Sir Clayton owned very little. The man was infamous for never passing up a card game or horse race, no matter how rigged the game or lame the horse.

Smith sat back when the barmaid returned and deposited two foaming pints on the table. She hovered, met Smith's gaze, and then scuttled back to the bar.

Red took a slurping gulp from his glass.

"What else?"

"Ee makes a fair living off black."

Smith sighed. "Yes, I know he engages in blackmail." He'd managed to purchased a copy of Clayton's list of victims—for an obscene price—earlier that day. Clayton's years at the Home Office had given him unparalleled access to dirty secrets, not to mention put him in a position to bury a goodly number of his own.

Smith would consider approaching some of the individuals on the list if nothing else yielded any results. Most of the names belonged to powerful people whom he had no desire to alienate. More importantly, Smith didn't want everyone in the city to know he was after Clayton. Right now, the only people who knew were his three friends and Red Jasper.

He could trust his three friends.

The man across from him…?

Well.

Red leaned even closer and it was all Smith could do not to gag at the smell of his body odor. "I've found somebody 'oo ain't on that list."

"Oh?"

Red nodded. "'Ee tapped the Earl of Selkirk for 'elp just yesterday."

Smith sat back, startled by the name.

He wasn't surprised to learn that the Infamous Earl would do plenty that was worthy of blackmail, only that the man would pay to hide anything. The rumors that swirled around the millionaire, dark horse earl were plentiful and murky.

Smith was intrigued. What, in the name of all that was unholy, had Selkirk done that Clayton could use as blackmail fodder?

"Do you know why Selkirk would pay him?" he asked Red.

Red snorted. "Naw, guv. 'is loreship don't confide in me since I gave 'im the cut direct." He cackled at his jest.

"So, that's all you have for me—that he sent a minion to Selkirk?"

Red wiped the foam from his lips with the back of his hand. "You know 'ow much brass I 'ad to spread about to get even *that*?"

Smith sighed, reached into his coat pocket, and produced the small leather pouch he'd filled with *brass* before leaving the house.

When Red reached for it, Smith trapped both the money and his hand on the table. "You know who to come to if anyone asks you about this subject, don't you?"

The smirk evaporated from the other man's face and a slight tremor passed through the hand Smith was holding down. Good, it was nice to know that some of his reputation from the *old days* persisted.

Of course, dropping Onions off on his street corner earlier that day—rather the worse for wear—would have also helped the criminal element remember Smith and what he was capable of.

"Aye," Red said, nodding. "I know what's o'clock."

Smith released Red's hand, pushed his untouched pint across the warped, sticky table, and stood.

"Oi, one more fing, guv."

Smith lifted an eyebrow.

"Nobody can prove nuffink, but Clayton's 'ad people snuffed. You might not need to find '*im*. Wouldn't be surprised if '*ee* sends somebody for *you*."

Smith smiled. "I hope he tries."

Chapter 24

Moira had just seen her sister off—a tearful parting, with Moira promising to visit Sandrine and her family within the next few weeks—when Luke brought a message to her sitting room.

"The master would see you now. He's in his study."

She looked at his impassive face, her heart pounding. "Did he just return?"

"No, Miss. He came home during the night."

Why had he not summoned her last night?

You know why.

Moira swallowed down her pain and nodded. "Thank you, Luke."

Once he left, she looked at her reflection; she was pale and there were dark smudges beneath her eyes.

At least her hair, freshly cut only a few nights ago, was neat and tidy. She smoothed the front of the soft, primrose skirt—yet another color she would have not dared to wear if not for Smith—and made her way downstairs, dread making each step heavier than the last.

"Come in," he said immediately after she knocked.

He stood up from the chair behind his desk—where he must have been working, although the surface was pristine—clear of even so much as a sheet of paper.

"Your poor face," Moira blurted when he looked up at her.

He smiled faintly. "It looks far worse than it feels." He gestured to the seating area in front of the crackling fire. Moira sat and he lowered himself into the chair across from her. "Would you like tea?"

"No thank you."

You killed my father.

The thought assaulted her like a brutal north wind, chilling her to the bone. What chilled her even more was that although she was deeply shocked, she felt no sadness, only a vague regret.

Moira dropped her gaze to his feet, fixating blindly on his glossy black boots as her emotions roiled and pitched inside her.

"How are you feeling today, Moira?" He asked, seemingly unaware of the turmoil inside her.

Moira forced herself to lift her eyes to his. He was looking at her with an expression of kind concern, not as if she were a traitor who'd betrayed his trust. Not as if he were the same man who'd cold bloodedly killed her father.

"I'm tired. I stayed up late to talk with Sandrine both nights."

The smile that curved his lips was fond. "Yes, she said you did a great deal of catching up."

"You talked to her?"

"She joined me for an early breakfast."

Suddenly it hurt to breathe; he had invited her sister to breakfast. Sandrine hadn't mentioned it, no doubt thinking to spare her feelings.

She swallowed convulsively, but the gritty envy or jealousy or whatever it was called stuck in her throat like a burr.

How can you care for his regard—in any way—after what he has done to your father?

Even though Marie was probably back in Paris by now, her voice was as loud as it had been when they'd stood in the same room. Not that her mother had said so much as a single word to her. Nothing.

You are in love with a man who killed your father!

Yes. I am.

It was a relief to admit it—if only in her head—and it seemed to banish her mother's shade.

"Moira?"

She wrenched her gaze up.

"You have been cleansing to prevent conception."

Moira could no longer work up any surprise that he knew. How he must have laughed at her puny efforts to deceive him.

"Yes."

"What would you have done if you'd become pregnant? Would you have aborted the child?"

"I—" she broke off, unable to finish what she needed to say.

"Yes?" He looked distant and reserved, like a stranger.

Only now did she realize just how warmly he'd always looked at her.

Only now did she understand how fortunate she'd been to have earned his regard.

Only to have thrown it away.

As she stared into his cool brown gaze she knew, without a doubt, that fury raged beneath his calm veneer.

"I'm pregnant."

He raised one eyebrow.

"It must have happened right after my last courses. I knew Luke had told you the last time—when I bled on the bedding, so I bought some blood from a butchers."

He didn't so much as blink.

"Did you already know?" she asked.

"No. So, you are pregnant. I repeat my question, what are you going to do about it?"

"I want to have it."

"Why? What has changed?"

Say it, Moira! Now is your chance. Probably your only chance.

She forced herself to meet his gaze. "Because I love you, Smith."

His face remained immobile and unreadable.

Moira wanted to melt into a puddle on the floor and disappear. But she had to do *something, any*thing, to make him understand.

"You don't believe me."

He didn't disagree.

"I wasn't even sure myself what I felt. I—well, I was so caught up in doing what I came to England to do that anything else seemed"— Moira stopped and searched his face for even a trace of understanding.

She found none.

How could she ever explain her life to him? The time to do that would have been before she'd betrayed him, when she could have put her trust in him and confessed.

"Your sister has told me a great deal about the way Marie and Blois raised you," he said. "I know the pressure they put on you and I know the misapprehension you labored under, specifically about Sandrine."

"Why didn't you *tell* me about Sandrine, Smith?" she couldn't help demanding.

"That wasn't my secret to tell, not when it would have put her life—or even just her happiness—in danger. But supposing I *had* gone against the promise I made to Sandrine. Suppose I *had* broken my word and told you about her. Are you telling me that you wouldn't have gone to your parents? Even if only to confront them on the issue?"

Moira opened her mouth to hotly deny it but stopped, because that is *exactly* what she would have done. Especially as she never would have believed her parents were capable of murder without seeing it with her own eyes.

It pained her to admit it, but she probably wouldn't have believed all Sandrine's story without some proof.

And all because she'd been so desperate to finally mean something to her parents. To do something that made them proud. That would make them love her.

"I don't know what I would have done," she lied, simply unable to admit the humiliating truth.

Rather than answer her, he went to his desk, took a fat bundle of paper from one of the drawers, and handed it to her without a word.

Moira recognized the top document as a copy of the contract she'd signed. She had an identical copy up in her chambers. Beneath it were several others, one of which seemed to be a deed for a house.

She looked up at him. "What is all this?"

"It is the deed to the house mentioned in your contract. It is only a few streets from here, on an excellent square with a delightful, fenced park. I will arrange for it to be made habitable and engage servants—"

Moira stood abruptly, the papers sliding from her lap onto the floor. "You are ending the contract?" Her brain scrambled for whatever she could find—any weapon, any tool. "Doesn't that make you in breach?"

For a moment he looked genuinely amused. "No, because there is a clause that reserved my right to do so without giving a reason. I marked it on that copy, but it is identical to the one you read that day—the one you signed."

Moira flinched at his not-so-subtle rebuke, not that she didn't deserve it.

"And what about me? Have I no right to know your reason?" Her entire body shook with anger—and fear. "I'm sorry," she said before he could answer "Of course I know your reason—I betrayed you."

He didn't speak.

She gave a laugh that sounded more like a sob. "You can't forgive me, can you?"

Something that looked like hesitation flickered across his face.

Moira struck as fast as an adder. "I—I made such a terrible mistake, I know that now, Smith. But I deeply regret what I did. And I'm having a child—*our* child—and—"

"No."

Moira's voice rose. "Do you really hate me that much?"

"I don't hate you, but I no longer wish to be your lover. And I don't want you in my house." He spoke quietly, but the words were like a thunderclap in her ears.

Hot tears slid down her cheeks. "Please tell me one thing?"

He nodded.

"Could you have loved me if all this hadn't happened?"

"We'll never know, will we?"

Moira flinched back from his quiet words, which were both more and less than what she deserved.

"I want to stay."

"But that decision isn't up to you."

"I will sign a new contract—one without money or payment of any sort. I will repudiate all you've given me, the house, the money. Just… don't make me leave."

Lines of irritation furrowed his forehead. "What would be the point of that?"

"To show you that it isn't for money that I offer myself. You can take everything back that you promised. I will stay and have the child with no assurances."

"You must think I am some sort of inhuman monster."

"*What?*"

"Do you really believe I would want to inflict such uncertainty on a child or the mother of my child?"

"No! I didn't mean that. I meant—" She bit her lip, unable to come up with the right words. She couldn't get past the regret—the burning, grinding regret—at what she had done to him. Even worse was what *might* have happened if Smith had not learned about the abduction plan beforehand.

He would be dead right now, and they both knew it.

And it would have been her fault.

Moira slid to her knees. She knew how to crawl and she'd done it times beyond counting in the past. But never before had she *needed* to abase herself for someone. She dropped to her hands, her eyes never leaving his as she crawled the short distance to him.

"Stop," he ordered, when she would have come close enough to touch him, his face a stern mask.

The knowledge that he didn't want her hands on him was like a needle-sharp blade sliding slowly into her heart; Moira suddenly couldn't bear that she'd thrown him away.

Hate and fear and jealousy had once been the worst emotions she could imagine.

But none of those could compare to regret.

Moira's hands closed around the supple leather encasing his ankle and she dropped her face to the toe of his boot, covering it with desperate kisses, even though she knew what a pitiful, disgusting sight she must be.

She rested her forehead on his toe. "Please, Smith, please." He didn't move or speak as she sobbed, her tears falling on cool leather when she yearned for the touch of his skin, the warmth of his breath.

Moira lost what control she had left and wept, crying as if her heart were breaking.

Because it was.

She cried until no more tears would come, until her eyes burned and her heart was empty and cold. Until the room was silent but for the ticking of the clock and the occasional pop of the fire, not even the street noises penetrated the well-insulated room.

"Sit up," he ordered quietly.

Moira rose up onto her knees. Her face would be hideous, her eyes red-rimmed; she was not the sort of woman who looked beautiful when she cried.

His gaze was hard; her weeping had left him untouched. "I don't trust you. And I don't think I ever will again," he said.

"I understand." And she did, no matter how much it hurt.

His jaw tightened and finally—*finally*—his mask slipped, giving her a glimpse of the anger and pain beneath. "I don't think you do, or you wouldn't keep asking me to allow you to stay. I want to hurt you, Moira—not for your own pleasure, but to feed my anger. I am disappointed and ashamed for entertaining such emotions. And I am furious at you for being the cause of them."

Moira shivered at the look of barely leashed savagery. "Then hurt me," she begged, a twisted but powerful bolt of lust shooting straight to her cunt at the thought of suffering for him.

His eyes were heavy and hooded, his normally full, smiling lips compressed into a cruel, cold slash. "If I start hurting you, I might not be able to stop myself." He frowned. "You should go."

"You really can't forgive me, can you?"

He sighed and reached out, as if to cup her face, but then lowered his hand without touching her. "I am sorry to cause you anguish. You deserve to be happy."

"But not with you," she whispered.

"No, Moira. Not with me."

Chapter 25

Luke hurried through the hushed corridors toward Mr. Smith's chambers, both anticipating and dreading seeing him.

The household, normally so comfortable and pleasant, had been tense and grim since Mr. Smith's abduction. Even though Luke hadn't asked Miss Moira about what had happened, he knew she'd played some part in it—a bad part if the distance between her and the master was anything to go by.

She'd moved through her days as though she were asleep, listlessly eating, bathing, going for her walks, and staring at books and never turning pages, merely existing, so broken and sad that it hurt to look at her.

What had Smith said to her three days ago when he'd called her to his study?

And where had the master gone immediately afterward?

None of this is your concern. He won't appreciate you prying into his affairs.

Yes, that was true enough.

Luke paused outside the master bedchamber, calmed his breathing, and knocked lightly.

"Come in!" a clipped voice called from within.

Mr. Smith was seated at a small secretaire desk, scribbling away on something and when he looked up, his stern expression eased into a weary smile. "Ah, Luke. Come in and have a seat. I'll just finish this and be right with you."

Luke slid into a chair and took the opportunity to stare at him. He looked thinner—as if he'd been going without meals—but of course that was ridiculous. He'd only been gone three days. The bruises on his face had turned from black and brown to a sickly purple and sullen yellow that looked far worse.

"There," Mr. Smith muttered, straightening the papers, and setting them to one side before removing his spectacles and looking up. "Miss Moira will shortly be moving to her own house."

Luke's eyes widened, but he nodded. "Yes, sir."

"There are matters that need seeing to before the house is habitable." He sounded distracted, almost as if he were speaking to himself. "Before you decide whether you will accompany her, you should understand the conditions."

Go with her?

Mr. Smith picked up a sheet of paper and held it toward him. "She agreed to the following."

Luke leapt to his feet to take the document. He sat and reached into an inner pocket to retrieve his glasses.

"I did not know you wore glasses," Mr. Smith said.

Luke flushed. "Just for reading, sir."

"You seem young to need them."

"I've needed them since I was a lad." He glanced down at the paper and his eyes widened a bit at the formidable list of requirements.

His head whipped up when he read the third item. "*Pregnant?*"

"Yes." He snorted softly. "She purchased blood to fool us."

Luke stared at Smith, trying to see how he felt about this development. He knew the other man would have been euphoric even a week ago.

But now…

Luke shook the thought away and focused on what was important: Miss Moira was pregnant with his master's child! He could only feel one thing—no matter what had gone wrong between the two lovers—and that was happiness.

"Congratulations, sir."

Smith smiled briefly. "Thank you. If you go with her, it will be part of your job to see that she complies with the list," he said, his fingers drumming on the desk in an unprecedented display of restlessness.

Mr. Smith said *if.* Not *you must go.*

This was Luke's chance, right *now.* He could say *no.* He could stay beneath his master's roof—perhaps they'd resume their relationship— and he could allow somebody else to care for Smith's discarded lover and unborn child.

Luke frowned. Why did that not feel quite… right?

"If I stay, then what would my duties be?" he asked.

Smith shrugged. "The same as before, if that is enough to keep you from getting bored. The house is so well-run I know there often isn't much to do."

Luke gripped the arms of the chair to keep from leaping up and capering with joy. They would return to their former arrangement!

But then Miss Moira's face—and her deadened gaze—flashed through his mind. She was pregnant and yet seemed to have lost her will to live.

Although Luke loved Mr. Smith, he'd grown quite fond of Miss Moira, and not only because of the child. She'd always been kind to him and friendly.

And she looked so very lost right now—so in need of somebody to care for her.

And the fact that it was *Smith's* baby in her belly, well…

"If I were to go with Miss Moira, could I—" Luke broke off, not sure how to phrase his desire.

"Could you still come see me?" Smith guessed, a faint smile curving his lips.

Luke nodded.

"Yes." Smith's smile grew into a fully-fledged smirk. "In fact, I might have to insist on it."

Luke's brain, already reeling, spun. Did Mr. Smith just say what he thought he'd said?

"If you don't wish to go, you must let me know now so that I might engage somebody suitable as soon as possible." Smith hesitated, looked Luke in the eyes, and then said, "She likes you and is comfortable with you. I would consider it a favor to me if you went with her."

And that was all it took.

"Of course, I will go with her, sir."

Smith's look of relief was all the gratitude Luke needed, but the other man smiled and said, "Thank you, Luke. That is a weight off my mind. I will want to speak to you at least weekly, primarily to check on her health and the condition of the child. She will also see the physician regularly, but he will report to me separately."

"Yes, sir."

"She is aware that you will report to me as it is part of our agreement."

"Of course, sir." Luke was relieved to hear that, because he didn't think that had been the case before.

"If there is anything else you wished to say—now is your chance, Luke."

Now is the perfect time to say it! Say it now! Say it now! This is your chance to at least tell him. And if he never wants to see you again… Well, you will already be gone.

Luke swallowed and forced himself to meet the other man's gaze.

Smith lifted his eyebrows. "Yes?"

"I have—" Luke's voice broke. "I have missed being with you," he said, his heart pounding so hard that his chest *hurt.*

But rather than look disappointed or disgusted, his master's stern expression softened. "And I, you."

Luke shoved down the deafening cheering in his head and hurried on, "It's more than that."

Smith waited patiently.

"I can't sign another contract agreeing to no emo—" his voice broke on the word. He cleared his throat and tried again. "I can't sign anything agreeing to no emotional attachment."

Mr. Smith's brow furrowed. "What are you saying, Luke?"

"I l-love you." It was so soft that even *he* could barely hear it. He raised his voice. "I *love* you, sir."

He'd never seen Smith looked shocked before—he assumed it was shock and not disgust—nor had he seen him at a loss.

The silence dragged between them.

Finally, Smith said, "I cannot give you what you want, Luke."

"You don't *know* what I want!" he retorted, his heated response startling them both. "You've never asked me what I wanted," Luke said, more quietly.

"No, that's true. Why don't you tell me."

Luke tried to compose his thoughts, but the words just began to leap out of his mouth, willy-nilly. "I *love* you. I have for ages—even before I accepted this position. It started when you used to come into the Briar Palace, and I looked forward to—" Luke stopped, biting his tongue to keep from just pouring everything out at the other man's feet.

Smith's eyes widened at his confession, but he nodded. "Go on."

"I've felt this way about you for a long time," he said, leaving the matter at that. "I suppose that makes me in breach of our contract—since I knowingly violated at least one section before even signing it."

Smith laughed softly. "I think I can let that go, under the circumstances."

Luke had to lower his gaze for this next part. "I'm *not* Charles." He glanced up from his clenched hands when Smith didn't say anything, relieved to see the other man didn't look angry at the mention of his former lover. He hurried on. "I want you to be happy because I love you, sir. I know how you are and I accept it. You're untamable and that's fine because I don't want to tame you. Or—or change you… I just want *you*." He swallowed. "As much of you as you can spare." He inhaled a shaky breath and stared at his tightly latticed fingers.

The room was so *quiet*.

When he risked a look at Mr. Smith, he saw he was smiling—this one genuine.

"You're not angry."

"How could I be, Luke?"

"But you didn't want—"

"Jealousy? Recriminations? Daily brawls?" Smith snorted. "No, I didn't. But I don't think that is what you are offering."

Luke shook his head. "No. But p-perhaps a bit of regularity?"

Smith chuckled. "I think that can be managed."

"How often may I come to you?" Luke persisted, wanting to have this issue settled and engraved in stone before he packed his bags.

"How often do you want?" Smith countered.

Every night rose to his lips, but Luke caught it. "I usually take Mondays as my free day."

"Then come on Mondays."

"Every Monday?"

"Yes."

Luke couldn't help from smiling, which then turned into a grin. He knew he looked like an idiot but couldn't help himself. "Very good, sir."

"If I am out of town on a Monday, we can make other arrangements." Smith cocked his head, a twinkle in his dark gaze. "Is that acceptable to you, Luke?"

"Very acceptable, sir."

Mr. Smith stood and came toward him.

Luke shot to his feet.

Smith reached up and cupped his face, and Luke heaved a sigh of contentment, nuzzling into his palm.

"I care for you, Luke. A great deal. I know I don't always show it—"

Luke leaned down and claimed Smith's mouth, cutting off his words.

Smith grunted with surprise but opened to him, his hand sliding behind Luke's neck and pulling him closer.

The kiss was tender and deep, like the sort between lovers, not the type between client and whore.

Smith could give Luke a piece of paper to sign—because that was what he needed—but their kiss was Luke's inarticulate way of sealing the deal they had just made.

Smith suddenly pulled away, his expression no longer civilized, his lips no longer smiling. "You know I don't like to share."

Luke couldn't help smiling at the other man's double standard. "I know that, sir."

"I allowed it before—with David, but not anymore."

"There is nobody else."

Smith nodded. "Good. You're mine."

"Yours," Luke agreed, happier than he'd ever been in his life.

Chapter 26

S mith's carriage rolled to a stop in front of the biggest mansion on Berkeley Square.

As wealthy as Smith was, the houses that lined the square represented ancient money and power and were—as yet—beyond his reach.

Many of the aristocrats who owned houses on this square were beneath water when it came to their finances, but the massive Portland stone Palladian belonged to Lord Jeremy Winters, the Earl of Selkirk.

Selkirk was many things the average aristocrat was not, and one of those things was an investment genius—and he was not ashamed of his financial acuity, unlike many others of his ilk, who viewed commerce as beneath them, even while their fortunes crumbled.

The earl was also a gentleman painter of some repute, although his pictures were not the sort to find their way into public galleries.

Smith had never met the man, but he'd had the good fortune to purchase one of Selkirk's paintings several years ago, a rather outrageous nude titled #6.27.

While Selkirk wasn't on the level of Nora Fanshawe, he had his own distinctive style and his work pulsed with eroticism, not to mention a healthy—or unhealthy, depending on where one stood on the matter—dollop of sadism.

The front door opened and a dignified butler greeted him. He gave the man a card. "Smith here to see the earl."

"Good evening, sir. His lordship is expecting you." He took Smith's hat and gloves before helping him out of his coat. "This way, sir."

He led Smith up to the very top floor, which was typically reserved for servants.

But the corridor was no servant hallway. There was a luxurious carpet runner and gleaming wood, not to mention a great deal of art—some hanging, some displayed in glass-fronted cases or shadowboxes.

Smith paused in front of one of the larger cases, whose contents were Peruvian, produced by the Moche, an Andean tribe. He could have spent hours looking at that display, alone.

"Right in here, sir."

He turned and saw the servant had stopped at a door at the end of the corridor.

"This is his lordship's studio, sir," the man said, and then opened the door.

Smith's eyes widened as he took in the north-facing room. Selkirk must have knocked the walls out of several rooms to create the giant space.

The earl was sketching a woman who was reclining on a chaise longue surrounded by strategically placed candelabra, the flickering candlelight creating a magical glow.

"Come in and have a seat," Selkirk muttered, his left hand flying over the large sketchpad. "I'll be with you in just one moment."

Smith lowered himself into the chair across from the earl and turned to the woman on the divan. She was nude except for a slender gold chain around her waist and a narrow black ribbon around her neck. Her knee was thrown out and exposed her sex. The pose should have been lewd, but instead she looked as if she'd simply sprawled that way—perhaps after a lover had finished with her—and was too content to move.

Her face was attractive enough, but not so distinctive that you would notice her in a crowd. Rather, it was her body that drew one's eyes—or at least it drew Smith's. She had exceptionally large breasts on a ribcage that was almost freakishly slender, her hips generously flared, her legs long and well-muscled; the legs of a woman who worked, Smith surmised.

There was a chill in the air and her skin had goosebumps, her large nipples puckered into pebbles. Her thighs were sheened and her sex glistened in the romantic lighting. As chilled and exposed as she was, the pose—or something—had aroused her.

The earl gave a low grunt of satisfaction, and then tossed the charcoal into a metal tray with a soft *tink* and set his sketchbook aside.

Smith watched with interest as Selkirk's mind came back from where it had gone—some place of pure artistic expression, the sort of place Smith would never know.

Jeremy Winters was a slim man, perhaps an inch or so taller than Smith's own five feet nine inches, with a shock of prematurely white hair and the finely drawn features of an aristocrat. His eyes were a pale, crystalline blue, made more striking by dark lashes.

"You may dress and leave, Ten," Selkirk said.

Smith frowned; not sure he'd heard the man's words correctly. Had he just called the woman *Ten?*

The model quietly and quickly slipped into a plain gray silk robe and moved across the room with exceptional grace, closing the door behind her without a sound.

Selkirk turned to Smith. "I was intrigued by your message—and your desire to see me." He employed the same crisp voice he'd just used with his model—probably the same one he used with his servants, as well.

Smith was accustomed to aristocrats speaking to him in that tone. To them he was a merchant, and therefore a social upstart, no matter how wealthy he was.

That was fine, Smith hadn't come to Selkirk to make friends.

"I am here because I am looking for Sir Clayton Tyler."

Selkirk didn't display so much as a flicker of surprise. "What makes you believe that I know anything about the man?"

"I know that you are acquainted, but you needn't worry that it is general knowledge," Smith assured him.

"Hmmm." Selkirk's frosty gaze slid across Smith's body in a way that left his skin tingling.

"I'm sorry that I must disappoint you," Selkirk finally said.

"Are you saying that you haven't had contact with him recently?"

"No, I'm saying that I don't know where he is *now*. A week or so ago he sent one of his minions with a demand for money."

"And you gave it to him?"

"I did. I also had one of my servants follow Clayton's man when he left with the money."

Smith raised his eyebrows. "And where did he go?"

"To a brothel." His thin lips turned down at the corners. "Unfortunately, Clayton outsmarted my man and slipped away. It is anyone's guess where he is now."

Smith swallowed his disappointment. "Why did you have him followed?" He couldn't imagine the earl planning anything violent, but one never knew.

Selkirk shrugged; the action sinuous—almost erotic. "Curiosity."

"Why did you agree to talk to me?"

"Curiosity."

He laughed. "You are a very curious man, my lord—you know what they say about curiosity."

"Yes, but then I am not a cat, Mr. Smith." Selkirk smiled coldly.

"You wouldn't have agreed to see me unless you wanted something," Smith said.

Selkirk didn't bother to deny it. He stared at Smith for a long moment, his gaze so opaque, his body so motionless, that he might have been a statue. Indeed, Smith had never met anyone as unreadable as the Earl of Selkirk. Whatever thoughts went on behind those remarkable eyes was anyone's guess.

Finally, the earl gave another of his elegant shrugs. "I knew you were looking for him before you contacted me."

Smith fought down a twinge of irritation. That would be Red Jasper's doing, the clumsy, careless bastard.

"You obviously know what Clayton has been up to all these years," Selkirk continued. "The list of his victims is a long one."

"It is," Smith admitted. "But your name is not on the list that I saw, my lord."

Selkirk's pupils narrowed slightly. "I somehow suspect that your name isn't on it either."

Smith smirked. "No, but I suspect I've made my way onto a far shorter, more exclusive list: Clayton's soon-to-be deceased list.

"You don't seem very worried about that."

"I'm not."

The earl nodded, his gaze speculative. "I know what you did to the Duke of Tarland."

Smith's systematic destruction of Tarland a year ago—not with a truncheon or a pistol, but with money—was not something he'd tried to hide, but neither had he advertised his actions.

"It's not exactly a secret," Smith said.

"You earned a number of enemies when you went after Tarland."

Smith shrugged. He'd ruined Tarland for Jojo, and he would never regret it.

"It just so happens that I approve," Selkirk said. "Tarland was an abomination."

"That… surprises me."

"You think I approve of a lord who rapes his servants and fathers children on them?" he asked, the faintest bite in his tone.

"I thought membership in your select group meant that you would be willing to overlook, the duke's, er, foibles."

Selkirk stared for a long moment and then—shockingly—grinned. "I do enjoy plain speaking."

"Perhaps you might return the favor," Smith said. Because he knew for a fact that Selkirk hadn't agreed to see him out of the goodness of his heart.

"I want you to kill Clayton for me."

"You weren't jesting—that *is* plain speaking."

"I've heard rumors about you—about your past."

Smith snorted. "Was one of the rumors that I am an assassin for hire?"

Selkirk ignored his levity. "I looked into your, er, *dealings* closely once I received your message. I know you want him. Badly."

Smith was not willing to discuss his reasons for seeking Sir Clayton with the earl. "Why don't you hire somebody to kill him? Somebody else," he clarified.

"Unfortunately, my problem won't end with his death."

Smith paused and then said, "Ah, I see. If he dies then your dirty secret gets sent where? The police? The *Times*?"

"The police could be bargained with. It is newspaper men that Sir Clayton has targeted."

That made sense. The names on Clayton's list would be wealthy, powerful men and women who the police—not known for their sterling ethics—would pander to. For a price.

But a list like Clayton's could keep a newspaper in business for a decade; there would be no buying any silence.

"I still don't understand what this has to do with me?"

"I think you are probably going to kill him." He paused for Smith to argue. When Smith said nothing, he continued, "If you kill him without getting that information first, you will ruin my life."

"I don't mean to be rude, my lord, but—"

"Why should you care about my life and whether it is ruined or not?" Selkirk asked, his pale eyes glinting with humor. "Well, let's just say I can be of more use to you unruined than ruined."

Smith crossed one leg over the other. "And how can you be of use to me?"

"One of your syndicate partners is the Earl of Taunton?"

Smith wanted to groan; what had Gideon done now? "Yes," he admitted cautiously.

Selkirk's humor spread from his eyes to his lips. "He has been generating *quite* a bit of amusement in Lords since taking his seat. Not exactly what I would call an *asset* to you and your partners."

"That is hardly news to me, my lord."

"I could smooth Lord Taunton's way considerably. I could do more than that."

Smith knew that Selkirk—with his impressive business acumen and connections—would be a powerful ally where he and the syndicate needed one the most.

Smith was intrigued by both the offer and the man. He appreciated the fact that Selkirk had offered assistance—rather than coercion—to get what he wanted.

Of course the man wasn't stupid. If he'd looked into Smith's background then he would know Smith didn't respond well to heavy-handed tactics. Not well at all.

"Do you have any information that might help me find Clayton's hiding place?" he asked after a moment.

"No."

Smith sighed.

"But I have somebody looking and I will tell you if I learn anything."

Well, that was the best he could hope for, he supposed.

"You've sat for Nora Hudson," Selkirk said.

Smith blinked at the complete change in the conversation. "Yes, I have."

"I own one of her paintings of you."

"Which one?"

"It is titled *Winter*."

Smith experienced a brief but sharp flare of annoyance. The painting in question featured Smith dressed for riding, the composition of the portrait charmingly old fashioned. Nora had sketched him one chilly winter afternoon when they'd all visited Gideon at his country estate.

"I tried to buy it only to learn it had sold even before the show opened," Smith admitted grudgingly.

Selkirk briefly flashed his teeth, his canines exceptionally pointy. "I saw it early, at a private showing. I have… connections."

"I don't suppose you'd consider selling it?"

"I'm afraid not."

Smith was disappointed, but not surprised. The painting was one of Nora's best, Smith just so happened to be the subject.

"If you agree to help me recover my information from Clayton, however, I will give it to you."

Smith couldn't help laughing. "You must think I want it very badly."

"Don't you?"

Smith mentally rolled his eyes at his own vanity. Yes, by God, he wanted that bloody painting with a vengeance.

The door to the studio opened and a woman entered bearing a tea tray. Only when she came closer did Smith realize it was the model from earlier. She was garbed in a severe black gown of the sort normally worn by housekeepers. Her long brown hair had been neatly plaited and wound into a tidy bun. Even her conservative gown could not disguise her magnificent figure.

Once again Smith was entranced by the woman's elegance and grace as she lowered the tray to the coffee table and then sank to her knees in a continuation of the motion.

Smith's cock twitched at a different image, that of her sinking to her knees before him, her pale slender fingers deftly opening his placket rather than fussing about with a pot of tea.

"How do you like your tea, Mr. Smith?"

It was the first time the woman had spoken and her voice was pleasingly low, not precisely refined, but inflectionless, like her employer's.

"Black, please."

"I can offer you one more incentive," Selkirk said.

Smith pulled his attention away from the kneeling woman. The earl's gaze was as opaque as ever, but his severe features were softened by an almost imperceptible curving of his thin lips, as if he knew what thoughts were going through Smith's mind and enjoyed them.

"More incentive?" Smith taunted. "Do you have even *more* portraits of me?"

"In a sense."

The woman rose and came toward Smith with a cup and saucer, two small biscuits perched on the side.

"Thank you," Smith said, taking the woman's proximity as an opportunity to look closer at her face. She was older than he'd first thought—closer to thirty-five than thirty. Up close he saw that her irises were an attractive pale brown, the only pretty thing about her rather plain face.

She turned to give the earl his tea—minus the biscuits—and then lowered to her knees beside his chair, her submissive pose sending blood rushing to Smith's cock.

He looked up to meet Selkirk's gaze.

Although the other man's expression hadn't altered, he radiated a smug dominance that Smith recognized given he was often guilty of feeling it himself.

"You were speaking of an incentive?" Smith asked, his voice rougher than normal.

"Are you familiar with my work?"

"I have the good fortune to own one of your paintings."

"Indeed? Which one?"

"It is titled #6.27."

"Ah, yes. Six was one of my favorites." Before Smith could ask him what *Six* meant, the earl went on, "So you are aware of my tastes and style."

The painting in question was one of the most erotic—and blasphemous—in his collection. It would probably land even an earl into hot water if the wrong people got their hands on it. Malcolm had given it to Smith as a birthday gift several years back.

"I have some idea," Smith said dryly.

"I would like you to sit for me."

Smith blinked. "You want to paint me?"

"I want to sketch you, and anything I draw will belong to me. But if I end up painting you then I will offer you first right of refusal."

Smith chuckled. "You've certainly taken my measure, haven't you, my lord?"

Selkirk merely smiled.

"I would be honored to sit for you," he said, not bothering to beat about the bush when they both knew bloody well that he would love it.

"Excellent. How about right now? If you have time."

Smith hesitated, a bit startled, but took out his watch. "I have an hour before I need to be somewhere. Would that be enough time?"

"That all depends on you, Mr. Smith." Selkirk turned to the woman still kneeling beside his chair. "I'd like to sketch you while Ten pleasures you."

The man had a knack for shocking him. "I beg your pardon, but did you say *ten*?"

"Yes, her name is Ten. I will make sketches until you orgasm. The number of sketches I make is, therefore, up to you."

Smith laughed. "You have managed to surprise me twice in as many minutes, my lord." He looked at the woman—Ten. Her gaze was as opaque as her master's. "I pride myself on my self-control… Ten."

There was a flicker of something that looked like humor in her brown eyes.

"Ten will test your restraint," Selkirk said, his long, slender fingers wrapping around the woman's throat and lightly stroking.

Ten's eyelids gave the faintest flutter at his touch.

The made an attractive pair and Smith couldn't help staring.

Selkirk dropped his hand. "Strip and go to Mr. Smith."

Ten's hands went to the high buttons of her gown.

Smith couldn't help wondering about the relationship between these two, but suspected the earl was not the sort to share such details— even if he clearly didn't mind sharing his lover.

Selkirk picked up his sketchpad and took a fresh piece of charcoal out of a tin while the woman calmly disrobed.

Smith shifted so that his cock wasn't jammed into his thigh and then relaxed and enjoyed the sight of her gracefully removing her bodice, skirt, petticoats, cage, corset, and chemise—no drawers— leaving only her plain white stockings, simple garters, and sturdy black ankle boots.

Once she was naked, she lowered herself between Smith's spread feet with the same grace that she did everything and unfastened his trousers with deft fingers, freeing his erect cock.

Smith hissed when Ten's cool, strong hand wrapped around his shaft.

He looked up and found Selkirk staring at his erection. The other man lifted his darkened gaze to Smith's and gave him a long, smoldering look before he began to sketch.

Smith's breathing quickened as Ten worked him with *exactly* the right pressure, her thumb teasing his frenulum with each stroke, dragging her short nail over his leaking slit and using his moisture to slick his shaft.

He forced his hands to relax on the arms of the chair rather than sink into her hair. His eyelids drifted shut when her other hand slid beneath his cock to massage his balls.

"Yes," he muttered, pulsing his hips slightly and fucking into her tight, slick fist.

Hot, damp breath was the only warning he had before she took him into her mouth.

Smith opened his eyes and stared down, locking gazes with her as she made love to the fat crown, her plush lips kissing and sucking at his slit while her hand pumped him with firm strokes from root to tip.

She swallowed him deeper, her jaws stretching wide to accommodate more.

"You look lovely taking me," he said, amused when her cheeks flushed at his praise.

He lifted his hips, feeding her the last few inches, until her lips were stretched thin around his thick root.

"So beautiful," he murmured, easing out to allow her to breathe.

Rather than gasp or cough, she inhaled silently and lowered her mouth again, swallowing him to the root each time, her pupils so huge that her eyes looked black.

Smith tore his gaze away long enough to glance at his host.

The earl's striking eyes were hooded and the front of his light gray trousers tented, but his hand still flew across the page.

"She is lovely, Selkirk," Smith said in a strained voice, his fingers sinking into her thick chestnut hair. "And so skilled that I'm afraid your time is almost over."

Selkirk smiled faintly, not stopping his work. "You have lasted longer than most."

Smith glanced down at the woman to see how she took such a comment—an admission that this wasn't the first time she'd serviced one of his guests—but her rhythm never stuttered.

"Going to come," he warned her with a groan, loosening his grip on her hair and giving her a chance to pull away.

Rather than withdraw, she swallowed.

"Fuck!" he shouted, his body jerking with each pulse of his cock.

She milked him gently, until even the slightest touch was too much.

Smith lowered his hips and she sat back on her calves as he caught his breath. Her pale skin was passion mottled and her lips were slick and red.

He slid a hand around one of her breasts and lightly thumbed the hard nipple. Her body shuddered in response, her back arching. When he lowered his gaze, he saw that her thighs were slick, and the pink tip of her clitoris was poking through the neatly trimmed curls.

Smith was just about to lift her onto his lap and see to her needs when the sound of a throat clearing shook him from his erotic daze.

Selkirk had set aside his sketchpad and was sitting back, one elegantly trousered leg crossed over the other. His face was as unreadable as ever, but his posture spoke louder than words: the sitting was officially over.

Smith shrugged slightly and then helped Ten to her feet, admiring her backside as she walked back to Selkirk and sank down beside the settee.

"So," Selkirk said, his hand resting on Ten's nape. "Do we have an agreement?

Smith laughed. "You drive a hard bargain, my lord. But yes—we have an agreement."

Chapter 27

One month later

Luke was heading toward his mistress's dressing room with an armload of linen when he heard the strange noise.

He stopped and paced up and down the corridor, listening at each door.

It was eight o'clock at night, too late for a servant to be on this floor. They would all be in the kitchen or their rooms.

Luke paused in front of one of the unoccupied guest rooms. He listened for a moment longer, until he recognized it as female weeping.

There was only one woman in the house, so it was easy to guess who was crying.

He stared unseeingly down at the folded linen in his hands, the doctor's most recent words going through his mind. "Miss Dunsmuir is losing weight—she doesn't look well. This is not good for her child." Doctor Felson had spoken to Luke after leaving Miss Moira's chambers yesterday.

"What can I do?"

"I don't know—you know her best. Make her happy, somehow."

Luke was sure that only Smith would make her happy, but he kept that observation to himself.

"If you don't do something soon, the fetus may suffer permanent damage," Felson had warned. "Women who are malnourished have difficult deliveries and underweight children."

Luke had nodded.

And now, after hearing her weeping, he knew he had to act fast.

He returned the linen to the closet and then went to his room and drafted a brief letter to Miss Moira's sister, Sandrine, asking her if she might visit, as her sister was lonely.

It took him several hours just to write a few stilted sentences.

Afterward, he'd sent the letter by messenger and then had worried all night and most of today.

Had he been too presumptuous? Would Miss Sandrine tell her sister? Would she be angry with him? Would—

"Mister Luke?"

He turned away from the chrome he was polishing to death at the sound of his name, and smiled at the youngest member of the household, eighteen-year-old James Whitburn. This was his first footman position and James glowed with enthusiasm.

"Yes, James?"

"There's a lady visitor sir. She says she's Miss Moira's sister. I put her in the small sitting room."

Luke sighed with relief and pulled off the cotton gloves he used for polishing. "Go and tell Cook to prepare tea and I'll find the mistress and bring her down directly."

"Yes, sir."

Luke entered Miss Moira's chambers to find her laying on her favorite chaise, a neglected book resting beside her.

"You've a visitor, miss."

The hope in her eyes was like a punch to the stomach, and Luke realized who she thought it might be. "Who is it?"

"It is your sister, miss."

Disappointment flickered briefly across her pale face, but a radiant smile replaced it. "Oh, what a lovely surprise." She leapt up and glanced in the looking glass and pulled a face. "You must help me, Luke! I look a mess. I think I'll change into the new rose silk that just came."

"Of course, miss."

She moved more quickly, and with more purpose, than she'd done in a month, fairly flying toward the dressing room.

Luke followed her into the other room, not realizing until he saw his reflection that he was smiling like a fool.

***

Mr. Smith,

Sir Clayton left the Duke of Linton's palazzo three days ago. I regret to inform you that I lost his trail. I followed his coach, servants, and baggage to Nice, where I discovered he was not inside the carriage. I backtracked to Turin, where I learned that he'd engaged an inn carriage to take him to Dijon.

I will report again once I have reached the city.

K. Fielding

Smith looked up from the message and sighed.

Who would have believed that his sixty-two-year-old quarry could be so energetic and slippery?

In the six weeks since learning the other man's identity Smith had also discovered plenty about what Sir Clayton Tyler had been doing for the past thirty-five years.

Clayton's story was one of meteoric rise and almost equally meteoric descent. His rise had begun over three decades earlier, after his superlative work suppressing Greek rebels. And his descent had begun three years prior, when Clayton had chosen the wrong man to blackmail.

John Hudgins—a wealthy shipping magnate—proved a disastrous choice for Clayton because he didn't give a damn who knew about his propensity for handsome young men.

Rather than pay Clayton any money, Hudgins had contacted several ambitious newspapermen and told them how a government official had tried to blackmail him.

And then he'd taken a long holiday to Paris, where he was still living happily and operating his vast shipping empire.

Clayton had lost his position and had almost taken down Prime Minister Smith-Stanley, 14th Earl of Derby, by mere association. Only Smith-Stanley's well-known loathing for Clayton had spared him and his administration.

Even so, twenty-seven government employees—from clerks to an assistant minister to several unnamed government agents—had been sacked along with him.

That meant twenty-seven men—not counting Clayton—were unemployed and looking for work.

Smith had only needed to find one of those men, but it had taken him weeks.

Kenneth Fielding was Smith's newest employee and had his own reasons to track down Clayton, the man who'd ruined his career.

Fielding was also an immoral, vicious killer, which meant he was perfect for the job of bringing Clayton back to England.

But even Fielding was having a difficult time getting the job done.

Smith had been impatient to begin with; there was no good word to describe how he felt after six weeks of looking for the man.

"Are you sure that you're irritated about Clayton? Or might it be something… else?" Malcolm had asked Smith the last time they'd seen each other, which had been at the christening of Mal's son, Alexander.

They'd been in Malcolm's study after the ceremony, sharing a drink, when Smith had confessed that he was in a vile mood.

"What are you getting at?" Smith had retorted.

"Don't you think that maybe part of your mood might be because you were too hasty with Moira?"

"I think I was remarkably bloody restrained," Smith had shot back, his fury surprising even him.

But Malcolm had known Smith too long to be frightened of him and had just clucked his tongue and given Smith a knowing—and annoying—look.

He'd dropped the subject, but Smith hadn't forgotten it.

Of course he was still angry—and hurt, dammit—at what Moira had done. But that had nothing to do with his fury at Clayton.

Smith glared down at the message from Fielding. The urge to get the hell out of London and scour the Continent for Clayton himself was strong, but he had too much work here as it was.

If Fielding couldn't catch the bloody man, then Smith would just have to wait until he returned to England, which he probably would when he ran out of money. The man had treated his blackmail victims like a bank for years—making withdrawals whenever he was skint. He wouldn't stop now, especially since he no longer had a job and steady income.

Yes, Smith just needed to be patient. He'd been waiting over thirty years already. What difference would a few more months make?

Chapter 28

Two Months Later

It's *him* you go to on these nights, isn't it?'

Luke froze in the middle of fastening Miss Moira's gown before she went down to dinner.

He realized that she was looking at him in the mirror and his face heated.

"Er—"

"It's all right, Luke," she said, a slight smile on her face, which was no longer gaunt. In fact, he'd even go so far as to say that she was glowing. "I'm not angry at you." She chuckled. "But I must admit that I'm *envious*."

Luke finished closing the buttons. "Yes, I go to him."

"You are lovers?"

He hesitated, again met her gaze, and nodded. "Yes."

"You do this after you give him reports about the health of the child."

Luke swallowed, squirming under her gaze. "Yes."

She nodded.

Luke didn't tell her there were occasionally other questions. He worried it would give her hope. Smith, he knew, had closed his heart to her, even if he could not quite close his mind and not be curious.

"I'm glad, Luke."

He looked up at her unexpected words.

"I… care for him." She grimaced. "Why am I bothering to lie? I love him."

Luke nodded, unsure of what she wanted him to say.

"You love him, too, don't you? You've loved him long before I came into your lives?"

"Yes, I love him." He hesitated and then added, "But he does not love me."

She snorted softly. "At least he still *likes* you. I think he hates me."

Luke didn't tell her what he thought, but she guessed anyhow.

"You are thinking I got better than I deserve." She waved to the beautiful house around them. "I betrayed him and ended up with this." She laughed, but there was no humor.

He *had* thought that, but not since the very beginning. Not for a long time.

"I am fortunate to have his child growing inside me."

Luke agreed; he would have given a great deal to be able to offer such a gift—a child—to Mr. Smith.

"You are very fortunate," he said.

He saw the words—and the force with which he said them—surprised her.

She turned away from the mirror to face him, took his hand, and laid it on the slight bulge of her belly. "I'm fortunate to have *you*, Luke. I think you like me—at least a little—and I think you will love my child because it is Smith's child." She smiled. "Your love is a constant and abiding affection. I saw it in the way you looked at Smith when you thought nobody was paying attention."

His face flushed.

She shook her head and held his wrist when he would have pulled away, pressing it against the surprising hardness of her stomach. "The way you look at him is beautiful, Luke. I'm sad for Smith that he can't see it. But maybe he will, one day."

Luke's heart rejoiced at her words, but he was quick to quash his joy.

When he didn't respond, Miss Moira rubbed his hand over her stomach. "I want to share the wonder of what I'm feeling with somebody, Luke. I—I—well, I've felt so alone. Perhaps, if it is not repugnant to you—you might stand as father while this child grows. I don't mean that you should be my lover," she said hastily, "I mean you would be somebody to share things with. My sister is a delight, of course, but she has her own life. You and I—we are together so much. I feel—"

She suddenly looked so young and so lost that he felt an almost suffocating wave of sympathy for her.

"I would be honored." He curled his fingers around her stomach and gently stroked her.

When she looked up at him, there were tears shimmering in her lovely sea green eyes, threatening to spill over, but they were happy tears.

"Thank you."

He smiled, removed his hand, and turned her back to the mirror to finish dressing her for her solitary meal in the glittering dining room below.

After she left, Luke went to fetch his hat, coat, and cane before walking the few streets that separated his new home from his old one.

The weather was bitterly cold, even for the end of January, but Luke had an extra spring in his step. He'd not realized that keeping his meetings with Smith from Miss Moira had weighed on his mind. It had been an uncomfortable conversation, but he was grateful the matter was now out in the open.

Luke made his way up the front steps, still feeling odd about not using the servant entrance, even though it had been months since he'd been a servant in the house.

"Come in through the front door, Luke," Smith had said on that very first Monday, his expression lazy with spent passion, his body naked in the sheets they'd spent all night tangling. "You are, after all, my guest." He'd chuckled at that, as if he'd made a joke. But Luke chose to believe he meant it—and felt warmed by his words.

He raised his hand to ring the bell when the door opened and he almost collided with a person coming out.

"Oops! I beg your pardon," he said, taking a step back.

Luke almost didn't recognize Charles Smith: it had been over a year—closer to a year and a half—and he'd been clean-shaven the last time Luke saw him.

Luke inclined his head. "Good evening, Mr. Smith," he said, even though using the man's surname felt odd.

"Oh," Charles said, his brow wrinkling, the quizzical expression making his angelic, gorgeous features look even more charming. "I know you—you are a footman here."

Mr. Smith appeared behind the younger man, his expression indulgent as he looked from the nattily dressed, golden-haired young man to Luke.

"This is Luke, Charles. I'm sure you remember him." His cut the younger man a sardonic look. "He works elsewhere, now. He is just paying a visit."

Charles's sapphire eyes opened wide; Luke couldn't blame him. Since when did footmen visit their employers? Former, or otherwise.

"Well," Charles said, his eyebrows arched, his expression condescendingly amused. "How nice to see you, I'm sure."

Luke read him like a cheap penny paper: he was jealous—fairly boiling with it, just as he'd always been when it came to Smith.

"I shall see you on Wednesday, then, Charles?" Smith said, his words a dismissal, no matter how polite.

"I look forward to it, darling." The younger man took his leave, his back stiff as he descended the stairs.

"Come in, Luke." Smith shut the door and then pulled a face. "I'm sorry about that. I'm afraid it was a surprise visit."

He held out his hands and Luke stared at them, confused.

Smith laughed. "Oh come, surely I am not so selfish as to not hold a man's possessions while he divests himself of an overcoat?"

Luke's face heated. "No, of course not. It is just, er, unusual to see you in the role of a servant, sir."

Smith took Luke's hat and cane first, and then returned for his gloves, his mouth curving into a wicked smile as he stepped close—far closer than was necessary to take the gloves Luke had just pulled off his hands.

"Tell me, would you enjoy having me be your body servant?"

Luke couldn't recall his cock ever becoming so hard, so fast before.

Smith chuckled and went around behind him, lifting his coat from his shoulders. "It would be my pleasure to serve you in any way… master."

Luke shuddered at the words and Smith whisked his coat away, handing it to David—who'd come hurrying into the foyer and was visibly stunned to find his employer playing at being a footman.

"Oh, sir. I'm terribly sorry."

Smith grinned, his eyes never leaving Luke. "Have Cook send up a tray in an hour, David. Do you want anything special, Luke?"

Luke's face heated under his former lover's scrutiny. "Er, some shortbread if he has it."

David's eyebrow was cocked mockingly as he bore Luke's coat away.

As they made their way up the stairs—which was not exactly comfortable with an erection as hard as the one Luke was currently sporting—he was intensely aware of the man beside him.

The thought of having Smith for a servant—no matter how temporarily—was one of his most private fantasies. Had he been serious? Or merely jesting?

Once the door closed to his bedchamber, Smith turned to him. "So, are you a kind master? Or a cruel one?

A startled laugh broke out of Luke at the question. "I suppose you'll find out," he managed to say.

He could see by Smith's delighted grin that was the right answer.

"Strip," Luke ordered, falling into his role with an ease that surprised him. "And then we will go into the gymnasium where you will exercise for my viewing—and touching—pleasure.

Smith's pupils flared in a way that told Luke he'd made a choice that would please them both.

A scant five minutes later, he was lounging against a wall—an erection jammed into the leg of his trousers—watching as Smith did some of the things he'd wondered about for so long.

"Tell me what you are doing," he said.

"These are weights." Smith held up a canvas pouch with buckles. "They are filled with sand and range from one to ten pounds. This one is five pounds." He fastened it around his ankle. "They offer more of a challenge to some exercises."

Luke nodded. "Some of the lads I spar with use those."

"So, you are a pugilist?"

"Not until I came to work here," Luke admitted.

"You've participated in some of the mills out in the stables?"

Luke blinked. "You know about those?"

Smith chuckled as he laid down on a tufted pallet on the floor. "I know about everything that goes on in my house."

Luke believed him. "Why have you never come to watch a bout?"

Smith shrugged. "I thought I might have a dampening effect on the entertainment."

"I think you should come and put your name into the hat," Luke said, and then was amazed by his own temerity.

Smith grinned. "I might do that." He clasped his hands behind his head, lifted his feet in the air and crossed them at the ankle, drawing his knees toward his bent elbows with smooth motions, holding the position for a count, and then releasing it.

Because he wore no clothing, the effect of the exercise on his muscles was gloriously evident.

Luke prowled around him, not wanting to miss any part of the view.

But he froze midway on his circuit, his gaze trapped by the exquisite sight of Smith's erect cock and heavy sac between his muscular thighs.

"See anything you like," Smith asked in a slightly breathless voice, his body quickly becoming sheened from his relentless exertion.

"How many of these will you do?" Luke asked, his own voice sounding considerably breathier for all that he was standing still.

"Fifty. Then a break, and then fifty more."

"What are you at, now?"

"Forty-three."

Luke unbuttoned his placket and let his drawers and trousers drop. Smith's gaze lowered to his swollen cock and his tongue darted out to moisten his lower lip.

Luke groaned at the sight and pumped himself a few times, savoring the way Smith's movements became jerkier, less focused.

"See anything you like?" he taunted.

Smith's laughter interrupted his smooth rhythm and he lowered his feet and began to stand.

Luke shook his head and pointed to the floor with his free hand, snapping his fingers. "Hands and knees. Crawl to me."

The flush that darkened the other man's face as he assumed the servile position was like a sip of the finest brandy.

"Slowly," Luke instructed. He wanted to savor this.

The muscles in Smith's shoulders and back shifted enticingly beneath his sweat-sheened skin. Luke shivered under his intent stare; the stare of a carnivore closing in on its prey.

"Up on your knees," Luke said when Smith was almost on the toes of his shoes.

When Smith complied, Luke pumped his cock in his face.

"Tongue my slit."

Smith's eyes smoldered as he extended the pointed tip of his tongue, penetrating the bead of moisture and pushing into the tiny hole.

Luke released an explosive groan, unable to tear his eyes away from the mesmerizing sight. "You love having a cock in your mouth, don't you?"

Smith's eyes blazed and he nodded.

Luke smirked and the monster that slumbered most of the time woke up and flexed its muscles, ready to play.

"That's enough," he said when his balls began to tighten. He fisted Smith's hair and jerked his head back. "I'm going to fuck your mouth. Make it good," he warned.

He hissed when Smith took him deep, sucking him hard enough to hurt. "Hands off your prick," he ordered. "You'll come when I tell you—*if* I tell you. If you're a good boy." He chuckled evilly. "Now, quit fucking about and suck me like you mean it."

The way Smith's eyes rolled back in his head, Luke knew he'd be a very good boy, indeed.

***

Smith could not fall asleep. He turned on his side, resting his head in his hand and looked at Luke's slumbering body beside him.

Tonight had been delicious. He enjoyed the spectacular transformation that took place inside the normally quiet, submissive man when he was given leave to pursue his fantasies.

He wondered if Luke knew how terrifying he appeared when he became cruel, cold, and brutal. It was hard to believe he was the same person. Although he supposed some people—the few who had seen both sides of Smith—would say the same of him.

But he didn't want to think about that right now.

Instead, he thought about Luke's face in the gymnasium earlier, when he'd been staring at Smith, who'd been shamelessly performing for him.

What Moira had always teased him about was true: he *was* terribly vain.

Moira.

Smith had worked hard to control his thoughts about the woman these past few months. After all, there could be nothing between them other than—hopefully—a mutually respectful relationship as parents in the future.

He knew that sending her away looked cold and unfeeling.

Nora and Edward and Malcolm had told him so repeatedly. But they only knew what they saw. And what they saw was, in the most cliched of terms, the tip of an iceberg.

Not only could Smith never bring himself to trust her again, but he had murdered her father—after she had begged him to show mercy. Each of those things, alone, was enough to keep them apart.

And then there were the other, more private, and more painful reasons.

Although he suspected that the human heart could recover from any damage or pain, he was not interested in testing that theory.

Quite honestly, Smith could not get past the fact that she gave him up to the *Comte* without even trying to speak to him.

He knew her parents had warped all their children almost beyond saving, but Sandrine had been in a similar position and yet she'd come to him and confessed, throwing herself on his mercy.

And he *was* merciful. To those who deserved it.

He was still stunned—infuriated and, yes, hurt—that Moira had never believed he was worth trusting.

That night, when he drank her drugged wine and submitted to being bound, he—stupidly—had continued to hope that she would not follow through with what she'd set in motion.

But she had.

Smith's heart—not the reliable organ that continued to beat and pump blood through his body, but the far more fragile part of a person that carried hopes, dreams, and yes, love—had taken a vicious beating that night.

So had his pride.

And yet here he was, not ill or dying from the blunt trauma of that night but lying beside a different lover.

Perhaps it was *only* his pride that had been damaged? After all, he'd moved so easily from one body to the next—perhaps he was, as Charles had always accused, not capable of deeper feeling?

Ah, Charles.

Smith laughed softly—and a little ruefully—to himself.

Seeing Charles today had reminded him of why it had taken so very long to extricate himself from that affair. He was a vibrant, funny, clever, and passionate man.

He'd gained polish during his year on the Continent and was even more attractive. Intellectually, Smith knew that Charles was trouble waiting to happen.

Unfortunately, his cock took a much more earthy view of matters and didn't care what sort of problems Charles might bring to his life.

For all his faults, Charles had been an insatiable and creative lover.

Whether Smith allowed Charles back into his life at this point—or at least into his bed—would have no effect on his arrangement with Luke. The one benefit of losing Moira had been realizing that Luke was important to him—far more important than he ever would have imagined possible—and he wouldn't risk losing him for anyone.

He might take a night or two of physical pleasure with Charles, but he would never again neglect Luke for any other lover.

He looked at Luke and leaned over, placing a feather-light kiss on his brow. Luke had remained steadfast, even when Smith had wandered, and he'd never betrayed Smith's trust in him.

In Smith's experience trust was something just as precious and even more rare than love.

Chapter 29

Six Weeks Later

Moira stared out the rain-spattered window. "I don't think it's going to get any better," she said. "We should go now."

Luke, who'd been cleaning her already spotless dressing room, came to stand beside her. She could *feel* his frown.

"It's cold. You know Doctor—"

She flopped back against the cushions that made the window seat such a pleasurable reading nook and glared up at him.

His mouth snapped shut and he lowered his eyes.

Sometimes—more than sometimes—she wanted to do something to get a reaction out of him—to get him to snap or snarl. He was such a tightly laced, self-contained, unreadable man.

Every time she thought about prodding him until he reacted, she felt contrite about having such aggressive thoughts toward such a kind person.

"You are restless," he said quietly. "It's been four days inside. I don't blame you."

"I *am* restless." She loved her walks and went half-mad without them. "But I shouldn't take it out on you." She held out a hand and he took it in his own far more quickly than he had the first twenty times she'd done it.

Moira hadn't realized how much a creature of touch she was, until the only person who touched her was Doctor Felson every week or Sandrine and her girls when they came to visit.

Sexually, she'd had nobody since that last catastrophic night with Smith.

She suspected her newer contract forbade it, just like the first one had—although she'd not bothered to read this one, at all. Not that she would have wanted a stranger around her body right now, in any case.

"Perhaps playing the piano might make you feel better?" Luke suggested. "The room is warm, I had Armand light a fire first thing this morning."

Armand was a young footman who'd come to work a few weeks earlier and had turned the house upside down with his gorgeous looks. It amused Moira to watch a houseful of men behave exactly like a houseful of women over a good-looking man. It restored her fractured faith in human nature.

"I never asked how your night out with Armand was?"

Smith had been out of town for almost two weeks, and Luke had said he didn't require his usual evening off, but Moira had insisted.

The poor man was already forced to spend too much time with her. And she knew that Smith being out of town caused him considerable anguish.

She'd been amused and titillated when he'd told her he'd accepted an invitation to go to a nearby pub with Armand.

Luke flushed, as he always did when any attention was focused on him. She knew he was older than her by a decade, but she sometimes felt ancient around him.

"We had a nice evening."

Moira groaned. "You are my only source of amorous entertainment, Luke. You must do better than *nice*."

"I have no *amorous* interest in Armand. We only had a few pints—nothing else."

"Oh, pooh! Surely you could make something up—just to entertain me?"

"You know what the doctor said, Miss—"

She narrowed her eyes at him and he sighed.

"You know what the doctor said, *Moira*, too much excitement is bad for the baby."

Moira laughed. "You are worse than an old woman, Luke."

He smiled, rather than look offended.

Her free hand drifted to her belly.

"Would you like me to rub you?" Luke offered.

Moira knew she should say no, she already relied on him for everything in her life. But his hands were magical and her body was so constantly aroused that she all but wore out her nub rubbing it most nights.

"Perhaps that might be a way of making it up to me."

He smiled, something he did more often after she'd cornered him one day and verbally battered him about treating her like she was the daughter of the Queen.

"We were both whores, for pity's sake. I need a friend more than I need my cunt shaved. If you can't be a friend to me, you might as well leave," she'd shouted at him, like a fishwife.

Moira had spent a horrible evening after that, locked in her room and buried under a pile of bedding, terrified that he would pack up his things and leave her alone, which is what she deserved. She had cried herself to sleep.

In the morning, she'd looked up to find Luke standing beside her bed.

"How did you get in here?"

He held up a key.

"I'm sorry for being such a wretched shrew."

"It's all—"

"No, it isn't all right. I was awful to you. And I ordered you around as if you were a servant, claiming I wanted a friend. I'm sorry."

He'd dropped the key in his pocket and held out a hand. "Come… *Moira.* A bath will make you feel better."

That had been the beginning in their changing relationship. It had coincided—rather uncoincidentally—with her mood improvement.

"Come," he said now, an echo of that morning all those weeks ago.

He helped her to her feet, as he would an invalid. She'd given up on arguing. Between Smith and Doctor Felson, she was securely packed in cotton.

He led her to the bedchamber and unbuttoned the back of the loose gowns she wore almost all the time, now, even when she went out to window shop or spend an afternoon in the reading room at the museum, which she'd grown to love.

Luke, it turned out, knew how to alter her gowns so that Moira could still wear them, even though she'd begun to get thick in the waist. He also knew how to trim hats, bake bread, and any number of wonderful things.

"Living in a brothel—as you know—is like living in a house full of sisters," he'd reminded her when she'd been amazed at his quick, perfect stitches when he'd mended something.

He also knew how to give the best massages she'd ever received.

Luke lifted the gown over her shoulders and she stepped over to the bed, climbing onto the delightful down mattress and lying on her back in her thin petticoat and chemise.

Luke sat beside her, his huge body tilting the mattress and making her laugh.

"Perhaps we should get you a table—did you have the padded tables at Bernina's?" he asked as he laid a big hand on her belly and began to rub her with a light touch.

She closed her eyes. "Yes, the ones for a massage. That is a good idea," she added dreamily, her body shifting and relaxing into his touch.

***

Luke stared down at her as he stroked her, ashamed by what he was doing. Oh, not the rubbing, itself—he knew she liked that and it relaxed her.

What shamed him was what it did to *him*.

He'd known it was a terrible mistake to give in and call her *Moira*, to chatter with her like they were friends—equals, to tell her bits about his life and ask bits about hers.

Of course, it led to *this*.

This being the monstrous erection tenting—and likely leaking on—his trousers.

If you had asked him the first time he met her, he would have said he thought his mistress very attractive, but not his usual preference when it came to females, which was for voluptuous, tall women. Luke was a big man and he'd always been attracted to big women.

Katie, the woman he'd loved—and still did, in many ways—was the exact opposite of Moira when it came to body type. Although, of course, he'd never seen Katie naked. He'd never seen more of her than a flash of ankle on a hot summer day and, on several memorable occasions, her forearms when he'd been invited into her mother's kitchen to watch her make bread.

He knew it was odd to find a woman's forearms sexually stimulating, but then—by that time, when he'd been meeting men in dark alleys regularly—he'd already known his sexual preferences had crossed well beyond *odd* and gone deeply into criminal.

He swallowed again, annoyed by how much he drooled like a lecher while performing this innocent task.

His eyes drifted from the low neckline of her chemise, to the twin points of her nipples, down to her hard belly, and lingered on the triangle of her sex.

Luke had become hard the very first time he'd shaved her—grateful that his heavy work apron had concealed his condition.

He still got hard each and every time. He'd been shaving her weekly although Mr. Smith had made no mention of it on the list of his duties. His mistress had simply asked him to continue doing so two weeks after they'd moved into the house.

"Do you mind?" she'd asked. "And could you do my legs as well?"

"Of course, I don't mind." Luke had wanted to suggest taking over shaving her legs. She was careless and cut herself at least once each time she attempted the task.

And so, the next time Luke had gone to see his master, he'd passed along a request for the table that was still in her bathing chamber.

Smith had looked nonplussed. "She asked for it?"

"She requested I continue to groom her and it would be far easier with the table, sir."

"Oh. Of course, she should have it," Mr. Smith had said. "I'll have it sent over tomorrow."

Something else had occurred to Luke, something his mistress had *not* asked for. "And perhaps she might have the piano?"

Smith had stared at him, not speaking.

The hair on Luke's neck had stood on end as he'd endured a look that had burned through his skin.

"Has she engaged a new tutor?" Smith had finally asked.

Luke took a deep breath and told his master what he'd long ago guessed. "I believe she plays rather well, sir. I think she did so before moving into your house." He'd felt increasingly uncomfortable as Smith had continued to stare at him. "I believe it might give her something pleasant to do on the days she cannot go out," he'd babbled.

Smith had stared for a moment longer, and then nodded. "I will have both sent over."

Luke didn't know if his requests had made the other man angry. But what he did know, was that his master had bound and whipped him that night, a treat Luke had only enjoyed once before.

He suspected there was a connection between asking for the table and piano and then receiving such a savage beating and fucking, but he'd decided not to examine it too closely.

If Luke had wondered whether he was doing the right thing by asking for the piano, his mistress's reaction had assured him that he'd done well.

When it had been delivered she'd clapped her hands and looked as gleeful as a young girl on Christmas morning.

"Oh, thank you, Luke. I know Smith sent the piano, but he would only have done so at your urging. I wanted to write him and ask for it, but"—she'd broken off and shrugged.

Yes, Luke knew why she hadn't asked. She was afraid of his response—not that he'd deny her the piano, but that he wouldn't respond to her letter and just send the instrument with no message.

The piano had made the days with bad weather more bearable for her. She really was an excellent musician and all the servants agreed it was divine to live in a house where such music was free to enjoy.

"Luke?"

He realized he'd closed his eyes and opened them. Somehow, his hands had slid beneath Moira's chemise. Somehow, they had slid higher than her belly. Somehow, they were resting just beneath her breasts.

He jerked his hands back. "I'm terribly sorry. I'm not sure what—"

"I liked it."

Luke's erection throbbed at the look that accompanied her words, his lungs freezing in his chest.

She gestured to his tented placket. "I didn't know—well, I thought—"

"You thought I did not like women."

It was her turn to swallow, and she nodded. When he didn't speak, she went on, "All those times you groomed me and I was aroused."

He took a deep breath and let it out slowly. "You were not the only one."

"But you never—"

"You belonged to Mr. Smith."

Belonged. The word clanged like a spanner tossed onto a tile floor. *Belonged.*

She took his hand by the wrist and lowered it over her sex. "I no longer belong to anyone."

Luke could restrain his curiosity no longer. "Will you tell me what happened that night, Moira? Why he sent you away?"

***

His question knocked the air from her chest. Moira swallowed and then said, "Smith has never told you?"

Luke shook his head.

Moira was surprised and relieved to learn Luke wasn't in Smith's confidence to that degree. It pained her to imagine the two of them talking about her—flushed from making love, their gorgeous bodies tangled together.

Well, thinking about that second part was quite nice, but the first part…

Moira pulled her attention back to Luke's request. "I want to tell you what happened. But only if you stay sitting here—beside me."

He nodded.

And so Moira told him an abbreviated story of her short, pathetic life, ending with that awful night in Smith's bedchamber.

By the time she'd finished, *he* had taken her hands and was holding them tightly. "Anyone might have done the same thing," he said softly.

"Sandrine didn't."

His full, sensual lips flexed into a frown. "But *she* hadn't been told by your mother and father that Smith had killed you."

Moira smiled and squeezed his hands in return. "Thank you for trying to make me feel better. I have so many regrets. Not just what I did to him, but also that I repressed my interest in him for so long, fearing I'd slip up. All those wasted opportunities to *know* him. Now they are gone forever."

"Have you ever considered that it might not be over?"

"What do you mean? Has he said something to you?" The hope in her voice was painful to her own ears. "I'm sorry," she said almost immediately. "I didn't mean to ask you that."

"Why don't you go to him. Tell him you regret what happened and want to try again?"

"I *have* apologized."

"I don't mean apologize; I mean tell him that you regret the loss of what you had with him. Tell him what you just told me."

"Tell him that I love him?" she asked, her voice slightly higher just thinking about such a conversation.

"Why not?"

"Because I already did."

He paused at her admission, but then said, "Maybe you need to tell him again, now that the waters have calmed."

Moira could still recall Smith's expression and flinched away from it. "It was agonizing

"Worse than what you are feeling now?"

Moira gave a startled laugh. "Things can always be worse."

"They can always get better, too. If he cares about you—and I think he does—then won't you regret letting him slip away? Don't you think he is worth fighting for?"

Her eyes narrowed. "Why are you so good to me? I know you love Smith. Why would you try to help me?"

"It is *because* I love him that I want him to be happy."

"Even if he is with somebody else?"

He sighed. "Even if he is with somebody else—somebody who makes him happy." He scowled. "Not somebody like Charles Smith."

Moira chuckled at the unusual animus he bore the other man. "And you think I can make him happy?"

"I think you have a better chance of doing so than I ever will."

Her eyes teared up.

"What is it?" he asked, alarmed.

"You. It's just—how did you get to be so good?"

"I'm not all that good, Moira. I feel pain and frustration at not being his first choice. He hesitated and said, "I was jealous of you when you came. I think I even h-hated you for a while."

Moira's lips parted, but she didn't know what to say.

"But I saw—rather quickly—that you made him happy. Much happier than he ever was with Charles and much happier than he was with me." Luke shrugged. "He cannot make himself love where he does not. Just because I am not his choice does not mean I want him to suffer. Don't you want the people you love to be happy? Even if you are not necessarily the reason for that happiness? Isn't that what loving somebody means?"

Moira smiled through a sheen of tears—she was so emotional of late!—and said, "I think it is supposed to be that way, but you are the first person—man or woman—I've ever met to truly put another's interests before your own."

"Well, don't put me on a pedestal. I do it for myself as much as I do it for Smith. I could never be happy with him if I knew he loved another. And I wouldn't do anything to keep him apart from such a person."

She gave a watery laugh. "You won't talk me out of believing you are one step from sainthood."

Luke snorted, his eyes flickering over her scantily clad body. "Trust me, the thoughts in my head right now are the farthest thing from saintly." He removed his hands from hers with obvious reluctance.

"But you won't act on it?" she said, warming at his words and hot look but just as quickly cooling at the determination on his face.

"No matter how much I might want you, I owe him my loyalty. And so do you."

Moira's face heated with mortification, not just because she'd tried to tempt a good man, but because she'd also tried to betray Smith. Again.

Luke didn't appear to notice her flushed face. "Besides," he said. "I doubt that sort of, er, behavior would be good for the baby." He stood and went to fetch her dressing gown.

Moira felt a slight smile tug at her lips. As far as a declaration of interest went, it wasn't much.

But it was better than nothing.

Chapter 30

Smith squinted, as if that would help him with defective hearing. "I'm sorry, what did you say?"

Doctor Felson swallowed. Again. "Er, Miss Dunsmuir wished to know if er, intercourse would damage the fetus."

Smith frowned; Felson knew he didn't care for that word. It was too... clinical. He didn't like it.

Felson cleared his throat under Smith's glare. "I mean the baby."

"Why?"

Felson blinked. "Because you don't care for the other word."

Smith struggled for patience. "I meant why did she want to know that?"

Felson's eyes went wide. "I don't know, sir. She simply asked me— she didn't say why or who—not that there is a who, of course."

As amusing as it was to watch the other man squirm, he decided to have mercy on him. "So, would it?"

"Would it?" Felson repeated.

"Would fucking her damage the baby?".

Felson flinched at the crude question. "Oh. Er, no. That is, not in my experience." An expression of horror seized his bland features. "I don't mean in *my* experience with Miss Dunsmuir. I meant—"

"I know what you meant." Smith drummed his fingers on his desk. His study, so coolly neutral and comforting with its elegant gray, ivory, and black suddenly glowed a dull, pulsing red.

Smith's body—encased in the same clothing he always wore—was hot and itchy. As if he were covered in ants or mites or filth.

He stood and Felson scrambled to his feet.

"You may go," Smith said, distantly aware that his tone was uncharacteristically menacing—at least for use with an individual who'd done nothing to deserve it—but he found that he didn't care. He went to the window and looked out on the day. It was a typical London spring, wet, miserable, and brown, the air as thick and slimy as treacle.

He took his watch out of his pocket; not because he wanted to know the time, but because he felt like he had to do *something*. Something that wasn't rending and tearing and breaking things.

Moira wanted to know if sexual intercourse would damage the child. Even an idiot could figure out what that meant.

Not to mention the fact that she would have *known* Felson would come to him with the question.

Smith unclenched his jaw and worked it from side to side.

The contract had been most explicit about bringing men to her house after the child was born—he did not think it unreasonable to wish to keep *his* child away from strange men—but it had not occurred to him until that exact moment to include anything in the new contract about *before* the child was born.

He gave a snort of laughter. "You devious little bitch," he muttered, not without admiration.

Smith had been the one to send her away, so why should he care if she took lovers, now—whether the contract forbade it, or not? He didn't want her.

Smith paused at the thought; it was patently untrue.

He didn't *want* to want her. But he did. All the time, in fact. While it was true that he wanted to hurt her, he also wanted to fuck her.

He wanted to ask her what was wrong with him that she'd been able to throw him away like rubbish.

And he certainly didn't want anyone else to have her.

He marveled for a moment about the unreasonableness of such a thought. He was behaving like a child who had tired of a toy but still clung tightly to it, not wanting anyone else to get pleasure from it.

But she wasn't a toy, she was a human being with emotions and urges.

It wasn't as if *he* hadn't been sating his urges.

He been gorging himself on sex, not just with Luke or at Bernina's, but also with Charles. Indeed, his resumption with Charles had a somewhat frantic edge to it.

Even Charles, one of the most self-centered people he knew—an amusing observation coming from *Smith*, he knew—had remarked on it the last time they'd been in bed. And by *last* time, Smith meant *last*.

He'd been an idiot to even let the man step over the threshold.

As ever, they'd had magnificent sex and had been exhausted afterward, Charles absently tracing the ridges of Smith's stomach. "You are even more exquisite than you were a year ago," he'd commented with grudging admiration. "What sort of man becomes more youthful as he ages?"

That had made Smith smile—and preen, he had to admit.

"But I can't help feeling there is a sort of… desperation to you now."

Ah, Charles—the master of the barbed, subtle insult.

He'd continued when Smith hadn't risen to the bait. "I've heard tales of you from a friend or two at Bernina's."

It had annoyed him that Charles was gossiping about him, but he'd kept it to himself. After all, he had no hold over the younger man, he wasn't paying him. Charles could do or say whatever he wanted. If Smith didn't like it, he could either suffer in silence or put an end to their occasional fucking.

His mood had been mellow at the time, so he'd shut his mouth and said nothing.

Charles had chuckled, not missing the tension in Smith's body.

"You hate that, don't you?" He'd dragged his nails across Smith's abdomen hard enough to leave scrape marks, the action drawing a hiss of pleasure.

When Smith had ignored his question, the younger man had continued.

"When we were together, I satisfied those hungers—did I not?" He'd begun speaking arrogantly but had ended with a pleading, wheedling note in his voice.

"You did," Smith had agreed. And that was the truth. It had never been Charles's ability to please and satisfy him sexually that had been their problem.

"We were so good together."

When Smith hadn't commented, Charles had applied his considerable talents to waking Smith's cock from its slumber.

"You said it couldn't happen," Charles had said after he'd drawn an unprecedented fourth orgasm from him. "Perhaps your… footman, could use a lesson or two from me." Charles had smiled smugly, his lips still slick with Smith's spend.

Smith had ignored the twinge of irritation his comment about Luke elicited. He'd also ignored Charles's obvious angling to resume their prior arrangement.

While he greatly enjoyed bedding Charles on occasion, he had absolutely *no* desire for anything permanent.

He'd not even wanted the other man to stay the night, but he'd allowed it, even though the following day was a Monday and he was leaving for Bristol for ten days on Tuesday. All of which had meant he had a great deal to do.

But he'd let Charles stay until the following morning.

"I can't see you tonight. I have plans," Smith had said early Monday. It had been later than he liked and he'd been itching to get into his gymnasium and spend an hour before his busy day consumed all his time.

Smith was always restless before he left on a trip and he'd needed time alone to think and prepare.

What he had *not* needed was an argument.

But that's what he got.

"Change your plans. I want to see you tonight," Charles had insisted, resting his hands on his hips, the action drawing Smith's attention to his exceedingly desirable cock.

Charles had an apradava piercing and Smith had always been a bit obsessed with it.

At that moment it had suddenly struck him: Charles's pierced prick was pretty much *all* that he still liked about the other man.

He'd been a fool to invite him back into his bed—into his life.

He'd looked up from Charles's groin to encounter his demanding stare.

"No."

Charles's jaw had sagged.

Before he could launch a harangue, Knox had entered, but had hesitated upon seeing Smith and Charles glaring at one another, naked.

"I'm ready for my shave," Smith said. "You may go prepare." He waited until his valet had disappeared into the adjoining bath chamber before turning back to Charles.

"No. I will not change my plans."

"You really are a pitiful man, Smith." Charles had shoved past Smith even though he was nowhere in his path and flounced into his dressing room, where Smith insisted that he put his clothing, rather than strewing everything all over the floor, yet another request that annoyed Charles.

Smith had considered simply leaving the room and joining Knox, but he knew Charles would just follow him and continue his ranting.

Charles had stormed back into the room and thrown his armload of clothing over the back of the chair, snatching up his shirt and ramming his arm into it so hard it tore.

"Fucking your servants." He snorted. "You *do* realize how pathetic that is, I hope? You must know that big lummox—*Luke*—can't say *no*, don't you?"

Smith had sighed and waited for him to finish.

Charles had jerked his head toward the door Knox had just gone through. "Are you fucking him too? Are you fucking *all* of them now? Some sort of servant harem."

Smith had just stared, biding his time until the other man left. And then he would never allow him back into his house. Ever.

Perhaps Charles saw his decision on his face.

"I'm not the only one who finds it pitiful, you know." Charles had shrugged into his vest, not bothering to button it before struggling into his coat. "I was in bed with one of my most loyal clients—the Marquess of Sale, perhaps you've heard of him? Although I doubt you move in similar circles." He'd shrugged, his smile petty. "In any event, I was telling him about your *arrangement* with your last valet. Who wasn't even—"

One moment Smith was waiting for the other man to finish and leave, the next, he had Charles pinned to the wall by the throat.

Smith thought he might have been more surprised than Charles, although nowhere near as scared.

"You have made several mistakes in the time we've been acquainted, Charles," he'd said quietly, slackening his hold on the other man's neck to allow him to breathe. Smith hadn't wanted to hurt him— or at least not much—he'd merely wanted to be sure he had his complete attention. "The biggest mistake you've made, by far, is your belief that whatever affection I once bore you still exempts you from my displeasure. You know my thoughts on being a subject for your pillow talk, so I won't belabor the point. I'm going to leave you to dress in private, so I'll bid you goodbye right now. And this *is* goodbye, Charles." He'd held Charles's bright blue gaze a moment longer, wanting to be sure the other man understood.

Charles had nodded shakily, his Adam's apple bobbing beneath Smith's hand, his throat as fragile as a cornstalk in October.

Smith had not seen Charles since.

While he was relieved, he couldn't help feeling a pang of regret that things had ended so badly. He could never love the younger man, but he'd enjoyed his company greatly at one time.

Unfortunately, Charles had become even more callous during his year away and Smith suspected there were darker reasons for his slender physique than merely a picky diet. He knew the look of a person's pupils on opiates, and he feared Charles had developed habits that would lead him to sorrow.

He suspected that his addiction had already led him to poverty as he'd somehow managed to piss away the money Smith had paid him— more than he'd make working for a decade—in addition to whatever his Russian prince had likely given him.

Charles, Jojo, Moira—all three gone.

If Smith ever needed evidence that he was meant to live alone, he needed to look no further than those three.

One embittered.

One with another man.

And one reluctantly carrying his child and seeking another lover.

Which brought him back to Felson and his visit.

Smith sighed and glared out his study window.

Moira wanted to fuck someone else. What was he going to do about it?

Smith noticed a familiar figure approaching the house and frowned; it was Luke.

But today wasn't Monday.

He was walking with the same dignified, almost stately, stride he always employed. But Smith knew Luke's body intimately. He could see his shoulders were tense even from this distance.

He looked like a man who had steeled himself to face an unpleasant task.

Smith's stomach, which had already been roiling, tightened with dread.

What now?

Chapter 31

This is a terrible, terrible idea, Luke.

It was. It was the sort of idea from which a person might not recover.

But he'd already taken the longest route to Mr. Smith's house, and then looped back around and taken another route. He could either wander the streets for the rest of the gloomy day, or he could be a coward and go back home, or he could do what he'd set out to do.

Mr. Smith doesn't want her. Why should it matter what you do? A quiet, greedy voice in his head muttered.

Luke suspected things were not quite so simple.

It was David, his erstwhile lover, who answered the door, his eyebrows lifting when he saw it was Luke. "Not normally your day, is it?"

"No, I just need a few minutes with the master. Is he here?"

"Yes, he's alone. The doctor just left." He paused. "How is Miss Moira? Nothing wrong, I hope?" All the servants knew about the impending baby, of course. Most were almost as excited as Luke about the prospect of a child in the house.

"No, nothing wrong." Luke suppressed a slightly hysterical urge to laugh.

"Why don't you wait in the small sitting room and I'll go and see—"

"Ah, Luke."

Luke's head whipped up to find Mr. Smith standing at the head of the stairs. His face was in shadow, but he sounded as pleasant as ever. So perhaps the doctor hadn't told him anything?

"Hello, sir. I'm sorry to come outside the appointed time, but I wonder if I could take a moment of your time?"

"You are always welcome, Luke. Come join me in the study." He turned and disappeared.

Luke handed his hat and cane to David and stripped off his gloves. "Should I send tea, do you think?" David asked.

"Er, I would wait to see if he rings for it."

Or if he just throws me out a second-floor window.

Luke climbed the stairs with the reluctant step of a man mounting a gibbet. But that did not mean he wanted to back out of his decision and run. He needed to sort this out; matters had become too complicated, emotions too entangled for him to continue as if he viewed Moira as nothing more than an employer.

All night long he'd pondered the situation. Finally, after taking out fear of what *might* happen, he had simply looked at what he would *like* to happen.

What he would like is for all three of them to be back under the same roof—even if that meant fewer nights alone with his master. But that wasn't going to happen.

So that left Luke and Moira.

And he liked her a great deal. More than liked her.

Smith had thrown her out. Why should she be alone?

As for Smith not liking to share… Well, that's where things became difficult.

Smith had left his door open so Luke entered and shut it quietly behind him. Smith was at his desk and gestured to one of the chairs across from it.

"You look upset, Luke."

Upset. Yes, that was probably as good a word as any.

"You have come about Moira," Smith said when Luke appeared incapable of speech.

"Yes, sir."

"You are the reason she has asked Doctor Felson about the health issues regarding sexual intercourse."

Luke swallowed and made himself raise his eyes to meet his master's. "Yes."

"I see." He remained inhumanly still, the air around him strangely charged.

Then suddenly he stood and Luke immediately followed suit. When the other man came toward him, it was all he could do not to back away. Smith didn't stop until he was almost standing on Luke's toes.

Looking into his master's eyes was like staring into a blast furnace.

"You've come to ask my permission to fuck the woman carrying my child."

Well, when you put it that way…

"Is that it?" Smith persisted when Luke didn't immediately respond. His tone was flat and emotionless but his smile was unlike any that Luke had ever seen. Seething and feral and *terrifying*.

"She is lonely, sir." It wasn't what he'd wanted to say, but he'd needed to say *something*.

"Is that why you would accommodate her? Out of pity?"

"No." He didn't hesitate with his answer. Maybe because it had been one that occurred to him, as well. Only after a great deal of self-examination had he discarded it. She had always aroused him, but only lately had his arousal been joined with a true emotional connection.

Luke inhaled deeply, opened his mouth … and then closed it.

"Say what is on your mind, Luke."

Never had his master looked so *coldly* at him.

Be a man, Luke.

"You have cast her out—of your heart and your house—do you also believe that nobody else should love her? Do you want her to be alone to punish her?"

They were the hardest words he could recall speaking and—for just a second—something flashed across Smith's face and Luke thought perhaps he'd broken through the thick wall of reserve.

But then Smith turned and went back to his desk. "I excuse both of you of any contractual obligations you might have. You must do what you feel is best," he said, opening the ledger on his desk.

Luke opened his mouth.

"I'll let you show yourself out," Mr. Smith said, putting on his reading glasses.

So, that was that.

***

As awful as Luke had felt leaving Smith's house, he was pleased about Moira's reaction to his news.

"*Luke!*" Moira shrieked, leaping into his arms.

Luke clutched her bottom and hitched her over his hips as she covered him with kisses.

Her body drove him wild, which probably meant that something was wrong with him, because he'd never before heard of a man being aroused by a pregnant woman.

But it had been agonizing keeping his hands off her. And now he didn't need to.

Smith's dead gaze flashed through his mind, but he pushed it aside. Being with Moira did not diminish his love for Smith. He would simply need to make the other man see that. He could begin working on him this coming Monday.

"I want you right now, Luke," Moira said, her voice pulling him back.

"Now? Er—" He glanced out the window.

"I don't care if is daylight. In fact, I would prefer it; I want to see you clearly when you fuck me the first time."

Luke's face heated.

She gave a delighted laugh. "You are embarrassed!"

Was he? He'd shown himself to thousands of people over the years and engaged in every sort of debauchery. Could he possibly be embarrassed to have sex during broad daylight with a woman he cared for?

"You are!" Her eyes widened and she smothered her laugh with a hand.

"Take off your clothes," he ordered.

Her pupils widened at his words and tone.

She nodded, but said, "I want you fully clothed. The first time." She fumbled with the buttons, so he shoved her hands aside.

"I want you fully naked. Every time," he replied, making her laugh yet again. He was generally not accounted the wittiest of men, so he appreciated her effort.

He'd seen her naked many, many times, but never with the knowledge he would soon be inside her.

He'd just lifted her chemise over her head when she slid to her knees. For a moment, he thought she'd fallen, but then he felt her hands on his placket and groaned.

"I shan't last long," he warned.

"I don't care—we've got all day. And all night. It's miserable weather and a perfect day to spend in bed."

"I'll need to work at some point—urgh!" His eyes rolled back in his head. "Hell, that feels—"

She sucked him down to the root, and he was not a small man.

Luke's hands slid into her curls, which she had decided to keep short.

"Mmm," he groaned, tightening his fingers, his hips bucking.

Her answering groan told him what she thought about that, so he pumped into her again, harder, earning a louder groan and writhing.

"You need a proper mouth fuck, don't you?" The filthy words just came pouring out and he immediately stilled, waiting for the backlash— he'd heard plenty of whores, men and women both, complaining about punters who couldn't keep their bloody hands to themselves and just enjoy a nob polishing.

But the effect of his words on her was electric, and she sucked him down to the root, choking herself with his shaft. Her shell-pink lips were stretched so thin around his prick that he looked as thick as a wine bottle.

She *wanted* his hands on her. And she wanted it *rough*.

"Look at me while you suck my cock," he snapped while he rolled his hips.

Moira's eyes turned wide and glassy at the violence of his use. Every time he pumped into her, the muscles beneath her pale skin tensed and tightened. She was slender, but strong.

She was also pregnant and he didn't like to see her kneeling so long.

He tightened his hand in her hair and pulled her off, enjoying her angry whimper.

"Enough," he growled when she tried to suck him back down. "Get on the bed."

She moved with economy and grace, all the more noticeable with the bulge in her middle.

"On your back, legs spread."

Luke stroked himself and watched with greedy glee as she obediently put herself in position.

"Please," she said when he just stared.

He let his dark side show, sneering down at her, pumping himself with slow, menacing strokes. "Please what?" he growled.

"Please fuck me."

Hearing the vulgar word on her tongue had the predictable effect.

Later, after he'd had her a few times, he could behave with more decorum. But right now, he just needed to get inside her.

He pulled her to the edge of the bed, spreading her lower lips before placing himself at her swollen, slick opening. Before he entered her, he met her gaze. "If you have even the *slightest* discomfort, you tell me."

She nodded.

"No, say it."

"If I feel even the slightest discomfort, I'll tell you."

"Good. Now, beg for my cock."

"Please, Luke—I need you inside me so badl—"

He entered her with a firm, smooth thrust, the tight heat of her body making him dizzy. "My God you feel good."

She clenched even tighter and grinned up at him.

"Witch," he muttered, lifting her hips and then slowly pulling out, aroused almost beyond bearing at the sight of her slick pink folds stretched around him.

The first few thrusts were careful—exploratory—but the expression of bliss on her face emboldened him.

He knew he wouldn't last, nor would he be able to make her orgasm in this position—at least it was rare in his experience.

"Bring yourself off," he ordered, smirking when her hand started moving before he'd stopped speaking.

Thank God she was skilled with her fingers because his crisis hit him only a moment later, the two of them climaxing within seconds of each other.

Luke held her tight against his groin while he pumped her full of his spend, her contractions milking him until it was painful.

He pulled out of her with a groan and then moved her up higher on the bed before lowering himself between her thighs and burying his tongue deep in her cunt, the familiar taste of his ejaculate mingling with hers.

Moira was right, Luke thought, today was a perfect day to spend in bed.

Chapter 32

Moira was at the piano when Armand entered.

Luke had given her a surprise gift yesterday, new sheet music from the composer Brahms. It was a challenging piece and had kept her riveted all morning.

"You've got a visitor, Miss Moira." Armand held out a salver and she picked up the card: Charles J. Smith.

She looked up and shook her head. "I'm afraid this must be a mistake. I don't know a Charles J. Smith."

The door opened without warning, clipping poor Armand in the shoulder, and Luke barreled into the room.

"Oh, I beg your pardon," Luke muttered when he saw Armand clutching his shoulder, his eyes swung toward Moira. "Do you know who that is downstairs?"

She shrugged. "Charles J. Smith."

"That is *Mister* Charles."

"You mean *The* Charles?"

"The same."

"Whatever does he want with me?"

Luke's normally smooth brow puckered. 'I don't know."

Moira studied him a moment, waiting for more. When he said nothing, she nodded at Armand. "Show him into the sitting room and tell him I'll be down shortly."

Once he'd gone, Luke stepped closer. "Are you sure about this?" he asked, setting a hand on her stomach, as he was prone to do now—as if he could not stop touching her—which Moira loved.

She put one of her hands over his. "Shouldn't I be?"

Luke absently stroked her belly as he considered her question. Now that he warmed her bed regularly, he'd stopped being so passive and often gave opinions before she sought them, which was exactly how she liked it.

If not for the brooding presence of Smith hanging over them both—or so she imagined, although he'd never once contacted her or bothered her in the months since she'd left—she might have imagined that Luke was her child's father. He was certainly more excited about the child than any father she'd ever met.

"Charles is not a restful man," Luke said finally. "And I believe he can only have come to make mischief."

"You think he has come to gloat?"

Moira had known that Charles had returned because Luke had briefly mentioned encountering him at Smith's house. She'd wanted to ask more—she was desperately curious about everything to do with Smith—but she knew Luke already straddled a delicate position and didn't want to make matters any more awkward for him.

"I think Smith might have only seen him briefly," Luke said. "I've heard from several of the servants that Charles has shown up uninvited and Smith has turned him away. I've also heard that he lost his position at Tosca's. He went to Bernina's and the Birch Palace, but neither place would have him."

"Why come here, though?"

"I think he is obsessed with the master and he'll have heard about you and the child." He stroked her belly and his eyes were the blue of a flame as he stared down at her. "I don't like thinking of you and the baby in the same room with him."

Moira stood up on tiptoe and kissed him, already wet from only a few minutes of his gentle caressing. "I'll be fine. I'll go and see what he wants. Why don't you knock on the sitting room door after a few moments and ask if I want tea. If I need help getting away from him, I'll mention macaroons." Moira had recently developed a loathing for the biscuits, which she'd once loved.

Luke nodded reluctantly, his usually sweet expression gone, the one that took its place grim, determined, and protective.

***

The man standing beside the large sash window looked like an angel.

"Thank you for seeing me, Miss Dunsmuir." Charles Smith strode toward her with the sort of grace that came with being completely at home in one's own body.

And what a body it was.

He had a sort of otherworldly beauty that was almost overwhelming, which she'd known that from the portrait over Smith's bed.

But as Charles came closer, Moira saw the signs of dissipation. While he might pass for twenty-five at a distance, he looked a good ten years older up close.

"You are probably wondering why I've called?" he asked, making her aware that she was staring rather rudely.

"I'm curious," she admitted, gesturing to the chair near him and then taking a seat across from him.

His smile was charming, but it never reached his eyes. Instead, his gaze wandered over her slowly and thoroughly, lingering on her midriff.

Moira didn't realize she'd laid her hand on her stomach.

"That is the reason I am here, too—curiosity," he said at her questioning look. "After all, we are members of a very small club, you and I—those people allowed briefly into Smith's life—and home."

Moira had nothing to say about that—she would hardly open her heart to this stranger.

Charles smiled, as if he could hear her thoughts, and then sighed. "I'll be honest. I just wanted to meet the woman fortunate enough to be carrying his baby. You see I've been bad and have been banished from his life—permanently, I fear." He gave a brittle laugh. "I'd thought perhaps…" He bit his lip, his flush making him look younger.

"You thought we might console each other?" she guessed when he didn't finish.

He laughed at her wry tone. "Now that I'm standing here, it does sound rather bizarre." He looked so embarrassed, lost, and alone that Moira's heart went out to him. She, too, knew what it meant to be cast out of paradise.

"Would you care for some tea?" she asked.

This time his smile wasn't just beautiful, it was genuine. "I'd adore some tea."

***

Luke had wanted to kick Charles Smith's scrawny arse down the front step rather than let him in the front door, but it wasn't his place to make that decision, which was something that rankled more than it should.

267

But he'd obeyed Moira's order and waited five minutes before knocking

"Ah, Luke. Could you have a tray sent up, please," Moira said, leaving macaroons out of her request and giving him a look that said she did not need any assistance ridding the house of the other man.

Charles looked at him and laughed. "Well, you are just *everywhere*."

Luke looked to where Charles was sprawled out in a chair, his eyes dancing with vindictive amusement.

"You know Luke?" Moira asked, as if she didn't already know.

"I wouldn't say I *know* him, but I certainly see him here, there, and everywhere."

Luke ignored his mocking. "I'll have a tea tray sent up right away." He bowed and left before he did something he oughtn't.

Charles didn't stay much longer, clearly disinterested in taking tea with Moira. Luke didn't relax until Armand had shown him to the door.

Later that night, in bed, they discussed Mr. Smith's erstwhile lover.

"He is just spoiled—as very beautiful people are often wont to be," Moira said, excusing him far more readily than the bastard deserved.

They'd been naked and sweat-slicked from their lovemaking, Moira relaxing on top of him. She had kissed his nose. "You are very beautiful, too, so I'm not sure why you're not spoiled."

She'd been amused that her words had embarrassed Luke.

He knew he was attractive, but he'd never been comfortable with hearing it. It was just a shell and it would age and crack and wear. He wanted somebody to love him for more than his face and body.

He'd also not wanted to talk about his *beauty*, but rather about Charles.

"I hope you did not encourage him to return," he'd said, and then had wondered at his own audacity at dictating to his mistress.

But Moira hadn't seemed to mind. "I don't think he'll be back," she said. "I think he was just curious. And lonely and perhaps a bit jealous."

Luke had been able to smell the spite on the other man at fifty paces.

"Promise me that you won't admit him if I'm not at home, Moira."

She'd sobered at his use of her name—which he employed rarely. Rather than tease him about being able to care for herself, she'd nodded and stroked his face. "Of course, I won't let him in if it bothers you."

Just thinking about the visit now, four days later, his skin crawled to think of Charles coming back to Miss Moira when Luke wasn't there.

As he made his way toward Mr. Smith's for their usual Monday evening, Luke tried to discern why he disliked Charles so much. He didn't know him—at least not more than a superficial knowledge—but there was something about him that had always been so acquisitive and self-centered.

Luke might worship and adore Mr. Smith, but he was fully aware of his flaws. Smith was selfish, vain, and wanted to have everything exactly the way he liked it.

At the same time, Smith did not manipulate people with lies into signing his contracts. Everything was laid out clearly and plainly. If Charles signed it, he should have agreed with what he was signing.

While it was true that Smith's demands were… well, *demanding,* a person always knew where they stood. And as much as he expected from his lovers, he always gave more; at least that was Luke's opinion.

As he walked through the late March evening, he wondered what he'd find at his destination. His last conversation with his master—the one about Moira and becoming her lover—had not gone well.

Smith had then been out of London for three weeks.

Tonight he fully expected to find that Smith had not yet returned. Or that he simply did not wish to see Luke.

But when David opened the door, he gave Luke his usual smirk and said, "He's waiting for you up in his chambers." He waggled his eyebrows. "A fine dinner he's ordered for your de-lec-ta-tion."

Luke laughed as he unwound his muffler. "Impressive. You must've been reading something other than the penny dreadfuls."

David grinned. "Thanks to *your* influence, if that's what you're asking."

It hadn't been, but Luke was pleased he'd given something to the other man, even if it was only better taste in books.

"You look well, Luke, working for Miss Moira suits you."

"Thank you. And yes, it does," he said, annoyed that his face heated.

But David gave him a genuine smile, rather than teasing him for his blushing. "I'm glad for you."

"How are things with you?" Luke asked.

"Good, good. I'm seeing Tony."

Luke grinned. Tony was one of the grooms, who was as well-hung as his equine charges. "Ah, lucky bugger."

"Exactly."

They laughed and Luke headed up the stairs.

He knocked softly before entering his master's chambers.

Mr. Smith was sitting in front of a crackling fire, smoking a cheroot and reading something—business papers, probably. He looked up and smiled—a real smile, one that reached his eyes. "Hello Luke, come warm yourself by the fire. There's a chill in the air tonight."

"Thank you, sir." He took the chair the other man indicated.

"How are you this evening?"

"I'm well, sir. And yourself? Did your out-of-town business go well?"

"I am well and yes, the weeks of negotiation were brutal, but my syndicate is now the owner of the largest tinned food processing facility in England."

"Congratulations, sir."

"Thank you. I'd like to apologize for my rudeness the last time we spoke."

Luke blinked, floored.

Smith laughed. "Oh come, do I really apologize so rarely as that?"

"No, sir, it's not that. It's just that you rarely have reason to."

Smith's expression became sober. "That is a very kind thing to say."

"It is true, sir. At least in my experience."

"Well, then. All is good between us?"

"It always was sir."

"Anything I need to be made aware of?"

Mr. Smith always asked the same question. Usually, Luke had nothing to tell him, but tonight …

"Actually, there is one thing, sir."

Chapter 33

The door opened barely a crack and Smith kicked it in.

"Bloody fuck!" Charles yelled when the thick slab of wood struck him in the forehead.

Smith leapt on him, bearing him down to the floor and landing on top of his far slighter body.

Charles gasped like a landed fish, his eyes going wide. "Smith! What—"

"What the devil is this?" an arrogant, upper-class voice demanded from somewhere beyond the small entry hall.

Smith looked up to see a large man dressed in a gaudy gold and red robe.

"Get out," Smith snarled. "Now."

The man's jaw dropped and he shuffled backwards. He was about the same age as Smith, a head taller and three stone heavier, but he had the pasty look of a man who lived a life of leisure. And drugs. Smith could only assume he was one of Charles's customers.

He turned to Charles, who was just getting his wind back. Smith leaned his forearm on Charles's throat and pushed. "You go near Moira again and the next time there won't be any conversation. At. All. Do you understand me?" He lifted the pressure just enough so that Charles could answer.

"Yes!" he gasped. "Christ, Smith. I wasn't doing anything wrong," he said in a hoarse voice. "I just wanted to see this woman you've fallen in love with—I could see it in your eyes the few times I got you to speak of her. You finally love somebody." He sobbed. "And it's not *me*."

Smith's mind snagged on his words. *The woman you've fallen in love with.*

Bloody hell.

"Smith?" Charles asked, his voice shaky and tentative. "I'm sorry. Please don't be—"

Smith shook himself and turned his attention back to Charles. "You've seen her," Smith snapped, glaring at the other man and briefly tightening his grip again. "So now you don't need to go near her again."

"I understand—I won't talk to her. I promise. Bloody hell!" he whined. "I think I cracked my head when you knocked me down."

Smith scowled and pushed to his feet, brushing off his clothing and staring down at the wreck of a man at his feet.

He was shocked by Charles's appearance. He was skinnier than he'd been even a month ago, but it was more than that. His skin was dull, his hair—once his crowning glory—was lank, and he stank of sweat and the sickly-sweet smell of his new lover—the one he smoked, not the one in the hideous robe.

Smith hesitated, and then said, "You'd better take yourself in hand soon Charles, or there won't be anything left of you." He turned toward the door, which was still hanging open.

"Smith."

"What?" He turned.

Charles was still sprawled out and his robe was parted, exposing his flaccid cock.

Charles slid a hand around his shaft, the gaslight glinting on the silver in the head of the crown. "How about once more? Just to say goodbye properly."

Smith snorted with disgust, spun on his heel, and took the steps two at a time.

Once outside he waved away his coach. "I'll walk."

His two guards hopped off the box and followed behind at a discreet distance.

It was cold, dark, and a goodly way back to his part of the city, but he needed the air and exercise.

He grimaced when he recalled that he'd left poor Luke sitting in his bedchamber, no doubt believing he'd gone mad.

Perhaps he had.

He had, quite literally, seen red when he'd heard Charles had gone to see Moira. It hadn't only—or even mostly—been fury that propelled him to Charles's house like a winged hangman of death. It had been fear.

Charles would have gone to see her for no good reason, but at least one bad one: to hurt her in some way because he knew it would hurt Smith.

He snorted at that. How was it that Charles, out of everyone he knew, was the only one to see into Smith's heart and realize that he'd fallen in love with the damned woman?

Well, he suspected Charles wasn't the only one who knew how much he cared about Moira. Luke knew how Smith missed her. But only Charles had seen the gut-churning anguish that had simmered within him those few times when he'd mentioned Moira's name.

Perhaps Charles saw those emotions in Smith because he'd experienced them himself—*about* Smith?

Smith grimaced. Christ. He didn't like to think of anyone suffering such emotional pain.

You *can alleviate your pain, while Charles doesn't have that option*, a voice at the back of his mind pointed out.

Smith scowled. *And just what does that mean?*

You were the one who sent Moira away. Why not let her come back?

Smith grit his teeth against the thought; it was not the first time he'd had to wrestle with it. And it never got any more pleasant—nor did he understand why he couldn't simply forgive Moira.

He *hated* how angry he became just thinking about what she'd done to him. And it didn't matter that she was obviously sorry. Extremely sorry.

Smith's thoughts churned around and around without ever resolving.

He realized he was cold and noticed that the streets had emptied and the sky was unusually clear, the air crisp.

A glance at his watch told him he'd been walking for almost two hours.

He slipped his watch into his pocket with a guilty grimace—the two guards must think he was mad.

Smith looked up when he paused to cross the street and realized where his feet had led him: this was the cross street that led to Moira's house.

He hesitated only a moment before turning right instead of left and heading toward the pretty square out in front of her house.

There were stone benches here and there and Smith took one facing the house, vaguely aware that his two guards were standing awkwardly near a lamp post, clearly uncertain of what to do.

As he stared at the house it struck him that it was missing something: guards at the front door.

He could have slapped himself! How had he neglected to provide her with protection? He might have warned Charles off, but in the years to come there would be others who realize that Moira was an excellent way to get back at him.

He would hire men tomorrow—and summon Luke so he could discuss the matter with him and make suitable arrangements.

Luke.

Bloody hell. Smith had run out of the house like a lunatic.

The front door of Moira's house opened and the man in question stepped out, as if Smith had summoned him with his thoughts.

Beside Luke was Moira and a third person. Smith squinted and then gaped; it was Nora Fanshawe, of all people.

What the devil was *his* friend doing there?

Smith snorted at the foolishly possessive thought. There was no reason that Moira and Nora couldn't be friends. Indeed, the two women chatted with the ease of longtime acquaintances and soon Nora's carriage came from the mews to pick her up.

Smith stared at Moira as she waved to Nora, Luke standing beside her in a way that seemed to lay claim, even though he wasn't touching her.

When the carriage disappeared Moira turned to Luke, said something to him that made him laugh—a sound that Smith had never heard the other man make in all the time he'd known him—and then Moira put her hand on Luke's arm and the two disappeared into the house, shutting the door on this brief, intensely painful, glimpse into their lives.

Smith felt dazed, as if he'd been struck in the head with a brick. She was too bundled up for her stomach to be visible—Luke would never let her step outside in the cold without proper protection—and he wondered if her pregnancy was obvious yet.

She'd been so at ease with Luke, and vice versa. They were very like a married couple, Smith realized.

The thought shocked him, and he waited for a red, raging wave of possessive anger—like the one that he'd felt the night Luke told him that he wanted to be Moira's lover.

But none came.

Instead, he felt a sadness that infused every part of his body and left him feeling as if he weighed a thousand pounds.

Only mere feet away—in a house that he'd provided—were the two people he liked most in the entire world, and they were together, without him.

And it was nobody's fault but his own.

Chapter 34

"Can I move now?"

Moira smirked at Luke's pained voice. "Fine," she said, looking up from the half-finished sketch. "You may take a ten-minute break."

Luke groaned and rolled his massive shoulders, the action causing the familiar tightening in her sex. He was a beautiful, beautiful man.

"I want to see it," he said, pushing off the chaise lounge where she'd had him reclining—unfortunately still clothed as he'd refused to be nude in the middle of the day.

"Not until it's finished," she said, pulling the sketchpad closer to her chest.

He winced. "You're going to get charcoal all over that gown and ruin it." A wicked gleam entered his sky-blue eyes. "I think you should sketch in the nude from now on."

Moira laughed. "I will if you will."

"You sound like my ten-year-old niece," he chided, his playful smirk positively adorable and so very, very rare. He bent to pick up his coat and slipped it on. "We're finished for today."

"Oh, we are?" she asked. Moira found it entertaining that her so-called servant managed to boss her around so thoroughly.

"Yes," he said, his long, thick fingers deftly fastening the buttons. "You wanted to go and listen to Mister Darwin talk about his new book and that means you shall have to dine early."

"Ah," Moira said, closing her sketch book. "I'd forgotten that was tonight. What time do—"

A series of shouts came from the corridor.

Luke frowned. "What was—"

The loud *crack* of a gun interrupted his words and Moira shrieked. "My God, what is—"

Luke moved toward her like a blur. "Get down behind the settee," he ordered, his eyes on the door.

"But—"

"Do it, Moira!" he ordered, gently but firmly pressing her down and then standing in front of the settee just as the drawing door opened hard enough to hit the wall.

"What do you want?" Luke asked whoever had entered the room, his tone so cold that it didn't even sound like him.

A hysterical laugh filled the room, the sound chilling. "You're not who I'm looking for, but you'll do."

Moira recognized the voice as belonging to Charles Smith, although he hadn't sounded so shrill and brittle—so *unhinged*—the last time.

"Where is she?" Charles demanded shrilly.

"She's not here."

"Quit. Lying."

"I'm not ly—"

Gunfire cut off Luke's words.

Moira screamed as he fell to the floor.

***

"I'll not be back for dinner," Smith told David, as his servant helped him into his overcoat.

"Very good, sir. And should—"

Somebody pounded on the door hard enough to make the windows rattle.

David looked at Smith. "Should I—"

"Open it," Smith said, pulling on his gloves.

A young, breathless man in livery stood in the opening—Armand, Smith thought his name was—and there was blood smeared over his cheek.

"What happened?" Smith demanded.

"There's a man with a gun and—"

Smith shoved past him and ran.

***

"Get up," Charles ordered.

Moira ignored him and pressed a torn piece of her day gown against the blood staining Luke's shoulder.

"I said get. Up." A boot struck Moira's lower back, knocking her over Luke's body.

She whipped around and glared up at the man holding the gun a few feet from her face.

"What is *wrong* with you? He will bleed to death if I don't—"

There was a light touch on her arm and she looked down.

Luke was smiling up at her, his hand fumbling with the cloth she'd been about to tuck under his coats and shirt to stop the bleeding. "I can do it, Moira. Do what he says."

She opened her mouth to argue and the boot struck her again, jolting her spine.

"Yes, Moira," Charles said in a mocking tone. "Do what I say."

Luke nodded again and Moira took a deep breath and pushed up slowly. The urge to hunch protectively over her midriff was almost crippling.

Charles grabbed her arm and yanked her toward the door.

"What do you want?" she demanded, her eyes flooding with tears while her chest filled with rage.

"What do I want?" His eyes pulsed with rage. "What do you think I want, you stupid bitch? I want Smith back." When he yanked open the door, she saw servants clustered in the hallway.

Charles pointed the revolver at Moira's head. "Any of you try anything and I'll kill her."

The servants scattered like pigeons before a cat.

"Go and help Luke," she called over her shoulder as Charles dragged her toward the stairs.

"Where are we going?" she asked when they reached the foyer and he yanked open the door, his head whipping back and forth.

When he didn't see what he wanted, he growled and slammed the door shut, pressing his face to the sidelight.

"May I please put on a cloak if we are—"

He spun on her and slapped her hard enough across the face to drive her back against the console table, sending a vase crashing to the marble floor.

"Shut up!" he snarled and then whipped back around and stared out the window. "Finally!" he muttered and turned back to her, grabbing her arm in a biting grip. "You try anything stupid and I'll shoot you in the stomach." He demonstrated by pointing the barrel at her stomach. "It won't kill *you*, but it will put paid to your precious baby. Understand?"

She nodded vigorously. "I won't do anything."

He flung open the door and pulled her toward a private carriage waiting in front of the house.

Somebody inside opened the door and Charles shoved her toward it so hard she stumbled. A gloved hand closed on her arm and pulled her into the coach, which took off before Charles was even fully inside.

"You imbecile! I told you not to make a scene!" a voice snapped in the near darkness of the carriage.

"I couldn't help it," Charles shot back. "One of the servants attacked me."

"He did not!" Moira said, and then yelped when Charles's fist clipped her shoulder.

"*Enough!*" the other man roared and Moira was vaguely aware of a scuffle underway, and then two loud slaps.

"That *hurt!*" Charles cried out.

"Shut up, you degenerate," the newcomer hissed, his voice pulsing with loathing. He was just a shadow to Moira, who could only see the outline of a top hat in the near darkness.

"I apologize if you've been manhandled, Miss Bardot."

It took her a second to realize he'd used her real name. "Who are you? What do you want with me?"

A low chuckle filled the small space. "I am a friend of your father's. Or perhaps I should say I *was* his friend, because I suspect he is no longer with us, although I've read nothing of his demise in any newspapers, I'm guessing that Nicolaides has disposed of him."

"Who?" she asked. "I don't know who you are talking about. Are you sure you have the right person?"

There was a pause, and then more laughter. "Oh, very good—almost convincing. But you know who I'm talking about. I spoke with your dear mother only a few weeks ago. Marie is not pleased with you, by the way."

"Smith won't be pleased with *her* once he learns you've been talking to her."

"What do you know about—"

A loud slap cut off the rest of whatever Charles was going to say.

"Please excuse Charles, Miss Barton. It has been some time since his last pipe, so he is even more uncivil than usual."

Moira knew people who used opium and was aware they could become quite erratic if they were deprived of the substance. It also explained Charles's sickly pallor and short temper.

"I want to talk to you about Nicolaides."

"I have not seen him in months. Not since my parents came to London—or didn't Marie tell you that."

"Your mother knew very little about what happened after she left, but Charles has helped fill the gaps."

"Who *are* you?"

"That hardly matters."

"I can't help you get into Smith's house, if that is what you want."

A chuckle came out of the darkness. "I won't need to get into his house because I have *you*, so he will come to *me*."

Moira didn't correct him—didn't tell him that it was the baby Smith would come for, not her. She wanted both these men to forget that she was pregnant. It made her sick to know that *they* knew.

"Why do you want him?" she asked.

"Because the bastard is trying to kill me. So I'll need to take care of him before he can succeed."

"What did you do? Why does he want to kill you?"

"You ask a great many questions." He didn't sound happy about that, so she closed her mouth.

The carriage wheels passed onto a section of road that was rough and Moira had to cling to the seat to keep from bouncing off.

The older man muttered something about a *bloody hovel.*

"Well, I'm sorry, but it is all you could afford," Charles snapped, unrepressed regardless of how much the other man obviously hated him. "I know you can get more money from that *list* of yours, you just don't want to share any of it with—*argh*!"

"Oh, *do* shut up," her host muttered.

The carriage abruptly came to a halt and then shook in the way that indicated somebody was hopping down.

"We are here, Miss Bardot," her unknown captor said. The door opened and admitted the light from the coach lamp, illuminating the man across from her.

He was older than her father—closer to seventy than sixty—and might once have been handsome but dissipation had turned his eyes into piggy blue glints hidden by waxy folds of fat. His skin was an unhealthy yellow, his hair a dirty gray beneath a hat that had seen better days.

A quick glance around outside showed them to be in a narrow alley. The man who'd opened the door was dressed like a clerk rather than a liveried servant.

He helped the older man out of the carriage and then gave him a look no servant would give an employer. "I'll be wanting my pay, Clayton."

Clayton scowled, his eyes sliding to Moira and then back to the other man. He dug into the front of his overcoat and came out with a battered envelope. "Tell Selkirk I want it ready and waiting no later than tomorrow morning. Understood?"

The other man snatched the letter from his hand, rolled his eyes, and stomped off.

"Get out," Charles ordered behind her, giving her a push.

Moira stumbled from the carriage while the older man, Clayton, stared after the messenger he'd just sent off, his gaze pensive.

"Are we just going to stand here?" Charles demanded.

When Clayton turned back around, he held a pistol, which he pointed at Charles, rather than Moira. "I don't really need you anymore, boy, so you might want to consider that."

Charles's mouth snapped shut, his blue eyes glittering with dislike.

"This way," Clayton said, gesturing Moira toward a door in the alley wall. Rats scurried beneath the ankle-deep rubbish and Moira bit her lip to keep from screaming when one clawed at her stockings.

Clayton unlocked the door and went in first. The lintel was so low that even she felt cramped, and she recoiled at the dank air that flowed out of the darkness.

If you go in there, you'll never come out again. Not alive.

Moira took a step back and bumped into Charles.

He grabbed the back of her neck. "Get in there," he snapped, and shoved her into the darkness.

Chapter 35

"Really, sir, I am fine," Luke insisted in a slurred voice while struggling to push himself up in the bed, and then just as quickly sliding back down.

"You need to lie back and relax, Mr. Cooper" Doctor Felson said. "I've just removed a bullet from your side. If you thrash about you will ruin all my careful work."

"But Miss Moira—"

"You've just been shot, Luke. You are going to rest," Smith said, using his firmest voice.

"But I could—"

Smith gave the younger man a stern look.

Luke opened his mouth a third time but nothing came out. Instead, his eyes slid most of the way shut and he grunted softly.

"That will be the second dose of laudanum taking effect," the doctor said to Smith in a quiet voice.

Smith turned to the footman hovering beside the door. "Stay here with him until somebody relieves you. If he wakes, make sure he stays put."

"Yes, sir," David said, his expression grimly determined.

Smith walked the doctor out of the room and then paused by the head of the stairs, far enough away from his bedroom—which is where he'd had Luke brought—so they wouldn't disturb the injured man.

"Is everything as you said? Or is it worse?" Smith asked.

"No, what I said was true—the bullet came out cleanly. It was a very close thing as it passed near one of his kidneys, but he was fortunate. Now what we need to do is stave off any infection.

Smith breathed a sigh of relief. "Thank you for coming so quickly."

"Of course, Mr. Smith."

"I want you to stay with him tonight."

"It's not necessary as he's not really in—"

"It will make me feel easier," Smith said. "And of course I shall pay adequately for your time.

The doctor hesitated, met Smith's gaze, and then nodded. "Certainly, I will stay."

"Good. I'll send my steward up to show you to a room where you may—"

The sound of running feet on the stairs stopped him and he turned to find the man he'd just been speaking of, slightly out of breath.

"What is it, Michael?"

"You've a visitor, sir."

"I want no visitors right now," he said, struggling to keep his tone civil.

"He said you'd say that, but—"

"Who is it?" Smith snapped.

"The Earl of Selkirk, sir."

***

Lord Selkirk was examining his own painting when Smith entered the sitting room a few minutes later.

"Selkirk, what a surprise," Smith said, not caring if he sounded rude or abrupt, since he was feeling both those things.

The earl didn't appear to notice his tone. "I sense that your house is in something of an uproar."

"Clayton kidnapped one of my people and another was shot during the abduction," Smith said, stumbling slightly on his description of both Moira and Luke. How did somebody describe a person who was more than a lover and yet didn't have the legal standing of a spouse? He shook the pointless thought aside.

Selkirk's eyebrows shot up. "*Clayton* abducted one of your people? It's not like him to get personally involved, he usually likes to allow others to do the dirty work."

"I misspoke—I should have said his henchman acted for him."

"Was it one of the agents who were sacked along with him?"

Smith pursed his lips in distaste. "Unfortunately, it was somebody I know—an ex-lover."

"Ah."

Smith was mildly amused by the other man's look of discomfort. One could speak of abductions and shootings in front of an aristocrat, but God forbid something even vaguely personal was mentioned.

Smith reached into his right front pocket and handed Selkirk the piece of paper Charles had left at Moira's house. "His messenger left a demand letter."

The earl read the few lines and looked up. "That is a great deal of money—will you give it to him?"

"Yes," Smith said without hesitation. The abduction had only occurred three hours ago, but it felt as if an entire epoch had passed. In the span of mere moments, he'd almost lost one lover and *had* lost another. And all because he was a grudge-bearing fool. If they'd been living with him, he would have had guards. If he'd knocked on the door last night and told Luke he was leaving his guards there—if, if, if!

"Mr. Smith?"

Smith shook himself from his pointless self-flagellation. "Based on your presence here, Clayton must have contacted you?"

"Yes, he sent a man for more money."

Smith snorted. "Greedy bastard."

"I think he's hoping to take all he can get and disappear permanently." Selkirk's lips curved into a smug smile.

"What?" Smith demanded.

"I know where he is hiding."

Smith's heart pounded almost painfully hard. "Where?"

"I want two assurances, first."

Smith's hands fisted, but his voice was calm when he spoke. "You are concerned about the documents you seek?"

"Yes."

Smith felt his mouth curl into an unpleasant smile. "If I get my hands on Clayton, he will give me whatever I want."

Selkirk gave him a long, searching look, and then nodded. "I believe that."

"What is your other demand?"

"I prefer to think of it as more of a request."

"I'm listening."

"I want to be there when you confront him."

Smith stood. "Fine. As long as you're ready to go right now."

***

Moira pulled the thin, smelly blanket tighter to her person but still couldn't stop shivering. She suspected it was more from fear, than from cold.

"You can't leave yet Grimes, you need to pick up Smith's money!" Clayton shouted, his angry, high-pitched voice making her jolt.

"I did what I said I'd do—Selkirk paid his part. I never agreed to tangle with Smith," Grimes retorted. He was one of the three men who'd aided in her abduction—not counting Charles and Clayton—the same one who'd left immediately after dropping them all off in this hovel.

"I can pay you more," Clayton said.

"I can't spend the money if I'm dead."

"I can meet Smith and collect the money," Charles piped up. "I'm not afraid of—"

Clayton turned on the jittery young whore and glared at him. "Shut. Up."

Grimes snickered. "That's a grand idea, Clayton, send *Charlie* here—he's not afraid."

"Don't call me that," Charles snapped.

"I'll pay you triple if you make the collection," Clayton said, ignoring Charles altogether.

Grimes gave Clayton a look so scathing it should have left the other man with singe marks. "I want *half* because I'm taking at least that much risk. Do you even understand who Smith is?"

"Of course, I'm familiar with his reputation," Clayton said.

Grimes laughed. "That's about as close as a man should get to him—his bloody reputation. I'd introduce you to the last man who touched *her*"—he jerked his chin at Moira— "But he's about as mobile and talkative as the vegetable he's named for."

Moira frowned; he could only mean the man who'd called himself Brown but was really Owen Onions. What had Smith done to him?

"I can hire somebody else to do this for less than half," Clayton blustered.

"Hire them, then," Grimes shot back. "But I think you'll be surprised, because nobody who works for Little will work for you—at least not when it comes to Smith."

Clayton scoffed. "Gerry Little runs this city! At least the criminal aspects of it. Are you claiming that *Little* is afraid of Smith?"

"Too bloody right I am. Anyone with a speck of common sense is." The look he gave Clayton said he didn't fall into that category. "So if you want my help, then I'll be wanting *half* and that's a bloody bargain," Grimes finished.

Clayton dithered and whined, but even Moira knew the older man had already decided to accept the counteroffer.

"Very well. But I want you to go early and show up before Smith does. It would be like him to have somebody tailing you."

"Don't try to teach me how to suck eggs, old man. I think I know how to spot a tail."

Clayton visibly restrained himself from arguing, keeping his mouth shut as Grimes gathered up his coat, hat, and a nasty looking pistol, which he tucked into his coat pocket.

Once he was gone, the tiny, filthy room seemed even more crowded for some reason.

Although Clayton and Grimes clearly didn't trust each other, Clayton and Charles *hated* one another. They reminded her of snakes, hissing and snapping. The minute one of them was distracted she wagered the other one would be on him.

"You promised me something when Grimes returned," Charles asked in a reedy, wheedling voice.

Clayton jerked his attention back to Charles. "There is a bottle of gin on the table. That will have to keep you satisfied until we leave this pesthole."

"If you just give me some money, I can go—"

Clayton pulled a pistol from his pocket and pointed it at Charles. "You will sit down and shut your mouth or I swear I shall—"

The door opened and Grimes hovered on the threshold.

Clayton cut him a glare and frowned. "What did you forget to—"

A voice that Moira didn't recognize said, "Drop it, Clayton. You know I'm a rather fine shot."

A slim man in exquisite dinner clothing stepped out from behind Grimes's large body.

"Selkirk!" Clayton hissed, the hand with the pistol wavering. His eyes slid to Moira and he hesitated.

The new man—Selkirk—made a clucking sound. "You'll be dead before you can even take aim."

"You wouldn't dare! You know what will happen if you kill me," Clayton said, smiling smugly.

"Selkirk might care about that, but I don't, Clayton." The calm, familiar, voice came from behind Grimes.

"Put the gun down," Smith said, entering the room, pushing Grimes ahead of him.

The bigger man stumbled and fell to his knees, which is when Moira saw his hands were tied behind his back.

"You stay down or I won't hesitate to put you down permanently," Smith said to the fallen man, his eyes on Moira.

"You'll get no struggle from me, guv," Grimes said.

"You filthy coward," Clayton snarled, glaring at his henchman.

"Put the gun on the table," Smith said.

Clayton took a step back and set the gun down.

"Good lad." Selkirk's lips twisted into an amused smirk. "Step away from it."

Clayton stepped back.

"Are you hurt?" Smith asked Moira, closing the distance between them in two strides, his brow furrowed with concern.

Moira shook her head, too stunned to speak.

Smith caught her up in a bone-crushing embrace, his voice low and husky, his arms like steel bands. "Thank God, Moira. I was so—"

"Let go of her!"

They both jolted and Smith half-turned at the sound of Charles's voice.

The younger man stood in the far corner of the room, holding the revolver he'd had earlier at Moira's house—which must have been on his person somewhere—and pointing it a Moira, or at least trying to. His hands were shaking too badly to settle his aim anywhere.

"What are you doing, Charles?" Smith asked calmly, easing his body in front of Moira, whose hands had already moved to protect her baby, as if they could stop a bullet.

"This all happened because you just never have enough!" Charles shouted, his voice raw with fury and pain.

"You can stop it right now—before somebody dies, Charles."

"I shot your other lover—I'll hang for what I did."

"The doctor removed the bullet, which didn't hit anything critical. With bedrest he will be fine in a few days."

Moira wanted to weep at his words; thank God!

"You'll be glad about that, won't you?" Charles shouted. "He can be warming your bed again soon." He laughed wildly. "Step out from behind him, Moira."

Before Moira could move Smith reached behind him with both his arms and held her.

"No."

"I'll shoot if you don't move, Smith!"

"Do it," Smith said.

For the second time that day a gun went off—this time it sounded like two.

Chapter 36

Smith spun around the instant Charles hit the floor. Moira was crouched over, her eyes squeezed shut, her arms covering her stomach.

"Are you hit, darling?" he asked her, gripping her shoulders. "Moira?"

Her eyes opened a sliver. "Did you get shot?"

"No. You?"

"No." She sobbed and then flung her arms around him.

Smith held her, keeping his back between her and the rest of the room, but turned his head to see what was happening.

Clayton was slumped in a chair, clutching his shoulder, and moaning loudly and Charles was on the floor, Selkirk staring down at him.

"Stay here," Smith said.

"No." She shook her head emphatically and clung to him like a kitten.

"I need to go deal with Charles, sweetheart."

"Don't kill him, Smith." Her fingers clutched at his arm. "Please."

"Alright, I won't."

"He's not worth it."

He smiled at her and smoothed her messy curls back from her forehead. "I won't kill him."

Smith tried to move away, but she shook her head. "I'm not letting you go."

He kissed her and said, "Very well, but stay behind me."

She nodded.

"I hit him in the leg," Selkirk said when they came near. "I'd prefer not to kill anyone," he added, as if Smith might have argued.

Smith dropped to his haunches beside Charles, who was weeping, his skin so pale he looked like a corpse.

"I'm so sorry, Smith." He clutched at Smith's hand and Smith didn't pull away, even though the other man's touch made his flesh creep. "I can't seem to stop myself. I don't want to do these things, but—" He sobbed.

Smith forced himself to nod and say. "I know."

"I'm going to die, aren't I?"

Smith tore open the bloody cloth to get a better look at the wound.

He looked up and met Charles's terrified gaze. "You will be fine as soon as the doctor stitches this up."

Charles cried. "I didn't mean any of it. I miss you so much. Do you forgive me, Smith? Please say you forgive me!"

The last words were so garbled Smith could barely make them out. Based on the way Charles was shaking and his physical condition, he was in acute withdrawal from opium.

"I forgive you," Smith lied, his anger at what Charles had done giving way in the face of this drug-addled wreck. He pulled his hand from Charles's clutches and stood, turning to Clayton, who was still sniveling and holding his shoulder.

Smith stepped closer and set a hand on Clayton's shoulder.

The older man stared up at him with wide, terrified eyes.

"Where do you keep it?" Smith asked.

"I don't know—"

Smith shoved his thumb into the bullet wound and winced when the other man screamed; Clayton could reach an impressively high note for such a large man.

He removed his thumb. "Where do you keep it?" he asked again once he could be heard over the screaming.

"What?" Clayton sobbed.

He shoved his thumb in again. This time, he rooted around until he could feel the bullet, which he pushed.

Clayton screamed and thrashed.

"Where do you keep it?" Smith asked, applying more pressure.

Still the man didn't divulge the hiding place.

"No?" Smith said. "How about a bit more persuasion—"

"Good God, *please* stop!" Grimes yelled. "I'll tell you where he keeps his stash of dirty secrets."

Amazingly, Clayton screamed louder than he had with a thumb in his shoulder. "You duplicitous bast—"

Smith pulled out the pistol he'd had tucked into the back of his trousers and held it at Clayton's head. "Shut up."

The older man's mouth snapped shut.

Smith turned to Grimes. "Where?"

"There is a false bottom in that rattletrap carriage of his—that way he always had everything with him. You'll find it stuffed full."

"Where is the carriage?"

"It's at the Barrow and Snake," he said, naming a truly vile inn two streets away.

Smith wiped his bloody thumb clean on Clayton's coat and turned back to Selkirk, who was watching the proceedings with interest.

"Take one of my grooms with you and send the other to fetch the doctor—tell him to come in my traveling coach."

The earl nodded, tucked away his gun, and left without another word.

If Selkirk wasn't already one of the richest peers of the realm, he could have had an excellent career ahead of him as a criminal henchman.

Smith felt Moira shiver beside him and cursed his stupidity.

He turned to her and unbuttoned his overcoat. "Here, sweetheart," he said, draping the coat over her shoulders and leading her away from the two moaning, bleeding men, but turning so that he could keep an eye on them.

"Is Luke really going to be fine?" she asked, pulling his coat tightly around her small body.

"Yes. He was angry that he couldn't come along to help. Doctor Felson had to give him enough drugs to knock out a draught horse to keep him in bed." He tucked a brilliant red curl behind her ear. "He was beating himself over the head that you got taken. He will be most relieved to know you are unharmed."

"He protected me and the baby with his life," Moira said.

Her words—and how close he'd come to losing her—sent a stab of fear through him, and Smith cupped her face. "When I thought I might lose you—" his throat constricted, trapping the words inside him.

"You must have been so worried about the baby. But I feel fine, nothing bad—"

"I worried about *you*, Moira—not just our child." Smith bent his head and claimed her mouth.

She groaned and melted against him.

Smith felt like a man who'd been deprived of a life-sustaining substance and suddenly had access to it again; he wanted to gorge on her.

But Clayton's rat's nest was hardly the place for a much-anticipated reunion, so he forced himself to pull away.

Moira stared up at him, her eyes huge. "I'm so sorry for what I did. I didn't—"

"I know you are." He pulled a rueful face. "And I apologize for being such a grudge-bearing arse. I know the pressure Blois and your mother exerted on you and your siblings. I knew how it was for Sandrine. I should have been kinder."

Smith took a deep breath and did what he should have done months ago: he told the truth. "I was so hurt that I lashed out. I was also too stupid to realize the only reason you could cause me such pain is because I'd come to care for you." He hesitated. "Because I love you."

She caught her lower lip with her teeth, tears welling in her eyes.

"I hope I haven't killed your feelings with all my—"

"I love you, Smith! I love you so very, very much." She threw her arms around him and Smith buried his face in her hair, closed his eyes, and gave a silent *thank you* to the powers that be.

When he reluctantly pulled away, he saw that she was biting her lower lip, her brow furrowed.

"What is it, darling?"

"It's just—well, you know that Luke and I—"

"I know."

"And does that make you angry?"

Smith's lips twisted into a wry smile. "I was angry at first. No," he corrected, "I was furious. And also jealous, which I didn't care for. At *all*." He framed her face with both hands. "But the more I thought about it and the more I *lived* with it, the more I realized it made sense that the two people who'd somehow stolen my heart—for lack of a better word—were together. I hope I've not burnt my bridges with the two of you."

She nuzzled her cheek against him and grinned. "I'm sure we will conceive of a way for you to make it up to us."

Smith laughed and pulled her into his arms. "I look forward to it with all my heart, love."

***

"You're sure about this?" Selkirk asked Smith, eyeing Clayton's shivering, sniveling form with open loathing. "I'd heard you weren't the sort of man who left loose ends. Ever."

Smith thought about Charles—whom he'd just sent off in his carriage rather than a sack filled with rocks in the Thames—and shrugged. "I'm trying to mend my ways and be more merciful."

Selkirk snorted, which Smith deserved.

"Besides," Smith said. "It would be too easy to kill him." He gave the eighth, and last, man on his ancient list one last look before closing the door to the hovel and leaving Clayton to his own misery.

The earl looked doubtful but shrugged. "Whatever you say. I have what I came for" he lifted an envelope—"so I don't care what you do with him."

As they walked back to the carriage Smith said, "He's poor, friendless, and he's lost the only way he has of making money. His life won't be worth living from now on."

"True," the earl agreed. "But he's still a snake. And he hates you."

"I suspect he'll soon be a snake without a head."

Selkirk's eyebrows raised.

"He owes some rather nasty people large amounts of money." Smith smirked. "I might have sent word to some of Clayton's creditors about where he could be found."

The earl barked a laugh, a genuinely amused expression on his austere face. "Remind me never to rely on your *mercy* for any reason."

Smith smiled and the other man climbed into the carriage where Moira was bundled in blankets, having refused to go home while Smith dealt with Charles and Clayton.

"Is it over?" she asked, her eyes a startling green today, her face far too pale.

Smith nodded. "It's over."

Selkirk leaned toward Moira. "We've not been introduced, ma'am. I'm Selkirk—it's a pleasure." He took Moira's hand and raised it to his lips.

Moira's eyes flared at the distinguished lord's courtly gesture and Smith had a sudden, violent, urge to open the door and chuck the peer out of the carriage.

"Moira Dunsmuir," she said, her voice composed, although her cheeks now had spots of color. "I've admired one of your paintings often. Smith keeps it in my favorite sitting room."

The earl shot Smith a sly look. "He might have another quite soon."

Smith tried to suppress his greedy excitement at the thought and failed. "I shall look forward to that."

"On another subject," Selkirk said, "Do you want to return the contents of Clayton's strong box, or shall I?"

"I will leave that to you—if you don't mind."

"I don't mind." Selkirk's lips twitched and Smith wondered if the man was pondering earning some *black* of his own. Well, it wasn't his concern—they were all the earl's friends and acquaintances. He could do what he wished with the evidence.

Smith looked at Moira. He, personally, was finished with revenge. For good.

He was also finished with hiding his love. He'd wasted too many years living for the past and he had two excellent reasons—soon to be three—to look to the future.

Smith intended to keep all three close.

Chapter 37

Luke opened his eyes and found two beloved faces looking down on him.

He blinked.

But when he opened his eyes, they were both still there.

Luke smiled. "Well," he said, the single word almost more than he could manage.

Moira's eyes widened and she glanced at Smith, who grinned down at him.

Luke had never seen such an open, joyous expression on his master's face before and it had the unfortunate result of causing his heart to pound, which *hurt*. He sucked in a breath and then tried to push himself up.

Hands landed on his shoulders when he whimpered.

"Let us help you," Moira said, reaching for a pillow while Smith stood, slid his arms carefully around him, and lifted him gently.

Luke stared at their intent, caring faces—*together* and in Smith's bedroom with him!—as they propped him up and plumped his pillows.

If he was dreaming all this it would kill him.

"Do you remember what happened?" Smith asked.

Luke tried to recall what was causing him such pain, but the last thing memory he had was sitting for Moira while she sketched him.

"You were drawing me," he said to Moira. "That's all I remember."

"You were sketching Luke?" Smith asked Moira.

She shrugged, her cheeks darkening.

"I want to see it," Smith said.

"I'm not very good."

"Yes, she is," Luke said, nodding at Smith. "She's very good—she can paint, too. And her piano playing is… exquisite."

They both looked at Moira, who'd turned a shade of red that clashed with her hair.

She pursed her lips and shook her head at them both, but Luke could see that she was pleased.

"What happened?" Luke asked. "Why don't I recall anything?"

"The doctor had to give you a great deal of laudanum." Moira said, her hand finding his beneath the blanket and squeezing. "Charles came to the house and you tried to protect me—he shot you."

Now it was coming back to him.

"The baby! Is—"

"Shh," Smith murmured, taking his other hand. "The baby is fine—Doctor Felson made sure of that." He smirked. "You two have kept the poor man busy. I'm beginning to think I'll need to hire him full time."

"I was shot? He operated on me?"

Smith nodded. "You were fortunate the bullet did not damage anything internal, but he had to dig around a bit to make sure."

Ah. That would explain the excruciating pain in his side.

"You need to make sure you don't disturb any of his work—which means resting. *Resting*," Moira repeated, giving him a stern look.

Luke smiled at her, amused by her attempt to look threatening. But then he frowned. "Wait—I remember now, Charles *took* you! Tell me what happened, please."

Moira looked at Smith and Luke saw a weighted glance pass between them. It was a look that caused a definite pang in Luke's chest, this one not the result of a bullet.

Something had happened to bring them back together, perhaps they had even mended the rift and admitted to the love he knew they felt for each other.

They were together.

Luke swallowed, grateful that neither expected him to speak because he wasn't sure what he would say. He was happy for them—of course he was—but…

Moira gripped his hand tighter and said, "Charles and a man named Sir Clayton Tyler abducted me."

"Sir Clayton is an enemy of mine," Smith added, an expression of guilt sitting strangely on his normally confident face. "I put you both in jeopardy with my quest for vengeance." He looked from Luke to Moira and back. "But that is over now." He hesitated and then said, "I will tell you both the truth—all of it. It is the least of what I owe you."

Luke stared, his breath freezing in his chest. "B-both of us?"

***

Smith looked at the two people he loved—yes, he could admit that what he felt for Moira and Luke was love—and it terrified and shamed him that it had taken almost losing them before he came to his senses.

"I want to apologize for putting both your lives in danger."

Moira dropped her gaze, clearly uncomfortable.

"Sir, you did nothing wrong," Luke said, looking just as unhappy about Smith's apology as Moira.

"Yes, I did. I should have known that Charles presented a danger." Smith grimaced. "He was never the most stable of men and I'm afraid my time with him did nothing to help that instability. He needed monogamy and security and I knew before I ever allowed our relationship to commence that I couldn't offer him the first of those things. As if that wasn't bad enough, I dallied with him again—because I'm selfish." He gave them both a wry look. "But then that is no surprise to either of you."

He reached out a hand to Moira, so that he held a huge hand in his right and a delicate hand in his left. "It's hardly original, but I've realized—long past the time that I should have—that my revenge is not nearly as important as some other things in my life." He smiled. "Like the two of you."

A tear rolled down Moira's pale face. "I'm *so* terribly sorry for what I—"

"Shhh," Smith murmured, lifting her hand to his mouth, and kissing the back. "You've already apologized—more than once. If anyone owes an apology, it is me. I was just so… *wedded* to my anger that I cut my nose off to spite my face." He squeezed Luke's hand. "With both of you. I held you at arm's length because of my experience with Charles," he said, his gaze locked with the other man's. "You paid for my inability to see what was right in front of my eyes."

Luke looked profoundly uncomfortable at his confession. "You have nothing to apologize for, sir."

"Yes, I do. But thank you for trying to defend me," Smith said, smiling like a fool for some reason. Perhaps it was simply the lightness he felt inside—the relief of sharing a secret long suppressed.

Smith looked from Moira to Luke and said, "I love you both—very much."

He looked from a stunned set of blue eyes to a stunned set of blue green eyes and laughed. "You should see your faces."

Luke glanced at Moira and something passed between them, and then they both turned to him.

"Yes?" he said, guessing what was coming.

"We both love you," Luke said.

"But we love each other, too," Moira added.

"Yes, I'd gathered as much." Smith inhaled deeply, and then let it all out. "I told Moira earlier that I was jealous when I knew the two of you were… together. It hurt—and I was angry." He snorted. "You know that," he said to Luke. "You were the poor bastard who had to beard me in my den."

Luke's cheeks darkened.

"I'm grateful you did, Luke. I went away to Bristol on that business trip not just to work, but to lick my wounds in private. Well," he snorted, "not *entirely* in private." Indeed, he'd engaged in an embarrassing amount of debauchery, none of which had satisfied him.

He looked at his two lovers. "You both know what I want—*you*, both of you—but it's time I knew what *you* wanted. Whether I can provide it?" He shrugged. "I can't know until you tell me."

Again, they exchanged a look, clearly at ease with each other and on this subject. Rather than the familiar jealousy, he only felt a yearning; a yearning to be part of what they shared.

"We want each other and we want you. Neither of us need anyone else." Moira's lips curved into a teasing smile. "We know you, Smith— we know who you are and what you need and want—and we love you. To us love means not trying to change you. It means wanting the people you love to be happy."

Smith was finding it difficult to breathe, his emotions so ferocious that he marveled he could possibly contain them all.

He glanced away for a moment, struggling to contain the burning behind his eyes. When he looked back, his mask of composure was once again firmly in place.

"Thank you," he said. "I will strive to deserve you both."

It was their turn to look flushed and giddy.

He cleared his throat. "There are a few things that I need to tell you. About me. About who I was and… and how I came to be Smith."

And then he took a deep breath and proceeded to tell his two lovers the truth, at least most of it.

There were parts of his past that he'd never tell—parts that nobody should have to know.

Smith would always try to protect them both from that sort of ugliness. Because that's what he did for the people he loved.

Epilogue

Two Years Later

It was past two o'clock in the morning when Smith entered the foyer of his London house.

"Good evening, sir," Walter, the lead guard on duty said. Both he and Daniel were seated at the small table that Moira had placed in the entry hall so that they might play cards, or read, and be more comfortable on their long nights.

"Please, don't get up," he said when they both made to stand. "Who is winning?" he asked, setting his hat on the console table and putting his stick in the brass holder before pulling off his gloves.

Walter grinned and jerked his chin toward the pile of pennies on his side of the table.

"Ah, I see," Smith said with a chuckle.

"He's too damned lucky," Daniel grumbled.

"Anything happen that I should know about?" Smith asked as he shrugged off his coat.

"No sir, all quiet."

Smith hung the snow-specked garment on the coat rack—also placed there by Moira—which held enough cloaks and coats and scarves and whatnot that the old Smith would have felt uncomfortable with the clutter. Even now he felt a bit of a twinge, but he was getting better. Every day he became a little better.

"Good night, lads," he said.

"'Night sir."

Smith took the stairs two at a time, for all that he was exhausted. He'd been traveling for ten days, but at least this would be his last journey until the middle of next year. Now that he had a family, the syndicate divided up the traveling more equitably, although Smith was always the one who managed any volatile situations.

He bypassed the third floor and continued up to the nursery. He opened the door slowly and entered the warm room on the toes of his shoes.

The glow from the fire was the only light in the room. The old nurse—a woman Luke had personally selected—dozed in her favorite rocking chair near the fire.

Smith headed straight for the magnificent bed that Edward and some of the boys from the carpentry school had built for his child.

Had Smith cried when the massive crib/bed was delivered? Perhaps there had been a tear or two in his eyes when he'd read the terse message that had accompanied it:

It is a bed fit for an emperor. Or an empress.

Smith paused and peered over the high side of the crib—which would be lowered in the morning so the current occupant, a miniature tyrant, could crawl out of his bed without any help from his nurse, thank you very much.

Right now, Smith's son was curled on his side, thumb between his lips, his shock of dark red hair a deceptive halo around his sleeping face.

Smith knew that he shouldn't, but he had to.

He reached down and lifted the boy, cradling him against his chest and burying his nose in his hair, filling his lungs with that sweet baby scent.

Alexander—appropriately named after an ancient Macedonian King—shifted in his arms. "Papa?"

Smith kissed his temple. "Yes, it's papa."

"I missed you."

"I missed you, too."

"Did you bring me a puppy?" Alexander asked, the last word swallowed by a big yawn.

Smith laughed. "I don't know. Have you been a good boy?"

Alexander nodded, his heavy eyelids already drifting shut.

Smith held him until his body was heavy with sleep and then gave him one last kiss before putting him back in his bed. Although he'd been gone less than two weeks the boy had grown. And he had missed it.

He sighed and covered Alexander with the blanket, staring for a long moment at his boy's sleeping face. It was difficult to leave him, even for the night, but leaving for weeks at a time was excruciating. Smith knew he wasn't a nine-year-old boy sneaking out to look for bird eggs. He knew he wouldn't return home to smoking rubble and the bodies of those he loved. But the fear—though faint, now—was always at the back of his mind.

As he'd predicted to Selkirk that day two years ago, Clayton Tyler had died a poor and miserable man, stabbed in a dark alley, either by a desperate criminal or his creditors, Smith neither knew nor cared.

With Clayton Tyler's death Smith had finally released the last of his anger.

Smith would miss his family until the day he died, but he had a new family now, and it was far more rewarding to live in the present than mourn the past.

He tossed a few more pieces of coal onto the fire and banked it before leaving, managing not to wake Nanny Keogh in the process.

Knox, who'd traveled with Smith on his ten-day trip, had come straight home from the train station while Smith had gone on to meet with his business partners at their club.

Smith had told Knox to go to bed and not wait up for him, but the blasted man was still puttering around Smith's dressing room when he entered his bedchamber.

"How is the young master, sir?" his valet asked as he quickly and efficiently stripped him.

"He says he's been a good boy while I was gone. What do you think are the odds of that?"

Knox chuckled. "Full of mischief, that one."

He took a quick shower-bath—he might have become better about clutter, but he still relied on frequent bathing to keep him sane, especially after a long trip—and once he was reasonably dry, he padded through his empty bedchamber toward the connecting door.

Smith blinked at the sight that greeted him, both his lovers, wide awake in Moira's bed.

Moira was engaged with a piece of needlework—something she appeared to enjoy doing a great deal—and Luke put a marker in his book and set it on the nightstand.

"What are you two doing awake at this hour?"

"Waiting for you," Moira said, putting away her work and then lifting the covers as Smith climbed up on her side of the bed, shoving her even closer to Luke in the process.

"Mmm, so warm," he said, running his chilly hands up her hips to her belly and earning a yelp.

"That's cruel," she hissed, offering up her mouth for a kiss while Luke removed his spectacles and dimmed the lamp on his side of the bed.

Smith came up for air and buried his nose in her hair, inhaling the sweet smell of her. When he looked up, he saw that Luke was laying on his side, head propped on his hand, watching them with a quietly smug look.

Smith took Luke's hand and pulled him closer, until the two of them met over Moira's body, their kiss speedily devolving from sweet to hungry.

It was Smith who pulled away when he realized they must be crushing Moira.

But she merely smiled up at them. "That was lovely, don't stop on my account."

Smith snorted and tweaked one of her nipples. "Has she been bossy like this while I was gone?"

Luke nodded, smirking. "She's been dreadful."

Moira gave a scandalized squawk. "I have *no—mmgmph.*"

Smith grinned as Luke swallowed her protests, kissing her thoroughly while one of his big hands tugged down the blankets, baring her body to Smith's hungry gaze.

He backed down the bed, pushed her thighs wide, exposed her shaved cunt—another preference he had no intention of abandoning any time soon—and buried his mouth in her sweet heat.

Between them, Luke and Smith teased two orgasms from her body, Luke tormenting her nipples while Smith sucked her bud until she begged for mercy.

He was capable of mercy—on occasion—so he released her over-sensitive bundle of nerves after the second orgasm and met Luke's eager gaze.

"You know what I want," Smith told the other man.

Luke smirked. "I prepared her for you earlier, sir. I was most… rigorous."

Smith gave a pleased growl as he envisioned it. "And you say she's been bossy, hmm?"

"Something terrible, sir."

They both turned to Moira, who wore a mulish, but sated, scowl that made Smith's already aching balls tighten even more.

"You can see how she is just by looking at her," Luke said.

"Yes, I can."

They grinned at each other and Luke rolled on to his back while Smith nodded at Moira. "Up you get," he ordered. "Straddle him."

She gave him a sullen look, but he saw the greedy eager glint in her eyes as she knelt over Luke and grasped his thick cock with her small hand.

Moira loved taking them both at once, even though she'd be walking a bit gingerly for the next few days.

"Lower yourself *slowly*," he ordered, leaning closely enough so that he could watch while Luke's fat cock stretched her tight entrance.

Smith groaned. "Fuck! That's beautiful. Hold right there," he muttered, pushing his head between her thighs and licking where his two lovers were joined.

Their mingled scent was the headiest smell in the world and he sucked and tongued while sliding his free hand between Moira's cleft and fingering her arsehole.

He groaned when his finger slipped into her oiled hole with little resistance, the thought of Luke stretching her for Smith's enjoyment was erotic beyond bearing.

As usual, he was torn between wanting to taunt and torment her and wanting to fill her full of his seed and claim her.

It would have to be the second one tonight because Smith needed to be inside her; ten days was too bloody long.

He gave their joined flesh one last, lingering suck and then reluctantly released them.

"Take all of him, darling," he said, watching until Luke disappeared completely before pushing up and kneeling behind Moira.

He reached around her and cupped her breasts, pulling her back against him and nodding to Luke, who commenced to tease her already over-stimulated clitoris.

Moira squirmed and whimpered as Luke played with her pussy and Smith sucked a bruise onto the pale skin of her throat, kneading her tits and pinching her nipples until her small body bucked and shivered.

Luke groaned when she came. "God, you should feel her, sir— she's so bloody hot and tight."

Smith kissed the bruise he'd just sucked onto her neck. "Is that what you want, Moira? To feel me?" He bit her earlobe and then whispered. "Can you take both our cocks?"

"Please," she mumbled, her body wracked with spasm after spasm as her orgasm ebbed.

"Lie down on Luke," Smith said.

He took a moment to appreciate the beautiful sight of Moira's small body spread out on Luke's far larger one, giving his prick a few hard strokes even though he was hard and running like a tap.

He raised his eyes to Luke's. "Open her for me."

Luke slid his hands down to her hips and spread her cheeks wide.

Smith grunted softly. "My God that's beautiful," he said, positioning himself at her slightly reddened rosette and breaching her, entranced by the sight of his fat crown stretching her.

Moira moaned and canted her bottom at him. "Please."

"So impatient," he chided, setting his hands over Luke's. They locked gazes while he eased slowly inside Moira, ignoring her begging to go faster and harder and taking his time, allowing her to stretch and accommodate the two of them—no easy task.

"I can feel you," Luke said, his lips curving into one of his rare smiles.

Smith gritted his teeth and pushed in the last bit, until his groin rested against her spread bottom. He exhaled the breath he hadn't been aware he'd been holding.

"How do you feel?" Smith asked Moira, caressing her back while Luke covered her face with kisses.

Moira tightened her inner muscles, earning groans from all three of them.

"Touch yourself," he ordered in a strained voice.

Moira pushed her hand between her body and Luke's and Smith withdrew from her slowly before sliding back in, faster this time.

Smith and Luke established a rhythm that kept her full of cock at all times. He knew he wouldn't last long—he never did when they reunited after one of his trips away—and he held Luke's gaze as his hips pounded harder, his thrusting deeper, but less controlled.

By the time her body stiffened and she cried out Smith's control was ready to snap and he fucked into her hard, until he felt Luke let go and cry out.

And then Smith drove himself deep, closed his eyes, and savored the unbearably intimate and erotic sensation of his two lovers climaxing along with him.

***

Moira woke up just before dawn, wedged between two hard, hot male bodies. She lay there in contented silence, reveling in the utter perfection of the moment.

Smith was home—at *last*—and Christmas was just a few days away. She and Luke—with some rather rambunctious help from Alexander—had enjoyed themselves so much decorating the tree, but they had all missed Smith.

He'd promised it would be the last trip for a long time and she was eager to have him at home.

Moira smiled; she had the perfect Christmas gift for both men, although it would only be a surprise to one of them.

The hand that had been resting between her breast and Luke's back began to move south, not stopping until it was cupping her mound.

"Good morning," Smith mumbled, sliding a finger between her lower lips and giving her core a lazy caress.

"Yes, it is," she said, purring with contentment and raising her upper leg over Luke's hip to give Smith better access.

"I'm going to fuck you," he said.

Moira smiled. "Stop talking about it, and do it," she taunted.

His chest shook with mirth as his fat crown pushed inside her. "Does that hurt?" he asked, stilling.

"It feels good." He felt better than good; he felt perfect.

Luke shifted and rolled onto his side to face them. "Morning."

"Did we wake you?" Smith asked, his hips moving in languid thrusts, his fingers stroking her engorged peak.

Luke blinked his bleary blue gaze—he was always so slow to wake up—and then his lips curved into a smile as his gaze moved from her to Smith and then back. "Yes. But I'm glad. This is better than Christmas."

Moira reached for Luke. "Come here."

Luke shook his head. "No, I just want to watch. I'm usually too euphoric to pay attention."

Moira relaxed back against Smith and let her eyes close, luxuriating in the touch of one man and the rapt attention of another.

As Smith's clever fingers and big cock worked her slowly toward orgasm she reflected, not for the first time, how very fortunate she was.

The number three was not an easy one when it came to love—or at least she'd never known anyone to make a success of it and she had grown up surrounded by people with a far more pliable notion of morality than most.

And yet she had never been happier. Especially now that Smith was back with them. Just wait until he found out…

Her pulse quickened as Smith began to ride her harder, the soft ball of his thumb speeding her toward bliss.

Moira forced her eyes open as the pressure built inside her, meeting Luke's gaze.

He smiled, the love in his eyes the last nudge she needed to go flying.

"Come for us, Moira," Smith whispered in her ear, and then he buried himself deeply and flew with her.

***

Luke took full advantage of both Moira and Smith's momentary loss of awareness to devour them.

The last two years had been the best of his life, far better than anything he'd ever hoped for—or even dared to dream.

While it saddened him that few people outside this house— excepting Smith's small circle of friends—could ever know that he had two such wonderful lovers, keeping the truth from his brothers and their families was a small price to pay for his happiness.

The only person he was concerned about—the only one who would be hurt if the truth of their lives ever leaked out—was Alexander.

And of course *now* there would be—

"What are you frowning about?" Smith asked.

Luke saw the other man had come back from his small death while his mind had been wandering.

"Was I frowning?" Luke asked.

Smith gave a soft snort but let him get away with the diversion.

Moira's eyes opened and she gave a slight nod—Luke knew what that meant.

He reached out and set his hand over Smith's, which rested on Moira's hip. He wanted to be touching both of them when he spoke.

"Moira is pregnant."

The look on Smith's face—full blown shock—was priceless. He pushed up onto his elbow so he could see Moira, who was grinning.

"Already?" he asked, breathless. "Is it safe?"

Moira chuckled. "It has been two years, Smith! Besides, Doctor Felson assures me that I am as healthy as a horse." She gave a slight shrug, the gesture so very French when she did it. "He said many women wait far less time."

Luke could see joy and concern warring within Smith and knew exactly what it meant because he felt the same thing himself. He wanted more children—he wanted to fill their house—but he was terrified for Moira. While her pregnancy with Alexander had been almost shockingly easy, Doctor Felson said a woman never knew and that it could be different this time.

But that was a conversation Luke could have with Smith later—without Moira present.

Moira groaned. "I can see what you two are thinking—especially you, Luke. Please stop fretting right now. Everything will be fine. I don't want you two working yourselves up into a lather like the last time and trying to confine me to bedrest. I won't tolerate it this time."

"She *is* bossy," Smith mused, caressing her flat belly and looking at it quizzically, as if he might have been able to see something at only six or so weeks.

"I don't think we fucked her hard enough last night," Luke said.

Moira gave a startled squeak and Smith pinched her nipple. "You'd better watch out, darling," he warned her. "You don't want to wake the dragon."

Luke snorted. That was Smith's nickname for the Luke's darker, filthier side—a side of him that was allowed to come out much more often these days.

Although they both teased Moira about being bossy, Luke knew that *he* was the bossy one.

The other two really did let him cajole and steer and manipulate them.

His lips twitched into a smirk. And he loved it.

But while they might allow Luke to run their household, Smith was still master of their home.

Luke had never even used Smith's real name—Maximus—even though Moira had experimented with it—to mixed effect—on occasion.

"I have grown into being *Smith*," Smith had admitted when Moira had pressed him on the matter.

"You don't want a first name? You want to be *just* Smith?" she'd persisted.

Smith had grinned. "Yes. *Just* Smith."

Luke thought Smith's childhood name would always be a reminder of the horrors he'd endured as a boy. Although Smith had shared his story with them, Luke knew there was a great deal he'd not told them—like the many years after that awful day, and how he'd made such a success of himself.

Perhaps Smith would never share everything about his past. Luke could understand the desire to leave such deep wounds untouched.

Besides, he didn't need to know every detail about either Smith or Moira to love them deeply. Indeed, he appreciated the aura of mystery and reserve they both carried with them.

Luke would always think of Smith as his master and Moira would always be his mistress. He had stop questioning the way he was made or his burning desire to serve or how differently he viewed love and family. He had finally learned to be happy that he could have what he wanted, no matter how unconventional his desires might be.

They were a family—he, Smith, Moira, and Alexander—and soon there would be another member…

Which meant they'd need to start thinking about baby names.

Luke smiled. "There will have to be another name-choosing tournament," he said, giving voice to his thoughts.

Smith and Moira groaned.

"But the last one went on for *three* days," Moira whined.

"And you won and got to choose the name," Smith said flatly, still annoyed that Luke had been victorious.

"I don't know why *you're* complaining," Luke said to Smith. "I've heard you telling Alexander that he was named after a Macedonian king when you know good and well that I chose the name to honor one of England's greatest poets."

Smith rolled his eyes. "Alexander wants to be named after a warrior, not some fusty old English poet."

"I cannot believe you two," Moira scoffed. "I think *I* should be the one who gets to choose the next name—*without* being forced to undergo repeated and systematic humiliation on a chess board."

Luke and Smith exchanged looks, and Luke knew what the other man was thinking—that they'd spared Alexander the ignominy of being named *Rupert*, which had been Moira's choice if the baby was a boy—and Lucretia, if it had been a girl.

Luke cringed at both her the choices, and he could see Smith felt exactly the same.

"Er, I think Luke might be right when it comes to this, darling," Smith said, winking at Luke. "We should have a tournament to pick the name. It's the only fair way to do it."

Sometimes, Luke thought, three really was the perfect number.

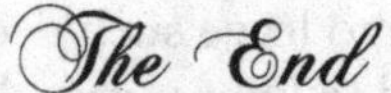

Dear Reader:

I hope you enjoyed my very first menage story. Wow, what a challenge it was to write a relationship with three lovers!

Smith being Smith (and I still can't think of him as Maximus) I wasn't surprised when this book progressed along—ahem—a non-traditional path.

Because I'm what is called a 'discovery' writer rather than an outliner or a plotter, I discover the story as I write it. Yes, that makes life interesting, to say the least.

I knew Smith's mysterious past would be a big part of this story, but I didn't want it to take over the romance. At one point I wondered if Smith wouldn't be better served having a 2-part book. But that would have meant 2 volumes, one with a cliffhanger, and I didn't feel I could do that to my readers.

I was concerned the book would be super loooong, but it turned out that my worries were unfounded and I was able to wrap the story up in about five thousand LESS words than my average book.

Of course, the book started off MUCH longer before edits. I don't think I've ever cut 8 sex scenes out of a book before, LOL, but I did with this one. What can I say? These characters just liked to hop in the sack. A LOT.

Going into this book, I was fully aware that a lot of readers really hate reading about infidelity. I'm not wild about it, myself, but I needed to stay true to Smith's character to be happy with his journey. And the guy is just constitutionally incapable of keeping that big pecker in his pants. But at least he is aware of his character flaws.

I knew he'd need a lover (or lovers) who understood him and loved him for what he was—flaws and all. Because there is definitely a lot to love, even though Smith doesn't make that easy for anyone.

When I started this series, I envisioned the 4 men—Edward, Stephen, Gideon, & Smith. But then Malcolm shoved his way in. And you might have noticed the appearance of a new character in this book… a certain Earl of Selkirk?

I've decided I'm not done with my decadent Victorians just yet…This series is one of my creative outlets, where I can have fun writing non-mainstream characters, so I anticipate there being at least a few more books.

I started Selkirk's book while I was in the middle of writing Smith's. I know, I know—*bad* author! I do that a lot—I just can't control myself when I meet an intriguing character, I need to write at least a few pages about them.

Selkirk is one twisted puppy, which is my FAVORITE sort of hero. Unfortunately, I'm not sure when his story will be published since I've got another busy year ahead for 2023.

Right now I'm busily working on Book 5 in THE ACADEMY OF LOVE, **DANCING WITH LOVE**. This book is scheduled to release December 27th, fingers crossed I can make that deadline. The reason I had to postpone **THEIR MASTER** was because I had surgery on my right arm. Of course, when one item gets off schedule the entire schedule goes out of whack, but I'm hoping I can make it.

I'm also working on some other fun stuff. A contemporary romance, a science fiction/post-apocalyptic/Regency Era mash-up, a new Victorian Era series called, THE HALES: AMERICANS IN LONDON, and **HYACINTH**, which is the second book in THE BELLAMY SISTERS.

WHEW! I wish there were more hours in the day.

I've also had a lot of requests for Jackson's story (he was the valet in **HIS COUNTESS**) and I've started his adventure, but—again—I'm not sure when that will get published. Don't worry, though, I won't forget about him.

I really DO pay attention to reader requests and it gets me all excited about a character when a reader is excited, so please send me an email and tell me if you think a character ABSOLUTELY must have their story told.

If you find typos, please do let me know and I will make every effort to fix them.

As always, I am grateful for reviews and I REALLY love getting emails: Minervaspencerauthor@gmail.com.

Until next time, happy reading!

S.M./Minerva

JOSS AND THE COUNTESS
HUGO AND THE MAIDEN

VICTORIAN DECADENCE: (HISTORICAL EROTIC
ROMANCE—SUPER STEAMY!)

HIS HARLOT
HIS VALET
HIS COUNTESS
HER BEAST
THEIR MASTER

THE ACADEMY OF LOVE:

THE MUSIC OF LOVE
A FIGURE OF LOVE
A PORTRAIT OF LOVE
THE LANGUAGE OF LOVE
DANCING WITH LOVE

THE MASQUERADERS:

THE FOOTMAN
THE POSTILION
THE BASTARD

THE WILD WOMEN OF WHITECHAPEL
THE BOXING BARONESS
THE DUELING DUCHESS*

THE HALES: AMERICANS IN LONDON
BALTHAZAR: THE SPARE

THE BACHELORS OF BOND STREET:

A SECOND CHANCE FOR LOVE (A NOVELLA)

ANTHOLOGIES:

S.M. LaViolette

<u>THE ARRANGEMENT</u>
<u>DUKE IN A BOX</u>

More books by S.M. LaViolette & Minerva Spencer
THE ACADEMY OF LOVE SERIES
The Music of Love
A Figure of Love
A Portrait of Love
The Language of Love
Dancing with Love*
THE OUTCASTS SERIES
Dangerous
Barbarous
Scandalous
THE REBELS OF THE *TON*
Notorious
Outrageous
Infamous
THE MASQUERADERS
The Footman
The Postilion
The Bastard
THE SEDUCERS
Melissa and The Vicar
Joss and The Countess
Hugo and The Maiden
VICTORIAN DECADENCE
His Harlot
His Valet
His Countess
Her Master
Her Beast
THE BELLAMY SISTERS
PHOEBE
HYACINTH*
SELINA*
THE WILD WOMEN OF WHITECHAPEL
THE BOXING BARONESS
THE DUELING DUCHESS*
THE HALE FAMILY: AMERICANS IN LONDON
BALTHAZAR: THE SPARE*